THE BRITISH EIGHTEENTH CENTURY AND GLOBAL CRITIQUE

THE BRITISH EIGHTEENTH CENTURY AND GLOBAL CRITIQUE

Clement Hawes

THE BRITISH EIGHTEENTH CENTURY AND GLOBAL CRITIQUE

First published in 2005 by
PALGRAVE MACMILLAN™
175 Fifth Avenue, New York, N.Y. 10010 and
Houndmills, Basingstoke, Hampshire, England RG21 6XS
Companies and representatives throughout the world.

PALGRAVE MACMILLAN is the global academic imprint of the Palgrave Macmillan division of St. Martin's Press, LLC and of Palgrave Macmillan Ltd. Macmillan® is a registered trademark in the United States, United Kingdom and other countries. Palgrave is a registered trademark in the European Union and other countries.

ISBN 1–4039–6816–0

Library of Congress Cataloging-in-Publication Data

Hawes, Clement.
    The British eighteenth century and global critique / Clement Hawes.
        p. cm.
    Includes bibliographical references and index.
    ISBN 1–4039–6816–0
        1. English literature—18th century—History and criticism. 2. Colonies in literature. 3. Literature and history—English-speaking countries—History—20th century. 4. Literature and history—Great Britain—History—18th century. 5. English literature—20th century—History and criticism. 6. Postcolonialism—English-speaking countries. 7. Postcolonialism in literature. 8. Imperialism in literature. I. Title.
    PR448.C64H39 2005
    820.9'358—dc22   2004059354

A catalogue record for this book is available from the British Library.

Design by Newgen Imaging Systems (P) Ltd., Chennai, India.

First edition: October 2005

10 9 8 7 6 5 4 3 2 1

Printed in the United States of America.

For Minnie

With thee conversing, I forget all time,
All seasons, and their change; all please alike.
—John Milton, *Paradise Lost*,
IV, ll. 639–640

CONTENTS

LIST OF ILLUSTRATIONS

ACKNOWLEDGMENTS

My thinking on the matters in this book has evolved in conversations with many people. My ideas have developed in dialogue with Greg Clingham over the years. I am grateful for his help with this book—he read earlier versions of the individual chapters and then a draft of the whole—but even more so for the pleasure and challenge of his intellectual companionship. I am indebted for the provocation of his written work. Rob Hume, most generously engaged of colleagues, read an entire draft with frighteningly meticulous attention. Rob's sinewy comments, ranging from the minute to the architectonic, have elevated my entire project. I thank Rob also for the example of his commitment to scholarship and teaching. Kit Hume's bracing comments helped me to rethink the book's title and conceptual grid. I have benefitted from the refining conversation of Joan Landes about the Enlightenment, and from the insights of Linda Selzer about Charles Johnson. Phil Smallwood sharpened my chapter on Johnson. Vin Carretta helped to keep me on track with Equiano. My ideas about Swift have been repeatedly sophisticated in exchanges with Hermann Real, Jim Thorson, and Don Mell.

I've been greatly lucky in having some hard-charging eighteenth-century graduate students as a sounding board. Many thanks to the following rigorous readers, of at least part of this book: Paul Odney, Srividhya Swaminathan, Elisabeth Heard, Gina Ercolini, and Lori Molinari. My current doctoral student and research assistant, Dannie Chalk, has lent me the use of her high-powered brain. Her conceptualizing abilities are especially imprinted on the index. The thoughtful words of Steve Schneider about Michel Foucault helped to keep me on my toes. Jessica Bailey, my undergraduate intern in 2003–2004, contributed intellectual energy and initiative beyond the call of duty.

I have received encouragement and generous support from several Penn State institutions. One of them is the Research and Graduate Studies Office. In particular, my research on the "Ossian" controversy would not have been possible without the support of Ray Lombra and the RGSO. To the Institute for Arts and Humanities, as personified by Laura Knoppers,

I owe my latest opportunities to research Swift. I would also like to thank the Office of Research and Development Administration at Southern Illinois University at Carbondale for its initial support in the making of this book. Charlie Fanning, Director of Irish Studies at SIU, inspired and supported my interest in the Irish Swift.

The Pattee Library at Penn State, a magnificent resource, is eager to make scholarship flourish. Many thanks to Bill Brockman and Sandy Stelts. The staffs of the British Library, Yale's Sterling Memorial Library, Yale's Beinecke, and Yale's Lewis Walpole have all contributed to my pursuits.

Mrinalini Sinha—partner and intellectual conscience—has read draft after draft, considered every issue that perplexed me, and has countless times sent me murmuring back to the drawing board. The germ of this book, an essay on Jonathan Swift published in 1991, brings us full circle. This piece was my first attempt to grapple with themes of empire and periodization—and, it so happens, the first piece of mine to bear the marks of her influence.

Problems and mistakes are mine alone.

PREFACE: FROM CRUX TO CRITIQUE

The British Eighteenth Century and Global Critique challenges the reigning clichés about "modernity" widely drawn from the writings of such contemporary thinkers as Michel Foucault and François Lyotard. The book locates in the eighteenth-century moment precisely what postmodern theory assumes to be absent: the basis for *modernity's self-critique*. That self-critique is possible, I contend, because as a transitional moment, the eighteenth century visibly exposes the highly contingent nature of modernity's origins. In essence, I trace the genealogy of a global postcolonial critique back to the British eighteenth century. My book intervenes in debates within current literary theory by means of a close engagement with texts from the British eighteenth century, the latter now viewed as a resource for the contemporary postcolonial moment. Indeed, rather than "applying" postcolonial theory to eighteenth-century texts, this book instead refines postcolonial theory by *using* eighteenth-century texts.

The liminal dynamics of eighteenth-century British culture does indeed afford many points of potential affiliation for critical reflection upon the imperial, the national, and the racial constitution of identities. Such pockets of critique, where the good and bad of modernity can still be disentangled, provide options unavailable to projects of nostalgic neo-traditionalism. Such pockets are, above all, potential launching sites for the urgent project of elaborating alternative modernities. These alternative modernities, indeed, must inevitably loom large in what ought to be the essential quest of the postcolonial project: the quest, I contend, for *a critical reappropriation of modernity*.

The History of Nation-Based Historiography

The moving arrow of secular time—so we think—points in one direction only. And yet as one approaches the new ideological dispensations associated with the eighteenth-century nation-state, the supposedly secular redactions of public memory turn out to be no less elastic than the back-and-forth temporality implied by Christian typology. Indeed, the quasi-religious fervor often inspired by such cultural nationalisms depends fundamentally on a sleight-of-hand that reads a supposed final purpose for the nation back into its supposed origins. Benedict Anderson observes that the key to the nationalistic appropriation of the sacred is, precisely, a sense of destiny. Nationalist ideology entails, in his words, "a secular transformation of fatality into continuity, contingency into meaning."[1] The rhetorical means of this magic trick, as I demonstrate, is best described as a special sort of self-referential trope: a *metalepsis*. This trope, to paraphrase Macbeth, murders time. Eighteenth-century British historiography makes for an especially privileged moment to observe the emergence of this dangerous hocus pocus and the cultural backlash it engenders. The eighteenth-century metalepsis of ancient Britishness, soon to achieve respectability, enters history sailing under the flag of humbug and fakery.

The later eighteenth century marks the chronological moment of a profound historiographical tangle: the dramatic shift in the writing of history when nation-based modes of legitimation began to eclipse dynastic ones. Dynastic historiography—mediated by religious institutions, Latinate high culture, and locally discrete social structures—was yielding to a more broadly based vernacular culture whose proponents struggled to articulate a radically new version of history.[2] Nationalism, in Ernest Gellner's words, "preaches and defends continuity, but owes everything to a decisive and unutterably profound break in human history."[3] The obfuscation bound up with antiquarian attempts to recover lost roots served in general to mask the historical break represented by the more egalitarian social relations, new divisions of labor, and increasingly secular politics associated with the structure of the modern nation-state. Writing about "the ruptures of the later eighteenth century," Anderson describes how these ruptures created a "new consciousness" afflicted by "amnesias and estrangements parallel to the forgetting of childhood brought on by puberty." Hence a backfilling operation: "at just this juncture," he continues, "emerged the narrative of the nation."[4] The familiar "awakening" *topos*, which imagines the nation as preexisting but dormant, serves to soften the discontinuity, even as it constitutes "the people" as a natural entity.[5] Even a pervasive pattern of fraudulent history-writing was not successful in patching up these gaps and lacunae. The sheer visibility of these ruptures, indeed, marks the eighteenth-century moment itself as uniquely liminal in the canonical sequence of literary-historical periods: an anomalous "Age of Forgery" that cannot be smoothly dovetailed with a continuous national history. Hence a notorious crux: the difficulty of arriving at a convincing way of characterizing this transitional era.

To be sure, certain elemental continuities in motives and strategy can be found between literary forgers in all ages: the *topos* of "ancient documents discovered," for instance, and the practices of "distressing." The latter involves simulating the ravages of time on material artifacts, as Thomas Chatterton doctored his "Rowley" manuscripts with ochre. The great arc of literary forgery arguably reaches from the esoteric wisdom ascribed to Hermes Trismegistus in late antiquity to the eighth-century *Donation of Constantine* to the nineteenth-century Book of Mormon and beyond. In this vein Anthony Grafton contends that the honor roll of eighteenth-century forgers—George Psalmanazar, Charles Bertram, William Lauder, Thomas Chatterton, and William Henry Ireland—belongs to "the *longue durée* of literary fraud."[6] Despite these continuities, however, a marked shift during the Enlightenment—what Susan Stewart terms "the rise in the legislation of originality, authorship, and authenticity"[7]—should not be minimized. As regards literary forgery, the particular legal and political developments of the Enlightenment confirm that the eighteenth century in Britain constitutes, as Paul Baines argues, "a defining period for concepts of fraud."[8] Both Baines and Stewart emphasize a newly inaugurated model of literary property: a forensic and economic nexus that brings together copyright law with a more individualistic notion of originality. Following Gellner, I contend that this accompanied the development of an anonymous, literate, specialist-transmitted culture based on a national metaphysics of "the people." The resulting conjuncture, as manifest in the moment of the first Celtic Revival, produced a distinctly *historiographical* mode of fraudulence. The most telling index of this sleight of hand is the ubiquity of metalepsis: a term that requires extensive definition. The eighteenth-century process of reappropriating the past—paradigmatic for subsequent myths of collective origins—amounts to a colossal *metalepsis*: a rhetorical figure of temporal reversal especially characteristic of the later eighteenth century.

What, exactly, *is* metalepsis? A premodern example of this self-referential trope, as Slavoj Žižek observes, can be found in a depiction of the Crucifixion by the medieval Dutch master Hieronymus Bosch. In this painting there is, in Žižek's words, a "nonsensical short-circuit" in that "one of the two thieves executed together with Jesus Christ confesses before his death to a priest holding a Bible under his arm."[9] The Church, according to the painting's uncanny logic, already existed as a fully developed institution at the very moment on which Christian theology is founded. Such a glaring metalepsis is perhaps unlikely to blend unobtrusively into the inert background of the "literal." Much of the New Testament, however, amounts to a subtler metaleptic operation on the Hebrew Bible. The latter, as Harold Bloom points out is not only recast as the superseded "Old Testament" but also repositioned by the Gospel of John as chronologically *later* than the eternal Christian Logos. "Before Abraham was"—as John's Jesus proclaims—"I am" (John: 8: 57–58).[10] By viewing biblical history itself as a

hermeneutic object—a typological "message" from a deity with foreknowl-
edge of the future—the New Testament willfully overcomes the unidirec-
tional limits of calendrical time. The arrow of Christian time, operating
according to an omnidirectionality that reads Christ the Logos into the
origins of the universe, metaleptically replaces the earlier with the later,
the Alpha with the Omega.

The dawning nationalism of the later eighteenth century is scarcely less
egregious in its anachronisms than the painting by Bosch. Despite certain
pathbreaking contributions, moreover—I think both of *The Invention of
Tradition*[11] and the companion volumes *Making History and Questioning
History*[12]—the process of national metalepsis has barely begun to be analyzed. Once the national metalepsis of "Britishness" became culturally
dominant, it tended to become invisible. A certain amnesia set in, also minimizing the extent to which the early precipitation of a "British" identity
was visibly global in its reach, visibly tied to its imperial annexations. Hence
the necessity of returning to the productive perplexities of the eighteenth-
century emergence of a British national culture. These perplexities constitute the story—a history of nation-based history-writing—that this book
will tell. But first we must stipulate a working definition of metalepsis: the
self-referential trope that murders time in the course of fabricating origins.

Metalepsis: A Definition

Metalepsis is an indispensable supplement to the influential concept of "the
invention of tradition." For a great deal of the fabrication that constitutes
invented traditions is structured by a specific figurative logic: namely, that
trope by which later *effects* covertly substitute for earlier *causes*. This metaleptic masquerade, while claiming to mediate the past, operates from and on
the present. The metaleptic reversal of antecedent and consequence, however, has a curious hall-of-mirrors quality that goes beyond the usual
anachronism of reading the present into the past: the phenomenon rou-
tinely denounced by historians as "presentism." The double figurations of
metalepsis seem more complex—more self-referential and more circular in
their logic—than the usual anachronisms of "presentism."

In speaking of fraudulent history, I deliberately risk provocation on
various fronts. I intend to avoid the conceptual confounding of truth and
fiction, pursued most eloquently by Hayden White, in many a contemporary theory. In the tracking of a course of events, it makes sense to mark a
spectrum that ranges from relative reliability, based on publically shared and
relevant evidence, to tendentious slanting, to outright fakery. Since few
historians have ever insisted that a literal access to the "raw" past is possible,
very little has been gained by bashing the straw man of an absolute positivism.

I likewise wish to avoid the opposite extreme: the position that the past is entirely a fictitious construct. As Noël Carroll points out, White's reiterated dichotomy between life (which is "lived") and stories (which are "told") simply cannot do justice to the historical effects of narrative itself. I concur with Carroll's contention that properly historical narratives, involving historical agents and their plans, require a sense of the overlapping stories that mediated their decisions and actions.[13] Because human life is experienced historically, one can study, as historical data, the archival layers of storytelling that constitute its horizons. To quote an elegant formulation: the complexity of "making history" in this sense has been summarized by Greg Clingham, who underscores the ambiguity created by the fact "of history and historical discourse being *at once* textual *and thereby* materially engaged and productive of new historical realities."[14] The notion of metalepsis, then, despite its apparent emphasis on figuration, in fact *returns* us to a certain reality: one that is neither "literal" (whatever that could mean) nor merely fictitious. Metalepsis is the concept that unlocks the very real distortions of historiography in the eighteenth century: distortions that mark the impact on historiography of British nation- and empire-building.

The expanded concept of the metaleptic process to be studied here involves a widespread and tendentious patterning of historical materials as regards the collective origins: the fabrication of roots. The recipe for a national metalepsis goes like this. In Phase One of the metaleptic process, one must convert some "relic" of the recoverable past into a magically flattering mirror: a trope that erases all traces of external derivation and contingency at the supposed foundations. An isolated element of the present is then *projected backwards* onto the past as a fictive moment of origination. This projection *repunctuates a diffuse series* by interrupting it with a spurious point of origin. Since excessive evidence of randomness or amalgamation must be purged from the repristinated origin, a massaging or outright *liquidation of extant historical sources* typically ensues. A *new terrain of argumentation* must often be established. Moreover, a half-buried chain of transmission, sufficiently intact to allow recovery, must also be salvaged: an illusion, as it were, *of restored continuity.* The direct line thus drawn establishes a regressive and overly immediate channel of identification between past and present. Time is murdered. This *collapse of middle terms*, a gerrymandered redrawing of the past, produces a supposedly organic chain of unbroken "roots."

In Phase two of the metalepsis, then, *the present is reconfigured* on the basis of the genealogical chain just fabricated for it. One earnestly "looks into the past," through a certain sort of antiquarian research; and then—behold!— one is immensely flattered by "recognizing" what a resplendent soul one was even in times long forgotten. Or, to translate it into the collective terms in which my examples of metalepsis operate: "We shall again be glorious, as we were in days of yore." From pre-cooked provenance, through an elaborate time-bridging operation by way of speculative or imaginary intermediate conduits, the metalepsis moves toward a thorough recasting of the present. A new and *more comprehensive saturation* of the "prefigured" present can now be attempted. The bridging operation—a narrative of corruptions, losses, purifications, and gapfilling recoveries—then permits the final stage. The completed metalepsis, tautological in its self-legitimating structure, *intervenes in actual conditions in the present.* A relatively frictionless narrative of collective origins and imminent arrival now encompasses past, present, and future. The collective "we, the people" so constituted—a transfiguration of the present—derives at one remove from a fabricated past. The metaleptic operation itself is designed to be a *vanishing mediator:* a scaffolding meant to disappear once the ideological edifice is securely in place. A new historical reality has been established and legitimated.

The nation-based metalepsis is precisely the recovery of meaning from the senseless: the recuperation of history's randomness, as Anderson would say, in favor of a spurious coherence. As a mode of mystification, the nation-based metalepsis that emerges in the Enlightenment is perhaps all the more beguiling to the extent that it mimics secular and rational forms of scholarly discourse. The value of anatomizing the covertly figurative dynamics of this discourse lies precisely in disclosing how such discourse legitimates the activity of national reinvention by way of fabricated origins.

Structure

The problem of metalepsis sets up the larger project of this book, which is to reread the British eighteenth century. In part I of *The British Eighteenth Century and Global Critique,* I show how an emerging idea of "Britishness" was being visibly made up in the eighteenth century: visibly cobbled together and, perhaps above all—visibly contested—before one's very eyes. Against this background, I investigate a key cultural phenomenon of the later eighteenth century: the metaleptic fabrication of national and racial pasts. I take the widespread eighteenth-century controversy over James Macpherson's notorious forgery of the pseudo-ancient "Ossian" epics as the epitome both of this activity and of its simultaneous critique.

In part II, I explore the enabling role of the British eighteenth century through paired readings of eighteenth century and contemporary writers. The section focuses on the decision of such authors as Salman Rushdie, Wole Soyinka, and Charles Johnson to affiliate with such eighteenth-century British authors as Laurence Sterne, John Gay, and Olaudah Equiano. The intertextual connections I explore below do not serve merely to aggrandize the present moment at the expense of a more benighted age. And the relationship involved between the juxtaposed texts involves far more than a mere "answering" or talking back. It involves a writing *through*, a writing *with*, perhaps even a writing *to*: relations of deliberate affiliation, extension, and elaboration that tend to escape the perverse logic by which nativism so often becomes merely the inverted mirror-image of imperialism. Each of the three chapters in this section consists of a reading that brings out the postcolonial logic of the pairing. When framed thus, the marked "turn to the eighteenth century" in the works of contemporary writers appears neither as a simple repudiation of the eighteenth-century moment nor as postmodern pastiche. A gesture of affiliation, this intertextual phenomenon marks an important difference between the postcolonial and postmodern projects. Affiliation, creatively cosmopolitan, takes one beyond identity politics.

In part III, then, I round out the revisionary reading of eighteenth-century British literature by demonstrating the eighteenth century's capacity for immanent critique. The focus is on the works of two major eighteenth-century writers, Jonathan Swift and Samuel Johnson. Their powerful attempts to disrupt imperial ideology—an achievement seldom given its due—gives the lie to contemporary habits of Enlightenment-bashing. To reveal the immanent critique of modernity disrupts the founding assumptions of a postmodernity defined over and against a supposedly monolithic eighteenth-century Enlightenment. Above all, this section makes the moment available as a critical resource for the future.

PART I

CANNIBALIZING HISTORY: THE PROBLEM
OF METALEPSIS

CHAPTER 1

THE GLOBAL MAKING OF THE BRITISH
EIGHTEENTH CENTURY

This book attempts, in the broadest terms, to lend analytical flexibility to current studies of the oft-bashed "Age of Reason." I am thus concerned with a problem of historical periodization: the perplexing sequence of historical changes known collectively as the British Enlightenment. To a surprising degree, moreover, this problem of historical periodization is linked to a terminology and to a geographical scale conspicuously wider than the territorial boundaries of Britain. Globalization itself has a history and that history, as Emma Rothschild argues, leads inexorably back to the eighteenth century.[1] For one thing, as the century in which "powerful quasi-European England becomes more powerful and imperial Britain"[2]— Howard Weinbrot's pithy formulation—the British eighteenth century offers an especially useful vantage-point for the study of modernity and for the expansion of geographical horizons that accompanied its arrival. For another thing, the antagonisms produced by this imperial process produced crucial anticipations of contemporary efforts to think beyond the horizons of the nation. Indeed, the eighteenth-century emergence of imperial Britishness, like its twentieth-century decline, problematizes the autonomy of the nation-state as such. And though the eighteenth-century moment is often cast as merely ancillary or reactionary, the period is better understood as a vital resource for complicating our own impoverished debates about the "Enlightenment project."

A great many readers of eighteenth-century British literature—even some specialists—are unwilling to see anything of interest or complexity in what they take to be the obvious and uninflected nature of eighteenth-century discourse. Against this pervasive stereotype, I contend that much in the eighteenth century challenges and exceeds the blinkered categories of historical periodization bequeathed to us by the successive redactions of empire- and nation-based historiography. I am thus especially interested in making visible the palimpsestic layers of nineteenth- and twentieth-century appropriations that have constituted the current positioning of the Enlightenment in narratives of cultural history. The importance of this problematic can be gauged by the pervasive framing function, for today's scholarly debates, of received cultural narratives about the Enlightenment. Both in the Humanities and the Social Sciences, several of the most urgent contemporary controversies are typically framed by distorted *ideés reçues* concerning the eighteenth-century Enlightenment. These controversies include the following: (1) debates about the political and aesthetic significance of rationality; (2) debates about the political and cultural significance of the "West," "Eurocentrism"; (3) debates about the definition of nation-based curricular fields, national "canons" of literature; and (4) debates about cultures and identities often defined over and against concepts such as, for example, "Western modernity."

Those in the field of eighteenth-century British literature have long been accustomed to schemas of literary history in which the eighteenth century features as an evolutionary stepping-stone. The eighteenth centuries of our literary anthologies and survey courses have evidently been constructed, as Lawrence Lipking has observed, "by the interests of a later time."[3] Moreover, a great deal of scholarship confirms that the cultural phenomenon we now call "Romanticism" marks the point of consolidation for the evolutionary formulas from which modern historical periodization itself derives. There is a sense, then, in which Romanticism—a self-proclaimed genesis—was, above all, a massively influential narrative.[4] Nineteenth-century Britain claimed to have achieved a triumphant shift from a vertical and class-ridden society to a significantly more horizontal and democratized one: a politically reformed and culturally "mature" nation. Douglas Lane Patey describes the resulting *nationalization* of the cultural past thus: "The history of any art becomes a history of stages—periods—corresponding to, because informed by, larger movements of the national mind and institutions."[5] The modes of literary-historical periodization we inherit from the nineteenth century thus articulate a developmental metanarrative of a national identity that has been retrospectively forged precisely from that era: the moment when a firmly secured "Britishness" was being consolidated over and against a disorderly past. Whiggish historicism cast the eighteenth century as representing the unnatural artifice of the *ancien régime*: the bewigged and decadent foil against which all later progress allegedly occurred. Such a narrative trivializes the significant ideological conflicts within the period. No wonder, perhaps, that scholars of eighteenth-century British literature have long grumbled among themselves about the discontents of working on a retrospectively constructed epoch.

To the familiar marginalization of "pre-Romantic" teleologies, however, there have now been added others. For contemporary theorists assert that postmodern thought has achieved a clean break with intellectual and political developments that are almost always traced back to the eighteenth-century Enlightenment. The Whiggish glorification of a continuous march of bourgeois progress has thus yielded to the postmodern laceration of a grand narrative of bourgeois hegemony. Once again, a historical break has been defined; and once again, the eighteenth-century moment figures as the devalued past to be broken from. As that which is made to stand for the origin and essence of modernity's undeniable violence, the period itself comes in, yet again, for a considerable drubbing. This postmodernist version of the eighteenth century does little more than invert the Whiggish "grand narrative," largely consolidated in the nineteenth century, which constructed the eighteenth century as the embryonic origin or harbinger—now surpassed and fulfilled—of all progress and reform. The crucial ruptures and obtrusive sutures in the cultures of the Enlightenment are papered over by many strains of contemporary theory, which depend for self-legitimation upon a monolithically baleful Enlightenment.

Hence a paradox: the eighteenth century does double duty in the broader sweep of literary and cultural historiography. The eighteenth century is made to represent simultaneously both the decadence of the *ancien régime* and the excesses of the French Revolution. Only a uniquely transitional century could require such a double negation: first as the quintessence of the Old Regime, and then again as the hateful epitome of "Violent Modernity." The leading feature of the British eighteenth century is indeed its conspicuous historical liminality as regards modernity. That liminal quality, as I argue in chapter 2, is everywhere evident and yet seldom fully acknowledged. It offers many compelling sites, moreover, from which a telling critique of the present can be launched. The abortive directions, the nipped buds, the roads not taken: precisely these possibilities that have been retroactively distorted, and that now appear in a very different light. Thinking back by means of the eighteenth century, with full attention to the threshold nature of its modernity, makes it possible to disaggregate concepts too easily lumped together. We achieve a sudden shift in perspective: a turn of the kaleidoscope that rearranges familiar elements. In historiographical terms, this means a reshuffling of several components of our current maps of literary history.

How can a single given period in literary history be made to represent both the evils of the past (in effect, the *ancien régime*) and the fearful violence of modernity? And what does it mean that in our broader accounts of literary history the eighteenth century continues to function in such a contradictory way? As I argue below, a figurative pattern of *metalepsis*—the retrospective fabrication of roots—constitutes a crucial part of the answer to these questions. The eighteenth century saw both the emergence of metaleptic narratives of the nation and of lacerating challenges to that emergence. We have failed to do justice to the useful messiness and agonizing contingencies that haunt the beginnings of such disciplines as history and literature. Both praised and damned for founding such nation-based disciplines, the cusp of the eighteenth century makes visible a key problematic for our moment: the challenges to nationhood both by fissures within the body politic and from more cosmopolitan perspectives. The resonance of such a conflicted beginning, its potential to outflank our own debates, has often been obscured by position-taking defined, in overly stark terms, either for or against "the Enlightenment."

As an era before "Britishness" could be invisibly assumed as natural, the eighteenth century is an epoch in which certain ideological patches and seams are crucially salient. Two powerful institutions—that of the national narrative, and that of history as a professional discipline—were gradually being assembled in a conspicuously awkward and often contradictory fashion. A reading of the eighteenth-century moment in more dialogical terms would thus serve to remind us that the oppositional themes of our own moment replay a great many eighteenth-century debates.[6] Indeed, the public culture of eighteenth-century Britain problematized historiography as such. For the eighteenth-century moment marks the emergence of the classic nation-building problematic of *making history*: a spectrum of "modernizing" narrative and publishing activities that encompasses outright forgery and archival fabrication as well as more productive enlargements of public memory. This problematic emerged as the potential vicious circle, as Greg Clingham intimates, lurking in the double sense in which history must be "made": a seemingly inescapable short circuit created by the fact, to invoke his words again, "of history and historical discourse being *at once* textual *and thereby* materially engaged and productive of new historical realities. . . ."[7] Clingham's companion volumes, *Making History and Questioning History*, register the extent to which current theoretical debates around such issues were first worked through in the course of confronting the emergence of nation-based historiography in the eighteenth century. The bumpy eighteenth-century process of "forging" Britishness thus produced a characteristic liminality that obstinately refuses to conform to the seamless logic of a later nation-based metanarrative.

Nineteenth-Century Appropriations

The initial debunking of the eighteenth century coincides with the moment of romantic nationalism. The writing of history, as a modern discipline, has been inseparable from the late-eighteenth-century rise of European nation-states.[8] What historians would then attempt to write, for the first time, is some part of the collective story of "we, the people": a process, despite the development of rigorous professional standards, that has been profoundly mediated by the need to *make*—in all senses of the word—easily consumable appropriations of a supposedly shared and supposedly self-legitimating past. In tracing supposed pedigrees of "the people," then, innumerable cultural historians, in disciplines as varied as historical linguistics, art history, literature, and folklore, have produced genealogies of collective identity: national museums, national curricula, national monuments, nation-based literary canons, and the list goes on. These genealogies have functioned to secure and harmonize the contemporary politics of national identification.[9] A centralized educational system is of course necessary to the production, through the harnessing of culture to pedagogy, of citizens. And so the later eighteenth century figures as the key moment, as Alan Richardson has emphasized, for the emergence of Literature as such: as "a cultural institution predicated on a canonical set of 'imaginative' works, disseminated through schools and centralized publishing venues, and managed by a professional group of critics and interpreters."[10] From the mid-nineteenth to the mid-twentieth centuries, according to Margit Sichert's review of numerous literary histories, such nation-based historiography played a functional role in disseminating pride in a distinctive and unified British character.[11]

It becomes obvious, then, why the so-called Whig version of history—that familiar account of the rise and cumulative progress of science, of the progressive increase of liberty, and so on[12]—has long been a favorite bugbear in eighteenth-century studies. As Norma Landau has observed, this is a version of history that sidelines the British eighteenth century as the interlude between the two great moments of the Glorious Revolution and the Reform Act of 1832:[13] a political history that evidently strongly overdetermines the familiar Classical-to-Romantic teleology in literary history. The nineteenth century claimed to have achieved a triumphant shift from a vertical and class-ridden society to a more horizontal and democratic one. This framing of history, however, allows the issue of domestic social stratification to eclipse other forms of oppression, and thus other modes of radical response, than those constituted by domestic class antagonisms alone. Such a nation-centered view of domestic reforms thus simply ignored how "parliamentary democracy," as defined by the boundaries of the nation-state, was constituted within a larger dynamics of imperial aggression and exploitation. Looking inward only, then, the Whig version of history refuses to engage with the significance of "external" victims of a material and social progress that was often built on their land, natural resources, labor, and military service; and at the expense of their autonomous economic, political, and cultural development.

The much-vaunted fraternal bonding evoked by the slogans of modernity—the universalizing language of rights—was thus shadowed by a racially exclusive definition of such rights: for *citizenship*, the only means by which one could exercise such rights, served precisely to mark the limits to such universality.[14] The Parliamentary Reform Act of 1867, one of the familiar milestones of domestic reform and progress in British history, specifically enfranchised only "Anglo-Saxon" males.[15] This racializing of citizenship is no minor aberration of history: it is intrinsic to the genealogical fictions of "common descent" used to legitimate the nation-state's coordination of the political structure with the cultural units of language, religion, and, of course, literary tradition. The Reform Act of 1867 marks the official arrival, in Britain, of the "racial state."[16]

The early- to-mid-eighteenth century was retrospectively defined in this nation-centered view, above all, in terms of elitism: as a class-ridden society and culture whose "artificiality" could be countered with a new order supposedly based on "nature." German *Geistesgeschichte* played a special role in paving the way for the reification of "peoples" into ethnically absolute cultural islands. Johann Gottfried Herder, for example, attacked as artificial monstrosities polylingual states like the Hapsburg Empire, which he described as a sort of Frankensteinian montrosity: the grotesque patching together of mismatched bodily parts from a lion, dragon, eagle, and bear.[17] This homogenizing gesture claimed to reject a classical heritage in the name of an authentic, natural, and unmediated language: the vernacular language of, as the familiar slogan has it, a man speaking to men. The often unspoken mediation was, of course, precisely the contours of a nation: a nation, indeed, that was, in the case of nineteenth-century Britain, learning to administer a global division of labor.[18] And the naturalizing language of the innate and self-evident was, notoriously, applied to the social categories that constituted this new order: above all, the intertwined categories of race, nation, ethnicity, and language.

Such organicist imagery for peoplehood, indeed, validates the insulation of local custom and tradition from rational critique. So the universalism of an earlier phase of the Enlightenment was pitted during the later eighteenth century over and against the heroic underdog of "local knowledge": that assumption, conveniently affixed to the name of Herder, that cultures are incommensurable. Such local knowledge, underwritten by appeals to authentic experience, authorizes an irrational epistemological immediacy. One should not, according to the more extreme versions of organicist politics, have to *reason* about political arrangements: one should just *intuit* political connections—and divisions—the way one feels the fated and unquestionable bonds of familial kinship. From this issues a tendency in Edmund Burke and numerous nineteenth-century thinkers, from Friedrich Schiller to Samuel Taylor Coleridge, toward the aestheticization of politics, and toward the "aesthetic ideology."[19] Perhaps for this reason Ivan Hannaford suggests that "race," as an ideology, was able to displace politics as it had been previously defined in the lengthy tradition of civic humanism, in which the definition of political life—however elitist—entailed articulate participation in a community self-consciously organized by law and forensic protocols of public debate.[20]

Hence a vast elaboration of vitalist and organicist metaphors for the "extended family" of the nation: a supposed kinship that anchored itself around genealogies of ethnicity and "race." Such localism, then—often hailed as an emancipatory breakthrough—in fact unleashed an irrationalist particularism whose regressive effects include the underwriting of ethnically exclusive nationalisms. By 1850, Robert Knox was prepared to declare in *The Races of Man* that "race or hereditary descent is everything."[21] And indeed, by the mid-nineteenth century one can scarcely find work in cultural historiography, whatever its immediate agenda, that does not think by way of a thoroughly racialized terminology. For liberals and conservatives alike, the ubiquitous and naturalized categories of mid-nineteenth-century historiography tend to be the "Hebraic," the "Hellenic," the "Celtic"—and, of course, the "Anglo-Saxon," the "Caucasian," and the "Aryan." Hippolyte Taine's *History of English Literature* (1863–1864) thus works from a dialectic of national temperament and the condition of the Norman conquest:

> The barbarous age established on the soil a German race, phlegmatic and grave, capable of spiritual emotions and moral discipline. The feudal age imposed on this race habits of resistance and association, political and utilitarian prepossessions.[22]

"Race" ("*la race*"), along with milieu and moment, are the three great historical causes that operate in Taine's account, which helped to establish a theoretical basis for nationalizing literature.

The Postmodern Dispensation

Such, then, were the race-tinted lenses through which the nineteenth century looked back at the eighteenth. Contemporary theorists, in an eerie echo of nineteenth-century self-periodization, like to imagine that postmodern theory has achieved a total break with modernity: a clean rupture, that is to say, with intellectual and political developments that are almost always traced back to the eighteenth century. Michel Foucault—his late self-fashioning phase notwithstanding—has promoted the notion of a sudden break with the subject of reason to great effect. In terms of literary history, this presupposes that various "Enlightenment categories"—typical examples would be aesthetic autonomy, rationality, authorship, disinterestedness, and gendered sexuality—are only now, in the wake of theoretically vigilant scholarship, being thrown into a belated but highly productive legitimation crisis. This crisis has supposedly hit the field of eighteenth-century studies with particular severity, in John Bender's words, "because this period more than any other produced the assumptions that have structured modern literary study."[23]

There are in fact several striking features to the importation of postmodern theory into the field of eighteenth-century British studies. One is the tendency to conflate the Enlightenment project with the eighteenth century as a whole.[24] Much of what Foucault has written about the "classical age," for example—from the triumph of the "great confinement" to the mutation of penology from bodily torture to rationalized psychic discipline—describes nineteenth-century Britain far better than it does the earlier Georgian era. Jeremy Bentham, who published his *Panopticon* in 1791, peddled his utilitarian views and surveillance scheme in the late eighteenth and early nineteenth centuries. The "science of man" to which Foucault bids such a grandiloquent farewell in *The Order of Things* signifies precisely those social sciences—and, above all, anthropology and sociology—that either simply do not exist before the nineteenth century or are at best nascent in the work of a few Scottish Enlightenment thinkers of the eighteenth century. One might argue that in generational terms Foucault, while actually slaying his nineteenth-century *grandfather*, has somehow been understood instead as slaying his eighteenth-century *great-grandfather*. In any case, the eighteenth-century Enlightenment remains perhaps the contemporary academy's most sacrosanct myth of origins: the site of a magically full-blown, self-present, and immediately reigning essence of all that has proven to be lethal or corrosive in modernity.

This contemporary failure—the reluctance to engage with the Enlightenment's capacity for self-critique—induces a certain intellectual and political stagnation. Indeed, the extent to which the "subversive" discourses of our own moment have now hardened, á la Flaubert, into a lexicon of *ideés reçues* is confirmed by the appearance in 1999 of *The Routledge Dictionary of Postmodern Thought*. One widely received such idea—François Lyotard's binary opposition between virtuously local "little narratives" and oppressively totalizing "grand narratives"—constitutes a monumental impediment even to grasping the structural effects of a genuinely global phenomenon such as several centuries of European colonial domination. Indeed, a politics whose legitimacy is explicitly restricted to local contexts can do little more than shrug when confronted with the systemic economic inequality—the global divide between rich and poor nations—that is surely the most brutal contemporary legacy of European imperialism. Far more forward-looking is Mrinalini Sinha's concept of the *imperial social formation*.[25] As an expanded field of analysis, the imperial social formation brings together violently discrepant, but nevertheless intersecting and ineluctably linked historical experiences. It provides a fresh perspective from which one can reexamine familiar problems of location, identity, historical memory, and historical periodization. To a surprising extent, moreover, the placidity enabled by a preoccupation with a local micro-politics of the subject is linked to the issue of historical periodization. "One shorthand way to define postmodernism"—so says the *Routledge Dictionary of Postmodern Thought*—"is as the end of the dream of mastery and a definitive improvement to human society through knowledge and technology."[26] Such platitudes conserve the monological authority of one historical moment over another. In doing so, however, they serve to erase precisely the distinctive and potentially productive *liminality* that is most characteristic of eighteenth-century public culture.

A second striking feature pertaining to the application of postmodern theory to the field of eighteenth-century British studies is the fallacious equation of a specifically Francocentric understanding of the Enlightenment, defined as a war of reason against clerical "tradition," with the very different trajectory of the Enlightenment in Britain. Here one can adduce Foucault's description of the classical episteme as an age constituted by the following discursive regularities: a rage for taxonomy and analytic nomenclature, emphasizing panoramic and synchronic maps of grammar-like tables; the purging, from natural history, of the lore of traditional commentaries; and the treatment of verbal signs as mere transparent instruments of representation rather than as part of the things themselves.[27] To be sure, these are all recognizable eighteenth-century British trends. Even so, however, Foucault's overly totalizing description of early science exaggerates its discontinuity, in the British context, from the Renaissance and its epistemological assumptions. Indeed, Foucault's periodization simply cannot reckon with physico-theology, a mainly British phenomenon that lingered well into the nineteenth century.[28] For the popularization of science, and especially Newtonian natural philosophy, developed during the British Enlightenment in the context of a prolonged "holy alliance" between science and Anglican apologetics.[29] Physico-theology was, in Robert Markley's words, "the quest for a single system of representation that articulates its equally strong commitments to experimental philosophy and to theology."[30] And there is little room in Foucault's periodization for the recognition that the influential Swedish botanist and taxonomist Linnaeus saw the world as ruled by a "divine economy" that linked sin and suffering; or that Sir Isaac Newton—"the last of the magicians," as John Maynard Keynes said in 1942—had strong hermeticist interests in alchemy, astrology, and Biblical prophecy.[31] The liminality of early science has been erased under the rubric of "discursive regularities."

Finally, there is the paradoxical way that the second or Postmodern break seemingly repeats many aspects of the now-familiar pluralizing gesture of romantic localism, even as it ascribes a very different valence to the eighteenth-century moment. For postmodern theory revolves around the declaration that the project of Enlightenment rationality and its discourse of universal human rights have proven to be a dead end: merely the lethal revelation that reason and domination are synonymous.[32] By effectively attacking the ontological basis of classical liberalism—that society is constituted by rights-bearing individuals—postmodern thinkers have mapped instead a world constituted by any number of incommensurable truth-regimes, discursive formations, and Wittgensteinian language-games.[33] "Postmodernist constructivism," as Satya P. Mohanty observes, "may be defined most basically as the idea that all those epistemological norms which were so dear to the Enlightenment—rationality, objectivity, and truth—are no more than social conventions, historically variable and hence without claim to universality."[34] Such relativism means, in effect, "that there can be no responsible way in which I can adjudicate between your space—cultural and historical—and mine by developing a set of general criteria that can have interpretative validity in both contexts."[35] Precisely this refusal of normative public standards is what has made the political significance of Foucault's work, at best, highly paradoxical.[36] Having turned his theoretical guillotine, as Thomas Keenan puts it, "on the individual, the human, and the humanism of human rights," Foucault simply cannot provide any compelling answer to the question: *why fight?*[37] Between Edmund Burke's horror of the abstract and Foucault's contemporary version of localism—his validation of "subjugated knowledges"—there may be, after all, less to choose than is commonly admitted or understood.

Liminalities

Both the Romantic and the Postmodern appropriations of the eighteenth century miss the abundant evidence that the eighteenth century is marked, on any number of crucial fronts, by a peculiar and distinctive historical liminality. The widely misunderstood liminality of its political economy is perhaps the best point of departure. This liminality can be glimpsed in the seeming anomaly of "gentlemanly capitalism," as P. J. Cain and A. G. Hopkins term it: a concept invoked to explain the values of the landed ruling class in

Britain at a moment when the country was still agricultural. The aristocracy was "shaped by merging its pre-capitalist heritage with incomes derived from commercial agriculture."[38] This is precisely why, as J. G. A. Pocock points out, that "the Augustan debate did not—as is often assumed—oppose agrarian to entrepreneurial interests, the manor to the market."[39] It was neither trade nor merchants that were the particular objects of controversy, but, rather, the *nationalization of credit*: the creation, that is, of the new Dutch-style institutions of finance capitalism, which permitted speculation with public funds.[40] England's "financial revolution" of the 1690s had enabled William III to establish new relations between politics and commerce. Adopting and sophisticating Dutch financial institutions, the English almost simultaneously nationalized the public debt (1693) and founded the Bank of England (1694) to manage it. By reorganizing its fiscal institutions, the English government increased its control over the minting of money, the legitimation of legal tender, and the availability of both money and credit. Whence a remarkable "lead," as Cain and Hopkins put it, "in the area of finance and commercial services": a lead that set the country apart from its rivals.[41] Colin Nicholson thus emphasizes the way that early-eighteenth-century satire responds to the founding of the Bank of England, the establishment of a national debt, and the revolutionary impact of paper credit on financial markets.[42] Precisely through the categories of legitimacy and criminality, then, one can see the liminality of early-eighteenth-century Britishness. In terms of its political culture, the age of the South Sea Bubble is distinguished by what historians have termed "Old Corruption": the reinflection of older cultural forms—above all, elite networks of patronage—to serve the interests of a new cash- and credit-based system.[43] And so it was, as Pocock likewise observes, that " 'bourgeois ideology,' a paradigm for capitalist man as *zoon politikon*, was immensely hampered in its development by the omnipresence of Aristotelian and civic humanist values which virtually defined rentier and entrepreneur as corrupt."[44]

The liminality of "Britishness"—its unfinished quality in much of the eighteenth century—has other coordinates as well. Critics otherwise as disparate in their views as Howard Erskine-Hill and Michael McKeon have warned against overstressing the familiar theme of "Augustan consensus."[45] On one side of the political spectrum, the supposed Whig consensus evoked by the term "Augustan Age" was disrupted by the once-revolutionary and still potentially subversive threat of "enthusiasm": the French Prophets, the beginnings of Methodism with that "reasonable enthusiast" John Wesley,[46] and the list goes on.[47] On the other, the consensus was riven by subcurrents of Jacobitism that twice erupted in armed rebellion: aftershocks of the seventeenth-century civil war. Britishness was, as Murray Pittock and Michael Hechter have insisted, thus simultaneously invented and resisted—and resisted not least by the regional popular cultures of Scotland, Ireland, and Wales.[48]

Given the nationalist project of coordinating the political and the cultural, our late-twentieth-century debates about canonicity are inevitably foreshadowed by the lengthy eighteenth-century struggles over vernacular canon-formation.[49] The emergence of a "British" literary tradition and curriculum, however, does not signify, even in historically relative terms, merely the democratic virtue of greater "inclusiveness." The episode that belongs specifically to the complex and highly ambivalent history of nation-building. And the particular role of eighteenth-century literature in nationalizing the British polity looms large in the work of many a contemporary scholar. What has seldom been adequately recognized even in the invaluable historical work, however, is the way that modern nation-building itself comes after, and is ultimately determined within, a global process of empire-building. The most significant exception to this rule is Kathleen Wilson's *The Sense of the People: Politics, Culture, and Imperialism in England, 1715–1785*. Wilson clearly demonstrates how an extra-parliamentary public culture, both invoking and inventing "the people," laid the foundations during the Georgian era simultaneously for "Britishness" and for Britain's nineteenth-century empire.[50] She has extended this anti-insular focus in *The Island Race: Englishness, Empire, and Gender in the Eighteenth Century*, which tackles the impact on domestic Britain of its growing empire.[51] To focus on the dynamics of this imperial process, which eventually touched even the most remote British village, immediately calls into question the commonsense boundaries of the nation.

The eighteenth-century moment stands out precisely in the way that empire and nation are so visibly *linked*. The umbilical cord, as it were, has not yet been cut: and precisely that visibility—often seized upon by the likes of John Gay, Jonathan Swift, Samuel Johnson, and other oppositional thinkers—which a fully matured imperial metropole would push into the deep background. In this sense, the category of empire serves to highlight precisely the liminality of eighteenth-century Britishness: for there was a considerable strain of thought in the eighteenth century that resisted, from various angles, the project of building an empire.

Precisely because the foundations of modernity are so messily and visibly contingent that a return to the eighteenth century provides an optimum site for the immanent critique of modernity. Virtually all of the categories currently privileged by way of ideological critique—race, gender, class, sexuality, authorship—are markedly liminal in this period. Above all, the recognition that nation and empire are mutually constitutive allows for the radical critique of "Britishness"—of national identities and national literatures *per se*—and of the category of "race."

The Emergence of "Race"

Perhaps the liminality of "race"—its visibility as an emerging construct—constitutes the greatest significance of the British eighteenth century for immanent critique. The focus in *The British Eighteenth Century and Global Critique* on the historical period during which an imperial discourse about the "Orient" was still emerging reveals the early "Orientalism" of the eighteenth century to be still conspicuously fluid and unstable—far more visibly contingent and vulnerable to challenge, in short, than is commonly assumed. By the same token, through the emergent historiographical project of the last quarter of the eighteenth century we can also trace the construction—the retrospective fabrication—of an essentialized and racialized "West." For modern racism has been, above all, a certain way of writing history: an evolutionary model that equates a preordained path of human development with the sort of technological "progress" represented by, say, the transition from the flint-lock to the repeating rifle.[52]

Racism, indeed, is at best, vaguely and intermittently surfacing throughout the period of Britain's "First Empire." Though "Black codes" were legally instituted by the slave-owning Caribbean plantocracy by the late seventeenth century, racism proper—the development of a coherent and formally elaborated ideology—can scarcely be said even to have emerged before the last quarter of the eighteenth century. The early ethnographic discourses that accompanied premodern conquest and slavery, in other words, long preceded modern racism, and simply did not coincide with it.[53] Indeed, throughout most of the eighteenth century, the debate within Britain over slavery generally turned, as Kenan Malik points out, on questions of economic utility and property rather than on questions of "race."[54] As Roxann Wheeler has thoroughly demonstrated, moreover, the differences in pigmentation and so on now ascribed to "race" had long been outweighed by other traditional categories of social division—notably, the aristocratic ideology of the "three estates"; the dynastic language of kingdoms; and the international discourse of religious communities and infidels. Indeed, throughout the first three quarters of the eighteenth century, the word "race" itself referred to family line, and simply did not refer to a biology-based division of the human population into four or five broad subtypes. Only a more rigorous periodization of racism can enable it to serve as a genuinely critical concept. Racism was at best *emergent*, as Wheeler demonstrates, and skin-color, in her words, "was not the only—or even the primary—register of human difference for much of the eighteenth century. . . ."[55] Though Wheeler's book miscarries badly in its chapter on Johnson's *Journey to the Western Islands of Scotland*, her contribution remains substantial.

A careful reading of eighteenth-century texts highlights precisely the process of racial *formation* rather than the achieved result. Such an approach is designed to counter the current conceptual inflation of racism to mean just about any discursive construction whatsoever, at any time, of an "Other." In Malik's words,

> The category of the Other is ahistorical and takes little account of the specificities of time and place in the creation of the discourse of race. Instead it steamrollers historical, social, and geographical differences into a single discourse of "the West and its Others."[56]

This inflation, for which Foucault-inflected discursive theory bears considerable responsibility, threatens to evacuate the concept of any critical force or historical significance. Only a more rigorous periodization of racism and Orientalism can enable them to serve as genuine critical concepts.

I borrow the term "racial formation" from theorists of racism in the United States, who define it as a concept that "emphasizes the social nature of race, the absence of any essential racial characteristics, the historical flexibility of racial meanings and categories, the conflictual character of race at both the 'micro- and macro-social' levels, and the irreducible political aspect of racial dynamics."[57] It should be noted here that discussions of race and racism have no real equivalent to the term "gender": a terminological resource adopted by feminist thinkers precisely in order to denaturalize ideologically produced difference—a construction imposed by cultural institutions—from a difference allegedly inscribed, by sexed bodies, into nature. Hence the recommendation by Henry Louis Gates, Jr. and other theorists that "race" be surrounded by defamiliarizing quotation marks. Such scare quotes serve as a distancing reminder that "race" is always rhetorical and figurative: "the ultimate trope," as Gates puts it, "of difference."[58] Gates has more recently recalibrated this nominalist position by giving due emphasis to the point that sociopolitical constructions are, after all, very real both in their lived effects and in their grounding of a certain political agency.[59] Even so, in a moment such as ours, which relentlessly plays out a logic of absolute incommensurability and difference, the recognition that race-based identities are ultimately contingent and constructed can only be salutary.

From Class to Race

The word *race* itself, as numerous cultural historians have pointed out, signified "lineage" throughout most of the century.[60] The history of the word, as Raymond Williams demonstrates, shows a transition during the 1700s from a class-based sense of ancestral lineage to the modern notion of a primary division of the human population based on visible biological characteristics.[61] The older sense of "race" refers to ancestral "blood," and hence ancestry in the narrow sense of familial clan: a small-scale group. As such, the term is imbricated in a classical ideology affirming aristocratic values: the unabashed rule of a nobility characterized, on the basis of its familial pedigree, by strength, courage, honor, and virtue. The reference in Aphra Behn's *Oroonoko* (1688) to the title character's being "the last of his great race" carries precisely this older familial significance: it is, as Fiona Stafford points out, "his royal lineage that is being emphasized rather than his color or ethnic group."[62] The Frenchified manners that enhance Oroonoko's prestige are in fact the very same that distinguished the Francophilic court of Charles II.

The older sense of *race*, which of course involved genealogical conceptions of identity, has certain very limited points of continuity with the modern sense: but one must nevertheless remember that the older sense lacked recourse to the particular ensemble of discourses—of modern divisions of labor on a world-wide scale; of modern domesticity and "normal" sexuality; of modern nationhood; of an imperial mission; of the pseudo-sciences of physiognomic measurement and biological destiny—within which "race" would come to refer to vast and yet supposedly distinct populations. As Jack Lynch points out, the "modern notion of race" is absent from Samuel Johnson's *Dictionary of the English Language* (1755).[63] The first modern usage of *race*, according to the *Oxford English Dictionary*, is found in Oliver Goldsmith's *Animated Nature* in 1774: a work which, nevertheless, still adheres to climatic theories of difference and assumes, as per the Biblical narrative, that humanity is descended from common parents.[64]

The late-eighteenth-century rearticulation of the meaning of "race" reflects a decisive historical change: the transition between what Hannah Arendt has identified as the two great ideologies: those based on class and race. Arendt goes on to describe the eighteenth century as a period of "race thinking before racism." Precisely the shift between these rival ideologies, then, explains the critical and ideological significance of eighteenth-century liminality. And the later eighteenth century, indeed, marks the consolidation of an ideological process by which traditional categories of social classification—above all, the opposition between aristocrats and commoners—began to be rearticulated in the unifying terms of ethnically homogenous "folk." Each folk, ineluctably bound by ties of "blood and soil," was held to possess an immutable soul or *Volksgeist*: so modern nation-alism, even as it attacked the mystique of aristocratic blood, allowed an ugly new metaphysics to enter through its back door.

In the making of "race," the significance of the historical break that occurs in the later eighteenth century is just beginning to be appreciated.

Romantic nationalism, and especially the nationalistic beginnings of vernacular canon-formation, cultivated a particularist fascination with linguistic and literary origins. What had been radical and revolutionary during the mid-seventeenth-century civil war, for instance—the notion of the "Norman yoke"—a class-based discourse which insisted, in Christopher Hill's words, "that before 1066 England was a free country with self-governing institutions"[65]—evolved by the early nineteenth century, under the pressure of British imperialism, into the very different concept of the "Norman race." This explanatory concept is utilized throughout Sir Walter Scott's novel *Ivanhoe* (1819), an early nineteenth-century historical novel that narrates the medieval basis of the modern nation. "Four generations," as Scott writes early in the novel, "had not sufficed to blend the hostile blood of the Normans and the Anglo-Saxons, or to unite, by common language and mutual interests, two hostile races, one of which still felt the elation of triumph, while the other groaned under all the consequences of defeat."[66]

Ivanhoe's "race-struggle" plot exemplifies the way notions of the nation mediated, as Kwame Anthony Appiah suggests, between the concept of race, on the one hand, and the idea of literature, on the other.[67] Nineteenth-century British historians, seeking to "reverse the conquest" by reclaiming the Saxon past, were immensely influenced by this racializing vision of history. Thus Macaulay, for example, in his *History of England* (1848), writes that the Norman Conquest "gave up the whole population of England to the tyranny of the Norman race."[68] By the later nineteenth century, as Appiah notes, Hippolyte Taine had identified the origin of British literature "not in its antecedents in the Greek and Roman classics that provided the models and themes for so many of the best-known works of English 'poesy,' not in the Italian models that influenced the drama of Marlowe and Shakespeare, but in *Beowulf*, a poem that was unknown to Chaucer and Spenser and Shakespeare."[69] The point, of course, is not to question the literary achievement of *Beowulf*: merely to note the poem's frequent use, in a factitious genealogy, for the purposes of a racial roots-finding exercise.

The threshold nature of the eighteenth century as regards "race" is everywhere visible once one understands its peculiar character. As Arendt points out, "race-thinking entered the scene of active politics the moment the European peoples had prepared, and to a certain extent realized, the new body politic of the nation."[70] One of the earliest debates involving the ambivalent politics of citizenship—at once more horizontal and normalizing—was the mid-century "Jew Bill" episode, when the Jewish Naturalization Act of 1753 was first passed and then repealed. This episode illustrates how a *religious* minority population born in England, given the homogenizing impact of nationalizing the body-politic, began to be discussed as in normative terms as an element that could never be assimilated. The Duke of Bedford thus argued in the parliamentary debate around the Jewish Naturalization Act that, as James Shapiro puts it, "Jewishness was an essence even more ineradicable than the blackness of colonial slaves."[71] A full-blown modern ideology of "race," however, was clearly not yet developed. Bedford argued that while blacks could be eventually assimilated through Christianity and intermarriage into the body politic, Jews could not: "whilst they continue Jews, [they] will be and will consider themselves as a people quite distinct and separate from the ancient people of this island."[72] The element that resists assimilation on this account is cultural—a question of tradition and religious belief—rather than strictly "racial."

The new politics of nationhood mutated into racism by way of a second "levelling" dimension. For the imposition of racialized identities on the indigenous peoples who experienced and resisted colonization entailed a highly consequential refusal to recognize distinctions among them of rank and class. Just such an acknowledgment of royal identity, of course, provides the pathos surrounding the title character of *Oroonoko* (1688). While Behn's late-seventeenth-century novella does not attack slavery as an institution, as is often pointed out, what it does resist is precisely *race-based* slavery. The recurring theme of the "royal slave" throughout the eighteenth century thus serves to mark a limit to the acceptance of a politics based entirely on race. Slavery itself had of course long existed in the context of many forms of unfree labor, and was only gradually refashioned as a racially marked practice.

From Biblical Narrative to Polygenesis

The crucial differences between premodern prejudices and modern racism, as well as continuities with it, urgently need to be understood. One simply cannot equate garden-variety xenophobia, ethnocentrism, and religious bigotries, from which no known culture has escaped, with the specifically Eurocentric white supremacist doctrines, buttressed by biological essentialism and a racist rearticulation of world history, which developed in the wake of modern imperialism. Premodern assaults on religious or ethnogeographic "Others"—framed as they were by theocentric or by climatic explanations for human variation—follow a very different logic. The sixteenth- and seventeenth-century rhetoric of colonial conquest and plantation, for example—often organized around notions of "election," on the one hand, and "accursed generation," on the other—does have a corporeal and genealogical component; but it does not, for instance, necessarily foreground skin-color.[73] *Robinson Crusoe* (1719), as Wheeler has recently shown—which uses a discourse about difference revolving around Christians, savages, and slaves—simply does not belong to a moment anchored by "race" as we understand it today.[74] Such prescientific rhetoric, above all, does not entail that hallmark of modern racism: a body-based essentialism that measured crania, weighed brains, quantified facial angles, catalogued the shapes of eyes and noses, classified hair texture, and thus donned the mantle of scientific authority.

Quasi-scientific taxonomies of humankind were of course emerging by mid-century in Linnaeus and others. The latter's schema, nevertheless, tries to map ethno-geographical divisions—Europe, America, Africa, and Asia—onto the traditional four humors.[75] This persistence of humor theory points to a considerable premodern element in Linnaean thought: and indeed, his entire notion of taxonomic hierarchy, as Gates points out, mostly emphasizes a metaphysics of gradations and unbroken continuities, as did the traditional *scala naturae* or "Great Chain of Being."[76] However, Linnaeus does begin to articulate for public consumption a minority view: that perhaps humankind, despite the monogenetic Biblical myth, comprises more than one species. Although this view can also be found in the unpublished papers of the seventeenth-century political economist Sir William Petty,[77] it was left to Linnaeus to popularize the idea. Thus in 1735 he makes the fateful move of classifying humanity into the two separate species of *homo sapiens* (which encompasses the five "varieties" of Africans, Europeans, Americans, Asians, and Wild Men) and *homo monstrosus* (which encompasses Mountaineers, Patagonians, Hottentots, Americans, Chinese, and Canadians).[78] Linnaeus also flirts with speculations about the boundary between humankind and apes, which he regarded as very thin.[79] Above all, perhaps, he attempts to correlate "inner" and "outer" characteristics. To that extent, Linnaean taxonomy probably deserves the responsibility often assigned to eighteenth-century classification more generally for constituting, as David Theo Goldberg puts it, the "primitive terms" or "grammar" of racial discourse.[80]

And so we catch a glimpse of the alternative to Biblical monogenesis: polygenetic theories of human origins, which had mainly emerged in the "progressive" or "free-thinking" context of natural history. The eighteenth century, with its interrogation of scriptural fact claims, the credibility of miracles, and the concordance between the Old and New Testaments, produced a gradual "eclipse," in Hans Frei's term, of Biblical narrative.[81] An exception to this rule is Henry Home, Lord Kames, who traces racial division back to the biblical Tower of Babel in his *Sketches of the History of Man* (1774).[82] More typical in his scientistic rhetoric, however, is Edward Long, the English judge who became a Jamaican plantocrat. Long insists in the *History of Jamaica* (1774), on the absolute separation of Africans from the rest of humanity, asserting that "they are a different species of the same genus."[83] Long manages to convince himself that the offspring of black and white sexual unions cannot themselves produce viable offspring.[84] His viciously brutal attitude toward those he enslaved and exploited is undisguised: "I do not think that an orang-outang husband would be any dishonour to an Hottentot female. . . ."[85] This dehumanizing attitude goes beyond even the paranoid view expressed two years earlier in his *Candid Reflections*. In this earlier pamphlet, Long expresses anxiety that lower-class white women—"remarkably fond of the blacks, for reasons too brutal to mention"[86]—will engage in wholesale miscegenation "till the whole nation resembles the *Portuguese* and *Moriscos* in complexion of skin and baseness of mind."[87] Such a fear of "impure" mixture would presumably be inoperative across the species barrier—in a world such as Long later claimed to believe in, that is, where "mulattoes," like mules, cannot mate.

Another decisive step along the path toward "scientific" racism can be found in Johann Casper Lavater's doctrine of physiognomy. The Swiss minister's four-volume work on this topic, *Physiognomische Fragmente* (1775–1778), elaborately catalogues a quantified version of national and ethnic facial features: a process by which aesthetic judgments, backed up by a scientist rhetoric of mathematical precision, are made to coincide with judgments about moral character and intelligence. Ominous as Lavater's work now seems, however, skin color, even at this point, is still of no interest in his considerations.[88]

As significant a turning-point as Long and Lavater would seem to be, however, the use of so-called scientific racism to justify race-based domination can be found in only a handful of texts from that moment. Their views were anticipatory: more typical of the age to follow than of his own.[89] Such "scientific" taxonomies of humanity still competed throughout most of the eighteenth century with climatic theories of differential skin pigmentation and with the lingering power of Biblical chronology—that is, the tracing of humanity's origins to the three sons of Noah. Premodern prejudices, moreover, did not purport to describe major subdivisions of the world's population. Nor did such ethnocentric prejudices attain anything remotely approaching the internal consistency codified in modern racism. Indeed, Benjamin Braude has demonstrated that classical, medieval, and Renaissance interpretations of the Biblical "Sons-of-Noah" narrative—the Noachic genealogy that is usually the prime evidence in attempts to write the continuous history of "races" in the modern sense[90]—were riven by several crucial inconsistencies. By examining such evidence as glosses on Genesis 9–10 itself and on *The Travels of Sir John Mandeville*, Braude demonstrates that Shem, Japheth, and Ham were neither always assigned to the same continents nor understood as representing ethnically homogenous regions of the world. Glossing the passage from Genesis, for example, Flavius Josephus in effect saw Japhet as Eurasian, Ham as Afrasian, and Shem as Asian.[91] Later premodern commentators, including Martin Luther, frequently assigned Ham to Asia.[92] Moreover, the representations of the continents themselves in the virtually mapless universe of premodern cosmology was so vague, arbitrary, and inconstant as to explode the supposed identity of, say, "Europe" across the centuries.[93] It was only in the later eighteenth century, according to Braude's research, that Ham—the son disfavored by a divine curse—settled firmly into his modern identity, often invoked in pro-slavery arguments, as the "African" race destined for slavery.[94]

The racial terminology that still prevails in many quarters, including that used in the United States census, was spawned in the 1790s. In the 3rd edition of his *De Generis Humani Varietate Nativa* (1795), J. F. Blumenbach introduced the term "Caucasian." Blumenbach's physical anthropology, promulgated at the University of Göttingen, mingled quantitative and aesthetic criteria—the wonderfully scientific notion, that is, that "Caucasians" are more beautiful. Blumenbach's four less beautiful races are thus described as having "degenerated" from the originary beauty of the white people dwelling in the Caucasus Mountains: a geography linked back to the Sons-of-Noah myth and to legends that Noah's ark had come to rest upon Mount Ararat. Thus did Blumenbach, still clinging somewhat to monogenesis, attempt to reconcile his quantitative science of mankind with his religious beliefs. The political effect of naming "Caucasianness," of course, would be overwhelmingly in the direction of racial separation and division. As Braude points out, the racializing of European identity—as an opting out of the Noachic genealogy—meant that Japhet, Ham, and Shem were "no longer in the same boat": no longer joined by a theological fiction of shared ancestry."[95] "Caucasian," despite its wholly mythical nature, persists as a favored way to identify those of European ancestry.

Genealogies of Whiteness and Blackness

Perhaps the most crucial step in the racializing process was the fabrication of the profoundly reductive and polarizing binary of "whiteness" and "blackness." "Whiteness"—a supra-national concept that served to minimize linguistic, religious, and ethnic divisions among European nations—was just emerging, by the mid-eighteenth century, in the context of imperial dynamics: the antinomy of core and periphery within a global system.[96] Among the earliest harbingers of racialized whiteness is the nasty footnote David Hume added to the 1753–1754 edition of his essay, "Of National Characters." This note, explicitly invoking the antagonisms of the colonial context, denies that non-white peoples ever produced any glimmerings of civilization:

> I am apt to suspect the negroes and in general all other species of men (for there are four or five different kinds) to be naturally inferior to the whites.

There scarcely ever was a civilized nation of that complexion, nor even any individual, eminent either in action or speculation. No ingenious manufactures among them, no arts, no sciences.[97]

Deceptively casual as Hume's aside is, its themes anticipate the later racial elaboration of Britain's fascination with liberty-loving Goths. Hume's own *History of Great Britain* (1754–1761), in fact establishes a pattern for the historiographical celebration of the Germanic—and especially the Saxon—contribution to British institutions.[98]

Hume's assertion of white supremacy is, nevertheless, far from a typical specimen of eighteenth-century discourse. Indeed, this egregious footnote was eventually challenged in print by Hume's fellow Scotsman, James Beattie, in 1770. Beattie, pointing out that the legitimation of slavery is what is at stake, begins by affirming "man's natural and universal right to liberty."[99] He goes on to flatly deny the truth of Hume's outrageous assertion:

we know that these assertions are not true. The empires of Peru and Mexico could not have been governed, nor the metropolis of the latter built after so singular a manner, in the middle of a lake, without men eminent both for action and speculation. Every body has heard of the magnificence, good government, and ingenuity of the ancient Peruvians. The Africans and Americans are known to have many ingenious manufactures and arts among them, which even Europeans would find it no easy matter to imitate.[100]

Beattie caps this refutation by imagining the depiction of "brute barbarity and sottish infatuation" that a hypothetical "Voltaire from the Coast of Guinea" would be able to render, as a merely factual account of European manners, to his own country-men.[101]

Hume's own essay *Of Commerce*, moreover, argues, in the usual Georgian terms, for an environmental explanation for human differences.[102] And his infamous footnote was most widely cited not in its own time, but, rather, in the early nineteenth century.[103] In any case, the pivotal decade for the polarization of "whiteness" and "blackness" would seem to be the 1770s, for a major burst of racialization attended the famous Somerset decision in 1772. Almost 60 years after Britain had become the world's leader in the slave-trade, the nation was finally forced by this case to confront the legal and political contradiction between "British liberty" at home and slavery abroad. James Somerset, the fugitive slave who was the catalyst for this legal conflict, resided within Britain when he was kidnapped and sold by Charles Stewart, the Scotsman who claimed to be his erstwhile owner. Somerset represented, in effect, a "black presence" of at least 5,000 in London: a population whose precise legal status was in limbo.[104] Lord Mansfield ruled, however narrowly and grudgingly, that slavery was incompatible with the national ethos of "British liberty." And it was precisely the Somerset decision that triggered Long's *History of Jamaica* in 1774. The launching both of so-called scientific racism and the counter-assertion of "black" intellectual abilities were directly tied to the Somerset case, as David Grimsted points out, and thus to a nationalization of the antislavery struggle: "the movement of antislavery from a Quaker to a general concern."[105]

The full development of a racist ideology required, as Nicholas Hudson points out, a totalizing suppression of ethnic, religious, and linguistic differences among communities that had hitherto been often regarded as multiple and distinct.[106] Edward Long makes precisely this homogenizing or "leveling" move as regards Africans in the *History of Jamaica*:

> In so vast a continent as that of Africa, and in so great a variety of climates and provinces, we might expect to find a proportionable diversity among the inhabitants, in regard to their qualifications of body and mind; strength, agility, industry, and dexterity, on the one hand; ingenuity, learning, arts, and sciences, on the other. But, on the contrary, a general uniformity runs through all these various regions of people; so that, if any difference be found, it is only in degrees of the same qualities; and what is more strange, those of the worst kind; it being a common known proverb, that all people of the globe have some good as well as some ill qualities, except the Africans.[107]

This brutal reification of "blackness" subsumes all differences between peoples of African descent. Absolutely nothing counts, for Long, except "race." Perhaps the stark violence of the white/non-white polarity enables such a logic of homogenization. Hudson notes a parallel reification in William Robertson's *History of America* (1770), which explicitly lumps together the hundreds of communities of Native Americans in the new world.[108]

The moment of the 1770s and 1780s also records the early adoption of a "black" identity by authors of African descent, most notably Phillis Wheatley and Olaudah Equiano. Both are authors who have subsequently been accused of being insufficiently "black." The ambiguities and conflictual elements in both Equiano and Wheatley are thus not to be understood as mere inauthenticity, as if "black" identity were a timeless given. What such ambiguities record, rather, is precisely the *liminality of racial formation*: the first literary efforts to reclaim an imposed identity and experience into a site around which solidarity could be organized, and from which political speech could be addressed. Wheatley and Equiano were both attempting to play the bad hand dealt to them by the history of slavery.

Nation-building rhetoric, invariably organized around categories which claim legitimacy precisely by way of natural authenticity and ancient origins, leads directly to factitious genealogies. Such exercises in rewriting the past have been less the sole prerogative of totalitarian regimes than the routine currency of nationalistic mythopoeia. And it was the modern nation-state—in the context of imperial expansion and rivalries—that invented "race." Race was also a motive for reinventing the actual status quo in the image of the invented past. The ideological need to eliminate the anomaly of white-skinned people living under the domination of darker ones was an umistakable inspiration for war when the Greek War of Independence (1821–1829) aroused fervent support all across Europe. Eugène Delacroix's famous painting, *Liberty on the Ruins of Missolonghi* (1826) turns precisely on the visual contrast between the personification of "white" Liberty and its dark-skinned Turkish enemies. And indeed, the Romantic philhellenism generated by this war, as Jennifer Wallace points out, became constitutive of the identity forged by post-independence Greece: an identity that minimizes all "eastern" elements of the national past. "The invented nation illustrates" as Wallace puts it, "in its constitution and self-perception, the aspiration of the west to re-imagine the past in its own image and to forge links abroad in order to gain a sense of identity."[109]

The vast historical continuities claimed in the name of "whiteness" grew most extravagant in the invention of the "Aryan" race. A number of thinkers from the north of Germany were apparently not displeased to think of themselves as belonging to a race which was both the most ancient and the most beautiful. Like "Caucasian," the term "Aryan," which developed in the discipline of historical linguistics, did not begin to circulate until the 1790s.[110] "Aryan" was introduced to the public in a translation from ancient Sanskrit by the Indologist and colonial administrator, Sir William Jones. The term had nothing to do, in its original Vedic context, with modern notions of "race." "The notion of 'race,' " as Romila Thapar explains,

> was embedded in the European intellectual consciousness in the nineteenth century. The universality of the concept was sought to be proved by translating various words as "race" even where the concept of race did not exist.[111]

The history of Indian civilization thus became so much fodder for a racializing historiography. By conflating language-families such as Indo-Germanic and Indo-European with the anachronistic notion of "race," such historical linguists as Friedrich von Schlegel and especially Karl Otfried Müller (another Göttingen-based scholar) contributed in the 1820s to the "Aryanization" of both the classics and, ultimately, of world history. Göttingen, a hotbed of new scholarship in classical philology, pioneered the establishment both of modern disciplinary scholarship and the "histories not of individuals but of races and peoples and their institutions."[112] And because the Vedic texts were far older than Biblical Hebrew, hitherto often taken to have been humanity's *Ur*-language, philology also created a well-nigh irresistible challenge to the premodern Biblical chronology. The "Aryan" pedigree trumped the Hebraic one. Aryanism persists, as Vasant Kaiwar shows, in the doctrines of some Hindu nationalists in contemporary India.[113]

Only by historicizing the categories which constitute the terms around which such identities are constructed can one lend some much-needed nuance and analytical flexibility to current discussions that are often severely limited by their neglect of the eighteenth century. For, precisely through encounters with *historical difference* can contemporary orthodoxies, including the political myths that now secure such social identities as "western," "oriental," "black," and "white," best be understood. Such identities, however politically enabling they may be for the oppressed at certain strategic moments, need in the long run to be interrogated in their fissured, materially constituted, and historically accidental beginnings. A full encounter with historical difference is thus precisely the opposite of a solipsistic and self-anchoring "recognition" whereby the prejudices of the past merge smoothly with those of the present, enabling a seamless closure whereby we know that "we are what we were." Such an encounter compels instead a far more unsettling recognition of the visibility of such seams, such ragged sutures: a recognition that means, in principle, that the cultural past, as Mark Edmundson puts it, may be in advance of our norms—may have, indeed, "the capacity to read and interpret us."[114]

Postcolonial Critiques in, and of, the Enlightenment

The apocalyptic break often claimed on behalf of postmodern theory tends to work against the possibility of a dialogue with the cultural past. Its own metanarrative, despite its claims to break with all grand narratives, is thus an extreme form of progressivist teleology. As Peter Osborne has observed, the narrative of the death of metanarrative is itself "grander than most of the metanarratives it would consign to oblivion."[115] Postcolonial literature and theory, however, has been somewhat warier of throwing the modernist baby out with the bathwater. Its project, I would argue, looks like the tentative and hesitant search for a "third way": an agenda defined, that is, neither by Eurocentrism (and the violence of modernity) nor nativism (which, as in the case of Afrocentrism, has too often been content to constitute itself merely as the inverted mirror-image of Eurocentrism). Too seldom recognized, moreover, especially within the discourse of multiculturalism prevalent in the United States, is the important strand of postcolonial literature and theory that has firmly repudiated any nostalgic "return" to a supposedly pristine, supposedly "pre-modern" tradition. The full implications of this repudiation, which point strongly to the need for a third way, remain to be fully developed. We need much more attention to *reappropriation*, a cultural process that produces the impure and layered artifacts.

I contend that such a third way can only come by way of a critique immanent to the Enlightenment. An immanent critique would have a great many advantages. Of these, the greatest is perhaps merely the refusal to surrender, as inherently "Western," the liberatory aspects of modernity: the egalitarian program of human rights; the constitution of a secular and democratized public sphere; the relative accountability that such transparency provides; and the commitment to material and intellectual progress. Such a critique also affords the hope of recovering an admirable cosmopolitanism that has yet to be clearly disentangled from its false and abusively Eurocentric versions. I concur with Kwame Anthony Appiah that most attacks on universalism really intend to target *false* universalism:[116] a confusion that breeds many errors of intellectual and political strategy.

The well-known intertextuality of much postcolonial literature has not yet received adequate theorization as a rewriting of literary and cultural history. Such rewriting, contrary to popular belief, has never been merely a matter of playful pastiche. The elements of such an immanent critique are perhaps already implicit in the peculiar resonance that the eighteenth century demonstrably has for a number of important authors writing out of the experience of twentieth-century decolonization and its aftermath. One can indeed discern a postcolonial *turn to the eighteenth-century* moment. And indeed, precisely in the complexity of its engagement with the eighteenth-century Enlightenment does a major strand of postcolonial literature differ most sharply both from most mainstream definitions of postmodernist writing and from the smorgasbord approach to multiculturalism widely practiced in the United States. The full significance of that turn—what it means both for eighteenth-century studies and for the postcolonial project—is a crucial subject of this book.

CHAPTER 2

WHEN FINGAL FOUGHT AND OSSIAN SANG: EIGHTEENTH-CENTURY METALEPSIS

> As the poems of Ossian are about to be published in Earse, their supposed original, some reason
> may be expected for transferring them from the third to the eighteenth century.
>
> —Malcolm Laing, *Dissertation on the Supposed Authenticity of*
> *Ossian's Poems*, 1804

Dynastic historiography was yielding in the eighteenth century to the influence of a more horizontally constituted and more secular vernacular culture. In historiographical terms, this produced both a rupture and many backfilling operations to disguise the rupture. Hence the familiar and interlinked phenomena of antiquarianism, forgery, and primitivism. Given the desire of nation-based anthologies of literature to emphasis continuity, the eighteenth century poses unique problems. Take, for example, a major shift between the sixth and seventh editions of the *Norton Anthology of British Literature*. The seventh edition of the *Norton Anthology of British Literature* undertakes a significant transfer of literary property. The editors of the first volume have moved the anthology's selection of popular ballads to the later eighteenth century. In the previous edition of 1993, these ballads had been tucked into the otherwise scantily furnished fifteenth century. Confronting the unsettling problem of folkloric origins, the editors of the seventh edition acknowledge in their headnote that it is "difficult to fit [the ballads] into an anthology divided into historical periods because their anonymity and provenance resist periodization."[1] The editors' unobtrusive decision to resettle the ballads in the later eighteenth century—the moment when the systematic collection and publication of *Volkspoesie* began—implies a recasting of literary history that deserves further exploration. By their act of chronological reassignment, the *Norton Anthology*'s editors have ceased treating the ballads as hallowed remnants from the nation's early times. They hint instead at a belated process of national invention. The Norton editors' revisionary dating, as the epigraph above from Malcolm Laing suggests, echoes dating controversies specific to the folkloric moment of such anthologists as Bishop Thomas Percy, Sir Walter Scott, and others. For the controversial dating practices of the later eighteenth-century ballad revival are but one strand of a messy chronological seam: the patch-job that accompanied the modern invention of "Britishness."[2] To engage with that unstable eighteenth-century moment is to foreground the awkward patchwork surrounding folkish ideas about "ancient Britishness."

No better opening into the historiographical fabrication of "ancient Britishness" can be found than the controversy beginning in the 1760s over Macpherson's "Ossianic" poems. The poems anthologized in Macpherson's various redactions of Ossian in the 1760s appeared before the public through the medium of a self-described editor, and surrounded by an "apparatus of authentication."[3] The full extent to which Macpherson defined himself as a historian is often either tactfully neglected or explained away as a regrettably dry and pedantic dimension of his essentially poetic achievement. "Ossian," nevertheless, epitomizes the specifically historiographic problems surrounding the emergence of modern nation-based historiography. The eighteenth century was "a great age of origin-seeking."[4] And indeed, nothing is more conspicuous, during the pivotal moment of the later eighteenth century, than a struggle over competing "discoveries" of antiquities retrospectively deemed national. A properly metahistorical narrative would need to give due emphasis to ruptures, seams, violent appropriations, and fabrications. To expose the mediation of such gaps by a retrospective backfilling operation restores a crucial element of irreducible contingency to the story. The name of "Ossian"—initially conjuring up wry notions both of forgery and of English Scotophobia—in fact epitomizes a phenomenon of far wider significance. "Ossian," indeed, provides the basis for surmising how the *Norton Anthology of British Literature* ultimately came in the edition of 2000 to redate its popular ballads to the age of Percy's *Ancient Reliques of English Poetry* (1765). "Ossian" is thus both the catalyst for, and epitome of, a much broader project of eighteenth-century cultural nationalism: the metaleptic fabrication of ethnic, national, and racial "roots."

Charles Churchill's Ossian and Lord Bute's Macpherson

An eminent historian sums up a common view of the Ossian controversy in this pithy truism: "The row was as much national as rational."[5] This smartly conveys a familiar canard about Anglo-Scottish animosities during the

1760s. Because friction between England and Scotland was an obvious feature of the mid-century political landscape, many succumb to the temptation of seeing "Ossian" only through the lens of the conflicts afflicting the precarious Anglo-Scottish union. This tunnel vision, indeed, accounts for the common understanding of the controversy as a pugilistic slanging match between James Macpherson and Samuel Johnson. Precisely in order to avoid this misleading and reductive impression, I have reserved my full discussion of Johnson's blunt but balanced interventions in the controversy for the final chapter of this book. Many other dimensions of the episode need first to be brought to the foreground. The tensions between England and Scotland, nevertheless, do require detailed exposition as an immediately surrounding micro-history.

When the 23-year-old Highlander James Macpherson (1736–1796) entered onto the metropolitan literary scene in 1760 with his anonymously published *Fragments of Ancient Poetry*, Anglo-Scottish relations remained vexed by several chapters of poorly digested history. Highland Scots themselves were still nursing the wounds left from the rankling events of 1745–1746, when the second Jacobite rebellion was crushed at Culloden by George II's son, the Duke of Cumberland. Macpherson, who was 10 years old during these events, came of age during a period of violent modernization and cultural disintegration. While chafing under such legal restrictions as the notorious ban on the wearing of tartan, the "pacified" Highlanders embellished folk traditions about the daring escape into exile of Bonnie Prince Charlie. The post-combat atrocities that "Butcher" Cumberland supervised—the systematic extermination of straggling Jacobites, the breaking of the clans, the burning of houses, the confiscation of cattle—likewise passed into legend both in Scotland and in England.

Meanwhile, the refusal of the British government to extend the national militia to Scotland—a topic of parliamentary wrangling from 1757 through the American War of Independence—especially aggravated nationalist sentiment among the otherwise loyally unionist Lowland intelligentsia, who felt mistrusted and exposed, against the odds, to invasion from France.[6] Indeed, the promotion of "Ossian," as Richard Sher demonstrates, was to a large extent the joint project of an Edinburgh clique deeply involved with the militia issue. This cabal orbited around William Robertson (author of *History of Scotland and History of America*); its members included John Home (author of *Douglas* and secretary to John Stuart, the Earl of Bute), Hugh Blair (the rhetorical theorist who would unconditionally promote Macpherson for some 40 years), Adam Ferguson (author of *Essay on the History of Civil Society*), and the above-mentioned "Jupiter" Carlyle (who published a pamphlet on the militia question). These high-flying literati commissioned Macpherson to recover an epic Scottish heritage, providing him "inspiration, incentive, financial support, letters of introduction, editorial assistance, publishing connections, and emotional support."[7] "They made it known what they were after," as Sher puts it, "and how important it was to them to get it; Macpherson gave them what they wanted."[8] Blair developed the habit, as Sher notes, "of referring to *Fingal* as 'our Epic' before Macpherson had even set out to recover it."[9]

John Home, who in 1759 cajoled Macpherson into his first "translation" of a supposed Gaelic antiquity ("The Death of Oscur"), is also the most likely to have introduced the impecunious young schoolmaster from Badenoch to Lord Bute. The Earl of Bute, George III's influential Scottish minister, soon became Macpherson's most prominent patron. Macpherson became a ministerial propagandist in the *Public Advertiser* and explicitly dedicated his second Ossianic epic *Temora* to Bute in 1763. The surname "Stuart" provided Bute's political adversaries with a convenient pretext for rehashing, with graceless crowing, the radical Whig version of the Rising of 1745: a tale of how the treasonous Jacobites were punished for provoking a civil war on behalf of the "Young Pretender," Charles Edward Stuart. Bute's prominence in public life thus became a lightning rod for English suspicions about a renewed "rising" of Scottish political and economic clout. This panic became a handy weapon for those who opposed Bute's most controversial policies: an excise tax on cider (to pay for the Seven Years War) and the Peace of Paris settlement of 1763 (which William Pitt and his allies deemed pusillanimous). The radical Whig MP John Wilkes, scoring easy populist points, relentlessly exploited the Anglo-Scottish rift in the British polity. Wilkes fanned the flames of anti-Scottish sentiment in his weekly journalistic organ, the *North Briton*, in the course of a well-orchestrated crusade described by Kathleen Wilson as "the most scurrilous press campaign of the century."[10]

Wilkes enlisted such talented allies in his demagogic campaign as the satirist Charles Churchill. Along with Churchill's *Prophecy of Famine: A Scots Pastoral* (1763), which was inscribed to Wilkes, a cluster of anonymous publications testifies to the prejudices for which Bute served as an expedient focus. The years between 1762 and 1764, in particular, were marked by the appearance of various uninhibited productions, including *The British Antidote to Caledonian Poison* (1762), the triumphalist frontispiece of which features a portrait of Cumberland; another, *The True-Born Scot* (1764), which is sarcastically dedicated to Bute; and a third, *The British Coffee House: A Poem* (1764), the title of which targets a coffee house in Charing Cross frequented by Robertson, Home, and Macpherson.[11] If many Scots were nevertheless hoping to harvest the benefits of Anglo-Scottish coalescence, an abrasive element in England manifested *Angst* about cultural usurpation from north of the Tweed. Those who fostered such phobic anxieties imagined the creeping of "Scotification" in such vivid fantasies as, for example, the replacement of the organ in St. Paul's Cathedral by bagpipes.

For a Wilkite satirist of Charles Churchill's skill, questions about the authenticity of Macpherson's "translations"—legitimate and rational in themselves—inevitably served as useful fodder for bashing Scotland and Bute:

> Thence [from Scotland] issued forth, at great Macpherson's call,
> That *old, new, Epic, Pastoral, Fingal*;
> Thence simple bards, by simple prudence taught,
> To this wise town [London] by simple patrons brought,
> In simple manner utter simple lays,
> And take, with simple pensions, simple praise.[12]

The attack on "simplicity"—implicating both Macpherson's retrograde "primitive" style and the theories of social and literary evolution adduced to authenticate Ossian—is quite effective. So is the portrayal of a Scottish nexus of patronage that also implicated Home and Tobias Smollet. Macpherson's connection to Bute "served to unite two prongs of Anti-Scottish attack."[13] While implying that Macpherson is the "willing slave" of a wire-puller, Churchill thus goes on to use the dubious Macpherson against the patronage-wielding minister, referring to "OSSIAN, *sublimest, simplest* Bard of all, / Whom *English infidels* Macpherson *call*."[14] For Macpherson, indeed, the direct association with George III's controversial minister was a "mixed blessing."[15] Bute, who was involved in securing a modest government pension for Samuel Johnson in 1762, must have winced also as "Ossian" developed into the stickiest of quagmires.

Metaleptic Mediations

The mutual antagonism of England and Scotland—supposedly mirror images of irrational chauvinism—is, in fact, ultimately of very limited value as a lens through which to interpret the nuances of "Ossian." The overheated extremism of Wilkite virulence against the Scots, as Linda Colley points out, "was testimony to the fact that barriers between England and Scotland were coming down."[16] Moreover, a merely bilateral conflict provides far too superficial an explanation for the multiple agendas, successive appropriations, and complexly motivated personalities that collided and overlapped as the controversy unfolded. Much more was at stake than the irascible jostling of the English and the Scots within the double yoke created in 1707 by the Act of Union. Among the various dimensions of the titanic metalepsis we call "Ossian," one must also factor in the following dynamics of the controversy:

1. *The Forging of Imperial Britishness*: the specifically imperial context, that is, for the eighteenth-century "forging of Britishness";
2. *The Massaging of the Archive*: the pressure to harmonize "Ossian" with the chronologies of human life described in ancient sources;
3. *The Sweeping of the Irish off the Board*: a concerted Scottish attempt to negate extant Irish antiquities (while appropriating others as originally Scottish);
4. *The Ethnic and Racial Appropriations*: the abuse of the Highland past by way of constituting ethnic identity (in the Lowlands) and racial identity (in northern Europe);
5. *The Linguistic Leaps*: the significance of philology as a new terrain of debate; and
6. *The Strange Loops and Vicious Circles*: a self-referential and self-confirming use of "evidence."

These features of the Ossianic phenomenon I treat in the order just enumerated, with a closing cadenza on their significance in regard to Thomas Percy's *Ancient Reliques of English Poetry*.

I make reference to the following texts by Macpherson, chronologically arranged below so as to provide a brief outline of Macpherson's career from pre-Ossianic poet to self-styled historian and translator:

1. *The Highlander* (1758), his six-book epic in rhymed couplets;
2. *Fragments of Ancient Poetry* (1760), his rather modestly produced and anonymously published anthology of translated Gaelic poetry (attributed to ancient Highland bards);
3. *Fingal* (1761), his much more elaborately produced prose translation of an epic attributed to the third-century bard Ossian, frugally recycling several of the "Fragments";
4. *Temora* (1763), his second translation of a pseudo-Ossianic epic, published with a small specimen of the "original" Gaelic;
5. *The Works of Ossian* (1765), which gathers all of the Ossianic "translations" and incorporates Hugh Blair's *Critical Dissertation on Ossian*;
6. *An Introduction to the History of Great Britain and Ireland* (1771), which elaborates his historical theories of ethnic origins;
7. *The Poems of Ossian* (1773), which (1) provides a new preface and revises the order of the poems; (2) eliminates the specimen of Gaelic; and (3) plays down the role of Ossian and seems to aggrandize the "translator";

8. *The History and Management of the East-India Company, from Its Origin in 1600 to the Present Times* (1779), which illustrates his hired propaganda for the Nawab of Arcot;

9. Malcolm Laing's edition of *The Poems of Ossian* (1805), which demonstrates that the poems are a vast tissue of *topoi* deriving from non-Gaelic and eighteenth-century sources; and

10. Sir John Sinclair's publication, in 1807, of the supposed Gaelic or Earse "originals" of Ossian.

Macpherson died in 1796, so Laing and Sinclair's dueling editions belong to his long cultural afterlife.

Forging Imperial Britishness

G. W. F. Hegel pointed to British national pride as an example of the historical self-realization of the national spirit (*Geist*).[17] "Britishness" was in many senses a global construction, and the ideology of Britishness, as Armitage demonstrates, provided "a link between the processes of empire-building and state-formation in the early-modern period."[18] The Second British Empire was beginning to demand a pedigree commensurate with its ascendancy. One conspicuous result was a nostalgic Celtophilia directed at borderlands being reconfigured as ancient origins: as, in Janet Sorensen's words, "a visible past at the edges of its geographically defined borders."[19] In the global making of "Britishness," moreover, Scotland played a central role. In the later eighteenth century, the word "British" itself, as Pat Rogers notes, was "a code-word for Anglo-Scottish."[20] Linda Colley points out that the empire—never termed *English*— "has always been emphatically *British*."[21] "A British imperium," in her words, "enabled Scots to feel themselves the peers of the English in a way still denied them in an island kingdom."[22] Indeed, the Scottish Enlightenment's precocious economic and intellectual success placed Scotland sufficiently near the core of the British empire to dampen the development of a full-blown desire for political independence until rather recently. "During the prolonged era of Anglo-Scots imperialist expansion," as Tom Nairn explains, "the Scottish ruling order found that it had given up statehood for a hugely profitable junior partnership in the New Rome."[23] The negotiated union of 1707 had established Lowland Scotland—a proudly defeudalized center of commercial enterprise—as a famous eighteenth-century hotbed of intellectual innovation. In his *Sketches of the History of Man* (Edinburgh, 1774), Henry Home, Lord Kames celebrates the advantages of the union with England in precisely these terms:

> Enmity wore out gradually, and the eyes of the Scots were opened to the advantages of their present condition: the national spirit was roused to emulate

and to excel: talents were exerted, hitherto latent; and Scotland at present makes a figure in arts and sciences, above what it ever made while an independent kingdom.[24]

In educational and cultural terms, Scots pioneered in the ideological forging of Britishness. The long-standing emphasis on "Britishness" at leading British universities, as Robert Crawford puts it, "harks back to the eighteenth-century origins of the subject when university teachers were training Scottish students in how to succeed in the increasingly unified British state and so gain access to the rewards in Britain and her formerly English colonies."[25] Though "South Britain" never made any headway in displacing "England" for the English, a comprehensive *Britishness*, incorporating both England and Scotland, became increasingly relevant to the making of an imperial national identity.

The cultural nationalism pursued by some Scottish literati during the "Ossian" tangle was less a blow to imperialism as such than the claim, by a dynamic provincial elite, to equal partnership in the imperial project. The following lines from the prophetic conclusion to James Macpherson's first publication, *The Highlander* (1758), illustrate the exact logic of this imperial coalition:

> See Scot and Saxon coalesc'd in one,
> Support the glory of the common crown.
> Britain no more shall shake with native storms,
> But o'er the trembling nations lift her arms.[26]

The Scots—victims of a certain internal colonialism during the First British Empire—would nevertheless be poised, in the wake of the Seven Years War, to take full advantage of the Second. To quote Colley again: "In terms of self-respect, then, as well as for the profits it could bestow, imperialism served as Scotland's opportunity."[27]

The most crucial impetus for the whole "Ossian" affair was linked to global expansion: the formation of specifically *British* cultural nationalism. This emerging ideology was informed by an intense rivalry with the legacies of antiquity. By about the 1750s, the famous "Battle between the Ancients and Moderns" had prepared the ground for an aggressively nativist appropriation of cultural production and dissemination. Thomas Gray's "The Bard" (1757), an acknowledged fiction, reimagined "Britannia's issue" through the prophecies of an ancient Welsh bard. Authors commonly celebrated homegrown poetry over and against the universalist claims of the classics. Such "native" poetry was often seen as authentic—as an unmediated expression of *British* genius—precisely because the author was supposedly unlettered, and thus had no burdensome debts to a classical (and Europe-wide) tradition centered in Rome. This redrawing of aesthetic horizons often entailed minimizing the actual education that such homegrown poets had in fact managed to acquire. Peasant poets, marketed as momentary novelties were lionized as strictly native voices, untainted by formal education.[28] It was indeed on the basis of the purity of the unmediated—a pristine ignorance of classical tradition—that the authenticity of "native genius" was ideologically founded. No arrival could be more fervently desired, more eagerly sought—more necessary, in short—than the advent of a "British Homer." The vacant slot, awaiting only a minimally plausible candidate, was already there. Hugh Blair made it his "self-imposed role," as Joan H. Pittock writes, "to find a match for Homer in the Scottish mountains."[29] *Ossian, son of Fingal* was to be that homegrown Homer. James Macpherson, was to be his eighteenth-century grandson—or, to speak more accurately, his eighteenth-century grand*father*.

Various zigs and zags nevertheless would attend the genesis and apotheosis of "Ossian." William Wilkie's *Epigoniad* (1757) though briefly promoted as a quasi-Homeric achievement, was a false start: too feebly imitative to qualify Wilkie for the post of "British Homer." Macpherson's openly contemporary epic, *The Highlander*, was another critical and commercial deadend: a failed "entrance" into a poetic tradition in which he likewise figured as a derivative clone.[30] We can infer what he learned from this abortive effort in 1758 from a grumbling sentence published in his revised prefatory dissertation of 1773: "Those who alone are capable of transferring ancient poetry into a modern language, might be better employed in giving originals of their own, were it not for that wretched envy and meanness which affects to despise contemporary genius."[31] He learned, that is, to recast the historical *moment* of his authorial entrance: to trade off personal claims to originality in exchange for the mystique of ancient origins. He would establish this false priority through stylistic analogues to the "distressing" of fake antiques. The dependence of *Comàla: A Dramatic Poem* on the Song of Songs makes Macpherson's debt to contemporary arguments about Hebraic "parallelism" unmistakable: he Hebraicized "Ossian." Such "distressing" techniques also include a remarkable footnote early in Fragment VII of *Fragments of Ancient Poetry* (1760) that identifies a passage about the suicide of Dargo's daughter as a spurious interpolation: a "forgery-in-forgery," as Ian Haywood puts it, that served to authenticate the "interpolation-free remainder of the text."[32] The preface to *Fragments of Ancient Poetry*, anonymously written by Blair, gives the following account of the cultural conduits that supposedly left Macpherson (as yet unnamed as the translator) positioned to act as the faithful channel of Gaelic tradition:

> There can be no doubt that these poems are to be ascribed to the Bards; a race of men well known to have continued throughout many ages in Ireland

and the north of Scotland. Every chief or great man had in his family a Bard or poet, whose office it was to record in verse, the illustrious actions of that family. By the succession of these Bards, such poems were handed down from race to race [that is, family to family]; some in manuscript, but more by oral tradition. And tradition, in a country so free of intermixture with foreigners, and among a people so strongly attached to the memory of their ancestors, has preserved many of them in a great measure incorrupted to this day.[33]

Fidelity extends, of course, to the "extremely literal" translation.[34] Although the theme of cultural purity is central to the authenticating enterprise, all the pieces of the metaleptic narrative are not yet in place. At this stage Macpherson "had not yet decided to assign the poems to a single poet."[35] Moreover, the vague mention of manuscripts would prove to be an irretrievable strategic error.

The mid-eighteenth-century vogue for bards was perhaps not as inevitable as it now seems. The Irish deist John Toland's *A Critical History of the Celtic Religion and Learning* (1740) had described bards—not quite extinct, as he noted without nostalgia—as overpaid flatterers often punished by banishment from Ireland to the Scottish Highlands. The possibility of such premodern "survivals," nevertheless, could easily be recuperated into an organicist myth, if not a cult. The trick, however, was to manage the metamorphosis from well-known oral genres, such as tales and ballads, to "the high-cultural clout of the epic."[36] Blair's preface does prepare the ground for that transformation, floating the tantalizing prospect that a heroic poem of considerable length remains in the Highlands to be recovered and translated "if encouragement were given to such an undertaking."[37] The contours of a rescue mission, the recovery of a dormant cultural treasure, began to take shape. Macpherson was to gain immortality as "*The Restorer of the British Homer*" (as the French translator of Ossian later put it): an epithet that "carried more of a punch than 'Scottish Homer,'" as Sher notes, "because it implied that the English had no poet to rival Ossian."[38]

Sponsors and subscribers rose to this bait. Macpherson duly made his famous collecting trip into the Highlands and Hebrides in the fall of 1760, accompanied by his kinsman Lachlan Macpherson. Lodged below Hugh Blair's residence in Edinburgh, he then quickly got down to the work of "translation": for the published version of *Fingal* (December, 1761) would be "very much a product of Edinburgh."[39] To "translate" his first epic, *Fingal*, Macpherson cobbled together the shards from some fourteen or fifteen extant ballads, perhaps a few centuries old, belonging to an almost entirely oral Highland tradition.[40] With cavalier freedom, he rearranged the themes and plots in these late-medieval materials for his own epic purposes.[41] Even this tenuous degree of dependence on Highland sources largely disappears, moreover, from the subsequent epic *Temora* (1763), Macpherson's sequel to *Fingal*. The contents of the Book of the Dean of Lismore—the valuable sixteenth-century manuscript that Macpherson did indeed rescue from likely oblivion—were not ideally suited to the specific agenda of an epic poet. The generative function of the collecting trip was a matter of authenticating the supposed context of a translation that, as a whole, lacked an original.

By the time his "translation" of *Fingal* appeared, Macpherson had crystallized his authorial fabrication around the name of his "British Homer." "An epic poem," as Stafford puts it, "required an epic poet, so Ossian, who had appeared in the Fragments as a character, was now placed firmly in the tradition of Homer and Milton as the blind bard of the Highlands."[42] Macpherson depicts "Ossian" in accordance with certain primitivist notions about ancient Greek rhapsodes set forth in Thomas Blackwell's *Enquiry into the Life and Writings of Homer* (1735). He annotates both *Fingal and Temora* (1763), moreover, by providing explicit comparisons between passages in "Ossian" and Homer. He lifts a footnote from Pope's translation of the *Iliad*, as Laing points out, in order to indulge in some learned remarks about the custom of hospitality amongst the ancient Caledonians.[43] In *Temora*, which Macpherson "translated" in London, the editor-cum-translator casts an admiring glance at the superior felicity with which "Ossian" handles a scene of single combat, veiling the petty details with an enveloping column of mist. "Not all the strength of Homer," Macpherson writes, "could sustain, with dignity, the *minutiae* of a single combat." In 1773, Macpherson published his own translation of the *Iliad* in Ossianic free verse: yet another gesture, one supposes, of linking Ossian and Homer as equivalent classics.

Blair insistently amplified Macpherson's self-canonizing commentary. While dwelling in *A Critical Dissertation on the Poems of Ossian* (1763) on Ossian's quasi-Homeric sublimity, Blair goes so far as to claim that the Caledonian bard also out-Virgils Virgil: "The tenderness of Virgil softens," according to Blair, but "that of Ossian dissolves and overcomes the heart."[44] If these classicizing parallels served as indices of epic value, however, they could also arouse suspicion of indebtedness. Malcolm Laing's edition of 1805 establishes the anachronistic debts of "Ossian" not only to the classics of Greek and Roman antiquity, but to many an early modern source: Shakespeare, Milton, Pope, Thomson, and Gray, among others. Laing's painstakingly collated evidence of belated production constitutes his reason (to reiterate the epigraph to this chapter) for redating the poems of Ossian "from the third to the eighteenth century." As for the crowning touch of Ossian's blindness, one cannot top Laing's dry conclusion of 1800: "We know that Homer and Milton were blind, but a third blind bard, like them the author of two epic poems, must be ascribed to imitation, not to chance."[45] Though James Beattie and Samuel Johnson rejected the hype promulgated by Blair, a chorus of adulatory applause greeted Macpherson across Europe and the Atlantic.

With his borrowed trappings of epic authority, James Macpherson supplied "a founding myth for the British empire rooted in native, not continental soil."[46] Yet the radical instability of the Ossianic foundation is obvious in Macpherson's own manifest ambivalence about having disclaimed authorship. Looking back to the road not taken after *The Highander*, he intimates in the 3rd edition of *The Poems of Ossian* (1773), for example, that he might be more than a mere translator. "Those who have doubted my veracity have paid a compliment to my genius," he writes, "and were even the allegation true, my self-denial might have atoned for my fault."[47] This coyness reached its zenith in the following masterpiece of equivocation, which concludes the prefatory dissertation of 1773:

> Genuine poetry, like gold, loses little when properly transfused; but when composition cannot bear the test of a literal version, it is a counterfeit which ought not to pass current. The operation, however, must be performed with skilful hands. A translator, who cannot equal his original, is incapable of expressing its beauties.[48]

Some spotted a confession in these words, whereas others angrily wondered if Macpherson were attempting to steal credit for the charisma of Ossian. Macpherson also arranged to have himself buried in Westminster Abbey, along with the likes of Chaucer and Spenser—hardly the final gesture of a humble translator. By 1805, Highlander Adam Ferguson—a major force in the nucleus that initially had commissioned Macpherson—had reached the following conclusion:

> If it should remain a question with many, whether [James Macpherson] collected or composed these strains [the poems of Ossian], I shall not be surprised; for I believe, that what he got in writing was unknown to those who gave it [the native Highlanders], and the merit of what was repeated scarcely felt. And, in short, that he himself was not averse to be thought the author of what became so much celebrated and admired throughout Europe.[49]

Ferguson's bleak tone acknowledges the telling discrepancy between Macpherson's "translations" and the vestigial sources left behind in 1796 for his literary executor.

In career terms, "Ossian" paid off handsomely. In return for Macpherson's heroic metalepsis, the Second British Empire eventually provided the former parochial tutor about a thousand pounds per year: the financial means to become a Highland laird and MP from Camelford (1780–1796). Macpherson's ties to the East India Company illustrate the prominence of eighteenth-century Scots more generally in that enterprise.[50] By the 1760s, after the Seven Years War had turned decisively in Britain's favor around the globe, the Company was beginning to attract unfavorable publicity: constant news, in P. J. Marshall's words, of "wars, famines, the overthrow of Nawabs, and the indiscipline of the Company servants."[51] In the wake of revelations about the scramble for wealth by Robert Clive and similar fortune-hunters, the misrule of Indian states by a private foreign corporation was coming under increasing scrutiny. James Macpherson—"building a reputation," as Daffyd Moore writes, "as one of the more formidable political fixers of the late eighteenth century"[52]—involved himself for over two decades in the Company's meddling in the internal politics of the subcontinent. Indeed, he made most of his considerable fortune acting as an agent and hireling writer for Mohammed Ali, the Nawab of Arcot: "the old and faithful ally of the company," as Macpherson describes him.[53] The Nawab was the Company's sponsored Muslim ruler of the Carnatic in southern India, and Macpherson wrote on his behalf against the interests of the Hindu Raja of Tanjore. Along with his protégé and ally, Sir John Macpherson— a governor general of India, and son of the Reverend John Macpherson— James Macpherson exploited public misgivings about the Company's machinations to create sympathy for the Nawab's debts. Their specific agenda was to build British support for the Nawab's scheme to seize Tanjore: an annexation that he desired in response to the burdens of taxation imposed on the Carnatic by the Seven Years War. Edmund Burke's response to the propaganda thus jointly produced by James and Sir John Macpherson sounds a note that recurs throughout the Ossianic muddle:

> They have been indefatigable in their intrigues and publications. They have filled the world with many new topics of argument, and new narratives of fact. They have even been at the pains of correcting and amending history in order to accommodate it to [the Nawab's] views. . . .[54]

One feels on familiar ground upon discovering that James Macpherson's final Indian pamphlet, *The History and Management of the East-India Company, from Its Origin in 1600 to the Present Times* (1779), lays claim to an unverifiable authority: "Private papers and documents, together with written evidences of a private nature, which unveil the springs of many measures, have come into [the author's] possession."[55] As regards documentation, Macpherson evaded all forms of transparency.

Massaging the Archive

The Ossianic metalepsis necessarily had to create, so far as possible, its own context. Grafton points out that forgers must fit their forgery "neatly into the ordered ranks of other sources, real, fake, and ambiguous, which readers may be expected to know."[56] He compares this archival context to "a chessboard full of pieces": a field of play in which, one way or another, the forger must devise a series of winning moves.[57] The sheer facticity of existing sources, like a partially assembled jigsaw puzzle, imposes substantial constraints on possible inventions. The attempt to synchronize new data with established sources, moreover, had become somewhat more systematic by the latter half of the seventeenth century, when a concentrated effort arose to collate the chronicles of antiquity into a synoptic and concordant history of the world. Sir Isaac Newton developed in his sophisticated *Chronology of Ancient Kingdoms Amended* (1728) a universal chronology based both on cross-verifying ancient sources and on calculating the precession of the equinox. Historians were becoming more critical of the partisanship and miracle-mongering habits of older chronicles, which they read with increasing skepticism. In 1729, Father Thomas Innes, a Jacobite antiquarian, published in London a skeptical analysis of historical annals that led to the rapid collapse, as Colin Kidd emphasizes, of the Scottish Whig mythology built around the notion of an ancient Gaelic constitution. Macpherson's various chess moves would respond to all of these conditions by purporting to correct and complete the archive.

By Macpherson's moment in the 1760s, moreover, the new philosophers of wealth and society had begun to theorize social evolution. The vector of progress produced a sequential spectrum of "earliness" and "lateness" along which coeval cultures could be relationally defined. In 1774, Lord Kames encapsulates the idea of "progress to maturity" that galvanized this notion of nonsynchronous coexistence among coeval cultures:

> Some nations, stimulated by their own nature, or by their climate, have made a rapid progress; some have proceeded more slowly; and some continue savages. To trace out that progress toward maturity in different nations, is the subject of the present undertaking.[58]

The spatial zones of palpably "uneven development" within the territory of Scotland itself surely stimulated the anthropological historicism for which the Scottish Enlightenment became especially famous. This evolutionary sociology tended to equate a preordained sequence of developmental stages with linear "progress."

The wide preoccupation with narratives of origin and progress, moreover, eventually sanctioned a certain latitude to speculate about "ancient manners" precisely because, "there were so many obstacles to recuperating remote ages."[59] The "conjectural history" practiced by such thinkers as David Hume, Adam Smith, and Lord Kames was methodologically oriented to overcoming a simple want of direct evidence: the fact that "one could not see, or read accounts of anyone who had seen, the transition from hunter-gatherer to agricultural society."[60] The data "contained enough 'slop,' enough missing intervals where a scholar must extrapolate across a gap, to provide a great deal of 'play' and plasticity for squeezing information into expectations."[61] James Macpherson, needless to say, would attempt to exploit this latitude as an indispensable opening for historiographical invention.[62]

The brief "Age of Fingal"—roughly speaking, the third century—was, so Macpherson claims, sandwiched between the extinction of the Druids and the arrival of Christianity. Limiting his supernatural characters to a few easily managed ghosts, he thus saved himself the difficulty of fabricating an epic pantheon based on Druidic metaphysics. In 1768, the Reverend John Macpherson improved on the rationale for the peculiar absence of religious references in Ossian by invoking a division of labor: "The Bard sang merely mortal subjects: hymns and anthems belonged to the more dignified race of *Faids*" [a branch of the Druids].[63] James Macpherson further kneaded his story-line so as to harmonize it with scattered references to the *Caledonii* by ancient Roman historians, also interpolating invented Gaelic cognates (such as "Caracul") for historical personages mentioned therein (such as Caracalla, son of the Roman emperor Severus). The anonymous author of *Fingal King of Morven, a Knight-Errant* diagnosed this belated interpolation in 1764: "From the single word *Carac-huil*, obviously the fictitious name of a Romantic champion, have they ["patrons of this new traditional history"] not had the art and address to extract the son of a Roman emperor at the head of a mighty army, and also a most glorious victory gained over this Roman general, and his mighty army, AD 210, on the banks of the Carron, by FINGAL King of Morven?"[64] Since the Roman historians had little to say about Caracalla—they left a "convenient chasm," as Laing observes—Macpherson massaged this gap accordingly: the silence, he says, reflects Roman reluctance to acknowledge the defeat of their mighty army at the hands of the doughty Caledonians. Though Roman historians in fact acknowledge plenty of defeats, Macpherson's manipulation of sources is impervious to such facts.

Above all, Macpherson invented a suitably defanged crew of Caledonian warriors—"noble, but not savage," in Weinbrot's phrase[65]—that compares very favorably with the gloating and plundering heroes of the *Iliad*. In one of his shrewdest chess-moves, Macpherson leavened the bloodthirsty and misogynist ethos of tribal warfare with a heavy dose of moistly tender "sensibility" themes.[66] Whether one reads this as a mediation of martial virtue and commercial politeness (Adam Potkay) or as a symptomatic incoherence that dismantles heroic values (Dafydd Moore), the strange conjunction is central to the significance of "Ossian." The combination of martial virtue

and chivalrous behavior is, of course, the epitome of a layering phenomenon Grafton describes as inherent to forgeries: "the forger's period super-
imposed upon the forgery's."[67] This sedimented fabrication Macpherson
then passed off as his "extremely literal translation"[68] of a quasi-Homeric
cycle of ancient Caledonian bardic poetry. For Lord Kames, the sheer
implausibility of such refined warriors was another argument for Ossian's
authenticity: "But if a forgery," he asked, "why so bold and improbable?
Why not invent manners more congruent to the savage state?"[69]

Macpherson ran into immediate trouble, however, with several angles of
his epic confabulation. In adapting the cycle of Magnus ballads to *Fingal*, he
introduced a blatant anachronism: a third-century Scandinavian invasion of
Ireland. With regard to this, Ferdinando Warner observed, in 1762, that no
such recorded event occurred "till the Irruption of the Danes which was
above Four hundred years after, the Aera of the Poem: and this alone is an
Objection to the genuine History of the Poem, which in my opinion is not
easily to be got over."[70] Further interference arose from Macpherson's
making Fingal and Cuchullin contemporaries. This required, as Charles
O'Conor points out, a sequence of generations averaging 57 years each
(from Trenmor to Fingal) and then a subsequent one averaging 19 years
each (Fingal to Ossian to Oscar). For the Irish Catholic O'Conor, widely
regarded as the best Gaelic scholar of his time, the archival massage has
deteriorated into a species of torture:

> How contrary such a Scheme is to Experience, and to the technical Canon
> established upon it by Sir Isaac Newton, and the best Chronologers, need not
> be shewn: But Mr. Macpherson has established a chronological Canon of his
> own, resembling the Rack of Procrustes, shortening or stretching the gener-
> ations of Men, as it best answered the Purposes, and fitted the Standard, of
> Ossian's genealogical Torture.[71]

O'Conor diagnoses the need in Macpherson, in the wake of Innes, to discover
"a *new* Monarchy of Scots in Britain, to make us Amends for the Ruins of the
old."[72] He likewise diagnoses the metaleptic operation as follows:

> The *modern Sentiments, Manners, Customs* and *Allusions* they contain, affix
> them to modern Times; and the Ignorance of Chronology, Geography, and
> antient History, shews that OSSIAN, the SON OF FINGAL, was in no degree fit
> to personate OISÍN, the SON OF FIONN, in the Description of Things to
> which that Prince was coeval. The Son of *Fingal*, therefore, lived near our *own*
> *Times*, and it is best known to Mr. *Mac Pherson*, whether he is not, in the
> Whole, or in Part, alive to this Day.[73]

The plasticity of the archive was, after all, far from unlimited.

Sweeping the Irish off the Board

The Ossianic metalepsis involved a risky and aggressive attempt to discredit, negate, and liquidate the Irish past: the strategic equivalent, to paraphrase Grafton's useful conceit, of sweeping all the chess-pieces off the board. All, that is, except for the few that Macpherson intended to filch: for the supposedly bilateral row involved crucial rivalries among Celtic antiquarians.[74] A great part of Macpherson's historiographical agenda involved an attempt to undo Irish antiquities. In his prefaces to *Fingal* and *Temora*, Macpherson engages a preemptive strike against well-attested Irish sources, attempting thereby "to undermine the potential of Irish literary and historical sources to demonstrate that his Ossian was fraudulent."[75] "The bards of Ireland," in the words of Macpherson, "by ascribing to Ossian compositions which are evidently their own, have occasioned a general belief in that country, that Fingal was of Irish extraction, and not of the ancient Caledonians, as is said in the genuine poems of Ossian."[76] The anti-Irish angle of Macpherson's project falsified Celtic history in general, recasting Scotland as the Celtic motherland and Ireland as the derivative colony. Macpherson coolly cannibalized such Irish figures as Fionn Mac Cumhal and Oisín, well-established in written Irish sources dating back as far as the twelfth century. These he purged of any tell-tale traces of Irish roots, such as St. Patrick: for Fingal and Ossian would now be shown orbiting around the mythical Scottish kingdom of "Morven" rather than Ulster or Connacht. Thomson establishes that Macpherson also raids the Irish histories of Geoffrey Keating and Roderick O'Flaherty for such details as the cookery of the Fian.[77] The three-sided context of this "Three Kingdoms" politics puts many aspects of the controversy in a rather different light, including the supposed struggle of an underdog "oral tradition" against a quasi-imperial written one.

In 1761, an advertisement appeared in the *Dublin Journal* casting doubt on Macpherson's translation. By 1762, Warner, an English scholar of Irish antiquities, asserted his opinion "that the Irish Antiquities here recited [in Macpherson's preface to *Fingal*] are authentic" and "that all the famous Champions, Cuchullin, Fingal, Ossian, Oscar, &c. were absolutely Irish Heroes. . . ."[78] In 1766, Charles O'Conor, weighed in with a sophisticated critique. O'Conor's own antiquarian pursuits were indirectly linked to a concerted political campaign, via the Catholic Committee, to repeal the vicious "Penal Laws" that disenfranchised Irish Catholics in virtually every sphere of life. O'Conor risked prosecution for public libel by publishing a series of four pamphlets between 1755 and 1771 on the deleterious consequences for Ireland of depriving Catholics of all rights.[79] He played an important part, in S. J. Connelly's words, "in recasting the Catholic case for relaxation of the penal laws in the language of orthodox Whig constitutionalism."[80]

The first edition of O'Conor's *Dissertations on the Ancient History of Ireland*, based on an extensive collection of manuscripts, was published in 1753. *Dissertations* asserts the value of a literate culture in pre-Christian Gaelic Ireland: a civilization that he traces back to Spain. O'Conor probes into and sifts historical sources, often conceding their discrepancies and limitations. "O'Conor's pride in his culture," as Thomas McLaughlin puts it, prompts "cautious scrutiny from the scholar in him, anger from the nationalist at foreign abuse, as well as a conciliatory vision of the future."[81]

In his second edition of 1766, O'Conor attached an essay to *Dissertations* dedicated to "Observations on the Poems of *Fingal* and *Temora*": the source of the quotations used above. The wittiest section of this scathing essay consists of a mock-dialogue between Ossian and James Macpherson, in which the latter attempts to persuade the former to collude in his fraudulent rewriting of history. Ossian expresses various misgivings and scruples, one of which involves the inconvenient existence of "the old Irish Chronicles and Language, which stand in the way."[82] To this O'Conor's ventriloquized version of "Macpherson" replies as follows:

> Leave that to me, Ossian: I will prove the *former* to be no better than a fardel of *crude* and *indigested* tales, and the *latter*, a corrupt *jargon*. Nay more: I will demonstrate . . . that all antiquity has been grossly mistaken, in peopling our Highlands from Ireland, or indeed, in peopling the British islands with different nations of Celts who spoke different languages. For, Ossian, it is for the interest of your scheme and mine, that they should speak *but one*, common to all. I will prove, that *oral tradition* alone is sufficient in *my hands*, for the setting aside all foreign and domestic accounts relating to our kingdom of Morven. With this tradition, I say, we will lay Lochlin waste, and people Ireland with our Highland colonies. Still more, Ossian, I will demonstrate, that your Earse is the pure Scotic, or Gaelic, spoken in the third century![83]

As regards Macpherson's tactics, the written Irish archive proved to be recalcitrant: not infinitely malleable. And yet there may be something to Maurice Colgan's argument that Macpherson's influence frustrated, for almost 150 years, the full recognition of the Irish epic *Táin Bó Cualnge* ("The Cattle Raid of Cooley"), possibly dating back as far as the first century BC.[84]

James Macpherson was anticipated to some extent in his attack on Irish antiquities by the Lowlander William Maitland's *History and Antiquities of Scotland* (1758), and he was reinforced in it by his fellow Highlander, the Reverend John Macpherson of Sleat. The Reverend Macpherson, with whom James Macpherson stayed during his fieldwork in the Highlands, reiterates in *Critical Dissertations on the Origin, Antiquities, Language,*

Government, Manners, and Religion of the Ancient Caledonians (1768) that the *Scoti* of ancient Ireland (*Scotia*) were originally from present-day Scotland: an egregious distortion. The anonymous editor who supplied the preface and annotations for this posthumously published book urges that James Macpherson not deign to reply to the critique of Charles O'Conor:"It is to be hoped Mr. Macpherson will not honor with a reply such an illiberal attack, which is as impotent as it is ungentlemanly."[85] Those acquainted with the self-referential texture of this controversy may be forgiven for suspecting that the author of this footnote is none other than James Macpherson.

In 1771, James Macpherson published *An Introduction to the History of Great Britain and Ireland*, which—rebutting O'Conor—attempts to codify the historiographical inventions that surrounded his presentation of "Ossian." While rehashing the Reverend John Macpherson's arguments, James Macpherson professes astonishment at continuing Irish credulity:

> It is a matter of some wonder that the Irish remain so long wedded to a ridiculous system of antiquities, which throws the reproach of credulity upon their nation. Every other polished people, who, in the time of ignorance, had set up high schemes of antiquity, have now extricated their history from the fables of their dark ages.[86]

In a truly Macphersonesque sentence, he writes of himself as follows:"An enemy to fiction himself, he [the author] imposes none upon the world." Not everyone was convinced. In 1773, the Reverend John Whitaker objected to the revisionist efforts of both the Macphersons in the following terms:"The whole current of history is to be violently opposed, the Ireland of the Romans is to be interpreted into the present Scotland, and the Scotch are to be made the aborigines of Caledonia."[87] William Shaw, the renegade Hebridean, sums up the entire historiographical project in 1781:

> the author [James Macpherson], in order to save his purpose, wrests facts as they may best serve his end, and, apprehensive of a future detection, labours with great zeal to destroy the credit of all Irish history, and, with a few bold strokes of his pen, obliterate all the Celtic learning ever known any where in order to make way for a new system of Celtic emigration and Hebridean and Fingalian history . . . of which nothing was ever heard before. . . .[88]

"Oral tradition" was not so much a heroic underdog as the solvent by which Macpherson proposed to decompose the most well-attested sources of Celtic history. Contemporary scholarly opinion largely accords with Shaw.[89]

Ethnic and Racial Appropriations

The Ossianic metalepsis involves further spirals of dissonant appropriations, by Macpherson, his immediate collaborators, and his various audiences. For one thing, the "internal colonialism" model for Scottish history goes, as they say, "all the way down." Eighteenth-century Scotland itself remained jarringly divided—linguistically and otherwise—between the increasingly prosperous, literate, and pro-unionist Lowlands (which sponsored and promoted "Ossian" from the commercial heartland of Edinburgh) and the recently conquered, poverty-stricken, residually feudalistic, and mostly unlettered Gaelic Highlands (which served, after brief interludes of "field-work," as the authenticating source). A good many Lowland Scots had wanted to vanquish the Jacobites; and some, indeed, had themselves used the fog of the punitive post-Culloden atmosphere to settle old scores. As late as 1763, the Presbyterian Scottish Society for the Propagation of Christian Knowledge (the S.S.P.C.K.) was still openly discussing their evangelical project of imposing English on the Highlands. Even after 1766, moreover, the S.S.P.C.K. promoted a Bible-based Gaelic quite different from the indigenous Earse. As Hugh Kearney points out, in the 1760s the Lowlanders began to romanticize and appropriate that which they had been irrevocably transforming for most of the eighteenth century: "the newly invented kilt and tartan were taken over by Lowland families as emblems of ethnic identity."[90] Given the obvious gulf between the Lowland literati and eighteenth-century Gaelic culture, the element of stark opportunism in this appropriation cannot be ignored. Literary regionalism, moreover, would find, or make, the marketable quaintness on which the genre thrives: "a setting outside the world of modern development, a zone of backwardness where locally variant folkways still prevail."[91] Sir Walter Scott, an author with whom one associates the early development of this genre, likewise popularized the invented tradition of distinctive clan tartans in *Sketches of the Character, Manners, and Present State of the Highlanders of Scotland* (1822).[92] Designed to influence a national pageant welcoming George IV to Scotland, this pamphlet emphasized the monarch's connections to the House of Stuart and passed over the unpleasant fact that "Butcher" Cumberland was his great uncle.

Macpherson's own appropriation and mediation of the Highlands has frequently been seen as essentially preservationist: a beneficial stimulus to Celtic revivalism. This view necessarily plays down the extent to which his war on "Irish corruptions" entailed a wholly arbitrary practice of "purifying" such Highland sources as he had. William Shaw reported, after his field-trip into the Highlands, that his informants there (among whom the name of "Fingal" was not in use) agreed that "Fionn" was an Irishman.[93]

Macpherson approached such sources as he possessed strictly as fodder for his Highland-based epic. In a letter published in the *Report of the Committee of the Highland Society of Scotland* (1805), Andrew Gallie—a diehard Ossian supporter—describes Macpherson's treatment of his Highland sources as follows: "I remember Mr. Macpherson reading the MSS found in Clanranald's, execrating the bard who dictated to the amanuensis, saying, 'D-n the scoundrel, it is he himself that now speaks, and not Ossian.' "[94] In one of his more revealing annotations, moreover, Macpherson writes as follows:

> Their [the bards'] interpolations are so easily distinguished from the genuine remains of Ossian, that it took me very little time to mark them out, and totally to reject them. If the modern Scotch and Irish bards have shewn any judgment, it is in ascribing their own compositions to names of antiquity.

Given the two-year period in which Macpherson churned out two full-length epics translated from a difficult language that lacked any settled spelling, one can readily believe that his editorial agonies were not prolonged. As for his comment about the wisdom of modern bards ascribing their own compositions to names of antiquity, one cannot improve on Laing's dry aside: "The unexpected truth contained in this strange note, is too important to be suppressed."[95] Jokes aside, the implications of Macpherson's interventions have a darker side. Stafford notes a subtle result of the dissonance between Highland source and English translation: a generally disappointed response in the Highlands to *The Poems of Ossian*, especially regarding Macpherson's use of Anglicized names (*Ossian* rather than *Oisín*).[96] One wonders, furthermore, how typical may have been the Reverend Archibald MacArthur's decision to *stop* collecting Gaelic poems "because he came to believe that those he was finding were of the kind Macpherson had denounced as spurious."[97] The description of Macpherson as a conjuror, reanimated ancestral spirits with his "ghostly muse,"[98] needs to account for ancestral traces lost in his wake.

Ironically enough, the agenda of the Edinburgh literati—to intensify Scottish pride, clout, and national unity through the vehicle of "Ossian"—backfired in unexpected ways. Macpherson himself took cover behind lofty patriotism while tainting, for the better part of a century, the legitimate study of Gaelic antiquities. Though a good many well-known Scots did initially close ranks around Macpherson, the issue gradually proved more divisive than unifying for them.[99] Such luminaries as David Hume, Adam Smith, and James Boswell, though initially inclined to enthusiasm, declined to jump on the bardic bandwagon. Macpherson's obstinate refusal to publish or even to grant access to his Gaelic "originals" irredeemably damaged his credibility. Even die-hard supporters began to fall back into positions more distanced from Macpherson's particular concoction of poetry and history, arguing either (1) that the aesthetic merit of *The Poems of Ossian* was independent of its historical provenance; or (2) that there could be no doubt, based on oral tradition alone, that "Fingal fought and Ossian sang." The Hebridean lexicographer William Shaw, originally a believer, courted Samuel Johnson's patronage and became a much-demonized "infidel" after his own collecting trip into the Highlands, in 1779, produced only fifteenth-century ballads with Irish heroes. The Scottish historian Malcolm Laing—attacked in some quarters as a Scandinavian outsider from the Orkney Islands—published, in 1805, the most meticulous demonstration of Ossian's eighteenth-century origins ever written. Above all, of course, the *Report of the Committee of the Highland Society of Scotland* (1805), commissioned and edited by Henry Mackenzie, established that, after a diligent collecting operation, "it [was] possessed of no documents, to shew how much of his collection Mr. Macpherson obtained in the form in which he has given it to the world."[100]

A further twist to the meandering controversy comes into view if one considers the Nordic overtones that "Ossian" acquired as it crossed the English Channel: a reception that had little to do with the interests of the Highlanders as such. Despite some painful retrenching on home turf, "Ossian" was an especially dazzling success in Germany and Scandinavia, where he was happily claimed as a northern Homer. Weinbrot's discussion of "Everyone's Ossian"[101] explores the rhapsodic reception of Macpherson in continental Europe. The democratizing element usually celebrated in Whiggish historiography, however, needs to be balanced with a recognition of the concomitant late-eighteenth-century making of Eurocentric ideology. The appeal of "Ossian" to collective identities wider than the nation-state serves to remind us that the politics of Ossian, as Colin Kidd points out, "are not reducible to an exclusively Celtic interpretation."[102] As Martin Bernal has argued, much of the energy for this northern European craze was derived from an emerging politics of racialized identities.[103] Blue-eyed warriors and white-bosomed maidens abound in *Fingal* and *Temora*: a physiognomical subtext that, when set alongside the emphatic claims to purity, encouraged certain "Nordic" appropriations. German and Finnish "fakelore" was shortly to follow suit: the *Kinder- und Hausmärchen* of the Brothers Grimm (1812–1822) and the runic epic *Kalevala* (1835). In 1782, William Julius Mickle parodies Ossianic Nordicism by posing as an editor who

> has the happiness of being long acquainted with a very ingenious and learned
> Antiquarian . . . a gentleman so very zealous in his researches for lost
> literature . . . that he is at this moment on his travels through Lapland on

purpose to discover proofs of the authenticity of his favorite Ossian. And his last letters assure his friends . . . that he is informed a fair copy of Ossian's poems, in the handwriting of one of his sons, is carefully preserved in the archive of the College of Bards in Iceland. . . .[104]

Popular as "Ossian" was, a skeptical diagnosis of the forces making him so dogged the myth at every turn.

The evolutionary framework of this cannibalistic historicism, moreover, could easily escalate into that "denial of coevalness" that Johannes Fabian has diagnosed in *Time and the Other* (1983) as haunting contemporary anthropology: the reification and exclusion of indigenous peoples consigned to an arrested stage of social development. Lord Kames embeds his defense of Ossian in a book that takes as its central argument that "there are different races of men as well as dogs: a mastiff differs not more from a spaniel, that a white man from a negro, or a Laplander from a Dane."[105] Charles Mackinnon argued for the authenticity of Ossian in 1785 precisely on the grounds of comparative primitivism: that as North American savages are known to be polished orators, so "as the Whites are superior to any other breed of human creature, it is no violent supposition, that the oratory of at least some varieties of Whites has also been much figured."[106] Even primitive "Whites," that is to say, are *already* essentially polite, essentially superior: a telling clue to the immense popularity enjoyed by the bowdlerized barbarians populating Macpherson's world. The ultimate zigzag in this maze of ironies lies in the fact that Macpherson—the proud Highland indigene—evidently considered himself of Germanic rather than Celtic descent. In 1771, he argues in *Introduction to the History of Great Britain and Ireland*, as Kidd's paraphrases it, that "the only people of ancient Caledonia of Germanic (though not Gothic) stock were the Catti, the ancestors of the Clan Chattan, a confederation of clans which included the Macphersons."[107] Even as he aggrandized Scottish Celts at the expense of Irish Celts, the ever-elusive Macpherson seemingly positioned himself as Teutonic. One must be alert indeed to follow every serpentine twist of James Macpherson's dance in and out of the oft-appropriated "Celtic Fringe."

Linguistic Leaps

The "Herderian moment" of the later eighteenth century marks the emergence of an ideological process by which divisive conflicts of class could be rearticulated in terms of ethnically homogenous "folk," each of which possessed an immutable soul or *Geist*. This spiritual essence was immediately accessible through language. A crucial element of the *odium*

Ossianicum thus concerns the rise of a specifically philological historicism: a field of play that proved to be no less elastic as regards metaleptic manipulation than had been the text of scripture. Though John Locke had powerfully argued at the end of the seventeenth century that language is constituted by wholly arbitrary conventions,[108] the new philology of the mid-to-late eighteenth century, as Hudson demonstrates, strongly recuperated theories based on the divine origins of linguistic signs.[109] The "Arch-Druid" William Stukeley, for example, attempted to derive the Welsh language from the sacred language of ancient Hebrew. His particular hobbyhorse was to trace the evidence in a vast array of ancient sources for a trinitarian mode of worship ("Patriarchal Christianity")—*preceding* the Mosaic dispensation—associated with serpentine or circular temples. He thus embedded his factual account of ancient megaliths, as Stuart Piggott writes, in "a strange mixture of fantasy and speculation about Druids and Patriarchal Christianity."[110] Admired even today for his archaeological surveys and perspective drawings of Stonehenge and Avebury, where he did extensive empirical fieldwork,[111] Stukeley argued in *Stonehenge* (1740) for the prehistoric colonization of Britain by the Phoenicians. The remnants of the original Phoenician colony, he speculates in *Abury* (1743), are "the *Irish* and ancient highland *Scots*."[112] Etymological leaps of faith constitute for Stukeley a wide-ranging mode of historical inquiry: "Thus we have sail'd through a wide ocean of antiquities," he writes in Abury, "and not without a compass. We set old things transmitted to us in writing, in parallelism with these we may now see at home, in such a manner, as I think, evidently shews them to be the same."[113] His extravagant romancing of the etymon permits him to connect, for example, *Hakpen* (the name of a ridge overlooking Avebury) both with Hebraic roots and with Greek *Parnassus*.[114]

As Locke had pointed out, if there were any "natural" connection between linguistic signs and the ideas to which they refer, "there would be but one Language amongst all Men."[115] Philology opened the door to the speculation that this had once been the case. For several decades in the mid-eighteenth century, "a veritable cottage industry of amateur philologists," as Sorensen puts it, sprang up to write histories of ancient Gaelic as the *Ur*-language.[116] A cadre of Welsh linguists, galvanized by the genuine scholarly accomplishments of Edward Lluhd in *Archaeologica Britannica* (1707), began publishing a mixture of legitimate literary antiquities and Celtophilic speculations. As Prys Morgan shows, these linguists—from Rice Jones to Thomas Richards to William Owen (self-named "Pughe" upon inheriting his estate)—converged in asserting the undefiled purity of Welsh, which, they argued, could be connected to the glorious history of the continental Celts.[117] An even more extravagant claim for Welsh as the Edenic language is reiterated in the amazing volumes of the Welsh antiquarian Rowland

Jones, who could afford to self-publish such idiosyncratic works as *Hieroglyfic* (1763), *The Origins of Language and Nations* (1764), and *Remarks on the Circles of Gomer* (1771). The special privilege of Celtic, as Jones explains, has to do with its having escaped any alteration during the Tower-of-Babel episode recounted in Genesis. Though such Celtomania apparently belongs to the wackier fringes of intellectual history, it enabled the establishment of a new terrain of argumentation.[118] Circumventing traditional historical sources, philologists could draw a direct line connecting whatever dots they wished to connect.

A Scottish philological tradition, emerging from the antiquarian specu-lations of William Maitland and Jerome Stone, likewise argued that Gaelic was the *Ur*-language. Such antiquarian projects blurred fiction and fact with varying degrees of self-consciousness, opening the door to poetic reinven-tions of "national genius." Maitland's *History and Antiquities of Scotland* makes explicit the turn to linguistics that drove this burst of antiquarian speculation. Maitland crucially argues that language itself is "a proof perhaps more certain than that of historical authority."[119] He anticipates several of Macpherson's ethnic speculations. Above all, he claims that the ancient Caledonians described by classic Roman historians were Celtae. "Scots" and "Picts," then, were names imposed from without on the Celtae. The present inhabitants of Scottish Gaeldom—residents of the northern and western regions—are contemporary descendants of the Celtae. In an espe-cially influential etymology, Maitland derives "Caledonia" from *Gael-duni* (Gaels from the *duni*, or hills). The etymological collapse of middle terms between past and present—a process of *disintermediation*—fostered competing claims among differently located Gaelic antiquarians, as Gauti Kristmannsson shows, about whose tongue was the closest to aboriginal purity.[120] John Clark, for example, attacks William Shaw's Hebridean dialect (from the island of Arran) as "so corrupt in the words, and so vicious in the pronun-ciation, as to be almost unintelligible in the other Western Islands and opposite continent of the Highlands, where the language is spoken with elegance and purity."[121]

Above all, linguistics provided the genealogical metaphors—cognate language families and family trees, branches with close and remote cousins, bifurcating twigs with common ancestors, and so on—that enabled nation-alism to mobilize metaphors of consanguinity for large populations. Macpherson and his allies got a great deal of mileage from tortuous etymologies of such key words as *Gael*, *Celt*, *Scotti*, *Pict*, *Morven*, and so on. Given the implied equation between language and national spirit, such "wild philology" enabled a new mode of nationalist historiography. These genealogical terms, which initially blurred the lines between language, cul-ture, and biological kinship, opened the door to "race" in the fully modern sense. By the early nineteenth century, a further step—a correlation of linguistics with the pseudo-science of "race"—would be taken, notably in the linguistics of August and Friedrich von Schlegel.[122]

Strange Loops and Vicious Circles

The Ossianic metalepsis provoked innumerable spasms of circular logic. The poems anthologized in Macpherson's various redactions of Ossian in the 1760s and 1770s appeared before the public through the medium of a self-proclaimed editor. Authenticating scholarly devices included introductions, learned dissertations, footnotes, and so on, all of which tended to "verify" the authenticity of their source materials by reference to a past inferred from those same sources. The metalanguage of Macpherson's scholarship explicates, as its object, the customs of the Ossianic days of yore; and the retrospectively fabricated "translations" of Ossian provide grist for Macpherson's historiographical mill. Hence a "strange loop": a paradox of self-reference that confuses logical levels, producing a sense of endless regress.[123] Consider the following line from an annotation to *Temora*, Book VII: "The description of the shield of Cathmor," writes Macpherson, donning his editor's hat, "is valuable on account of the light it casts on the progress of arts in those early times."[124] The passage is, as Laing points out, an imitation of Homer's description of the shield of Achilles. The self-referential split between Macpherson-the-editor and Macpherson-in-Ossianic-costume makes O'Conor's imaginary dialogue between the two especially telling. In this dialogue, Macpherson (the editor) explains to "Ossian" the advantages of this split as follows:

> Deal you in *Generals*, as much as possible: Should your *Commentator* mistake, in descending to Particulars, he alone will bear the Blame. If *Carachuil* be not *Caracalla*, or *Caros Caraisius*, the Fault will be mine, not your's.[125]

O'Conor's "Ossian" and "Macpherson" eventually work things out. O'Conor prepares us not to be surprised that the actual Macpherson finds in *An Introduction to the History of Great Britain and Ireland* (1771) that there is a "perfect agreement" between his history and the poems of Ossian.[126]

The great exemplar of this *circulus vitiotius*, however, is Hugh Blair's *Critical Dissertation on the Poems of Ossian* (1763; expanded in 1765), usually included in subsequent editions of *The Poems of Ossian*. Blair invokes the Scottish Enlightenment's pet theory of the four stages in the evolution of society—hunting, pasturage, agriculture, and commerce—to authenticate the antique manners described in Ossian. He then cites the (translated) works of Ossian as evidence to validate the corollary that the most primitive age is the most favorable for poetic sublimity. One might have expected the sophisticated rhetorical theorist, self-conscious denizen of so belated and rational an age, to spot the tautology in the following passage:

> What we have long been accustomed to call the oriental vein of poetry, because some of the earliest poetical productions have come to us from the East, is probably no more oriental than occidental; it is characteristical of an age rather than a country; and belongs, in some measure, to all nations at a certain period. Of this the works of Ossian seem to furnish a remarkable proof.[127]

The methodological problem manifest here, made glaring by the issue of fraud, in fact belongs to historical inquiry as such. If one subdivides history into discrete periods (of which a small portion only may be known of even one), then the act of understanding older texts and artifacts must confront the "hermeneutic circle" that has long haunted philosophical hermeneutics and German *Geistesgeschichte*.[128] Understanding the surviving part would seem to demand a contextual grasp of the whole (the named epoch); and yet the period as a whole must necessarily be reconstructed from very partial evidence. The act of historical reconstruction, moreover, like the mentality of the interpreter, is bound by its own historically contingent existence. The deepest historicity of the "Ossian" controversy lies precisely in its perplexing revelation of this hermeneutic circle. "Ossian" short-circuited relations between the past and the present. As should be clear by now, the more egregious tautologies and closed loops were sharply challenged at the time by a wide spectrum of intellectuals. To rehabilitate Macpherson in our own time as an heir of the Scottish Enlightenment—representing the forces of vernacular revival against linguistic normalization, of oral tradition against print-culture, and so on[129]—may involve a disservice precisely to those many Scots who proved most faithful to the Enlightenment ideals of transparency and cosmopolitan sensibilities.

To an incredible degree, of course, the self-confirming nature of Ossianic ideology reached far and wide. In 1763, Stukeley enthusiastically hailed the publication of Macpherson's second epic with *A Letter from Dr. Stukeley to Mr. Macpherson on His Publication of Fingal and Temora*. Stukeley supplemented his warm affirmation of Ossian with an engraved illustration of the shield of Cathmor. This lively drawing (see figure 2.1), not clearly marked as less empirically grounded than Stukeley's painstaking renderings of Stonehenge, is an early example of the stupefying number of spin-offs provoked by the rage for things Ossianic: parodies, rhymed versions, an opera, even a play produced in Edinburgh. The controversy also sparked something of a "cult," as Thomson puts it, of fabricated Gaelic verse.[130] Copycat bogus "Gaelic

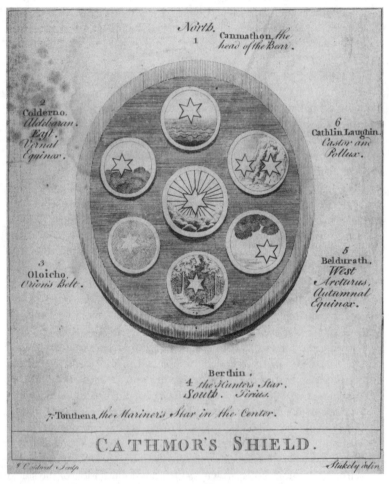

2.1 Drawing by William Stukeley, "The Shield of Cathmor."

antiquities" issued forth from the pens of the Reverend John Smith (in *Galic Antiquities*, 1778; and *Sean Dàna*, 1787); from Macpherson's pupil and kinsman John Clark (in *The Works of the Caledonian Bards, translated from the Galic*, 1778); and from the Reverend Duncan MacCallum (in "Calloth,"1821).[131] Chatterton's "Rowley" forgeries (written 1764–1770) are, of course, part of the Ossianic tidal wave.

The Ossianic rewriting of history fed back into the Highlands, illustrating how an actual place can become marked, through the leisured consumption of "local color," as *local*: the object both of tourism and of regional literature produced for a metropolitan audience.[132] As the quiescent Highlands of the 1760s became safe for tourists, Ossianic references increasingly began to permeate the names and features of its landscape: a discursive phenomenon driven by commercial as well as nationalistic motives. Ossian, as Paul Baines writes, became "an inescapable literary companion on the tour."[133] "Fingal's Cave"—later described in a novel by Sir Walter Scott, and hailed musically by Felix Mendelssohn—became a stop on a tourist's itinerary. Tourists of the Highlands, hungering for experiences of enclosed authenticity, wanted to encounter a trace of Ossian. Though Pat Rogers suggests that Samuel Johnson would have been more tactful had he delivered his acerbic views on "Ossian" separately, in an essay kept discrete from his *Journey to the Western Islands of Scotland* (1773),[134] the landscape itself had in effect been retrospectively Ossianized by the time Johnson traveled into the Highlands. The topic could scarcely be avoided, and Johnson was not the man to tiptoe around it.

The penultimate phase of Macpherson's personal metalepsis came in response to the unanswerable trump card that his doubters could always play: *produce the originals*. Just as Johnson famously defined patriotism (of the Wilkite variety) as "the last refuge of a scoundrel," so he described Macpherson's "stubborn audacity" in refusing to provide evidence as "the last refuge of guilt."[135] Eventually, however, Macpherson was in fact driven to a still more desperate shift: the fabrication, through a laborious reverse translation, of a Gaelic pseudo-original. A brief specimen of this "original Gaelic" (possibly back-translated by James Macpherson's cousin, Lachlan Macpherson) had appeared in the seventh book of *Temora* (1763). This minuscule sample, as Groom observes, merely intensified the demand to see the original manuscripts.[136] By 1783, a group of India-based Scotsmen had raised a thousand pounds, which they sent to the Highland Society of London, in order to enable Macpherson to fulfil his oft-delayed promise to publish all of his Gaelic "originals."[137] This gesture, done in a well-wishing spirit of Scottish solidarity, made Macpherson's position even more awkward than it had already become. Distracted by politics and a string of mistresses, he accepted the inconveniently helpful subscription while continuing to stall and temporize, toying for some years with the idea of transliterating his supposed originals into the Greek alphabet. Macpherson's compatriots, smelling fraud, tried unsuccessfully to recover their money through a lawsuit. Macpherson, whose knowledge of Gaelic seems to have been less than perfect, returned to the dogged task of backward translation, possibly with some trusted collaborators. One of his memoranda, as Thomson points out, reports delivering three books to his literary executor, John Mackenzie, of the Gaelic version of Cathloda that were "as complete as the translation." This seemingly backwards locution—normally *translations* are measured for completeness against their original—in fact shows Macpherson "gradually fulfilling what he regarded as his obligations: namely to provide a Gaelic original, since his friends expected it of him, and since he had accepted a subscription for publishing it."[138]

Macpherson's final act of metaleptic self-confirmation required still more trusty henchmen, for it was posthumous. Macpherson did leave some manuscripts behind upon his death in 1796. John Mackenzie informed the Committee of the Highland Society of Scotland "that the manuscripts left by Mr. Macpherson were not ancient, but those of the handwriting of himself, or of others whom he had employed. . . ."[139] In any case, Mackenzie passed along some sort of unfinished Ossianic gleanings to Sir John Sinclair, historian of the Highland Society in London in 1803. As Laird had foreseen in the epigraph to this chapter, Sinclair—financed by the subscription mentioned above—duly published a version of them in 1807, along with a facing Latin translation and yet another dissertation "proving" them the authentic Gaelic sources of Ossian. Rather than solving "the problem of origins," Sinclair's edition, as K. K. Ruthven observes, merely rendered the text of Ossian more polyglot.[140] One is struck by the very different conduct of the two Highland Societies—tactful disenchantment (from the Highland Society in Scotland in 1805) versus forgery (from the Highland Society in London in 1807).

Macpherson's holograph "transcriptions" were lost or destroyed: another ladder kicked away. Macpherson's understandable ambition to be regarded as an author, moreover, now served to recuperate the perversity of his conduct as regards his "originals." Sir John Sinclair explains that Macpherson finally overcame his reluctance, as a translator, to give Ossian his due credit:

> Elevated, by his connection with Galic poetry, to a respectable rank, both in literature and in society, his pride made him wish to believe, that he owed that elevation more to his own talents, than to the genius of an old bard, whom he had rescued from oblivion. But notwithstanding every motive which pride or vanity could furnish, a conscientious regard to truth, induced him at last to leave behind the original Galic poetry *expressly for the purpose of*

being published, though, by destroying it, his claims to be considered as the real author, would have received such additional confirmation, that it would have been extremely difficult indeed, at the present moment, to have refuted them.[141]

Thomson notes that this collection "shows the strong influence of Macpherson's English of 1762" and that "it must be concluded that it was translated from that English."[142] He does, however, observe that "there are ample grounds for saying that the Gaelic 'originals' of 1807 constitute a more complete forgery than the translations of 1760–63."[143] Hugh Trever-Roper is characteristically blunter, ascribing the entire enterprise of 1807 to "the Macpherson mafia in London."[144] For Sinclair's pseudo-originals of 1807, as Howard Gaskill notes, "the versions left behind by Macpherson were re-transcribed, using the conventions of the Gaelic Bible of 1767."[145]

Bishop Percy's Metalepsis

A refrain that has become quite fashionable of late offers the "balanced" observation, as if this were truly revelatory, that Macpherson was not *entirely* a charlatan.[146] The soft-focus treatment of Macpherson blurs the question of imposture by way of arriving at a sentimental appreciation of, for example, his understanding of "the value of art in ensuring the survival of civilization."[147] Bernard Bailyn and Philip D. Morgan blandly credit Macpherson with ensuring "the survival of elements of national and local culture in the collective consciousness."[148] However one parses the degree of authenticity involved, the exercise can easily seem a matter of measuring the exact length of Pinocchio's nose. Moreover, since not even Macpherson's severest critic ever denied that he made *some* use of Highlands traditions, the argument that he was not a "complete charlatan" seems to be wrestling fiercely with a straw man. In the face of all this, one feels that Macpherson's obituary might be better written in terms of Oscar Wilde's praise for the "the true liar, with his frank, fearless statements, his superb irresponsibility, his healthy, natural disdain of proof of any kind."[149] Wilde, whose middle name was "Fingal," of course entirely denies that art "belongs," in the *Zeitgeist* sense, to historical periods: a cogent challenge to evolutionary historicism and its historical typologies of art. Although I admire Wilde's insouciance, my own point is different: to argue that the rewriting of cultural history in terms of national identities produces the unacknowledged fictions of ethnic and racial metalepsis. Anthologies are often framed in ethnic and national terms to manifest the unfolding of peoplehood. Their organicist claims, however, are belied by metaleptic fabrication.

The lesson to draw from "Ossian" is surely not that Macpherson is on the side of the angels. He does have a good deal of company, however, in his lack of authenticity. The eighteenth-century ballad revival, for example, was profoundly Macphersonesque: rather than authentic artifacts, it yielded, as Stewart writes, "distressed" genres as a whole, "newly minted souvenirs of periodization."[150] Moreover, Johnson's *Journey to the Western Islands of Scotland* (1773), does not best serve to illustrate the tit-for-tat response to Macpherson on the English side. That dubious honor goes instead to Thomas Percy's *Reliques of Ancient English Poetry* (1765). Percy, Bishop of Dromore after 1782, was among the most influential figures in the eighteenth-century process of antiquarian ballad-collection. The early antiquarians who collected such materials "chose to believe," as the *Norton Anthology* delicately says, that their materials were "very old."[151] Percy's *Reliques*, a collection of apparently tangible artefacts, enacts an attitude of religious veneration toward fragments of an old manuscript rescued from a fireplace. Yet Percy was strongly pulled, as Nick Groom explains, between the opposing tugs of diplomatic editing and author-like reinvention.[152] The extent to which Percy bowdlerized and "improved" his sources is thus the crux of the dating problem noted in the *Norton Anthology* One feels sobered to come across, in Percy's correspondence, the following advice from William Shenstone as regards the chronological arrangement of the ballads in the collection that would appear as *Reliques*:

> If you consider improved Copies as the *standard or principal* ones, and give *them* a first place, I do not see that you need hereby violate your purpose of arranging according to date.—They may still rank as old Barons, let the robes they wear be ever so modern.[153]

Encouraged by Shenstone to "let the Liberties taken by the translator of the Erse-fragments [that is, Macpherson] be a Precedent for you,"[154] Percy sanitized and amended his originals, even inventing spurious archaisms. He succumbed to the temptation to "eliminate what he considered as imperfect grammar, to exaggerate heroic effects, to emphasize medievalism, and to soften what may have been considered vulgarity by his readers' delicate tastes."[155] Percy also interpolated freely, adding more than 150 lines, for example, to the fragmentary "Child of Elle."[156] Joseph Ritson, Percy's rival antiquarian, delivered in 1792 a definitive judgment on the latter's failures to specify exactly where he had "improved": "no confidence can be placed in any of the 'old Minstrel ballads' inserted in that collection, and not to be found elsewhere."[157]

Percy yielded to Shenstone's pressure toward author-like tampering in the name of taste, and so lapsed into an unflattering resemblance to

Macpherson. Thus Percy—though quick to assert the greater validity of written over oral sources—found it expedient to behave as evasively as Macpherson in keeping his folio manuscript "carefully hidden."[158] Percy was painted by Sir Joshua Reynolds with an awesomely hefty volume labeled "MSS": the classic instance of a mediator that would vanish, albeit not permanently.[159] Exactly like Macpherson, Percy felt compelled to keep his much-ballyhooed source—the bound "Percy Folio" teasingly displayed in the painting—safely hidden away in Ecton Hall from public scrutiny. Percy's descendants continued this reticence for a century, first allowing the Folio to be published in 1867–1868. When *Bishop Percy's Folio Manuscript* finally did appear, the nineteenth-century editors—while acknowledging that Percy had pandered to public taste with some regrettable tampering—credited him with nothing less than awakening the nation:

> The nation lay in prison like its old Troubador king; in its durance it heard its minstrel singing beneath, the window its old songs, and its heart leapt in its bosom. It recognized the well-known, though long-neglected, strains that it had heard in its youth.[160]

This typical "awakening" *topos* inevitably wraps up with a reference to an enlarged destiny of "more comprehensive joys."[161] The publication harmed Percy's reputation, however; and a different sort of awakening presumably underlies the fact that "Sir Patrick Spens"—originally published in Percy's *Reliques*—is among the ballads now redated in the *Norton Anthology* as an eighteenth-century production.

Percy, who investigated the alliterative basis of Old English poetics, did make several genuine scholarly contributions. One does not find in him a settled intention to deceive. Though he wisely refrains from claiming in *Reliques* to produce "regular and unbroken annals of the minstrel art,"[162] however, his editorial framework is scarcely more palatable than Macpherson's. *Reliques of Ancient English Poetry* generated the figure of the medieval minstrel, of pointedly Saxon ancestry, as an English mirror image of Macpherson's ancient Caledonian bard. Laura Doyle has recently argued that *Reliques*, a ballad anthology framed by the agenda of aggrandizing a people named as *Anglo-Saxons*, constitutes "a new narrative for English culture: a racial narrative."[163] Even those who eventually conceded Percy's editorial tampering, moreover, often harped on his signal contribution to ethnography: the drawing of an aboriginal boundary (in his 1770 transla-tion of Mallet's *Northern Antiquities*) between Anglo-Saxon and Celtic peo-ples. In the preface to the 1841 edition of *Northern Antiquities*, for example, I. A. Blackwell, makes a point of contrasting the "Teutonic Race" and the "Celtic Race." This comes in the context of a lengthy excursion on the eight ethnological subtypes of the human species. Philology, fully absorbed into a quasi-scientific anthropology, serves an agenda of differentiation and exclusion: a severe pruning of the human family tree.

Percy's anthology featured ballads geographically centered in the northern border country, some of them Scottish, while claiming the resulting mix as staunchly English. "It was precisely at the borders," as Groom observes, "that Percy discerned the most defining characteristics of national literature."[164] As Groom points out, a degree of "internal colonialism" may be discerned in Percy's Anglocentric handling of the northern frontier. The politics of Percy's *Reliques*, however, cannot be strictly confined to a "national row" between England and Scotland. For one thing, the anthology extends and thus blurs the boundaries of Englishness by including a gory modern ballad from the West Indies, "Bryan and Pareene," in which Bryan, the English lover of an Indian maid, regrettably encounters a shark while impatiently swimming to shore to meet Pareene. This doleful ballad, now immortalized in *The Stuffed Owl: An Anthology of Bad Verse*, was provided to Percy by James Grainger, author of the pro-slavery poem *The Sugar-Cane* (1764). To search for one's roots in a colony seems a telling symptom of confusion. More crucially, in pointing to "Anglo-Saxon ancestors" who came from "German forests," Percy invokes a theory of racial migration to establish the "roots" of English literature.[165] The Danes and the Dutch also get mixed into the international solidarity. As Kwame Anthony Appiah points out, the nineteenth-century result of all this, in disciplinary terms, would be a national canon of literature undergirded by the concept of *race*.[166] Doyle likewise attributes to Percy's moment the seeds of the racialized mythology "of an ancient soil-rooted folk fit to become modern, global conquerors. . . ."[167]

We arrive, in the globalizing eighteenth century, at the tradition of the Saxon minstrel, organic medium of the Teutonic tribes. Percy shows us how the folkloric nationalists, in the context of empire-building, could act globally while containing critical thought within a very local horizon. A merely priggish response, however—as in the case of Macpherson as well—seems banal. A more productive lesson to draw from the folkloric tsunami involves the scandalous contingency of social identities made from ragged scraps and patches. To unravel the legitimating seams of ethnic genealogies requires irony rather than piety. One of the better commentaries on eighteenth-century mode of roots-mongering comes from Horace Walpole in 1772, in a letter to William Mason:

> Somebody, I fancy Dr. Percy, has produced a dismal dull ballad, called "The Execution of Sir Charles Bawdin," and given it for one of the Bristol Poems, called Rowley's—but it is still a worse counterfeit, than those that were first

sent to me; it grows a hard case on our ancestors, who have every day bastards laid to them, five hundred or a thousand years after they are dead.

Walpole encapsulates the entire moment in his closing line: "Indeed Mr. Macpherson, etc. are so fair as to beget the fathers as well as the children."[168]

PART II

GLOBAL PALIMPSESTS: PRODUCTIVE AFFILIATIONS

CHAPTER 3

LEADING HISTORY BY THE NOSE: READING ORIGINS IN *MIDNIGHT'S CHILDREN* AND *TRISTRAM SHANDY*

Every novelist's work contains an implicit vision of the history of the novel.

—Milan Kundera, *Aspects of the Novel*, trans. Linda Asher
(1986; New York, Harper & Rowe, 1988)

If Ganesh breeds with Tristram Shandy to hatch Saleem Sinai, then who is the butt of the joke?

—Kumkum Sangari, "The Politics of the Possible"

What possibilities emerge when one begins to *use* the British eighteenth century, with full attention to the threshold nature of its modernity, as an artistic and conceptual resource? What perspective can be hatched as regards nation-building projects and their associated questions of representation? What take on the retrospective invention of roots is so conspicuous in the "Ossian" controversy? A sophisticated answer to these questions appears in a twentieth-century novel marked by a pointed turn to the eighteenth century: Salman Rushdie's *Midnight's Children* (1980). Although widely assimilated to the shibboleths of postmodernism, Rushdie's project in *Midnight's Children* cannot be fully understood outside its dialogue with the eighteenth-century moment that produced, in its marked liminality, both *The Poems of Ossian* and *Tristram Shandy*.

Midnight's Children has usually been seen as typifying both postmodernism and postcoloniality. As such, it has been taken to represent a new, "de-totalizing" way of writing history: specifically, the history of India as a modern nation-state. The novel figures prominently, for instance, in Linda

Hutcheon's *The Politics of Postmodernism*, where it exemplifies a structure that both installs and subverts "the teleology, closure, and causality of narra-tive, both historical and fictive."[1] Rushdie's postmodern techniques of nar-ration, in this view, express a self-reflexive and wary detachment from all totalizing modes of historical thought. For Hutcheon, the combination of a contemporary self-reflexivity plus the relativizing juxtaposition of "Eastern" and "Western" modes of thought seems to sum up *Midnight's Children*. Rushdie's novel "works to foreground the totalizing impulse of western—imperialistic—modes of history-writing by confronting it," in Hutcheon's words, "with indigenous Indian models of history."[2]

Rushdie's way of engaging these histories, however, seems both more subtle and more forceful on the whole than the mere juxtaposition of contradictory "Eastern" and "Western" models. Hutcheon's analysis relies on a polarization of terms that Rushdie's novel is at pains to undermine. For one thing, the narrator Saleem Sinai is more the unreliable narrator than the spokesperson for some tradition or culture. Raised a Muslim in Bombay, he claims to write as someone "well up on Hindu stories."[3] Just previously, however, Saleem has made a two-fold error in identifying which epic per-sonage (Vyasa, not Valmiki) dictated which epic (the *Mahabharata*, not the *Ramayana*) to that patient stenographer, elephant-headed Ganesh.[4] For another, "traditional" indigenous epics would not necessarily function as the most suitable antidote to the political iniquities of "Western" narratives. It is not possible to read the *Mahabharata*, as Aijaz Ahmad remarks, "without being struck by the severity with which the *dasyus* and the *shudras* and the women are constantly being made into the dangerous, inferiorized Others."[5] And, for a third, it is not entirely clear what the value would be, beyond a rather banal relativism, of staging such a confrontation. Such a confrontation, indeed, could easily reinforce the ideological theme of an essential and unbridgeable gulf between "East" and "West."

I contend instead that Rushdie's novel exemplifies the potential of a more nuanced politics of literary affiliation and periodization. His politics explores the retrospective fabrication of origins in the intersection of sev-eral different kinds of historical duration: (1) in the arrangement of novels into a developmental sequence; (2) in the division of literary history into an ordered sequence of distinct epochs; and (3), ultimately, in the narrative ordering of history itself. In each of these time-shaping domains, Rushdie's gesture of reaching back to *Tristram Shandy* can be seen as a fitting strat-egy of cannibalizing the European past for the political and cultural pro-ject of postcoloniality. As such, *Midnight's Children* opens up a dialogue with the eighteenth-century critique of roots-finding historiography found in *Tristram Shandy*.

Stories of the Novel

According to a broad critical consensus,[6] the main literary precursors of Salman Rushdie's *Midnight's Children* are *One Hundred Years of Solitude*, *The Tin Drum*, and *Tristram Shandy*. The usual emphasis on Rushdie's post-modernity[7] has obscured the full implications of his turn, via *Tristram Shandy*, to the eighteenth century. Criticism still needs to explain why a novel published serially between 1760 and 1767 should be so central to an important postcolonial novel in the late twentieth century. Critics have not explained what meaning, as a gesture of revival or return, such an affiliation might have. The insistent allusions to *Tristram Shandy* have received only a perfunctory interpretation as a way of pointing to "the imperialist British past," as Hutcheon puts it, "that is literally a part of India's self-representation as much as of Saleem's."[8] Criticism, furthermore, has not closely considered why Rushdie should feel an elective affinity, remarked upon but little elaborated, for the eighteenth century in general. In an interview with Una Chaudhuri, Rushdie mentions this unexpected affinity:

> I'm very keen on the eighteenth-century in general, not just in literature. I think the eighteenth-century was the great century.[9]

Rushdie again looks back strongly to *Gulliver's Travels* in the weaker *Fury* (2002), featuring violent ethnic strife on "Lilliput-Blefescu" (Fiji) and exploiting a possible "egg-wars" pun on "Big Endians/Indians." His partiality to the eighteenth century resonates with far broader implications.

The intertextual borrowings between *Tristram Shandy* and *Midnight's Children* are indeed many. As Keith Wilson notes, the origins of both Saleem and Tristram are linked to the striking of a clock. Wilson also observes that the noses of both have an "epic centrality." Saleem, furthermore, like Tristram's Uncle Toby, reenacting the Siege of Namur on his bowling green, attempts to translate public history into private obsession; both Saleem and Tristram make metafictional references to the titles and contents of their chapters; and both, construing narration as a race against mortality, frequently interrupt the narrative to record their own physical decay.[10] To Wilson's list of parallels, Robert Alter adds the following: in both novels, a jumpy, digressive narrator is reconstructing problematic origins. In both novels, the narrator uses a tone of "edgy hilarity" in response to "maiming and death." In both, once again, the narrators write "under the shadow of impotence." Both Tristram Shandy and Saleem Sinai address themselves to a dramatized female reader/listener: for Tristram, Jenny; for Saleem, Padma. Both novels so conspicuously prolong their accounts of the narrator's birth that the inaugural "event" threatens to dissolve into an endless regression of prehistories. Both novels culminate in a confrontation with a formidable Widow.[11] Even Rushdie's "obstetrics" theme, as Damian Grant points out, owes something to the conflict around midwifery in *Tristram Shandy*.[12] In short, *Midnight's Children* "begins," in every sense of the word, with *Tristram Shandy*.

The gesture of making *Tristram Shandy* a prime model for an emergent postcolonial literature, a beginning for a new and energetic artistic sequence, forces us to reframe the history of the English novel. The publishing event called *Tristram Shandy*, which occurred over two centuries ago, suddenly manifests itself again. It is as if the old light from a dead and distant star has reached us only now.[13] The resulting interplay between early and late is not merely a defensive denial of Rushdie's own chronological "belatedness," however, the issue is not so much about individual "originality" as a heightened awareness of the novel's developmental history.

Although the English novel has Elizabethan and even classical precursors, its historians generally agree that it was first created, along with the Enlightenment and its characteristic concerns, in the eighteenth century. The novel, itself one of the earliest cultural commodities, seems linked to these three broad historical phenomena: the rise of capitalism, the emergence of the European nation-state, and the consolidation of modern imperialism. Many of the familiar achievements of the genre—above all, its rendering of individual experience in particularized and historically specific detail— correlate in resonant ways with these broader historical currents. The motif of individualism informs the influential work of Ian Watt on the genre. Long after its publication in 1957, Watt's *The Rise of the Novel* continues, as David Blewett observes, to cast a very lengthy shadow on studies of the early novel.[14] Indeed, the rise-of-the-novel story counts as one of the "grand narratives," in William Beatty Warner's words, "of British literary studies."[15]

The "grand narrative," however, requires considerable nuancing. An explosion of variant accounts—emphasizing ideological conflict, prenovelistic fictions, subversive plots, spatial ideologies, legal subjectivity, domestic conduct, pedagogical aims, amatory fiction, historiography, political economy, and reified inwardness—has raised many questions about Watt's relentless emphasis on individualism and on the corollary technique of "formal realism."[16] The perspective conveyed by Watt threatens to elide the peculiar liminality of the eighteenth century, which simultaneously embraced and resisted the social relations and ways of knowing associated with commercial society. Consider the following passage from Charles Johnstone's *Chrysal: or, The Adventures of a Guinea* (1760–1765), in which a father lecturing to his son dissociates private and public interest: "The real strength of a nation consists in the prevalence of disinterested spirit, which, regardless of *self*, throws its weight into the public fund; as may be proved by many examples of small, poor states, conquering large wealthy ones." By centering all in *self*, however, the "spirit of commerce" breaks national solidarity: "that unanimity which is the very essence of power, and only can give it success."[17] The speaker goes on to advise his son to retire from business. As John Richetti is right to insist, the ideology of individualism is precisely what the eighteenth-century novel examines and puts into question.[18]

A parallel liminality may be observed in the relation of the eighteenth-century novel to national and imperial modes of identification. According to Benedict Anderson, the novel, along with print journalism, was an agent as well as a manifestation of nationalism. The novel, in this view, provided the technical means for representing the special kind of imagined community— "a sociological organism moving calendrically through homogenous empty time"—that is the nation.[19] Suggestive as this formulation may be, however, it underestimates the extent to which eighteenth-century novels imagine overlapping and international communities that in their religious or dynastic or regional loyalties resist a smooth alignment with the horizontally constituted nation as such. Such competing loyalties, indeed, often coincide with the vertical frictions of a stratified society. The Francophile aristocracy posed an obstinate impediment to the integration of Britain's national culture. Frances Burney's satire on the English chauvinism of boorish Captain Mirvan in *Evelina* (1789)—a chauvinism blended with class *ressentiment*— makes clear the extent to which one's attitude toward all things French mediated social divisions within late-eighteenth-century England. Moreover, the fictional marketplace was markedly international. Up through the early nineteenth century, literary historians of the age, as Warner points out, "discuss the novels of Cervantes, Marivaux, and Rousseau within the same conceptual coordinates as they discuss the novels of Richardson and Fielding."[20] Warner thus describes a nineteenth-century process during which the novel was nationalized.[21] Through his work on the novel as a genre institutionalized by such canon-makers as Anna Laetitia Barbauld and Sir Walter Scott, Homer Obed Brown adds the related insight that there is a sense in which "the eighteenth-century English novel was invented at the beginning of the nineteenth century."[22] The nation, in the eighteenth-century novel, remains more of a problem than an answer.

Finally, there is imperialism: for an equally crucial dimension of the novel has to do with its capacity to organize space. To be sure, the representation of geographical territory within some strands of the English novel began early on, in such texts as *Robinson Crusoe* (1719), to incorporate certain features of a colonial logic.[23] The emergence of this perspective, however, does not constitute an immediate consensus. Consider the following observation by Matthew Bramble in Tobias Smollet's *The Expedition of Humphrey Clinker*

(1771), who complains that the city of Bath is teeming with riff-raff and upstart nabobs. A sample of his rant against the "tide of luxury" demonstrates contemporary doubts about the imperial project:

> Clerks and factors from the East Indies, loaded with the spoil of plundered provinces; planters, negro-drivers, and hucksters, from our American plantations, enriched they know not how; agents, commissaries, and contractors, who have fattened, in two successive wars, on the blood of the nation . . . and no wonder that their brains should be intoxicated with pride, vanity, and presumption.[24]

Paradoxically, moreover, the overflow of territorial boundaries is precisely what finally gives the lie to notions that the novel, as a genre, is *essentially* bound to Britain or Europe. However oppressive and alienating, empire implies contact and exchange: connections rather than hermetic insularity. Such connections are, to be sure, often neglected. As David Armitage points out, contemporary historians who wish to minimize the domestic significance of the British empire often invoke as an excuse "the aggressive amnesia of eighteenth and nineteenth-century Britons"[25] as regards the colonies. That ideologically sanctioned amnesia, however—what Armitage terms "isolationist imperialism"[26]—is far more characteristic of the nineteenth century than the eighteenth, which had not yet consolidated the quarantine that would conceive of "British" and "imperial" history as things apart. Indeed, the eighteenth century's much fuller registration of global entanglement, as well as its critique of that entanglement, was precisely what the nineteenth century had to repress. Sterne's dedication of volumes 1 and 2 of *Tristram Shandy* to William Pitt, early in the Seven Years War, seems, as Tom Keymer argues, to urge a "Little-Englander" attitude on the aggressively expansionist Prime Minister. The Uncle Toby plot, as Keymer also points out, highlights the lingering psychological and material costs of war.[27]

The eighteenth-century moment has its uses as a fulcrum for unsettling the assumptions of a later moment. Lennard J. Davis, who celebrates Laurence Sterne's refusal in *Tristram Shandy* to reify either time or personality into manageable fictions such as "character" (a threadbare list of traits) and "plot" (a retrospectively reassuring explanation for change), points out that Sterne's consciousness was "purely eighteenth century."[28] What gives Sterne imaginative leverage over novelistic conventions is not some precocious modernity or postmodernity, but rather his emergence at a pivotal moment. "It is precisely my point," as Davis says, "that only at the beginning of the development of the novel could an observer be far enough outside what was going on to notice the change."[29] In this view, it was Sterne's liminal historical position that enabled him to be the novelist, in Davis's words, "who revealed the most about the ideological workings of the novel."[30] Sterne's moment comes just prior to the deluge of bourgeois realism: "In this sense, he could see the conventions of the novel without having come to the point that Austen reached some fifty years later of assuming that those conventions were virtually universal forms."[31] Davis begins to provide a strong historical rationale both for Sterne's seeming contemporaneity and for Rushdie's decision to reach back to him. Keymer, more nuanced, rightly refuses to caricature Sterne's contemporaries. Henry Fielding and Samuel Richardson, as Keymer points out, were grappling intelligently with the same set of problems.[32]

Tristram Shandy, at least until the canonization of High Modernism, has indeed seemed to stand outside the mainstream development of the novel. On the one hand, Samuel Johnson's notorious requiem on *Tristram*, "nothing odd will do long,"[33] has proven false. On the other hand, and despite Shklovsky's famous paradox, that *Tristram Shandy* is "the most typical novel of world literature,"[34] few literary historians have centered their accounts of the novel around *Tristram*. F. R. Leavis, notoriously, excludes it altogether from his Great Tradition. Watt, rather awkwardly tucking *Tristram Shandy* away in a concluding "note" to *The Rise of the Novel*, sees it merely as a parody that confirms the conventions of formal realism. And Richard Lanham confirms that Sterne "did not extend the domain of the novel."[35] Only recently, in an age of metafictions and postmodernism, has *Tristram Shandy* seemed truly central: "the prototype," as Patricia Waugh writes, "for the contemporary metafictional novel."[36] Unfortunately, however, in making Sterne "our contemporary," we risk domesticating the past. As Davis makes clear, we need to understand the self-reflexive techniques of *Tristram Shandy* as belonging to an early moment in what Milan Kundera calls the "sequence of discoveries"[37] that makes up the novel's history. Keymer elaborates on the specific elements making up Sterne's book, describing *Tristram Shandy* as "a close engagement with the novel in the crucial period of its formation," a quasi-Swiftian satire, and "a self-conscious exercise in metafiction."[38]

Rushdie's Shandyism, then, is best seen as a critical return to the novel's beginnings. The urgent point for Rushdie in turning to the eighteenth century in *Midnight's Children* is to uncover the process through which the novel's conventions were first constructed. In particular, Rushdie looks back to *Tristram Shandy* to denaturalize the conventions by which origins are made the "natural" bearers of causality and identity—the same conventions, indeed, that inform many attempts to write literary history more generally. It should come as little surprise to find that many of the English novel's historians agree that it really "matured" only in the nineteenth and twentieth centuries. In *The Rise of the Novel*, for example, Jane Austen's novels figure as the climactic achievement toward which all the previous novelists, lacking her ability to combine "internal" and "external" orientations, are merely evolutionary steps along the way. In the context of a teleology of progressive development, the eighteenth-century novel as a whole tends to be marginalized within the English canon. The point is not merely to cash in on the fetish of marginality; it is, rather, that eighteenth-century literature, ever since the manifestoes of the nineteenth century, has served as a historical foil—the site either of backwardness or excessive polish—for later and supposedly better developments. A dismal effect has been, until recently, the marginalization of issues often most visible in eighteenth-century texts.

Literary Epochs

As a historical epoch, the eighteenth century, precisely because it antedates the full-blown constitution of an English canon, makes the imperial process by which the canon formed quite visible. The theory of literary originality proposed by the country cleric Edward Young shows a marked fascination with images of empire, a desire to aggrandize England's territorial influence. The value of Young's essay in this context lies in its naked self-incrimination: for the project of postcolonial critique, it furnishes the proverbial smoking gun. Indeed, in his *Conjectures on Original Composition* (1759), Young seeks to define and to celebrate the "modern" precisely through an international power to disseminate the fame of English authors. Young not only demonstrates the deep connections analyzed by Benedict Anderson between print-capitalism and the "imagined community" of nationhood, but also lays out a blueprint for reconstituting literary texts as "Literature": that is, as a school-based discourse of English nationalism and imperialism. Young connects British colonialism with its supposed literary self-reliance. Young makes usefully explicit a possible link between authorial originality and the centrifugal influence of an ascendant culture. Literary originals, he writes, "extend the republic of letters and add a new province to its dominions." They colonize:

> *Bacon, Boyle, Newton, Shakespeare, Milton* have showed us that all the winds cannot blow the *British* flag farther than an original spirit can convey the *British* fame; their names go around the world, and what foreign genius strikes not as they pass?[39]

This link is especially crucial because the canon, in the case of English literature, was in part developed and institutionally defined, as Gauri Vishwanathan demonstrates, precisely in the crucible of colonial administration in India.

The canon-making process, essentially an experiment in sociopolitical control in India, began as early as the 1820s; the result, as Viswanathan shows, was only "imported" some fifty years later for home consumption. Policy decisions concerning the actual administration of colonial India were tactical decisions made in the context of more localized factional disputes and bureaucratic infighting. Even so, however, it was ultimately a grand strategy like Young's that in 1835 impelled Thomas Babington Macaulay, the East India Company's arrogant promoter of English literature over Indian classics, to write his infamous minute on education. According to Viswanathan's analysis, the canon of English authors functioned in India precisely to aestheticize domination, to transmit "Christian culture" and displace indigenous cultures without the controversial appearance of overt religious indoctrination. Thus institutionalized as "master" authors, Milton, Shakespeare, and the rest—better and wiser, no doubt, than the average imperial bureaucrat—became, in Viswanathan's telling phrase, "masks of conquest." The complex legacy of this curriculum in India has been examined from many angles in Rajaswari Sunder Rajan's edited volume, *The Lie of the Land: English Studies in India* (1992).

Viswanathan also points to a further historical irony, often neglected in citations of her work: that given the absence for even the most impeccably Anglicized Indians of opportunities for upward mobility, a curriculum that celebrated values of moral autonomy and self-sufficiency inevitably led to discontent and insubordination—the beginnings of resistance among the Indian elite to national dependency.[40] *Midnight's Children* represents the dangerous ambiguity of such an inheritance through the trope of blue eyes and mistaken ancestry. The novel, as Una Chaudhuri argues, depicts the imperial legacy as an unconscious way of seeing:

> *Midnight*'s hero Saleem has many surrogate parents, but his literal and clandestine father is a departing colonist. From him Saleem gets his blue eyes—mistakenly credited to the Kashmiri ancestry he never had. The Raj, that is, surreptitiously bequeaths its vision—its psychological structures, its institutions, its habits of mind, its language.

"Thus, for decades following the death of the Raj," she continues, "a class of Indians continues to collude, unwittingly, in a spectral colonization of India."[41] Although this seems to be a compelling reading, Chaudhuri's reading puts excessive weight on the "literal" (biological) filiation between William Methwold and Saleem Sinai. Moreover, the back-and-forth nature of Viswanathan's account reveals *both* a global making *and* a specifically Indian appropriation of British literature. As part of the formation of Indian nationalism itself, the English curriculum produced results that were unintended by the British. This historical irony is of course not very compatible with the nativist desire within India, after decolonization, to assert an absolute cultural autonomy. Given such a tangle of intertwining histories, questions of cultural agency and autonomy become exceedingly difficult to adjudicate. Rushdie's critical meditation on the artificiality of nationhood is meant to create space for critical reappropriations of Britishness, and thus to acknowledge the force of *chosen* affiliations that are not presented as "organic." Indeed, one wonders if Anderson, who published *Imagined Communities* in 1983, had read *Midnight's Children* (1980). The latter, in a highly resonant formulation, describes the birth of independent India in 1947 as "quite imaginary" and as a "collective fiction."[42] If this seems to anticipate Anderson, it likewise gives depth to Grant's central argument: that Rushdie's novels pursue "the critique of the imagination."[43]

A two-sided cultural weapon, as Rushdie knows from his own Anglicized intellectual heritage, was what English literature became: not at the level of authorial intentions, necessarily, but as a colonial institution. This is why one does not get far by reproaching Rushdie for satirizing phony populism and sectarian nationalist clichés. Rushdie does indeed refuse to affirm, as Timothy Brennan dogmatically complains, such nationalist slogans as "discipline," "organization," and "the people."[44] Rushdie's sensibility, to the considerable advantage of his art, resists the lure of bumper-sticker populism. This does not in any way diminish, for Rushdie or his readers, the mystique of the struggle led by Gandhi and Nehru. The point is what came after that struggle. In 1980—a full two generations after India achieved independence—Rushdie chooses to direct attention to more current issues as regards the collective project of imagining a national community in India. However unheroic as themes, religious fundamentalism, class divisions, political corruption, and nuclear arms are urgent topics in South Asia. Rushdie likewise refuses a naive affirmation of pristine folkloric traditions, emphasizing instead the cynical use of such traditions for sectarian or commercial ends. His turn to the eighteenth-century moment is a self-conscious alternative to false claims to the immediacy of folkloric roots, whether in India or Britain. And if this gesture mutes any easy celebration of Indian "roots," it likewise serves to challenge prevailing notions of "Britishness." What Victorian British culture tended to sweep under the rug was quite precisely the history, with all its glaring contradictions and contingencies, of its own production. Rushdie's novel can be seen as lifting up the rug. For *Midnight's Children* insistently points to that transitional century in which the potential for an abusive link between canonization and imperialism became visible.

Rushdie's gesture of reaching back to the moment of *Tristram Shandy* can be seen, finally and most crucially, as a fitting postcolonial strategy for reappropriating the practice of history-writing. This project converges with a more obvious one: the attempt by Rushdie and other South Asian writers to imagine an India beyond the stifling stereotypes recycled in the fiction and films of contemporary Raj nostalgia: *The Jewel in the Crown, Indiana Jones and the Temple of Doom, Heat and Dust, Gandhi, A Passage to India*, and so on.[45] According to Chaudhuri, the motive for creating an alternative to such Raj revivals "is not revisionist desire, not nostalgia. Rather," she says, "it is the opposite." It is "desire for a new account of experience that will not so much overthrow the imperial model as *place* it—that is, account for it—and subdue it."[46] This project of situating the Raj is, precisely, metahistorical. It requires something like the political history of history-writing. Its strategy of historical placement, moreover, is to be sharply opposed to other possible gestures: notably, constructing oneself, in the name of some tradition or fundamentalism, as the inverted mirror-image of the "West." The eighteenth century, like *Tristram Shandy*, can stand in this metahistorical strategy of placement as a figure for a certain turning point. It stands for a contingent and historical beginning for a mythology that never tires of elaborating timeless differences, of colonizing time as surely as it colonized territory.

Historiography, Metalepsis and the "West"

Midnight's Children is about nothing, of course, if not the questioning of myths of origin. Rushdie manipulates two stories familiar in the West to make room for his own mythologies of India's genesis and multiple identities.[47] These two stories are the Biblical account of Genesis (echoed in Aadam Aziz's origins in the Edenic Vale of Kashmir) and the fairy tale "Snow White and Rose Red" (echoed in the three drops of red blood falling from Aziz's nose and freezing in the snow). According to Karamcheti, Rushdie juxtaposes these two stories, sacred text and Märchen, to level their authority.[48] This account, however, does not exhaust the meaning of a complex trope such as this one. This double allusion points to the later history of Christianity in which, removed from its Asian context, it became a major signifier of the spirit of the "West." *In the beginning*, according to Rushdie, *was Snow White*: a character named for the emphatic whiteness of her skin. In a novel that also describes an icon of a blue Jesus, Rushdie's juxtaposition here parodies later efforts at whitewashing the origins of Christianity. By the nineteenth century popular images of Christ in Britain emphasized blond hair, fair skin, blue eyes, and (in depictions of the infant Jesus) a penis unmarked by circumcision.[49] At about the same time, Snow White (*Schneeweisschen*) emerged into print in the context of a scholarly enterprise involving linguistics, folktales, lexicography, and medieval studies, all of which Jakob and Wilhelm Grimm believed would reveal the essence of the Germanic *Volksgeist*. The other name for this moment—this colonial "genesis"—is the period sandwiched between the late eighteenth and the early nineteenth centuries. For it is precisely in the late eighteenth century that we can locate a radical change in dominant historiographical procedures. These procedures involve the central issues of the demarcation of East and West, especially as defined by such categories as Western humanism, Western science, Western rationality—and, of course, behind it all, "Aryan" racial superiority.

As Vasant Kaiwar demonstrates in an important review article, several important works of scholarship in the past two decades have converged in demonstrating that a qualitative break from past procedures occurred in the historiography of the late eighteenth and early nineteenth centuries. This new scholarship by Samir Amin, Martin Bernal, and St. Clair Drake has thoroughly exposed how a new way of writing global history fabricated an ahistorical "West" always defined, from Athens to Albion, by its links to rationality, progress, and science. Kaiwar synthesizes these works into a powerful commentary on the genesis and development of a vastly influential historiography founded, for the first time, and at a particular historical conjuncture, on the fabrication of an ancient "West." Above all, the revisionism described by Bernal and others involved the "Romantic-racialist" rewriting of history "in terms of immutable national essences."[50] Through such supposedly scientific academic disciplines as philology and anthropology, not to mention the physiognomical measurement of skulls and noses, history became "the biography of a people."[51] An acknowledged Afro-Asiatic-European confluence in the world of mediterranean antiquity got ruthlessly remapped in terms that eliminated traces of Egyptian and Semitic influence at the supposed origins of the "West."

Hence the origin of a fallacious myth of origin: that of the continuous "Western tradition." It is a myth that continues to frame, and thus debilitate, even progressive political projects that intend opposition to imperialism. As Aijaz Ahmad has observed, the myth of a continuous "West" undermines current studies in colonial discourse. Such studies often revert to the mirror-image of this same fallacy: namely, the demonization of a homogenized "West," from classical Greece to the postmodern United States. Ahmad demonstrates that this fallacy greatly weakens Edward Said's influential denunciation of the discourse he calls "Orientalism." As Ahmad shows, Said wavers incoherently between mutually incompatible definitions of Orientalism. Said's broadest definition traces Orientalism all the way back to Greek tragedy, and constructs an uninterrupted continuity from then to now: "from Aeschylus to Dante to Marx to Bernard Lewis," as Ahmad says.[52] This definition turns Orientalism into an essential pathology of a homogenized "Western" thought: an inverted mirror-image, as Ahmad points out, of Auerbach's account in *Mimesis* of "the seamless genesis of European realism and rationalism from Greek antiquity to the modernist moment."[53] Far more useful is Said's narrower definition, which, emphasizing the post-Enlightenment moment of the late eighteenth century, sees Orientalism rather "as the ideological corollary of colonialism."[54] Ahmad's main point, as he says, "is that Said takes a fantastic, and rather late, fabrication for a real genealogical history, hence disabling himself as regards the history of fabrication *qua* fabrication and settling down, instead, to reading modern history back into Antiquity, as is the wont of humanist scholars."[55]

Meera Nanda, like Ahmad, has been further exploring the implications of the new scholarship about Aryan historiography. For Nanda, a scientist, the chief point is to reject the demonization of science (as "Western" and/or "masculine" rationality) by Third-World ecofeminists. Nanda's critique, a scathing review of Vandana Shiva's *Staying Alive*, urges against the gesture of repudiating science on the basis of an ahistorical construction of the "West." Such a demonization, aside from continuing a tradition of reactionary indigenist obscurantism, is based precisely on the historical fallacy of equating "science" and rationality with the fabricated "West": now a synonym for white and male supremacist horrors. Such gestures of purification, in attempting to make a total break, lapse into nostalgia for a past that never was. To yield reason and science to the enemy camp, moreover, as Nanda persuasively argues, amounts to an excellent prescription for self-marginalization.[56] If reason is abandoned, even as an ideal, then little is left, as she points out, by means of which one can challenge the institutions and practices of arbitrary power.[57] In *Prophets Facing Backwards: Postmodern Critiques of Science and Hindu Nationalism in India* (2003), Nanda has fully developed her critique of so-called ethno-science.

Such debilitating errors as Said's and Shiva's demonstrate the importance of looking back to the historical timing of the Aryan historiographical enterprise. It should come as little surprise that the vast rewriting of history was done in the service of a political agenda that belonged to the late eighteenth and early nineteenth centuries. The broad agenda, as Kaiwar explains, is all too clear: "The elimination of these two [Phoenician and African civilizations] from the ranks of great civilizations, and from having made any contribution to Greek language and religion, coincided temporally with Black slavery, imperialism, and subsequently with anti-Semitism in Europe."[58] The fabrication of this notional "West" was indeed, as Kaiwar writes, "centrally connected to the cultural identity of modern Europeans," and it turned upon a supposed distinction between mythopoeic thought—characteristic of ancient peoples and modern savages—and "the rational thought of Greeks and later Europeans."[59] So an unbroken chain of Western reason was constructed. This genealogical rewriting of cultural history, it must be remembered, involved above all the suppression of the mixed and multicultural nature of mediterranean antiquity—purified, as it were, of all traces of African or Asian cultures. The long-standing prestige of the ancient Egyptians had to be violently debunked, even at the expense of the credibility of ancient sources; centuries of medieval Christian metaphysics had to be skipped over lightly; and the contribution to world civilization, for example, of Ibn Rushd (Averroës), the Spain-based Islamic rationalist cited by Chaucer, had to be reduced to the role of a mere passive "transmitter" of Aristotle.[60] In this sense *the West* was always the creation of the nationalism that spread across Europe after the late eighteenth century.

It was not only the history of the "West," moreover, that was thus grossly distorted by Aryan revisionism. To take a crucial example, the Aryan model, as Kaiwar points out, "was deployed during the colonial period in the construction of a racist model of Indian history, initially in the different editions of the *Cambridge Ancient History* series, but later picked up and amplified by Hindu-nationalist historians."[61] It suited the British, in their self-proclaimed role as restorers of India's classical glory, to present the Muslim Mughals as alien invaders and oppressors of "Aryan" Hindus. Contemporary communalist conflicts make all too clear the ongoing consequences in India of such versions of "Aryan" history. The origins of caste in India were likewise given a racial explanation based on various anthropometric calculations (see figure 3.1). Consider Herbert H. Risley, who presided, as census commissioner, over the 1901 census in India. Risley did a great deal to establish caste "as the single most important trope for Indian society, and the complicity of Indian anthropology in the project of colonial state formation."[62] A telling example is Risley's comment in *The People of India* (1915) about the anthropometrical implications of noses in the historical works of the ancient Greek physician, Ctesias (early fourth century BC), fragments of whose *Indika* still survive:

> when Ctesias speaks of the small stature, black complexion, and snub noses of the inhabitants of India, we feel that the description is precise enough to enable us to identify them with the *Dasyus* and *Nishādas* of early Sanskrit literature, and we are almost tempted to wonder whether the Greek physician, who was doubtless acquainted with the canon of Polycletus, may not have devised some accurate method of recording the racial characteristics of which he was so close an observer.[63]

Risley's work is, literally, a textbook specimen of nasal metalepsis. Because contemporary communalist conflicts underscore the potential complicity of nationalist "revivals of the past" with imperial distortions, they emphasize

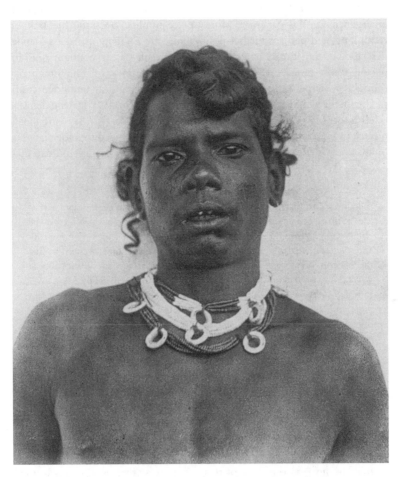

3.1 Photograph used by Herbert H. Risley to illustrate "Dravidian" nose.

all the more what is salutary about *Midnight's Children*: the close questioning of "origins" as they are reconstructed, afterwards, by the successive "winners of history."

What is most interesting for our purposes is that such scholarly develop-ments revise not only the racist legacy of cultural history, but also our own understanding of the Enlightenment. For in pinpointing the moment of emergence for this Aryan revisionism, we implicitly assume the task of rethinking, and perhaps further periodizing, the Enlightenment. As Nanda describes it, the Eurocentric myth was "a result of the constant tension between the progressive and humanistic aspirations of Enlightenment thought (which emerged as a challenge to the universalism and dogmatism of Christianity) and its recognition of its own superiority."[64] Having demys-tified a terribly oppressive medieval metaphysics, that is to say—no small service to humankind—Enlightenment culture proceeded to understand its own achievements through the Romantic categories of racial and national essences:

> the rationalism that flowered into the Enlightenment was claimed as a part of the "national character" of the west: Ancient Greece then became merely the childhood of this inherent European cultural trait. Consequently, rationality and science came to be seen as purely Greek and therefore "western" while the "orient" became associated with metaphysics at best and irrationality at worst. This construction of "essences" of nations and civilizations, as Kaiwar shows, was not a result of the much-maligned rationalism of the Enlightenment but came about with the rise of Romanticism (evident in the ideology of organicity, purity of the "people" and pre-industrial imagery) in Germany and elsewhere in Europe in the late eighteenth century and after.[65]

The assumption that science was "created by western man" "rests on an Aryan construction of ancient history put forward by European historians during the nineteenth century when imperialism was at its zenith and, incidentally, when the Enlightenment world-view was giving way to Romanticism."[66] Romantic Hellenism thus contributed to a reinvention of Greece around the time of the Greek War of Independence.

It is the horrific outcome of this vast process that usually gets blamed entirely on the Enlightenment. A distinguished intellectual tradition stretching from Adorno and Horkheimer's *Dialectic of the Enlightenment* to the contemporary work of Foucault and Lyotard has made a formidable case against the Enlightenment. Lipking observes that eighteenth-century studies as a whole has been strained by the ambiguities of the Enlightenment and its legacy. "If a proud commitment to enlightened values is one great legacy of the century," he writes, "so is a deep disappointment with the failure of that enlightenment to live up to its promise."[67] That ambiguity, however, is precisely what makes the century so crucial, and so subject to reevaluation.

Kaiwar praises Bernal's critique as providing what he terms "a revised Enlightenment view—Enlightenment universalism stripped of its incipient racism."[68] And indeed, it is precisely because various dubious historical processes began in the eighteenth century that they were still more visible and open to contestation than when they had become fully dominant. *Tristram Shandy* itself, which refuses to naturalize the nascent conventions of realism, is an ideal example of such contestation. Not only is *Tristram* itself about contingency, but it exposes as contingent "evolutionary" models of, for instance, the history of the novel. The significance of *Tristram Shandy* to *Midnight's Children* thus demonstrates that the eighteenth-century novel need not be rejected as the mere harbinger, more or less imperfect, of Victorian developments, good or bad. It should be seen, rather, as a site where a modern, supposedly secular notion of origins, as identity and causality, is still visible, still in the process of construction.

Tristram Shandy and *Midnight's Children*

Of all the intertextual relationships between *Tristram Shandy* and *Midnight's Children*, none better illustrates this broader historical point than the theme of noses. The centrality of Saleem Sinai's nose in *Midnight's Children* alludes not only to an amusing part of the body but to a certain history of physiognomic conventions of representation. Those conventions, in turn, are imbricated in ideologies that undergo a telling shift in the late eighteenth century, moving from the feudal arena of aristocratic and common blood to the imperial one of racial essences. Rushdie's rewriting of noses in *Tristram Shandy* serves in this context to make some telling points about the writing and rewriting of origins. It is now something of a truism that *Midnight's Children* recounts origins—ultimately, of course, of modern India—that are pointedly multiple. Rushdie's particular concern, however, seems less well understood: to unmask discourse about origins that disavows its own figurative ground. Hence *Midnight's Children* works above all against the retrospective conversion of an "effect" or "consequence" into a supposed "cause": the often unacknowledged trope of metalepsis.

The basis for Rushdie's anti-metaleptic theme is subtly present in *Tristram Shandy* in the fate of Tristram's nose. As is well known, Tristram's father Walter consults and invokes such sources as the learned Hafen Slawkenbergius in order to support his own theory that "long noses" are essential to good character. Along with the importance of names, this fascination with the size and shape of noses is one of Walter's several "hobbyhorses." Walter Shandy is convinced, indeed, that "the greatest family in

England" could not withstand "an uninterrupted succession of six or seven short noses."[69]

The learned lore parodied by Sterne reaches back, as Alfred David shows, to late antiquity. The valorization of the aquiline nose as a sign of noble magnanimity can be traced back as far as a text of the third century, long attributed to Aristotle.[70] By the twelfth century, the "well-made" nose had become, in the aristocratic literary portraiture of medieval France, "one badge of social class"[71] The patrician nose, as an index of social classification, found its hideous opposite in a vulgarly oversized nose. The sexual valence attributed to large and uncouth noses likewise derives, according to David, from aristocratic self-definition. A crudely bestial phallicism, in supposed contrast to courtly refinement and *fine amour*, was attributed to the commoner.[72]

For Walter Shandy, then, the nose is the physiognomic mark of aristocratic lineage. The fate of *Tristram Shandy*'s nose, crushed flat as a pancake by an obstetrician's forceps, therefore crushes his father's hopes for the family line. As a plot device, this mutilation emphasizes the impotence of Walter Shandy's various attempts to master reality through systematic knowledge. But nothing in *Tristram Shandy*, including causality, moves in a straight line. For it is only after Walter Shandy learns that Tristram's nose has been crushed (chapter 27 of volume III) that we learn of a second possible origin for the supposed ruin of Tristram's nose. As we learn in chapters 32 and 33 of the same volume, the whole inspiration for Walter Shandy's obsession is the fact that Tristram's paternal great-grandfather was quite flat-nosed. The nose in question, we are told, was shaped like "an ace of clubs."[73] And Walter Shandy, indeed, attributes the family's entire decline in fortune since the time of Henry VIII, as Tristram writes, to "the blow of my great-grandfather's nose".[74] Walter Shandy's fabrication of origins is not just a case of multiple factors and overdetermination. Much more interesting is the *metaleptic reversal of cause and effect*. What seems like an "effect"—the condition of *Tristram Shandy*'s nose—motivates, and thus is the cause for, a certain act of genealogical reconstruction. The "blow" of the forceps, though chronologically later, in some sense "causes" Tristram to have a snub-nosed ancestor. Sterne's theme of undecidable origins decisively challenges retrospective acts, whether biographical or collective, of narrating the progress of some essence. The trait of noses does not define, anchor, and cause social identity; rather, the activity of searching for social identity in terms of origins "causes" a focusing on nasal physiognomy.[75]

Reading *Tristram Shandy* through the lens of nationalist cock-and-bull stories accomplishes a more nuanced understanding of the nature of Sterne's achievement. For certain elements of *Tristram Shandy*—above all, its deliberately contingent and messy plotting of character and story—have often been misappropriated in ways that fail to recognize their significance in Sterne's own moment. On the one hand, these formal elements have been seen as a mere function of the novel's "primitive" moment in the developmental history of the genre: its status as a "pre-Romantic" stepping-stone to better things. On the other hand, these same elements have been repeatedly taken as "Postmodern" experiments somehow ahead of their time.[76] Yet Sterne's engagement with the rhetoric of an emerging nationalism suggests that the novel is informed by a specifically eighteenth-century problematic. And indeed, *Tristram Shandy* is, precisely in its experimentalism—in its demonstration, above all, of the wounding processes that underwrite acts of naming and identification—a quintessentially eighteenth-century critique of nationalist rhetoric. And it is not the least significant aspect of *Tristram Shandy*, then, that it gives the lie not only to nationalist teleologies, but also to later modes of Romantic and Postmodern literary-historical myth-making. What *Tristram Shandy* reveals is the more complex truth of the eighteenth century's historical liminality: a moment indelibly marked *both* by modernity's violence *and* its self-critique.

Tristram Shandy provides a crucial starting point for Rushdie's critique of metaleptically constructed origins precisely because Sterne's critique was written before the themes of so-called scientific racism had become dominant. The importance of ancient Egypt, as in a great deal of eighteenth-century speculation about "civilization," is simply taken for granted. Sterne mocks a foolish obsession, a neurotic "hobbyhorse." It was not until the late eighteenth century, however, that metalepsis as a grand strategy for delineating the "West" became fully systematized. Rushdie's later critique of metaleptic historiography, therefore, must address physiognomy as a quasi-scientific racist ideology as well as a foolish mode of snobbery.

The later eighteenth century thus proves, once again, to mark a crucial point in the punctuation of this historical shift. According to David, Sterne's mockery of nasal taxonomy occurs just before a break between a traditional sort of snobbish nasal lore and a newer quasi-scientific physiognomy:

[Walter Shandy's] *ideé fixe* . . . anticipates the serious endeavors of people who would be measuring skulls, feeling cranial bumps, and scrutinizing the angles of noses. The main difference between the old physiognomy and the new lies in the latter's claim to empiricism and mathematical objectivity. Once people had learned to measure such things as facial angles, it was a short step to their declaring that certain angles are superior to others. Winckelmann is one of the first to find a perfection in Greek statues that serves as an ideal type against which to measure other physiognomies. The type of the Greek nose, he found, was inherently more beautiful than the type of the Semitic nose.[77]

The most famous physiognomical work was published in four volumes between 1775–1778 by Johann Casper Lavater. Lavater's achievement, according to David, was "to make physiognomy fashionable and to give it the appearance of a science by documenting its 'laws' with hundreds of examples."[78] Amidst Lavater's voluminous speculations there is such discourse as the following about ethnic noses:

> The Tartars, generally, have flat, curved noses; African blacks, snub noses; Jews, for the most part, hawk noses. The noses of Englishmen are seldom pointed, but generally round.[79]

Such writings, as David says, "are symptomatic of intellectual, social, and political attitudes during the prerevolutionary, preromantic period that paved the way for modern racism."[80] By 1915, it was possible for Herbert H. Risley to publish the following analysis of the Indian caste system:

> Even more striking is the curiously close correspondence between the gradations of racial type indicated by the nasal index and certain of the social data ascertained by independent inquiry. If we take a series of castes in Bengal, Bihar, the United Provinces of Agra and Oudh, or Madras, and arrange them in the order of the nasal index, so that the caste with the finest nose shall be at the top, and that with the coarsest at the bottom of the list, it will be found that this order substantially corresponds with the accepted order of social precedence.[81]

Risley's faith in the significance of noses—an imaginary system badly in need of critique—tops even the nasal fixation of Walter Shandy.

The premodern and aristocratic projection of crude hyper-virility onto the subordinate classes established the pattern by which noses, in the discourses of modern racial bigotry, began to stand both for "excessive" sexuality and "ugliness" of racial character. Moreover, as Sander Gilman points out, the nose of the Jew, in particular, became "the polite anti-Semitic reference to the phallus."[82] That nose, indeed, "is the iconic representation of the Jew's phallus throughout the nineteenth century." The prevalence of this latter trope is quite staggering. Even relatively sympathetic portraits of Jews, such as George Eliot's *Daniel Deronda* (1876), cannot resist the occasional witless harping on such themes as a Jewish character's "chosen nose."[83] To all of this Sterne's Uncle Toby makes a reply in advance: "There is no cause but one . . . why one man's nose is longer than another's, but because that God pleases to have it so."[84] This view is obviously Sterne's own. The parody in *Tristram Shandy* of nose lore, as Sterne writes in a letter, "is levelled at those learned blockheads who, in all ages, have wasted their time and much learning upon points as foolish."[85] The names *Hafen* and *Slawkenbergius*, according to Howard Anderson's note, are derived from colloquial German words meaning *chamber-pot* and *pile of manure*, respectively.[86] Such is Sterne's critique of unconscious metalepsis: an analysis of the Shandy family's snobbish, egocentric, and retroactive revisions of the past.

The mobilization of *Tristram Shandy* to mock physiognomy has precedent in the eighteenth century. In October, 1790, the *Gentleman's Magazine* published a parody of physiognomy derived from the Shandean "nose" theme and pseudonymously signed "Slawkenbergius." Responding to a passage in Lavater in which he claims that a certain gentleman, forced by disfigurement to acquire a prosthetic nose, could not have chosen otherwise than he did without violating the "homogeneity" of his features. Those features, moreover, Lavater reads as expressing "astonishing faculties," but "without energy": a combination that signifies "voluptuousness." To this "Slawkenbergius" responds by the whimsical visual experiment of drawing different noses on the face in question. Slawkenbergius confesses that, to his eye, each of the three sketches displays an equal degree of homogeneity. His parting shot, alluding to the well-known damage done by syphilis to the nasal organ, suggests that it requires no uncommon skill to conjecture that "a man deprived of his nose had found the task of resisting the allurements of sensuality rather too severe for his philosophy. . . ."[87] Like *Tristram Shandy* itself, this little joke also plays on the implied analogy between nose and phallus lurking in Lavater's analysis. The bagatelle demonstrates both the oppositional implications of Shandean nasal science and the incomplete triumph, as late as 1790, of the project of modern physiognomy.

Tristram Shandy ultimately engages the problematic of "national origins" at several levels. *Tristram Shandy*'s disruption of origination myths is, first of all, a function of the novel's very structure: of its displacement of narrative progression by endless curlicues of digression and regression. But it is the effect, above all, of the novel's steadfast refusal, in the end, to suture together the time of writing (in which Tristram is our present narrator) with the time told about (in which Tristram's prehistory and childhood are described). In thus refusing to make Tristram's past and present cohere, Sterne does a certain violence to the conventions of the novel itself: a genre, on Anderson's account, whose commitment to the realist presentation of calendrical time and cartographic space has functioned historically as a binding force for the collective fiction of the national print-culture. The novel as a genre typically depicts the process by which a leading character develops and matures—and thus, by that rugged but necessary process, appropriates and naturalizes a stable sense of identity. The child, as Wordsworth puts it, is father to the man: but not in *Tristram Shandy*. In refusing to render Tristram's story as a *Bildungsroman*, a "coming-of-age" story, Sterne foregrounds the gulf between Tristram's experiences as a minor and his mature writing voice. Sterne thus refuses precisely that organicist grounding of identity on the recovery of origins that David Lloyd describes as a leading characteristic of the sort of narrative deemed "major" by nation-based institutions of canon-formation: the "narrative of ethical identity."[88] In leaving this gap unbridged, Sterne forecloses the moment when Tristram "comes into his own": when he achieves his majority, as it were, and declares his autonomy. In *Tristram Shandy*, characters are catastrophically malformed by mutilating accidents rather than informed by the organic unfolding of an essential nature. Indeed, Sterne points to a violent break between incommensurable temporalities: a broken story whose traumatic form could not possibly follow a linear progress. The disruption of the linear model of character development in *Tristram Shandy*, then, functions also to defamiliarize the historicist nostalgia of nation-building rhetoric.

It is no accident that the theme of civilization's westering progress is in fact explicitly mocked in *Tristram Shandy*. Consider the following little digression, which has most often been noted in passing as one more example of Sterne's spoofing version of "learned wit":

> No—there I mistake; that [one of his father's lofty tidbits of classical learning] was part of *Eleazar's* oration, as recorded by *Josephus*. . . . *Eleazar* owns he had it from the philosophers of *India*; in all likelihood, *Alexander* the Great, in his irruption into India, after he had overrun *Persia*, amongst the many things he stole,—stole that sentiment also; by which means it was carried, if not all the way by himself, (for we all know that he died at *Babylon*) at least by some of his maroders, into *Greece*,—from *Greece* it got to *Rome*,—from *Rome* to *France*,—and from *France* to *England*:—So things come round.—
>
> By land carriage, I can conceive no other way.—
>
> By water the sentiment might easily have come down the *Ganges* into the *Sinus Gangeticus*, or *Bay of Bengal*, and so into the *Indian Sea*; and following the course of trade, (the way from *India* by the *Cape of Good Hope* being then unknown) might be carried with other drugs and spices up the *Red Sea* to *Joddah*, the port of *Mekka*, or else to *Tor* or *Sues*, towns at the bottom of the gulf; and from thence by karrawans to *Coptos*, but three day's journey distant, so down the *Nile* directly, where the SENTIMENT would be landed at the very door of the great stair-case of the *Alexandrian library*,—and from that store-house it would be fetched.—Bless me! what a trade was driven by the learned in those days![89]

Given the overall context in which this appears—a novel that demonstrates the utter impossibility of reconstructing pure and unmediated origins from the endless regress of history—this passage functions as a laughing demystification of that sort of roots-finding, identity-imposing exercise. It is no more likely that the origins of Tristram's "sentiment" could ever be definitively tracked to its origin than it is likely that Tristram, who requires a full year merely to record a single day of his life, can adequately reconstruct his own history.

Midnight's Children, coming after the great Aryan metalepsis, further develops the Shandean demystification of retrospectively constructed origins. A second reading of *Midnight's Children* makes clear the extent to which "origins" in Saleem Sinai's life are the secondary effects, rather than the causes, of his history. For we learn at the novel's conclusion that Saleem's livelihood, his work in the Braganza Pickle Factory in Bombay, depends on his extraordinary sense of smell. Indeed, the activity of writing itself, which Saleem refers to as the "pickling of time" and the "chutnification of history," occurs in this factory.[90] It is thus the origins of his olfactory powers for which Saleem feels compelled to account. That he begins his story with the wonderful "probocissimus" of Aadam Aziz, whom he claims as his grandfather, should therefore come as little surprise. Apparently taking such dynastic notions at face value, so to speak, the narrative allows the reader to understand for some seven chapters that Saleem Sinai has inherited his badly congested "cyranose" directly from Aadam, his appropriately named Kashmiri forebear. The nose, containing both dynasties and snot, is flamboyantly phallic and patriarchal. In the eighth chapter, however, we are told that Saleem was not after all the biological son of Ahmed Sinai and Aadam Aziz's daughter Mumtaz/Amina. Saleem, through a melodramatic changeling plot, was swapped at birth with his alter ego Shiva. His "true" parents, according to biological descent, are Vanita Winkie, who died giving birth to him, and William Methwold, the departing imperialist.

The logic of this baby-swap is precisely against the grain of the conventional "birth mysteries" in such authors as Shakespeare, Dickens, and even Eliot. In *The Winter's Tale*, for example, blue blood will eventually tell: no rags can permanently obscure the royal origins of Perdita, the princess cruelly exposed as an infant. In *Midnight's Children*, however, the baby-swapping, which in fact reveals the narrator's "low birth," ultimately makes no difference.[91] Here the example of Tristram's retrospectively significant ancestor is pushed still further. An ancestor, for Saleem, is something one openly chooses; a usable past, necessarily selective and arbitrary, is something one self-consciously invents. "Giving birth to parents," as Saleem writes, "has been one of my stranger talents."[92] The point is less a postmodern sense of confusion as to whether Saleem's nose derives from the line of Aadam Aziz or William Methwold than a conspicuously figurative metalepsis. For Saleem's great emphasis on the magnificent noses of both his possible forefathers works as an openly avowed metalepsis, as an acknowledged and self-conscious figuration of origins.

The further point, for Rushdie, writing in the wake of pseudo-scientific racism, has to do with what the nose is not allowed to mean. Saleem refuses to permit the revelation of Methwold's role in his family line to become a peripatetic revelation of "race." This is in sharp contrast to the central moment in *Daniel Deronda*, for instance, when Deronda, finally confronting his biological mother, speaks the fateful words, "Then I *am* a Jew?"[93] Consider the following passage early in *Midnight's Children* describing Methwold's nose:

> And his nose? What did that look like? Prominent? Yes, it must have been, the legacy of a patrician French grandmother—from Bergerac!—whose blood ran aquamarinely in his veins and darkened his courtly charm with something crueller, some sweet murderous shade of absinthe.[94]

In some sense, of course, this passage foreshadows the revelation that Methwold is Saleem's biological father. At the same time, however, it pre-emptively subverts the force of that revelation. For instead of relocating the nose's point of origin in Methwold, it simply displaces it yet again, to a French ancestor.

The grandmother from France, moreover, needs to be read against the practice of Aryan history-writing, in which the historical novel has played its part, of understanding history through a single lens: the Anglo-Saxon "race" and its tribulations. Sir Walter Scott's *Ivanhoe*, in depicting the feudal antagonism between Norman French lords and Anglo-Saxon serfs, establishes a whole set of conventions for representing "race" in Anglo-American novels. For Scott, "race," in a profoundly reactionary substitution, supplants social class as a historical explanation. In *Ivanhoe* "race" is essentialized precisely in physiognomic details: hence the influential contrast, for instance, between an opposed pair of "dark" and "light" heroines. *Ivanhoe's* "race-struggle" plot exemplifies the way notions of the nation mediated, as Kwame Anthony Appiah suggests, between the concept of race, on the one hand, and the idea of literature, on the other.[95]

In *Midnight's Children*, Methwold's patrician nose works against this tradition. Although Methwold's nose stands for an imperial legacy, the French grandmother ensures that it cannot be made into a simple figure of "Anglo-Saxon" inheritance. So Saleem, though he writes, punningly, in a pool of "Anglepoised light," refuses to accept Padma's reclassifying of him as "Anglo-Indian."[96] The point has less to do with any simple fact of hybridization than with the uncovering of the post-Enlightenment fabrication of racial origins.

It might be argued that my single-minded emphasis on the eighteenth century, given the mixed or "chutnified" nature of intertextuality in *Midnight's Children*, is capricious. For allusions in *Midnight's Children* are not much limited by time or space. They range across high and popular culture both in Asia and in Europe, borrowing from Bombay "Talkies," from the *Ramayana* and the *Mahabharata*, from children's genre fiction such as science fiction and superhero comics such as *Superman*, from the *Arabian Nights*, and from twentieth-century novels such as *The Tin Drum*. And indeed, even Saleem's nose is implicitly traced back ultimately to "roots" that are literary: the character Cyrano de Bergerac, whom Saleem studied in school and also knew, as he mentions, via the *Classics Illustrated* comic book version.[97] Not one of these allusive patterns, however, not even the insistent invocation of the *Arabian Nights*, amounts to anything like the novel's formal and thematic debt to *Tristram Shandy*. The Bragenza Pickle Factory, moreover, is named for Catherine of Braganza: the Portuguese royal whose marriage to Charles II (1662) made Bombay an English possession.

Indeed, that "beginning" in the late eighteenth century serves, for reasons that are historically overdetermined, as the context for most of the others. It reminds us, for example, that the Brothers Grimm collected, edited, and published "Snow White" in the early nineteenth century in the context of cultural valorization of the German folk. And it reminds us as well that the *translation* of texts such as the *Arabian Nights* and the *Mahabharata* was a central aspect of the Orientalist project of textualizing the Asian cultures under the "indirect rule" of European domination: it was, indeed, "a significant technology of colonial domination."[98] The epics and legends of Indian antiquity, therefore, have less oppositional force than a nativist reading might suppose. If Rushdie's project were merely to challenge Western modes with "indigenous" ones, as Hutcheon seems to imply, he would risk invoking what amounts to a tradition that began to be "invented"— textualized, harmonized, canonized, and thus artificially frozen—by Orientalist scholars in the late eighteenth century: Charles Wilkins's *Bhagavad-Gita*, William Jones's *Śākuntala*, and so on. Ironically enough, as Rosane Rocher points out, this strain of scholarship resulted, in India, is a British promotion of "the distant past as normative."[99]

Midnight's Children, it has been said, is weakened by a "failure to disturb."[100] Such a charge misses the essential point of its postcolonial strategy of reading and writing, which proceeds subtly rather than crudely, domesticating its enemies rather than attempting to stand for their essential opposite. Rushdie pursues a strategy of historical differentiation and placement: of the novel, of the eighteenth century, of the Raj, and, ultimately, of Aryan historiography itself. *Midnight's Children* works, above all, as a multilevelled attack on the metaleptic rhetoric of self-legitimation. The trope of nasal origins in *Midnight's Children*, for instance, unmasks metalepsis not only in autobiographical history-writing, but in larger social processes as well. It is in this context that we can see the special value of Rushdie's gesture of turning back to *Tristram Shandy*, and to the eighteenth century in general, for his attempt to create a postcolonial novel. For it can be no coincidence that his critique of disavowed metalepsis focuses on the eighteenth century. This trope, as Martin Bernal and other historians are teaching us, found its largest and most scandalous instance in the late-eighteenth-century fabrication of Ancient Greece as the origins of "the West."

The central lesson of Bernal, Amin, and the rest is the delinking of rationality, or, more generally, Enlightenment values, from any racial or hemispheric essence and the situating of it instead in a particular material history. To think otherwise, as this work makes clear, forces anti-imperial opposition to repeat that historical fallacy which annexed science and rationality as the essence of an ahistorical "West." Thus glib attacks on the Enlightenment, whether postmodernist or neo-traditionalist, often merely invert the values of Eurocentric historiography without challenging its fundamental premise. *Midnight's Children*, in showing how history has been led by the nose, provides a far more successful challenge to the rhetorical strategies of Eurocentrism.

CHAPTER 4

SINGING THE IMPERIAL BLUES:
READING NATION AND EMPIRE IN
JOHN GAY AND WOLE SOYINKA

I've got the imperial blues
I'm as blue as I can be

— "Mackie's Farewell,"
Opera Wonyosi

Echoes from the eighteenth-century Scriblerians abound in the works of the contemporary Nigerian playwright, director, poet, novelist, journalist, editor, translator, autobiographer, and cosmopolitan scholar, Wole Soyinka. Like Salman Rushdie's engagement with Laurence Sterne in *Midnight's Children*, this pattern of allusive encounters bespeaks a significant gesture of affiliation. In particular, the resonance of Soyinka's *Opera Wonyosi* (1977)—a powerful act of affiliation both with John Gay, and with Gay's historical moment—deserves to be teased out in its full complexity. For it is certainly by way of Gay's duology, *The Beggar's Opera* and its sequel *Polly*, that Soyinka, with admirable self-consciousness, lays claim to a legacy from the British eighteenth century. The special liminality of the eighteenth-century moment as regards narratives of empire and nation makes it possible to understand Gay and Soyinka as fellow travelers. This threshold quality of the moment allows writers such as Soyinka and Rushdie, among others, to affiliate with key figures within it in the act of constructing a shared history.

Soyinka's *Opera Wonyosi* is far more than a Nigerian appropriation of a British text: *Opera Wonyosi* is a multilayered critique of national cultures as such; and it looks back to John Gay's plays precisely because, among other reasons, it finds in them an essential precursor for such a critique. Rather than reinforcing nativism, Soyinka's gesture of affiliation with Gay invites us to read both authors together in terms of a more global model: the transnational narrative of capital and its relentless expansion from northwest Europe. West Africa, then—already deeply involved in this narrative by the eighteenth century—serves for Soyinka less as a pristine source of cultural identity than as a space where various histories collided. In choosing to write through Gay, however, he foregrounds the eighteenth century as a promising site for the immanent critique both of the imperial project and of nationalism.

Soyinka's Scriblerian echoes make up the matter of perceptive essays by Peter Sabor and Aparna Dharwadker. In his "Wole Soyinka and the Scriblerians," Sabor scrupulously documents Soyinka's extensive engagement with both John Gay and Jonathan Swift: in Soyinka's prison poem "Gulliver" (1972); in his *Opera Wonyosi* (1977), which takes off from Gay's *Beggar's Opera*; in his satirical play *Requiem for a Futurologist* (1983), which rewrites Swift's "Bickerstaff prank"; and in his pervasive motif of cannibalism, which looks back to Swift's "A Modest Proposal."[1] Yet Sabor stops short of teasing out the full historical resonance of what is in fact a crucial strand in Soyinka's complexly braided *oeuvre*. He concludes, rather diffidently, that the Scriblerians do not ultimately constitute any sort of "master key" to Soyinka's *oeuvre*.[2] In her more recent essay, "John Gay, Bertolt Brecht, and Postcolonial Antinationalisms," Aparna Dharwadker goes much further in demonstrating the significance to Soyinka's postcolonial politics of the latter's intertextual dialogue with Gay's *The Beggar's Opera*.[3] Despite Dharwadker's valuable emphasis on Soyinka's critical distance from nationalist rhetoric, however, she fails to make explicit the particular resonance, for a postcolonial politics, of the eighteenth-century moment. For the dialogue between Soyinka and his eighteenth-century satiric forebears serves to illustrate not only the generally intertextual nature of much postcolonial writing, but specifically the crucial significance, for contemporary postcolonial politics, of the eighteenth-century moment.

Indeed, I argue that reading the Scriblerians through and after Soyinka's engagement with them opens up a vital new context for situating their work. For only in the wake of Soyinka's particular contextualization of their work can one appreciate the true significance of the challenge posed by Swift and Gay to an emerging British national identity. Soyinka's gesture of reaching back to the eighteenth-century Scriblerians points to a more complex genealogy for critical resistance than a contemporary monopoly on counter-hegemonic critique would suggest. As a gesture of affiliation, Soyinka's dialogue with Gay enforces the point that canonical texts, in Dharwadker's words, "may themselves be subversive rather than hegemonic. . . ."[4] Diane Dugaw, who explores the twentieth-century uses made of *The Beggar's Opera* by Bertolt Brecht, Vaclav Havel, and Alan Ayckbourn, likewise emphasizes the productive way that Gay's work "opens to scrutiny" enduring features of a modern commercial society: the "mercantile order and sensibility" so conspicuous in his works.[5] The location of a meaningful critical resistance within the eighteenth century is crucial precisely because of the polarized and reductive nature of current debates about the field. A rereading of the Scriblerians through the Soyinkan connection, however, demonstrates that the historical moment in question produced more than, in John Bender's phrase, "the assumptions that have structured modern literary study."[6] Indeed, the eighteenth century itself also produced some of the earliest and most telling challenges to those same assumptions. That is precisely why Soyinka chooses at times to write, again in Dharwadker's words, "*through*, not *against*, canonical texts that are already deeply subversive."[7] Soyinka, while exploring Yoruba metaphysics and ritual drama throughout his career, simply declines to position himself entirely "outside" the Anglophone literary traditions that partially produced him. Early and late in his career, as in his recent musings on L. S. Senghor and the Negritude movement, Soyinka has emphasized histories and traditions that can serve as bridges between cultures.[8]

Although Soyinka has passionately defended his "selective eclecticism" as "the right of every productive being,"[9] his intertextual engagement with Gay and Swift is not mere artistic eclecticism. Indeed, precisely by means of his Scriblerian palimpsest that can one best see how Soyinka's work provides the basis for recasting such sterile dichotomies as nativism versus Eurocentrism or tradition versus modernity. For in turning to such carefully selected eighteenth-century precursors, Soyinka is in fact thematizing a more general critique of national cultures as such, inviting an analysis in terms of the imperial social formation.[10] Soyinka's reworking of the Scriblerians asks us to rethink the supposedly discrete "national" traditions of both British and Nigerian letters in the supra-national context of an imperial history that in fact constitutes them both. Soyinka's gesture of affiliation, emphasizing the imperial corruption of nations, serves to open up a dialogue with the global making of the eighteenth century. Indeed, just as John Gay serves Soyinka as a *historically* located vantage-point from which to write, so Soyinka's intertextual satire should serve in turn to complicate and challenge the boundaries of the "British" or "Western" eighteenth century.

Reading Soyika after Gay

Soyinka's Scriblerian genealogy includes John Gay, Alexander Pope, and Jonathan Swift. For the purposes of this chapter, however, I have chosen to focus on Soyinka's use of Gay: for only through Soyinka's engagement with Gay's *Beggar's Opera* and *Polly* can an oppositional reframing of literary nationalism be fully realized. Only when *The Beggar's Opera* is given its due as the key for understanding *Opera Wonyosi* does it become possible to see how the latter provides an alternative unit of analysis for framing the histories of nations in the age of empires. The eighteenth century, of course, figures centrally in most influential discussions of modern nation-building. The particular role of eighteenth-century literature in nationalizing the British polity looms large in recent scholarship. What has not been adequately recognized even in this valuable historical work, however, is the way that modern nation-building itself comes after, and is ultimately determined within, the overarching structure and dynamics of an imperial social formation.

The English had slave-plantations in the West Indies by the latter half of the seventeenth century; the British became the leading global trafficker in slavery after acquiring the Asiento in 1713; and by mid-century they were building military forts along the coast of west Africa to protect their trading posts there. (Lagos, former capital of modern Nigeria, was one of those trading posts.) The British, moreover, were simultaneously educating African princes, with whom the slavers found it convenient to negotiate, in British universities;[11] and by the late eighteenth century Christian missionaries from Britain, who brought their own avenues to literacy in English, had arrived in west Africa to join with the traders. Accordingly, a wave of recent scholarship has thoroughly documented a substantial "Black presence" *within* the borders of Great Britain during the eighteenth century: a presence that is *not* the product of recent immigration patterns, but, rather, an important index of the impact of empire on the very shores of Britain at least since the Georgian era.[12] Paul Gilroy's *The Black Atlantic*, moreover, has now provided a far more suggestive model than Linda Colley's nation-centered account—even for the British eighteenth century—for coming to terms with the historical significance of this Afro-British presence. By expanding his unit of analysis to a trans-Atlantic African diaspora that overflows all national boundaries, Gilroy exposes the exclusions practiced by traditional nation-centered accounts. And Gilroy, then, gives due emphasis to "the special position of Britain within the black–Atlantic world, standing at the apex of the semi-triangular structure which saw commodities and people shipped to and fro across the ocean."[13]

Soyinka refers to the Atlantic slave trade as "an inescapable critique of European humanism."[14] The literary legacy of Gilroy's "Black Atlantic" experience, however ambivalent, constitutes a good portion of Soyinka's inheritance. Even his own educational trajectory, indeed, reminds us that the histories of west African and European literatures were increasingly embedded, by the middle of the eighteenth century, within a shared global process. After all, the same historical process that would produce an Anglophone Nobel Laureate from Nigeria in 1986—namely, Soyinka himself—had already produced, by 1789, Ibo author Olaudah Equiano's autobiographical slave-narrative in English.[15] What Soyinka's gesture of affiliation with the Scriblerians does, therefore, is to challenge the project of nation-building by thematizing the alternate and supra-national trajectory of imperial expansion: a trajectory that both includes and supersedes the usual way of organizing knowledge around nation-based categories.

Understood thus, Soyinka's purpose in drawing so heavily on John Gay's *The Beggar's Opera* cannot be reduced to the mere recognition of his belated condition as a postcolonial author. The point of such an affiliation, rather, is to bring together the moments of nation-building in both the metropole and the periphery within the same imperial continuum. The resonance for Soyinka of Gay's *The Beggar's Opera* (1728), a play about Britain in the 1720s, lies in the latter's stinging critique of British nation-building. This critique, for Gay, is manifest in the delineation of a corrupt state in which an oligarchic elite masquerades as the supposed representative of a general national interest. Gay's bitingly topical satire of this society was widely understood to have scored direct hits on Prime Minister Robert Walpole and the chicanery of his bribery-based patronage machine. Although Gay's play generated various highly partisan "keys" purporting to unlock the veiled identities of its highly placed targets, the satire was most fundamentally directed, as David Nokes insists, at a "wider political culture."[16] According to *The Beggar's Opera*, Hanoverian courtiers differ from common criminals only in their freedom from legal consequences. Macheath's penultimate song in *The Beggar's Opera* puts this levelling logic best:

> But Gold from Law can take out the Sting;
> And if rich Men like us were to swing,
> 'Twould thin the Land, such Numbers to string
>   Upon <u>Tyburn</u> Tree![17]

No wonder that Dugaw suggests that "the mirroring oppositions in Gay's works—indeed, the opposition intrinsic to burlesque as a strategy—pose the dialectical premises by which social class has subsequently been understood in the Marxist tradition."[18] Although *The Beggar's Opera* derives its primary momentum from a critique of the emerging British nation-state, it does prefigure the imperial motifs that are more fully developed in the play's less-known sequel, *Polly*. The imperial context thus casts its inescapable shadow both in the prospect of penal transportation and in the various "bubbling" allusions to the South Sea Bubble.

Soyinka does for twentieth-century nation-building in post-independence Nigeria what Gay did for British nation-building in the 1720s. Soyinka's *Opera Wonyosi*,[19] heavily indebted to *The Beggar's Opera*, was first performed in 1977 at the University of Ife. It portrays the amoral society of Nigeria's 1970s oil-boom under the name of the "Centafrique Empire." The main characters, the members of a bandit gang, are Nigerian expatriates who live in the Nigerian quarter and terrorize the local population. The play's criminal protagonist, with a nod to Bertolt Brecht as well as Gay, is variously called Macheath or Mack the Knife. Like *The Beggar's Opera*, *Opera Wonyosi* depicts a virtually total coincidence of the most vicious criminal transgressions with the highest legal authority. And just as Gay's play is centered around the theatricalized spectacle of public executions at Tyburn gallows,[20] so Soyinka's play emphasizes the festive nature of the public executions at Bar Beach, the arena for public executions in 1970s Lagos. Both plays, then, feature a systemic corruption that links all of society, with high differing from low only in scale and degree. The "Dee Jay" who speaks the prologue to *Opera Wonyosi* suggests that *The Beggar's Opera* could be an alternative title for the play. He cannot decide, however, as Mpalive-Hangson Msiska points out, *which* "beggar" after whom the play should be named since the whole nation is begging for a slice of the action.[21]

Opera Wonyosi thus illustrates Soyinka's grim view that the political and cultural aftermath of the Nigerian civil war (1967–1969) represented, as his prison memoir puts it, a consolidation of crime. After a coup (January 1996) and a counter-coup (July 1996) led to the secession of Biafra from newly independent Nigeria, a grim civil war ensued. *The Man Died* (1972), written while Soyinka was incarcerated in Kaduna Prison for publicly opposing the Nigerian government's prosecution of the civil war against Biafran secessionists, suggests much about his affinity for Gay's themes:

> The vacuum in the ethical base—for national boundary is neither an ethical nor an ideological base for any conflict—this vacuum will be filled by a new military ethic—coercion. And the élitist formulation of the army, the entire colonial hangover which is sustained by the lack of national revaluation will itself maintain and promote the class heritage of society. The ramifications of a corrupt militarism and a rapacious Mafia in society are endless and are nearly incurable.

"The war," Soyinka concludes, "means an acceptance of the scale of values that created the conflict, indeed an allegiance and enshrinement of that scale of values because it is now intimately bound to the sense of national identity."[22] *Opera Wonyosi*, the work of a great satirist, burlesques a national culture of corruption that, in Msiska's words, "makes it difficult to separate the criminals from the lawmakers."[23] An ugly and frightening continuity between past and present atrocities rears its head. Corruption in this sense is the deepest thematic link between *The Beggar's Opera* and *Opera Wonyosi*.

The reincarnation of the eighteenth-century *Beggar's Opera* as the twentieth-century *Opera Wonyosi*, however, does not imply Soyinka's support for a strictly linear notion of historical progress: the reenactment in decolonized Nigeria, that is, of the "birth-pangs" of European modernity. Soyinka has elsewhere referred to the notion of such birth-pains as "that near-fatal euphemism for death throes."[24] More crucially, his consistent critique of European imperialism and its "stages-of-development" paradigm does not allow the relationship between *The Beggar's Opera* and *Opera Wonyosi* to be figured simply in terms of a Nigerian time lag. The trajectory of European modernity in independent Nigeria recognizes instead the *coevalness*, in Johannes Fabian's sense,[25] of European and Nigerian time. Soyinka's awareness of such coevalness serves, more crucially, to distance his work from simplistic prescriptions for Nigeria to travel the path already traversed by Europe.

Opera Wonyosi thus highlights the profound ambiguity of the modernist legacy to which some contemporary west African leaders are laying claim. The character of Soyinka's murderous military dictator, Emperor Boky, makes it clear that Soyinka's agenda cannot be a mere fulfillment of the modernist project, now epitomized by the French Revolution. Emperor Boky is a hilarious portrait of the historical personage, Jean-Bedel Bokassa, Emperor-for-Life of the Central African Republic, who was deposed a few years after the play's production. Soyinka's depiction of Bokassa includes a scathing reference to an actual atrocity: a scene in which schoolchildren are punished, by death, for refusing to wear the uniforms he had prescribed for them. An "imperial infanticide," as Soyinka writes in 1999,[26] Bokassa/Boky is likewise a parody of the wrong turnings of modernity. Boky, who sees himself as locked into a medal-wearing and title-mongering contest with Uganda's Idi Amin, repeatedly voices the desire to outclass Amin by becoming a "Black Napoleon." Here is Boky's spiel on Napoleon:

> And he was a revolutionary. You may not remember, but France is the cradle of revolution. Every revolution in the world began in France. And Napoleon it was who eventually placed our mother country on the map. We have to emulate him. Enough.
>
> I have condescended to be with you today not to talk politics but culture. You must know that our mother country, not content with being the cradle of revolution, is also the cradle of culture. So understand this—in this empire . . . em, nation, culture is on our priority list.[27]

Boky's fawning Francophilia, a colonial hangover, meshes seamlessly with his violent ambitions. The play is set on the eve of Boky's imperial coronation, and the amnesty by which gang-leader Macheath is spared from the firing squad at Bar Beach—structurally equivalent to MacHeath's escape from Tyburn at the conclusion to *The Beggar's Opera*—provides, *á la* Gay, an extremely sardonic "happy ending." Specifically, the amnesty is, as the police chief explains, a corrupt act of imperial patronage: "We men of influence—of power if you like—respect one another. We speak the same language, so we usually work things out."[28]

Emperor Boky, a shameless spouter of egalitarian slogans, tries to lay claim to the revolutionary heritage of the Jacobins. As we have seen, however, "Folksy Boksy" calls his domain an "empire," and then—correcting the telling slip—hastily revises his terminology back to the more homey-sounding "nation." Indeed, precisely in that slippage between nation and empire, in that terrible swerve from "liberty" to "glory," does the French Revolution give way to Napoleon's autocratic empire: a slippage marked by the transition in official insignia from the red phrygian bonnet to the imperial eagle.[29] Given *Opera Wonyosi*'s African location, moreover, we should not forget that Said's early scholarship places the inauguration of modern Orientalism in Napoleon's Egyptian Campaign of 1798–1799: an unprecedented invasion of some 200 experts and intellectuals—encyclopedic imperialists, in short—surely more significant, in retrospect, than the rather brief military intrusion.[30] The military campaign failed, but "Egyptology," as an imperial discipline, was launched upon the world.

Napoleon, as Said points out, liked to imagine himself, in reconquering Egypt, as a second Alexander the Great: for precisely the appalling scale of such violent "greatness" is of satiric concern both to Soyinka and John Gay. *The great man,* a reiterated catchphrase in both *Polly* and *The Beggar's Opera*, does of course refer ironically and obliquely to Walpole.[31] But it serves as well to delegitimate the whole notion of "greatness." To quote the insouciant lyric that opens *The Beggar's Opera*, as sung by crime-boss Peachum, "And the statesman, because he's so great, / Thinks his trade as honest as mine" (I.i.7–8). What occurs in *Opera Wonyosi*, then, is not so much a simple reenactment of an eighteenth-century nation-building project as the underscoring of a parallel, and symptomatic, *slippage between nation and empire* that has haunted nation-building, whether in eighteenth-century Britain, nineteenth-century France, or twentieth-century Nigeria, from its founding moment.[32]

Especially suggestive in this regard are the closing moments of *Opera Wonyosi*, when Macheath must face the firing squad at Bar Beach. He then achieves a certain bravado by singing the "imperial blues." In the first degree, the reference to blues is perhaps a commemoration of the blues-based poetry from Langston Hughes' *The Weary Blues* (1926) that was read during the inaugural address marking the occasion of Nigerian Independence.[33]

The further irony—an irony that challenges any glib fossilizing of such a countercultural tradition—is that the "imperial blues" is *now*, under Boky's cruel regime, a truly fitting song for the occasion. But even as the "imperial blues" motif points to the extraordinarily harsh political dilemmas of post-independence Africa, it simultaneously evokes the sedimented cultural memory of the earlier "imperial blues" experienced by diasporic Africans during some three centuries of transcendent cruelty in the south Atlantic. Soyinka here pays homage to Gay's device of an opera based on vernacular ballads by pointing to the stubbornly defiant musical counterculture that produced not only blues music, but also the jazz by which Brecht updated Gay's ballad opera in *The Three-Penny Opera*.[34] Soyinka's reliance on Gay points to a context that exceeds all nationalisms, whether in Europe or Africa, and which must be seen as logically prior to and constitutive of them. As a rewriting of the end of *The Beggar's Opera*, moreover, Macheath's *imperial* blues song is prefigured in the supra-national logic of Gay's own sequel to *The Beggar's Opera, Polly*. For in *Polly* Gay already depicts the inseparably related histories of nation and empire. John Gay, then— no less than Wole Soyinka—provides the basis for a radical alternative to nation-centered approaches to literary texts.

Reading Gay after Soyinka

If *The Beggar's Opera* is a key for opening up *Opera Wonyosi* as a parable about the inadequacy of nation-centered cultural institutions and approaches, then *Opera Wonyosi* returns the favor to Gay. For turning back to Gay after *Opera Wonyosi* compels us to read *The Beggar's Opera* and *Polly* together, and, hence, rather differently. In so doing, we become fully aware of the extent to which Gay's duo of linked plays comments on the character of a specific moment in the history of capitalist accumulation. For taken together, *The Beggar's Opera* and *Polly* are not only critiques of nation-building but also resonant documents, as Diane Dugaw and others have noted, for constructing a global narrative of capital expansion from northwest Europe.[35] *The Beggar's Opera* on its own has been discussed as a "capital satire" that demonstrates, above all, the saturation by a ruthlessly monetary language of all civic and social values.[36] Taken together, however, *The Beggar's Opera* and *Polly* unmistakably depict an early moment of finance capitalism: a period marked, as Nicholson emphasizes, by the founding of the Bank of England, the establishment of a national debt, and the revolutionary impact of paper credit on financial markets. The "national contours" that the English gentry had been able to derive from a land-based "insular system of propertied independence" began to be swamped by new historical forces.[37] In terms of its political culture, moreover, the age is distinguished by what historians have termed "Old Corruption." Inaugurated by the catastrophe of the South Sea Bubble in 1721, the decade of the 1720s is a cultural moment in Britain that seems peculiarly marked, above all, by a pervasive and disorienting sense of criminality. Government patronage and influence, now commodities on a highly visible marketplace, permitted the self-serving to buy Parliamentary seats and even peerages.

Polly rearticulates the "criminality" themes of Old Corruption quite specifically in terms of imperial aggression and plunder. *Polly* was banned from production by the Walpole government, and though Gay did make a fortune selling printed copies, *Polly* was not performed until 1776. Picking up the subsequent story of the bigamist highwayman Macheath and his much-betrayed wife, *Polly* utilizes the plot-device of penal transportation to unfold the links between criminality and colonial settlement. Gay's inside critique delegitimates precisely the trajectory whereby, as repeatedly in Daniel Defoe's fiction, settlement in the New World provides an avenue for moral and material redemption for transported criminals. Both Moll Flanders and Colonel Jack thus ultimately prosper as Virginia planters: a plot that points to the trans–Atlantic context within which Defoe's own nation-building,[38] as in his *A Tour thro' the Whole Island of Great Britain* (1724–1726), needs to be mapped. For Gay, however, the whole project of colonial settlement merely enlarges the scope of criminal endeavor, enabling the petty criminal to aspire to a spurious "greatness."

The highwayman Macheath, protagonist of *The Beggar's Opera*, reappears in *Polly* stripped of any residual rakish glamour. Macheath, a convict, has been transported as a slave to the West Indies. As the play begins, Macheath has now escaped his master, married the prostitute Jenny Diver, and disguised himself in blackface as the pirate chief "Morano." Polly, meanwhile, runs into immediate peril in her nobly deluded quest to find and reclaim the incorrigible Macheath. Upon arrival in the West Indies, she is immediately sold as the servant-cum-mistress of a lascivious colonial planter, and her asking price—equivalent to that of "half a dozen negro princesses" (I.vi. 26)—marks the intersection of slavery proper with a broader exploitative traffic in women. Her escape from this situation entails her disguise as a boy-warrior, in which masquerade she evinces considerable courage. In the end, Polly—having inadvertently captured "Morano" in battle without having recognized him as her errant husband—narrowly fails to save him from the death sentence to which her military victory has delivered him. His last defiant words, perhaps the play's finest line, are "*Alexander* the great was more successful. That's all."[39] In the play's final sardonic scene, the widowed Polly opts out of European society altogether, making an alliance instead with the noble, if parodically sententious, Indian prince Cawwawkee.

Polly extends the notion of legalized crime to British violence and greed in the colonial context of the West Indies, retrospectively highlighting the trans-Atlantic and imperial context in which the predatory society of Walpole's London arguably found its deepest significance. Gay's second ballad opera, indeed, defines colonialism as nothing more than glorified piracy. As Diane Dugaw shows, *Polly* is a caustic deflation of the heroic ethos once popular on the Restoration stage. Polly herself flatters the pirates as "those brave spirits, those *Alexanders*, that shall soon by conquest be in possession of the *Indies* (II.ii. 123–124). The pirates themselves, meanwhile, see the "greatness" of their chosen profession as its universal aggression:"Our profession is great, brothers. What can be more heroic than to have declar'd war with the whole world?" (II.ii. 25–27). In Dugaw's words, "The European presence in the New World, Gay insists, is a chaotic state of war between divergent 'Alexanders': rapacious planters and squabbling buccaneers, all of whose conquests stem from racism, pillage, cowardice, and greed."[40] So much for colonial modernity.

That Gay's political resistance is ultimately ineffectual and evasive— John Richardson's argument[41]—ignores the specific angle of his satirical attack. In perhaps Gay's most sardonic commentary on the relationship between the national and the imperial contexts, Macheath's pirate gang comprises members whose surnames—the Dutch Vanderbluff, the British Hacker, the French Laguerre—connote both the violence and the specific national backgrounds of those European powers that were mucking about in the Caribbean. Each personified nation thus represents, in the imperial context, a principle of piratical violence writ large. In one especially caustic scene, this gang fantasizes about the heroic colonial exploits that will ensue if only they can disentangle their chief from his distracting "Cleopatra," Jenny Diver.

Hacker. That inveigling gipsey, brothers, must be hawled from him by force. And then—the kingdom of *Mexico* shall be mine. My lot shall be the kingdom of *Mexico*.
Capstern. Who talks of *Mexico*? [*all rise*] I'll never give it up. If you outlive me, brother, and I dye without heirs, I'll leave it to you for a legacy, I hope now you are satisfy'd. I have set my heart upon it, and no body shall dispute it with me.
Laguerre. The island of *Cuba*, methinks, brother, might satisfy any reasonable man.
Culverin. That I had allotted for you. *Mexico* shall not be parted without my consent, captain *Morano* to be sure will choose *Peru*; that's the land of gold, and all of your great men love gold. *Mexico* hath only silver, nothing but silver. . . . (II.ii. 92–104)

The gang's rapacity inevitably escalates into a potentially fratricidal squabble over their imaginary possessions. The fact that they are presided over by a

British criminal in blackface makes all too visible the viciously exploitative relationship on which the imperial fraternity of nations depends. Macheath's masquerade is, in Dugaw's words, "an icon by which Gay metaphorizes his analysis of European heroism as racially embodied slavery."[42] Moreover, the prejudice which at least part of the gang evince toward "Morano"— one objects to being commanded by a "Neger" (III.v. 12)—might serve as a cautionary check on overly utopian reimaginings of pirates in the cultural imagination. However cosmopolitan the Algerian "Renegadoes" studied by Peter Lamborn Wilson may have been,[43] it should not be forgotten that the European tradition of celebrating pirates belongs primarily to a discourse of colonial romance. A West Indian planter such as Edward Long, whose pro-slavery *History of Jamaica* (1774) is a notorious landmark in the history of racist propaganda, is thus unstinting in his support for Henry Morgan and his fellow pirates in the Caribbean: "It is to the Bucaniers," Long claims, "that we owe the possession of Jamaica at this hour. . . ." Conversely, when Peter Hulme reminds us that Sir Francis Drake, Sir Walter Raleigh, and sim-ilar brave Elizabethan buccaneers were bloodthirsty pirates and robbers,[45] he elaborates an anti-colonial *topos* already well-developed not only in Gay but in Swift and Samuel Johnson as well. Taken together, *Polly* and *The Beggar's Opera* thus foreground and delegitimate the same conflation of nation and empire that is thematized in *Opera Wonyosi*. The import of read-ing Gay after Soyinka, then, is precisely to highlight the ways in which Gay had already prefigured the inseparability, from the very founding of the British nation, of the imperial context.

Polly, for its part, enables us to read Old Corruption in its British mani-festation, and, by extension, in its Nigerian incarnation as well, as a by-product of imperial capitalist expansion. As a moment in the history of modern capitalist expansion, and in the formation of nation-states, Old Corruption can then perhaps best be understood not as a remnant of feu-dalism but, rather, as the *modern* reinflection of older cultural forms—above all, elite networks of patronage—to serve the interests of a new cash- and credit-based system.[46] This redeployment of residual cultural forms for a modern (and now dominant) capitalist logic is confirmed in *The Beggar's Opera* by the fate of the word "honour." Far from evoking a cavalier bastion of resistance to market forces, or even a sense of solidarity among thieves, "honour" seems already to have been fully absorbed within the atomizing logic of such forces.[47] By the same logic, then, post-independence Nigeria— struggling at this writing to emerge from a series of abortive civilian admin-istrations, a grisly civil war, and more than a generation of military dictatorships—cannot be properly understood as an atavistic throwback to a premodern Nigerian past. Rather, this oppressive historical pattern is pre-cisely an index of neocolonial modernity. For it is only through billions in oil-export revenues from such multinational corporations as the Royal Dutch Shell Company that the various military dictatorships have thrived since the coup of 1966, in parasitic opulence, despite the various modes of ruination that their terrifying irresponsibility has wrought.[48] *Opera Wonyosi*, then, depicts yet another moment in the global history of capital accumulation.

Resituating the Enlightenment

The juxtaposition of Gay and Soyinka ultimately produces a more nuanced reading of the eighteenth century both as a literary and a historical period. For the model of the imperial social formation that implicitly provides the basis for Soyinka's most powerful critique of imperialism, with its accompanying Eurocentrism, relies crucially on its prior articulation in the eighteenth century by writers such as Gay. It was indeed much more possible for Gay, writing in the earliest phases of the historical process of forging the nation, to document the implication of this process within the dynamics of an imperial force-field: for it is precisely the still-visible contingency of emergent nationalism—its umbilical link to the imperial womb—that is evident in Gay's duology of *Polly* and *The Beggar's Opera*. Later scholars and writers, operating from within a fully codified imperial hegemony, would learn to accept "nation" and "empire" as things apart. It is precisely such a rigid compartmentalization of nation and empire, however, that allows, in Gilroy's telling example, the assignment of slavery to the history of Black people exclusively.[49] Such a sanctioning of historical ignorance has serious consequences for the historiographies both of Europe and the imperially constituted "Third World." The lesson that Soyinka teaches us via Gay, then, is the need to return to the eighteenth century to document the origins not just of a Europe-dominated imperial system but also the lineage of its most powerful critiques.

This rethinking of the eighteenth century via Soyinka not only heralds the need for a more sophisticated reading of the period but also points toward a revaluation of contemporary scholarship on the period's most familiar icon: the Enlightenment. Soyinka has already warned elsewhere that "Icons can be positive or negative; a blanket iconoclasm is an undialectical proceeding on a par with blanket fetishisation of myth and history."[50] And the need for dialectical nuance is precisely Soyinka's lesson for current debates organized around the negative iconography haunting eighteenth-century studies. His work challenges the negative origination myth that haunts the academy: the bashing of the eighteenth century for all the woes of modernity. In fact, as Soyinka's thematizing of the imperial social formation through Gay demonstrates, it is precisely at the moment of their origins that culturally dominant discourses are most vulnerable, most visible. As Gay illustrates, the eighteenth century points not just to the formation of British nationhood but also to the ways in which British identity was so embedded within the empire as to be its derivative and secondary precipitate rather than its source and center. A practice of critique, then, must begin by affiliating with the iconoclasts generated from within the period of that destabilizing moment of origination.

Though Soyinka is far from an uncritical apologist for modernity, it must likewise be recognized that much of his political, intellectual, and cultural work in Nigeria does fall precisely under the heading of attempting to fulfill in Nigeria the unfinished project of modern democratization. Certainly Soyinka's most obvious sacrifices on behalf of public concerns in Nigeria— his 26 months as a political prisoner, his considerable time in exile, his principled resignations from academic posts, his various skirmishes with state censorship—all bespeak costly positions taken on behalf of "Enlightenment" values. As an agitator for democratic election and freedom of the press, moreover, Soyinka has insistently enunciated a language of universal human rights.[51] Soyinka publicly defended Salman Rushdie in 1989 after the notorious *fatwa* issued by Iran's Ayatollah Khomeini. For this stand, a defense of Rushdie's right to have published *The Satanic Verses*, he himself promptly received a death threat. While certain self-proclaimed progressives prattled about sensitivity to cultural differences throughout the controversy over *The Satanic Verses*; and while certain bookstore chains dithered about whether to sell such a controversial book, Soyinka put himself in harm's way for the sake of a universal principle. Even Soyinka's tenure as president of the Nigerian Federal Road Safety Commission, which eventually inspired his extraordinary play *The Road* (1965), was an exercise in Enlightenment rationality: an attempt to discipline the notoriously chaotic and deadly conditions, in both traffic and infrastructure, for drivers on Nigeria's main arteries.[52] It is a telling commentary on the limits of multiculturalism, especially as practiced in the United States, that Soyinka is typically slotted into survey courses to represent, usually on the basis of *Death and the King's Horseman* (1979), something like "the voice of African tradition." Brian Crow and Chris Branfield thus characterize Soyinka in terms of a "Nigerian theatre of ritual vision."[53] Even *Death and the King's Horseman*, which indeed features a challenge to individualistic sensibilities, represents the character who fulfills a tradition of Yoruba self-sacrifice as England-returned. Olunde is a voluntary and cosmopolitan participant in the ritual rather than a culture-bound naïf.

The current critical fashion of repudiating the Enlightenment wholesale—a veritable throwing of the baby out with the bathwater—can stand to learn a great deal from Soyinka's dialectical engagement with the period. For in *Opera Wonyosi*, at least, Soyinka leaves little doubt as to where he stands as regards the demystification of "traditional" metaphysical world-views made possible by Enlightenment values. In *Opera Wonyosi*, the public execution with which Macheath is threatened is attended by official representatives of all the local organized religions: a Roman Catholic priest, an Anglican priest, an Imam, a Sango priest, and the charismatic Protestant, Prophet Jeru. These characters replace the multiple wives who confront Gay's bigamous Macheath at the end of *The Beggar's Opera*. Like those wives, each of these religious functionaries claims Soyinka's bandit-leader as his own. The figure who represents an "indigenous" religion in this sanctimonious ensemble, the Sango priest, is by no means spared from Soyinka's withering satire. Macheath acknowledges the justice of the Sango priest's claim on him—"I like his style"[54]—after hearing his openly voiced desire to appropriate the bandit-leader's property: one bandit, in other words, recognizes another. The point of Soyinka's revision, then, is not primarily to mock infidelity to organized religion; for organized religion itself has become nothing more than a tool by which the state and its grotesque actions are sanctioned. Soyinka's critique, located firmly within the Enlightenment's assault on corrupt priesthoods, attacks mystification rather than supposed inauthenticity: an attack developed at great length in his two "Brother Jero" plays and *Requiem for a Futurologist*. Given the perversion of nationalist chauvinism in Nigeria, as in many a newly independent state, Soyinka simply cannot afford the luxury of an anti-rationalist posturing in the name of a supposed anti-imperial critique.

Indeed, Soyinka, who is widely known for experimenting with the theatrical resources of Yoruba metaphysics and ritual,[55] must also be seen as repeatedly demystifying easy counter-nationalist appeals to a reified "tradition." Such nativist reifications of tradition, which replicate a codifying and mummifying strategy frequently pursued by colonial rulers around the globe, lead directly to that most modern of phenomena, the "invented tradition."[56] It is precisely to identify the consequences of assuming that "tradition" is continuous, transparent, and traceable to a single geographical origin that Soyinka has coined such satirical epithets as "Neo-Tarzanism" and (from *Kongi's Harvest*) "glamourized fossilism."[57] Such a facile assumption leads directly, as the subtitle of his acerbic "reply in kind" to Chinweizu puts it, to "the poetics of Pseudo-Tradition." It is no small irony that invented traditions seem so compatible with postmodern theories that court absolute difference and incommensurability at the expense of some demonized modernity. In so far as these postmodern currents of thought reflect the influence of Foucault, moreover, their lapses may also reflect the short shrift that Foucault, for all his brilliance in elaborating a micropolitics of spatial domination, gives to such macropolitical topics as the narrative of empire and its related questions of sovereignty.[58]

Reading Gay after Soyinka, we are enabled to read the Scriblerians as having also gone before him: as having provided, that is to say, the basis for a critique that is not external, but, rather, thoroughly immanent to that which it criticizes. Soyinka has thus served to reconstellate the Scriblerians as among the important points of reference and departure for an emergent postcolonial literary tradition. Even more significantly, such a reading of Soyinka and the Scriblerians provides a site for rethinking the role of the eighteenth century in literary history and criticism. That is a larger achievement than many debates about the pointedly intertextual nature of much postcolonial writing have hitherto allowed; and it is one inseparably linked to the creative use of a historical vantage-point, in the liminality of the eighteenth century, rather than a merely geographic location.

CHAPTER 5

RUTHERFORD'S TRAVELS: THE PALIMPSEST OF CULTURE IN CHARLES JOHNSON'S *MIDDLE PASSAGE*

if the multiculturalists are using an outmoded notion of race, then their categories are problematic for me.

—Charles Johnson, *I Call Myself an Artist*

I had to listen harder to isolate him [his father] from the We that swelled each particle and pore of him, as if the (black) self was the greatest of all fictions; and then I could not find him at all.

—Rutherford Calhoun, *Middle Passage*

Charles Johnson's *Middle Passage* (1990) is a neo-slave narrative: a stellar member of the flourishing subgenre of contemporary novels that fictionalize stories of slavery. Johnson describes his purpose in *Middle Passage* as attempting to use the vehicle of the slave narrative, with its formal progression from bondage to freedom, to explore concepts of liberation "in a spiritual, in a sexual, in a metaphysical sense."[1] In so doing, he excavates the older tradition of spiritual autobiography, from John Bunyan to St. Augustine, that persists as a sedimented layer in a great many slave narratives. Given Johnson's own spiritual practice, however, *Middle Passage* invites comparison more with distinguished narratives expressing Buddhist ideals such as Herman Hesse's *Siddhartha* (1922) and Peter Matthiessen's *The Snow Leopard* (1978). Apparently working with materials that speak for themselves, Johnson insists on bringing philosophical scrutiny to bear both on their representations of reality and of the recording self. In *Middle Passage*, he combines the witnessing or transcribing project often ascribed to the slave-narrative with a meditative exploration of concepts so foundational that they provide the basis for classifying, for instance, "first-person narratives."

The self-conscious texture of his novel thus points to the fictive nature of identities constituted—as reified "facts"—by such alienating social institutions as slavery.

Johnson observes in *Oxherding Tale* that "the Age of Reason overlaps the age of slavery,"[2] and he looks back to the Enlightenment in *Middle Passage* in part to interrogate this conjunction. Johnson's response to this overlap, however, is neither to condemn wholesale the well-documented rationalizing of everyday social life as such nor to minimize slavery as an unfortunate anomaly in the grand march of progress. *Middle Passage* is too subtle to trap itself as merely "for" or "against" modernity. *Middle Passage* explores, by way of a Hanoverian context, a rich body of historical, generic, and allusive links to the eighteenth century. In returning to this moment, Johnson evokes the trans-Atlantic tradition that links Thomas Jefferson to John Locke, and colonial America to Great Britain. The Lockean social contract, which links property rights to sovereignty over oneself, makes property as such central to slave narratives. Johnson's exploration of these issues, however, complicates a more obvious trajectory of individual fulfillment—from chattel to self-determination—in order to explore questions of ownership as regards the writing of history.

Middle Passage compels reflection on the contested moment when human achievements began to be subjected to modern, nation-based institutions. *Middle Passage* thus opens up a broader meditation on the concept of ownership that is explored from unexpected angles and on unfamiliar scales. In writing against the lure of romantic nationalism, moreover, Johnson revisits central conflicts of the British eighteenth century. His approach to writing novels celebrates cosmopolitan intertextuality in deliberate opposition to folkloric essentialism and false claims to immediacy. Such claims often serve to short-circuit the writing of history. More than any other single issue in *Middle Passage*, questions about historiographical assumptions link the work to Olaudah Equiano's *Interesting Narrative* (1789). By way of this marked act of affiliation, Johnson develops his literary project in *Middle Passage:* the attempt to imagine a truly common history. The transitional quality of the eighteenth-century moment, especially as regards narratives of empire and nation, creates intellectual space for Johnson to make an exceptionally acute commentary on the American version of modernity. Johnson looks back to the eighteenth century precisely for purposes of a certain liberatory *dispossession*: to dislodge easy illusions about unreflective claims to the "ownership" of experience.

In Johnson's novels, links to the eighteenth century and its metafictive literary techniques thus serve to distance the reader from illusions that are self-centered and circular in their logic. In 1995, Johnson recalls, in his introduction to a new edition of *Oxherding Tale*, a wide-ranging appropriation of literary devices in the creation of that novel. Defiantly eclectic, he mentions devices that hearken back to Fielding and Sterne as well as elements drawn from Buddhism, Hinduism, and Chinese philosophy. "For," he asks rhetorically, "isn't all of human history—the effort of all men and women, East and West, to make sense of the world—our inheritance?"[3] Johnson's intimacy with the eighteenth-century moment is deeply marked and richly significant. In "The Manumission of First-Person Viewpoint," one of his "intrusive-narrator" chapters near the conclusion of the *Oxherding Tale*, he uses a Fieldingesque manner to disenchant the "I" as an illusory category of narrative focalization. *Oxherding Tale* also begins, as does *Tristram Shandy*, with the circumstances of the protagonist's conception. Hence a notable aesthetic coup: Johnson in effect finds in the British Enlightenment intellectual and spiritual tools congenial to his poetics of Buddhist non-attachment.

Historical Mediations

The earliest signal that Johnson intends a deliberate affiliation with the British eighteenth century is found in the prefatory acknowledgments giving us the original—and perhaps we may now say the alternative—title: *Rutherford's Travels*. Set in 1830, *Middle Passage* evokes the era of the four Georges: the Hanoverian period during which Britain dominated the slave-trade and, eventually, generated the political will for its abolition. Since the official trade had become illegal after 1808 both in Britain and the United States, the ship featured in the novel is a contraband slaver. The book deliberately recollects the rough maritime ethos of the Enlightenment. Harsh as this maritime culture could be, it revealed the porous nature of national boundaries. Given that modernity is defined in no small part by its unique ability to transplant and transform vast populations, "Blackness" itself in that sense epitomizes the "modern," as Paul Gilroy has argued. The anguished quandaries explored by artistic and philosophical modernism—the rampant themes of alienation, doubt, dislocation, and so on—might be said to find their most poignant harbingers in the African diaspora and its countercultural creations.[4] Hence the special significance of "Black Jacks": black sailors, both free and enslaved, whose large presence both in British and American history is finally getting attention. "Seafaring men were in the vanguard," as W. Jeffrey Bolster argues, "of defining a new black ethnicity for the many African persons dispersed by Atlantic slavery."[5] Johnson's act of affiliation with the eighteenth century thus serves to highlight the historical liminality of the Georgian era: its obstinate tendency to trouble the micro- and macro-political categories that define the modernity that would, for better or worse, finally arrive. The nation and the individual, by way of the political categories of subject and citizen, go hand in hand, and *Middle Passage* sets out to unsettle both.

Johnson enters the topic of property, as well as that of collective identities, as a philosophical problem. *Middle Passage* seems written to explore, from every possible angle, the question of who "owns" Olaudah Equiano's story. *Middle Passage* is of course titled so as to conjure up the unspeakable experience of enslaved Africans on the way to the new world, jam-packed like sardines into the foul hold of a slave ship. In that sense, the "middle passage" names the historical background to which a term such as "African American" alludes. Equiano's *Interesting Narrative* contains the single most influential description ever written of the "middle passage." Here is how Equiano describes it:

> I was soon put down under the decks, and there I received such a salutation in my nostrils as I had never experienced in my life; so that with the loathe-someness of the stench, and crying together, I became so sick that I could not eat, nor had I the least desire to taste anything. I now wished for the last friend, Death, to relieve me. . . .[6]

Laconic as it is, Equiano's description of the middle passage approaches the limits of what can be told or even imagined. For Johnson, the later recep-tion of Equiano is likewise at stake: the further and ongoing appropriations of his story, after his death, for various agendas.

Through the exploration of concepts of ownership, *Middle Passage* reworks the slave-narrative as a genre. *Middle Passage* audaciously refuses to recuperate the mental universe of the contemporary moment—its categories of private possession, cultural patrimony, and ascriptive identities—through a more nuanced dialogue with the past. Can history be written without reifying it as the experiential property of a particular group? Johnson writes in the neo-slave narrative genre precisely in order to explore the philosophical questions, for such corporate entities as nations and races, lurking in the middle passage. Equally crucial to Johnson's enterprise, however, is a philosophical era many might find surprising: the British Enlightenment.

In a novel so preoccupied with the many implications of ownership, the "ownership" of the colonial American period itself quickly emerges as a historiographical issue. *Middle Passage* insistently points to the way that nation-making in the crucible of the new world—the imagining of a specifically *American* community—extended the British imperial enter-prise. Even before the American Revolution, the supersession of one empire by another was foreseen by Bishop George Berkeley, whose "On the Prospect of Planting Arts and Learning in America"—using the familiar "westering" trope—concludes as follows:

> Westward the Course of Empire takes its Way;
>   The first four Acts already past,
> A fifth shall close the Drama with the Day;
>   Time's noblest Offspring is the last.[7]

In 1752, Berkeley, with sunny optimism, celebrates the prospect of an American empire. Eminent historians sometimes agree. Henry Steele Commager has presented the United States, precisely in this vein, as fulfilling an Enlightenment that began across the Atlantic. Indeed, to epitomize the Enlightenment was to be the "special destiny"[8] of the United States: Commager's version of American exceptionalism.

While claiming the achievements of the Enlightenment, American exceptionalism simultaneously serves to disown an unpalatable history. "A preoccupation with the exceptional elements of the American experience," as Eric Foner writes, "obscures those common patterns and processes that transcend national boundaries, most notably the global expansion of capitalism in the nineteenth and twentieth centuries and its political and ideological ramifications."[9] And given the imperial history of the United States—from colonial genesis through slavery, westward expansion, Latin American adventures, cold-war proxy conflicts, and hyperpower muscularity—sunny optimism cannot be sustained two and a half centuries later. The historian Francis Jennings is refreshingly lucid about the actual birth and development of America by way of a racially exclusionary land-grab: "By the great power of racial conceptions, varied Europeans are merged as 'whites' to share in what has been called *herrenvolk* democracy, and it was in this form that governmental power spread across the continent as legal institutions."[10] Prevailing public memory in the United States has yet to find a graceful way of owning up to the implications of having dispossessed Native Americans on a continental scale. Even earnest pieties around the issue of racial slavery often betrays the jingoistic assumption of an exceptional American destiny. After the North's victory, the same federal army deployed against the Confederacy and its slave-based society would be used against Native Americans. *Middle Passage* is specifically "postcolonial" in the extent to which it insists on addressing the particular implication of the United States in a global narrative of colonial aggression.

Empire-building has long accompanied nation-building in the United States. Joel Barlow's epic *Columbiad* (1804–1807), an American text devoted to propagating the "Manifest Destiny" myth, imagines that the Genoese explorer is granted a vision of the future to which he contributed so materially. Despite dark passages about slavery and the conquest of America, Barlow's Columbus is consoled by the triumphant progress of arts and science on the North American continent. Columbus observes the events of the American Revolution and learns that the citizens of the United States, like the Israelites, have a divinely sponsored mission to perform. Indeed, the entire world will eventually be united by commerce, joined beneath "one white flag of peace triumphant."[11] *The Columbiad* mediates between past and future by defining a utopian break between the old world and the new. That break is of course also the subject of *Middle Passage*, which is necessarily less utopian. Such issues are inevitably implicit in the texture of the Neo-Slave Narrative. *Middle Passage*, takes up these issues with cool lucidity. *Middle Passage* looks back across the Atlantic to eighteenth- and early-nineteenth-century Britain to comment on the United States of America, then a "fledgling republic."[12] Describing a ship named the *Republic*, the novel plays with the ship-of-state *topos*, depicting the American ship/nation as riven by mutinies, buffeted randomly to and fro by the currents of history, zigzagging without much discernible progress, constantly "flying apart," and constantly being "re-formed." In bringing skeptical scrutiny to bear on the communities imagined in the name of nation and race, *Middle Passage* goes beyond a concern with slavery only, as a unique and isolated phenomenon. From his location as an African American in the late twentieth century, Johnson revisits the larger imperial process imagined by Berkeley and Barlow. He insists on complicating the question of who can be said to "own" the experiences of slavery, and westward expansion, and imperial conquest.

The day-by-day "journal of the Republic"—a trope, of course, for America's slavery-ridden past—includes ledgers toting up the economic value of gold, ivory, and enslaved Africans. This log is eventually "bequeathed" to the novel's narrator, Rutherford Calhoun, by its original author, Ebenezer Falcon, who commissions Calhoun to be his biographer. Falcon, a monstrous amalgam of brutality and knowledge, was born "when the nation was but a few hours old."[13] Though a physical dwarf, he is a titan of linguistic expertise (like such imperial polymaths as Sir William Jones and Sir Richard Burton, among others). Like James Bruce and Mungo Park, among others, he searched for the source of the Nile in the interior of Africa. Like too many European "explorers" and archeologists to name, he has ruthlessly plundered the sacred treasures of other cultures. Indeed, in the novel's most daring twist, he has highjacked the living deity of the tribe of sorcerers—the Allmuseri—who constitute the "live cargo" trapped in the hold of the ship. A parodic embodiment of the Enlightenment at its most warped, Falcon has a "great bulging forehead."[14] Linked to famous pirates such as Captain Blood (a fictive character based in part on Sir Henry Morgan) and Captain Teach,[15] his greatest act of piracy is of course carried out in the name of "manifest destiny": for, above all, he is a builder of empire. Like Cecil Rhodes, who regretted his inability to colonize the stars, Falcon burns with a passion to "Americanize the entire planet."[16] Marc Steinberg sees Johnson, via Rutherford, as "overwriting the tradition of the slave narrative and historical writing about slavery that claims to be 'true.'"[17] It is also Ebenezer Falcon's blood-stained story, reaching far beyond "America" as such, that Rutherford Calhoun "inherits," and must rewrite.

Middle Passage, as a fictive artifact, explicitly presents itself as a palimpsest. Rutherford Calhoun writes his journal-like reconstruction of the voyage *over* the logbook of the *Republic*: the ship's official record, and thus an archival source constituted by and for the powerful. A rich and triumphant appropriation, Calhoun's writing is, nevertheless, also explicitly commissioned by Falcon. Badly maimed during the mutinies, Falcon—apparently still keen on posthumous fame—admonishes Calhoun to keep the log so others will know "the truth of what happened on this voyage."[18] Calhoun accepts this charge, promising himself that he will tell the story "first and foremost, as I saw it since my escape from New Orleans."[19] The layerings and mediations made explicit in this genesis of the story highlight the complexity of biographical, artistic, and cultural "ownership." Rutherford begins as a thief (a false species of transcendence) and ends as a writer (a truer one). Johnson thus inscribes his novel with a carefully crafted stance as regards the writing of history, which is ultimately figured not as a mere witnessing, but, rather, as a *reappropriation*.

The many ironies of this situation are foreshadowed by Falcon on his deathbed, where he confesses to an apocalyptic nightmare—"the last hour of history"—that involved the inversion of his entire world. "Hegel," he tells Calhoun, "was spewing from the mouth of Hottentots."[20] *Middle Passage* is perhaps intended as an extended reflection on the historical significance of this particular nightmare: Africans who not only reason, but have the temerity to appropriate precisely that philosopher who denied them that human faculty. As a theorist of the geographical basis of world history, Hegel traced the progress of "Reason" from east to west, a narrative shoe-horned into rough alignment with the hemispheric "progress" of certain civilizations. The result of this narrative was the capstone of modern Eurocentric ideology: the official claiming, as specifically "Western," of the faculty of rationality. Africa, writes Hegel, is "an unhistorical continent, with no movement or development of its own."[21] This "spatial vision of history," as Martin W. Lewis and Kären E. Wigen point out, "was tremendously influential through the mid-twentieth century."[22] Yet the master–slave dialectic in Hegel's thinking offers more to alternative versions of history—versions emanating from epistemological standpoints of the oppressed—than Hegel himself may have anticipated. It is clear that Rutherford Calhoun subverts the "Westering-of-Reason" narrative proposed by Hegel. Making provisional use of the dialectical method, however, he produces an alternative understanding of history that embraces impurity and flawed intermeshings. Rutherford is indeed symbolically "married" to Captain Falcon, who gives him a ring in exchange for acting as his spy; and he switches allegiance several times during the chaos of the successive mutinies. Rutherford's story, then, is conspicuously impure; but the success of his reappropriation of history perhaps lies in establishing the universality of such hybridity. Such impurity, indeed, is posed over and against the secularized Puritanism of Falcon, whose Emersonian "self-reliance" is manifest as lunatic perfectionism, bleak solitude, self-flagellation, and suicidal tendencies.[23] With only one working eye, Falcon "lacks binocular vision," and he confesses that other people are not real to him.[24] Captain Falcon does eventually die by his own hand: an act that fulfills his denial of intersubjectivity. No less than it rejects a reified "West," *Middle Passage* rejects any such atomized understanding of an "individual."

The relation of "ownership" to history involves both the sharing of human achievements and assuming responsibility for particular barbarities. To disown complicity is to lie: a vice, according to *Gulliver's Travels*, that afflicts the whole world, but especially the Europeans. Rutherford thus sometimes feels "cool" toward Peter Cringle, the otherwise likeable first mate, "who would never in this life see himself, his own blighted history, in the slaves we intended to sell. . . ."[25] The middle passage must be owned by all who participated in it. In the cast of characters that makes up *Middle Passage*, the culpable include not only the obvious suspects—every sailor aboard the *Republic*, starting with Captain Falcon—but also some less obvious ones: an Arab slave merchant (Ahman-de-Bellah), for example, and the English-educated Owen Bogha—son of an African princess and a Liverpool slave-trader—who owns and supervises the trading post on the Guinea coast. Then there is Phillipe Zeringue, the Creole gangster who dominates his neighborhood in New Orleans, where he is something of a folk hero. Papa Zeringue proves to be one of three owners of the *Republic*: investors in the sordid traffic. Though the great preponderance of guilt lies with greedy whites—the other two slave-trade speculators are white—the world of *Middle Passage* leaves very little room for unsullied innocence. Johnson refuses to launch his critique of the past from a standpoint of imagined innocence. Since very few people truly qualify as innocent—as free of complicity with structures of oppression—the demand for innocence is, at best, politically self-defeating. Moreover, those who genuinely believe in their own innocence are often profoundly dangerous: willing to kill in the name of their version of the truth.

Middle Passage makes clear why narrowly communal claims to the ownership of a certain historical experience lead to a political and philosophical cul-de-sac. Though Rutherford Calhoun is changed by his encounter with the African Allmuseri, he discovers that he does not automatically "belong" to their culture, and he does not construct them as any sort of origination myth. The Allmuseri, in any case, are themselves visibly changing under the pressure of the middle passage: "Stupidly," Calhoun writes, "I had seen their lives and culture as timeless product, a finished thing. . . ."[26] Since the Allmuseri language emphasizes process over abstraction, and exalts verbs over nouns, they would seem to well-equipped to handle change. The horrific violence that they experience, however—and especially the violence that they commit—inevitably alters the balance of the culture they had brought aboard the *Republic*. That culture had so abhorred divisiveness that its members had lacked even the individuating symbol of fingerprints. The Allmuseri had constituted their reality as a unity of being: precisely what the "American crimes" of the middle passage disrupt. This moral and epistemological rupture may be Johnson's most profound attempt to grasp the significance of the middle passage. The Allmusseri— "No longer Africans," as Rutherford observes, "yet not Americans either."[27]—are not a suitable vehicle for the recovery of "roots."

As the Allmusseri change before Calhoun's eyes, they produce a violent leader, Diamelo—heretofore considered a wastrel and bully by his fellow Allmuseri—who emerges as the ruthless counterpart to harsh new realities. Diamelo, moreover, defines himself by the experience of oppression during the middle passage:

> it was easy to see his bondage in the barracoon, then, as the most significant, the most memorable, even the finest hour of his life, a memory to safeguard and strengthen, to designate as the anno Domini demarcation since his birth two decades before.[28]

In this case, the "ownership" of oppression becomes a sort of fetish. Though Ebenezer Falcon is dead, moreover, Diamelo defines himself over and against the continuing influence of his spirit. Falcon is the unexorcised "Other" that validates his new regime—an inverted mirror-image and alter ego:

> But there, in the barracoon Diamelo found his long-delayed focus: Ebenezer Falcon, a true (godsent) devil to despise. A dragon so exquisite in his evil that Diamelo, never a boy to impress his people by his skills or social contributions, discovered that no one spoke of his flaws and personal failings when all their lives were wreckage.[29]

A deliberately anachronistic parody of decolonization ensues: new rules about language, religion, songs, stories, eye-contact with women, and food. Diamelo's inflexible rules, largely ignored by the starving and battered crew, prove to be futile in a broader sense. They could not undo history, and they could not restore the "four-dimensional" set of equations that previously constituted Allmuseri culture.

To claim ownership of a narrative, it seems, may mean to be possessed by its power. Rutherford's hair begins turning white after he witnesses the events of the middle passage, and he recalls wondering

> how, in God's name I could go on after seeing this? How could I feel whole after seeing it? How could I tell my children of it without placing a curse on them forever? How could I even dare to have children in a world so senseless?[30]

Such questions obviously inform the genres both of the slave-narrative itself and that of the fictive neo-slave narrative. If the cruel story is, in current parlance, "sensitizing," it may likewise be heart-numbing. It seems especially salutary, in this vein, to note that Olaudah Equiano marks the fact that his suffering is not entirely unique:

> but still I feared I should be put to death, the white people looked and acted, as I thought, in so savage a manner; for I had never seen among any people such instances of brutal cruelty; and this not only shewn towards us blacks, but also to some of the whites themselves. One white man in particular I saw, when we were permitted to be on deck, flogged so unmercifully with a large rope near the foremast, that he died in consequence of it; and they tossed him over the side as they would have done a brute.[31]

Such moments avoid making a fixed identity out of one's suffering.

Middle Passage does not claim merely to represent a neglected "black experience" or to articulate a lost "black voice." The specific philosophical point of *Middle Passage* revolves around the dialectical mediations of experience: experience that must be first made into a discrete entity *before* its history can be made, or told, or indeed sold, as a commodity. Even shipboard cannibalism, as Calhoun notes, can be recuperated as a perversely exotic "experience." Captain Falcon likes to boast, amongst genteel land-lubbers, of having eaten a black cabin-boy. The significance of this shocking boast expresses an intersubjective desire for recognition: the desire, which Rutherford reads in Falcon's eyes, to be a fascinating object "in the eyes of others."[32] Johnson approaches the task of writing a neo-slave narrative precisely through this insistence on a dialectic of intersubjective recognition—whether mutual and reciprocal, or asymmetrical and "monocular"—as a prevalent dynamic of history. "Race," however, is not presented as a given or self-evident category of human experience. Skin-color notwithstanding, the Allmusseri do not see Rutherford Calhoun as one of them. Calhoun writes of the most prominent Allmusseri elders, Ngonyama, "the distance between his people and black America was vast—his people saw whites as Raw Barbarians and me (being a colored mate) as a Cooked one."[33]

Johnson is not advocating here the bad-faith position of "color-blindness." The point—aside from a sly parody of the famous distinction in Claude Lévy-Strauss between "Raw" and "Cooked"—is more subtle: a demonstration that color as such, as an artifact of perception, is mediated by the cultural mapping of insiders and outsiders. In this specific sense *Middle Passage* illustrates a tendency common to the genre of the neo-slave narrative: critical engagement with "the anthropological idea of race" as a category of social performance and regulation.[34] By analyzing the points of exchange between "inside" and "outside" racialized positions, *Middle Passage* undermines overly easy the immediate notions of racial history. Peter Hallward, one of the novel's most acute readers, suggests that Johnson's critique of "enforced placement" risks affirming "displacement pure and simple."[35] To this issue we shall return later.

Claiming Equiano

Can identities be owned? The slave-narrative involves the attempt, through reflection and memory, to appropriate one's individual history as one's own. A politics of memory and re-telling is thus heavily invested in the genre as such, and the question of "owning" one's story has an especially potent political charge. To some extent, of course, similar paradoxes of voice emerge in connection with biography and autobiography more generally. The retrospective recounting of anyone's individual memory is universally a mode of pattern-finding that simultaneously secures—and threatens to reify—identities that are constantly being remade. The trajectory of a slave-narrative, however, involves accounting for the conditions of its existence as an "owned" story. By definition, the story involves an experience of slavery, where one's life is not one's own, and where the means to record that alienated existence are largely absent. The story arcs toward a more or less perilous achievement of legal freedom, whether by manumission or by the underground railroad. Finally, and almost by definition, a slave-narrative must recount the hard-earned acquisition of literacy that makes the former slave the conscious subject—and not just the mute and reified object—of the narrative. In the famous chiasmus devised by Frederick Douglass, his goal is to show how a man became a slave, and a slave became a man. To an acute degree, the genre of the slave-narrative evidently involves *reappropriating* an identity that has been grievously violated. And because that recreated identity is inevitably hybrid, there can be no seamless narrative—no smoothly sequential experience of one human life cycle—that can easily encompass the conflictual series of appropriations and reappropriations that constitute the struggle to possess, in all possible senses, one's own history.

Literacy itself is central to the story. It often marks a moment when the narrator can "belong," at least to the republic of letters; and can thus become an autonomous cultural agent, qualified to intervene in public debates. The genre thus inscribes an intimate link between "freedom" and the acquisition of literacy. Such an acquisition is necessarily a moment of acculturation as well, however, and this acculturation necessarily raises new questions of identity about collective belonging and ownership on a wider scale. Moreover, it is inevitable that reception history—the incorporation of slave-narratives into later written traditions and contexts—raises all sorts of urgent questions about the institutions, such as literature, that shape national cultures.

The original question of the ownership of Equiano's life has been replayed, through various cultural cartographers, on the familiar terrains of nation and race. Equiano "belongs" not to a single discrete history, but to a welter of competing histories and agendas. The question of his "race" simply cannot be entirely solved by brisk appeals to common sense. Equiano, like Wheatley, has frequently seemed marginal to critics engaged in constructing a "Black" tradition. His other identities—as Christian, as British sailor, and as quoter of British authors—seem to interfere with the desire for cultural autonomy often involved in tracing racially marked traditions. He did not have the same set of priorities later associated with "proper" black identification. Like Wheatley, for example, he apparently valued Christianity more than the indigenous religion of his youth. Despite his pointedly dark-complexioned portrait on the frontispiece of his autobiography, and despite his calling himself "the African" on the title page of his book, Equiano has sometimes been found, in effect, "not black enough." A recent edited volume seems to update this approach by considering him in the context of "passing."[36] Such a judgment smacks of "premature normativity": an "all-too-quick reification," in the words of Seyla Benhabib, "of given group identities."[37]

Who owns Equiano's story? The case for thinking of Equiano as Afro-British initially seems quite strong. Having publicly advocated interracial marriage in Britain, he married an Englishwoman, Susan Cullen, in 1792; (their surviving daughter, Johanna Vassa, inherited the considerable sum of 950 pounds in 1816); he converted to a Methodist mode of evangelical Christianity based in England, apparently with great sincerity; linguistically, his accent was undoubtedly "British"; he constructed his own written text so as to include many allusions to English writers; he fought on the British side against the French during the Seven Years War; and—perhaps above all—he directed his political activism for the cause of abolition to the centers of power in Britain, petitioning Queen Charlotte in 1788 and addressing his autobiography to Parliament in 1789. Equiano's involvement in abolitionist politics was reinforced by his connection with radical workingmen's correspondence societies in the 1790s—a fact that adds a black dimension to the "making of the English working class." As Walvin likewise points out, Equiano's involvement with the London Correspondence Society in the early 1790s reflects the extent to which Equiano was a product of the Enlightenment.[38]

Did Equiano really belong to any country? It must also be remembered that he probably spent more days of his life aboard a ship than on land in Britain or elsewhere. He preferred to remain a sailor after gaining his legal freedom, and probably found, as Angelo Costanzo suggests, a masculine camaraderie in life aboard a British ship that was more flexible than British society as such.[39] Perhaps Equiano, as a representative of an African diaspora, simply falls between the cracks of national identities. Since he was involved, somewhat abortively, in the Sierra Leone project of resettling free Africans (and lascars) in Africa, it could be argued that he flirted with a separatist impulse. Had he himself relocated in Sierra Leone, his hard-earned acculturation to Britishness would have surely undergone yet another metamorphosis. When Equiano reports being rebuked for talking "too much English," he marks the limits to his ability to assimilate on equal terms. His fascination with Turkey, where dark-complexioned people ruled over lighter ones, is another telling symptom of his dislocation. Above all, one would have to note that his tentative "belonging" to Britain was the product of kidnapping; and that he could scarcely have felt that his legal rights and cultural status in England were firmly secured.

A literate Equiano was, in effect, an unintended consequence of the imperial circulation of peoples. His acculturation into eighteenth-century "Britishness" was a hand dealt to him by the vicissitudes of a harsh history; and he played that very difficult hand with considerable flair and rhetorical self-awareness. There is thus something liminal as well about Equiano's relation to blackness and whiteness as seamlessly naturalized identities: a "transgressive" quality celebrated by some for its subversions of our contemporary habits of thought. I would add that it is precisely this—a provocative liminality as regards certain key issues of identity—that marks Equiano as a specifically eighteenth-century writer. His earliness, as regards the ideological construction of modern racial identities, is everywhere visible in the pages of his autobiography. Along with Wheatley, he is just beginning to create "blackness" as an identity that is claimed rather than merely imposed. Like Wheatley again, he refers rather casually to his dark complexion as "sable." His autobiography never suggests that he finds the inner meaning of his existence to reside in this particular complexion. Beginnings—as opposed to mystified origins—expose perplexing contingencies, and that is precisely what makes them so significant.

Equiano's *Interesting Narrative*—with two names on its title page, "Gustavus Vassa" and "Olaudah Equiano"—makes painfully visible the extent to which the claimed ownership of a former slave's autobiography stands at the margin of institutions surrounding literacy and authorship. The deeper interpretive questions begin, however, with the question of audience. Most students of slave-narratives understand them as urgently addressed, in their own time, to a society that condoned slavery and prospered from its effects. Such narratives are usually described as seeking to get across an abolitionist message through a powerfully compelling representation of the experience of slavery. In this view, the individual biography assumes a responsibility to speak on behalf of the vast numbers whom the institution of slavery have rendered politically inaudible. Such an instrumentalist view of the generic "message," whether seen as activist virtue or propagandistic defect, constrains readings of slave-narratives. Another burden for the genre springs from the situation of addressing a readership implicated, at least to some extent, in the very institution the author proposes to abolish. A degree of ingratiation seems intrinsic to the genre: a mode of indirection, or doubling of voices, that invites critical sensitivity to irony. We understand the irony involved when Equiano blandly addresses the British parliament as representatives of a nation renowned for "its liberal sentiments," "its humanity," "the glorious freedom of its government," and so on, even though it participated in tearing him away from "all the tender connections naturally dear to [his] heart." The dedication to Equiano's *Interesting Narrative* (1789) begins, quite appropriately, with this telling contradiction.[40]

The paradox of "voice" in a slave-narrative, however, often goes beyond the relatively readable trope of stable irony. That paradox has to do with the logic of ownership, as it applies at multiple levels: first of all, the legal status of the enslaved person as the property of another; next, the former slave's relationship to a disrupted past; and, finally, the selective appropriation of that individual act of remembrance itself within broader narratives of collective history. Those collective narratives involves boundaries, however they are drawn and redrawn; and they necessarily involve acts of selective remembrance based on what "belongs" to the broader story. We are less immediately certain how to read the closing exhortation in Equiano's *Interesting Narrative*, which looks forward not only to the replacement of the slave-trade by legitimate commerce, but also to the impact of "free-trade imperialism" in Africa: the insensible adoption by Africans—now consumers, rather than commodities—of "British fashions, manners, customs, &c."[41] This liberal discourse of expansionary commerce is a function of Britain's late-eighteenth-century rise to world economic dominance, and Equiano's text is indeed situated "at the focus of a profound cultural transformation."[42]

In appropriating this discourse—an economic argument against slavery—Equiano seems to position himself as a spokesman for the British empire. Indeed, Equiano's emphasis on commercial and entrepreneurial virtues, as Abbe Henri Gregoire pointed out long ago, link his story to that of Robinson Crusoe.[43] If Equiano's narrative invites comparison with Crusoe's, the basis for such a comparison lies precisely in the especially marked way that the British eighteenth century in general registers the awkward—and often brutal—transition to capitalist modernity. Crusoe's tremendous guilt over having disobeyed his father, and his pattern-finding search for providential significance amongst the episodic incidents of his life's story, register another version of that rugged transition. The overlap, needless to say, troubles familiar categories of identity.

Equiano's *Interesting Life* was skillfully used by the social movement, institutionalized in 1787 by the Society to Abolish the Slave Trade, to abolish slave-traffic. Like Phillis Wheatley's *Poems on Various Subjects* (1773), it was an obvious success as abolitionist propaganda, and clearly served to invigorate domestic opposition to Britain's involvement in the slave-trade. Though it went through many editions, however, Equiano's *Interesting Life* was not until rather recently incorporated into prevailing notions of British literature. A certain racialized notion of "Britishness" preemptively served to relegate Equiano to a history deemed "external" to the British nation. One consequence is that Equiano's role in the political achievement of abolition has often been neglected. Times are changing. Equiano is now often included in anthologies of British literature; he figures in monographs like this one about the eighteenth century; and he certainly counts as the prime example of eighteenth-century black British writing. The belatedness of Equiano's inclusion ought to be set alongside the stubborn fact of a long-standing "black presence" within the boundaries of Britain. As scholars now agree, a population of some 5,000 black Britons existed in London alone in Equiano's own time. The inclusion of Equiano two centuries later—a gesture enabled by the dynamics of a moment needing to stretch the prevailing definition of British national culture—ought to remind one of that earlier "black presence." Not recent immigration alone, but imperial relocations dating back to the Georgian era and before, produced the current cultural mix of Britain. Equiano exemplifies the need to enlarge our categories of Britishness.

One can also read Equiano's story in a Heinemann's edition that claims him, above all, as an *African* writer: part of a highly distinguished Anglophone tradition in Nigeria that also includes Wole Soyinka and Chinua Achebe. Following Nigerian independence in the early 1960s, Thomas Hodgkins, Philip Curtin, and Paul Edwards had all discovered Equiano, as James Walvin points out, "in and from Africa," where he was viewed as "a major figure in both Nigerian and, more generally, West African literary and historical culture."[44] Paul Edwards likewise suggests that Equiano's notably fatalistic Methodism, usually ascribed to Calvinist tendencies, might owe something to the West African theology of "Chi."[45] This West African contextualization aims to reveal continuity: the possible persistence of Ibo frameworks in the sense Equiano made of his life.

In a very different vein, however, the most skeptical critique of Equiano's fidelity to personal authenticity comes from the pen of an Nigerian critic, S. E. Ogude, who casts doubt on Equiano's claims to remember the sociological nuances of the Ibo culture he involuntarily left behind at age 11. Equiano's reconstruction of his African childhood, as a man in his forties, based in London, is likely to be compromised by the impact of a traumatic break. His act of recollection—he terms it "the imperfect sketch, with which my memory has furnished me"[46]—is, at the very least, oriented to the purpose of making Africans seem more familiar and less strange to a particular audience. It may also have been, as Ogude argues, mediated by details taken from contemporary European travel narratives.[47] Equiano's memories of such adult issues as customs regarding adultery and menstruation, for example, seem to have been filtered through some sort of ethnographic model. Ogude leans heavily on the fictionalizing aspect, suggesting that Equiano also drew on legends about Africa current among his fellow slaves. While this need not be construed as deliberate falsification, it does highlight a tension between neutral reflection and creativity. The pressure to be scrupulously mimetic collides with the demands of emplotment, and the fact/fiction issue inevitably emerges. The abridged edition of this work issued under the title *Equiano's Travels*, with its echo of the Gulliverian fiction, might be more suggestive than intended.[48]

Equiano quite possibly did not after all have *any* direct experience of the middle passage, and the account of his African boyhood may have been a fabrication. The meticulous archival research of Vincent Carretta, while providing independent verification of almost all of Equiano's autobiography, has unearthed unsettling evidence as regards his place of birth. According to extant parish records, one "Gustavus Vassa," baptised at age 12 in 1759, was "born in Carolina"; and a ship's muster book, from a ship mentioned in Equiano's autobiography, likewise records a South Carolinian origin for a sailor named Gustavus Vassa (with "Vassa" spelled "Weston").[49] This evidence of North American origins, as Carretta emphasizes, cannot be considered conclusive. The discovery nevertheless compels sober speculation, and seems likely to demand a somewhat different way of understanding the *Interesting Narrative*. Certainly the question of the author's intimacy with the reader—one of the strongest effects of the *Interesting Narrative*—might require qualification. Even the name "Olaudah Equiano" may turn out to be an imaginative act of self-naming: not an identity *revealed*, as Carretta puts it, but one *assumed*.[50] Perhaps "Olaudah Equiano" did not exist, as such, until Equiano began to advertise for subscribers to his *Interesting Narrative*. Perhaps the name is a fictive invention designed to guarantee that the author is an eye-witness to the middle passage. Such a demand for immediacy and authenticity—the first person account—was of course exactly the logic by which, in the later eighteenth century, all sorts of peasant poets were valorized, as supposedly unlettered. Such a demand for authenticity implies, as Charles Johnson writes in *Oxherding Tale*, that "what we value most highly are precisely the *limitations* imposed upon the narrator-perceiver. . . ."[51] If Equiano's African boyhood turns out to be a retrospective fabrication in the course of a story that is otherwise forthrightly told, that exceptional fabrication bespeaks the authenticating pressure to "make history" in a certain way. Equiano's rhetorical ethos, as Carretta emphasizes, "was dependent on the African identity he claimed."[52] The day may come when we will read most of Equiano's *Interesting Narrative* "straight," so to speak, while analyzing the "African boyhood" section as itself a historical artifact of a different order: the fossilized trace, in effect, of the reliance of public memory on metaleptic fabrication.

The refusal of mediations, as often occurs in a culture revolving around the ethos of authenticity, leads directly to the reification of histories and identities. The contemporary American context, where the racializing of identities seems most relentless, provides the most dizzying ironies for consideration of these difficult issues. Well before Carretta's questions about Equiano's birthplace had been published, excerpts from Equiano's *Interesting Life* had begun to appear in some anthologies of American literature. *The Heath Anthology of American Literature* shoehorns him in as "African American." The anthology apparently assumes that the color of Equiano's skin is sufficient to confer upon him a "representative" status as regards a minority conceived as a micro-nation within the larger American nation. In the course of his travels in the United States, Equiano did set foot in American ports from New York to Savannah, and he was briefly enslaved on a plantation in Virginia. He encountered friendly Quakers in Philadelphia, but left Georgia—resolved never to return—having been beaten, cruelly strung up, and threatened with murder there. Chapter 8 concludes with his bidding farewell to "the American quarter of the globe."[53] The relative brevity of his encounters with the American colonies, in the overall chronology of his life, would seem to make any specific claim to his being an American rather tendentious. Nevertheless, assembled thus, such an anthology of "American" literature inevitably brushes aside the far greater centrality to Equiano of a British context.

A much sounder logic might have been that Equiano, by writing the first important slave-narrative, in many ways *founds* the trans-Atlantic written tradition on which later American writers of African descent would build. *Classic Slave Narratives*, the anthology edited by Henry Louis Gates Jr., uses precisely this logic to juxtapose Equiano with the better-known slave-narrative of Frederick Douglass. An anthology of "American" literature, however, is likely to resist giving due emphasis to the centrality of British sources: hence the awkward solution of "Americanizing" Equiano. It seems ironic in the extreme that Equiano's inclusion in future anthologies of American Literature may hinge on a scholarly consensus that he was not after all, when all the evidence is in, actually born in South Carolina. The more "American" he becomes—in terms of literal nativity—the less symbolic resonance he will carry as an immediate eye-witness to the middle passage. If one sets aside the metaleptic quest for roots here and now, in the present, then a more judicious assessment of the *Interesting Narrative* will still be possible.

Middle Passage anticipates—and inoculates itself against—the possibility that Equiano is unreliable when it comes to his African boyhood. The narrator, Rutherford Calhoun, is a black man, born in the United States, where Johnson's novel both begins and ends. *Middle Passage*, then, declines merely to reimagine the original crossing from Africa to America. The novel deliberately starts instead with the narrator already in the New World; the trip is voluntary; it does not purport to recover lost "roots" in any simple way; and it concludes with a qualified affirmation of the narrator's American identity. Fritz Gysen's suggestion about contemporary African American fiction more generally holds true here: that the middle passage is treated, in his words, "as a boundary permeable only in one direction."[54] For Calhoun, to go "home" means to return, quite pointedly, to America, not Africa. Perhaps the middle passage, even in terms of its accessibility to recoverable memory, really must be understood as a one-way trip, always reimagined from the American side. Fictive mediations may be inescapable.

Wherever Equiano was born, his narrative does unquestionably have a certain "American" resonance. If we do grant that Equiano in some sense wrote an American book, however, then we ought to attend fully to his impersonation of Columbus, who, in his fourth voyage, famously overawed some hostile Indians in Jamaica by foretelling a lunar eclipse. Whether this story is true or not, it has become, as Aravamudan points out, a familiar staple of colonial discourse, repeated ad nauseam in later popular culture. Equiano repeats this mystifying gesture while quelling a minor riot during his interaction with the Miskito Indians on the Caribbean coast of central America:

> Recollecting a passage I had read in the life of Columbus, when he was amongst the Indians in Jamaica, where, on some occasion, he frightened

them, by telling them of certain events in the heavens, I had recourse to the same expedient, and it succeeded beyond my most sanguine expectations. When I had formed my determination, I went in the midst of them, and taking hold of the governor, I pointed up to the heavens. I menaced him and the rest: I told them God lived there, and that he was angry with them, and they must not quarrel so; that they were all brothers, and if they did not leave off, and go away quietly, I would take the book (pointing to the bible), read, and *tell* God to make them dead. This was something like magic. The clamour immediately ceased. . . .[55]

Neither absolute outsider nor absolute innocent, Equiano "plays" Columbus: a gesture that, when recounted in his *Interesting Narrative*, reveals the positional nature of racially constructed identities. Equiano carefully revised this passage in the course of multiple editions.

Such rich moments in the *Interesting Narrative* evoke meditations about contingency and alternative histories: the serious game of "What if?" The whole "Age of Discovery" could have worked out differently, given that the large Chinese fleet led by Zheng He made it to the east coast of Africa in the early fifteenth century. What if the Chinese had pursued a policy of colonization? Or what if European powers had decided, like the Chinese, not to molest the rest of the world? Such speculation destroys the illusion that the status quo is so "necessary" that it would be true in all possible worlds. For Rutherford Calhoun, such counterfactual speculations emerge in response to Captain Falcon's astonishing declaration that he has captured an Allmusseri deity:

> Could it be that in a dimension alongside this one I was a dwarf sitting in a Chinese robe, telling a white mate I had captured a European god, and, below us, the hold was crammed with white chattel? Preposterous! Considering thoughts of this sort was like standing on the edge of a cliff.[56]

Beyond the cliff's edge lies the recognition of contingency—accident rather than essence—in the racialized positions that make it seem normal for one culture to display the treasures of others in its museums and archives.

The British eighteenth century's most vivid rehearsal of the Columbus fantasy is to be found in *Robinson Crusoe*. That fantasy, as V. S. Naipaul suggests, is Adamic: "the dream of being the first man in the world. . . ."[57] By the same token, *Robinson Crusoe* can be seen as an "American" book, and *Middle Passage* invites us to consider exactly what this might mean. The initials *R. C.* and the syllabic cadence of Rutherford Calhoun's name, like other aspects of his story evoke that most famous eighteenth-century castaway, then: but they also evoke Crusoe's subsequent personification as *homo economicus*, champion of individual self-maximization. Fairly or not, the spirit of possessive individualism is often understood to be epitomized, on a mythic scale, by Defoe's protagonist. Robinson Crusoe's disobedience to his father's wishes, as Robert Wess observes, introduces the shift in priorities that the "new subject of individualism" required.[58] Defoe's novel, indeed, became the Bible, as Alasdair McIntrye remarks, of a generation including both Adam Smith and Jean-Jacques Rousseau.[59] Crusoe, moreover—despite his hardships on the Atlantic—remains confidently and imperviously "Crusoe."

What, then, might Charles Johnson have in mind with "Rutherford Calhoun"? Why invoke the initials of Defoe's protagonist? Calhoun, we notice, is *not* given the patronym of his relatively benign former master, the tobacco planter and minister Peleg Chandler. Instead, *R* and *C* seem to be filtered through the subsequent history of the United States. "Calhoun" evokes John Calhoun, the pro-slavery and states'-rights ideologue from South Carolina, who was also instrumental in the annexation of Texas. Still more disquieting, if one looks beyond the Civil War, are the overtones of "Rutherford." The disputed election in 1876 of Rutherford B. Hayes marks the moment when Reconstruction was rolled back, insuring that some 90 more years of official and legalized second-class citizenship for African Americans—betrayed by the federal government—would ensue. Known to his political adversaries as Ruther*fraud*, Hayes supervised this renewed national complicity in officially sanctioned racial oppression. Just as Ebenezer Falcon was born on July 4, 1776—in tandem with the new nation—so Rutherford Calhoun seems to have been named after two white personages who conspicuously prolonged national agonies around slavery and its aftermath. By virtue of connections that seem ironic at best, Rutherford Calhoun does "belong" to America. But America itself, despite its well-documented Adamic fantasies, names a continent laden with the baggage of history. Whatever we take "Robinson Crusoe" to signify through its accreted historical connotations, "Rutherford" and "Calhoun" both seem worse. Johnson's way of reading *Robinson Crusoe* as an American book is precisely to guffaw at American pretensions to Adamic innocence. If America "owns" the story of Olaudah Equiano in any sense, it is by way of a grotesque mediation: the lengthy shadow of such figures as Rutherford B. Hayes and John Calhoun.

Love and the Oceanic Feeling

The theme of domestic and sexual relations marks yet another dimension of Charles Johnson's implicit engagement with the British eighteenth century and its liminal literary products. Johnson "domesticates" his hero, so to speak, in a turn that seeks to repair the familial institution that slavery had split asunder. By rethinking ownership in terms of domestic belonging, *Middle Passage* finds a middle ground between the specious kinship of nationhood and the imaginary insularity of the atomized individual. Exploring the reification of the self is a primary concern of Johnson's thought and art. His interview with Jonathan Little suggests how he brings Humean skepticism together with his long-standing interest in Buddhism:

> It's very interesting to me where we get the notion of the self. Hume, with his radically empirical approach, looks into experience to see if there's anything that corresponds to the idea of a self. What he finds are memories, impressions, sensations, but no self. For Hume the self is inferred as a thing that holds all of this together. It's much the same in Buddhism, where the self is an illusion. In Buddhism all you have is this flow of impressions and sensations.[60]

The force of the term "illusion" in Johnson's work draws on this double tradition, providing epiphanies for characters who experience emancipatory disillusionment.

The protagonist Rutherford Calhoun initially suffers from a bohemian version of possessive individualism, which involves the greedy reification of sensations and experiences, in his words, "as if *life* was a commodity, a *thing* we could cram into ourselves."[61] Calhoun's "escape" to sea, such as it is, conceals an inability to love that is resolved only in the book's conclusion:

> Did I love Isadora? Really, I couldn't say. I'd always felt that people fell in love as they might fall into a hole; it was something I thought a smart man avoided.[62]

In this sense, the title clearly refers to the domestic trajectory of Calhoun, who ultimately accepts, as a freely chosen limit on his personal autonomy, the intersubjective role of husband and adoptive father. Celebrations of autonomy can disguise an inability to connect, and Calhoun is known among his shipmates as a drifter with nothing to lose: "believin' in nothin', belongin' to nobody."[63] His philosophical musings finally reframe the issue of freedom in terms that go beyond strictly legal issues. Calhoun is liberated, that is to say, from a phobic wariness toward commitment that is no doubt overdetermined by his previous experience of legal bondage. By reframing ownership in terms of mutual domestic belonging, *Middle Passage* works toward a resolution beyond the mere affirmation of individualism.

Calhoun's self-transcendence seems to fulfill a quotation from the eighteenth-century theologian William Law (1686–1771), cited in a description of Calhoun's education by Peleg Chandler. "Love," according to Law, "is infallible; it has no errors, for all errors are the want of love."[64] The demanding version of Christianity that Law advocates in, for example, his *Serious Call to a Devout and Holy Life* (1728) is incompatible with all forms of selfishness: ambition, social climbing, luxury, and so on. Placing love above an illusory autonomy, Calhoun chooses daily intimacy with others over his previous existence as a thief and vagabond. This exceedingly hard-earned approximation of bourgeois domestic norms will, no doubt, strike some critics as a rather conservative conclusion: an endorsement, in effect, of "family values." The ending, however, does not pretend that Rutherford Calhoun now fully belongs, by way of the institution of marriage, to a society that validates him or his family. Unresolved alienation on that front persists in Calhoun's description of himself as a "wreck of the *Republic*."[65] The conclusion instead marks a healthy softening of Calhoun's ethic of self-ishness. Unlike his father, Riley Calhoun, who had abandoned his family after the death of his wife Ruby, Rutherford Calhoun elects—despite obvious adversity—to stick around. Johnson's conclusion does not affirm "displacement pure and simple." On the contrary, Calhoun's choices affirms the grounding potential of love and intimacy.

Rutherford Calhoun's domestic middle passage likewise entails a rene-gotiation of his relationship with his older brother, Jackson: a relationship frayed precisely by issues of domestic property and order. Jackson, whom Rutherford recognizes as resembling an Allmusseri priest, quietly operates a commune in Makanda, Illinois: a practice of shared ownership that he finds more congruent with his understanding of Christianity than the exclusive ownership of the farm for which he might have asked. Precisely this deci-sion to disperse their inheritance from Peleg Chandler, a relatively benign slave-master, infuriates Rutherford (who calls Jackson a fool) and leads to their estrangement. Rutherford, however, is eventually compelled to engage more deeply with the harsh mysteries of property. At the climax of *Middle Passage*, when Rutherford's confused loyalties get played out in a double mutiny, a conversation with Ebenezer Falcon readjusts his vision. Falcon, who reveals that the Creole gangster Phillipe Zeringue is a part-owner of the ship, tells Rutherford Calhoun about "[A]n invisible economic realm— a plane as distant from me as the realms of religion and physics—behind the sensuous one I saw." The result is an insight into the systemic forces that constitute their world: "Suddenly the ship felt insubstantial: a pawn in a larger game of property so vast it trivialized our struggles on board." The game extends from New Orleans to "the remotest villages of Africa."[66] By the end of his harrowing journey, which involves surviving a shipwreck, Calhoun's perspective seems considerably altered in the direction of his brother's: "The voyage had irreversibly changed my seeing, made of me a cultural mongrel, and transformed the world into a fleeting shadow play

I felt no need to possess or dominate, only appreciate in the ever extended present."[67] From the transgressive acquisitiveness of his earlier career as a petty thief and sensation-hoarder, Calhoun outgrows possessiveness as such. *Middle Passage* achieves, by its exploration of the fictions and illusions of individualism, a challenging critique of reification.

In the reunion with his fiancée that concludes the novel, Calhoun's greatest desire is not for a union of bodies but, rather, of histories: "I wanted our futures blended, not our limbs, our histories perfectly twined for all time, not our flesh."[68] Though only private histories are immediately at issue, the desire for transparency—the freedom not to lie—resonates powerfully with the book's more public grappling with discrepancies in memory. And though Rutherford has a rather more rewarding homecoming than does Swift's Gulliver, who famously resides in a stable, the theme of lying in *Middle Passage* marks another dimension of Johnson's engagement with the eighteenth century. Rutherford Calhoun confesses to frequent mendacity in terms that recall Gulliver's encounter with the Houyhnhnms. "As a general principle and mode of operation during my days as a slave," Calhoun explains, "I always lied, sometimes just to see the comic results when a listener based his beliefs and behavior on things that were Not."[69] The Houyhnhnms, it will be recalled, lack a word in their language for lying, and thus can express their incredulity toward Gulliver only by means of a clumsy circumlocution: they accuse him of saying *the thing which is Not*. The negation of truth shades incrementally into the negation of society as such. Calhoun later confesses that he viewed all social bonds as lies, forged for the sake of convenience and easily broken for the same reason.[70] During the chaos of the mutiny aboard the *Republic*, Calhoun seems to act on this principle, first betraying the mutineers above-deck to Captain Falcon, and then betraying both Falcon and the sailor-mutineers to the Allmusseri mutineers, who escape from the hold. Only by the end does he clarify his own need for trust and sincerity.

Domestic space seems to offer a certain chance to create blended histories. The evocation in *Middle Passage* of Samuel Johnson's biography recalls the latter's unconventional household: his adoption into his household of the young Jamaican black boy, Frank Barber—eventually his sole heir—whose education he oversaw, and whose brief career as a sailor caused him great anxiety because he viewed ships as especially risky prisons. Early on in *Middle Passage*, the first mate Peter Cringle responds as follows to Calhoun's explanations (debts to Papa Zeringue, woman-trouble, the threat of jail) as to why he has stowed away aboard the *Republic*:

> "Half the crew's here for those reasons, or some other social failure on shore," he laughed. "But I'll tell you true: Jail's better. Being on a ship *is* being in jail with the chance of being drowned to boot."[71]

Cringle self-consciously quotes almost verbatim one of Johnson's familiar quips as immortalized in James Boswell's *Life of Johnson*. For readers of Charles Johnson, if not for Cringle, the allusion to Samuel Johnson also brings to mind the latter's famous toast, at Oxford, to the next slave-insurrection in the West Indies.

If eighteenth-century narratives arguably contributed to a cult of domesticity, they could also render, especially through lurid tales of pirates, the alternative maritime ethos of "rum, sodomy, and the lash." The texture of seafaring life, which mostly excluded women, was indeed potentially different in its arrangements of eros. Tobias Smollett's *Roderick Random* (1748), a satire periodically gibing at sodomitical phenomena at sea and on land, depicts something of this alternative ethos in his broadly drawn portraits of the heavily perfumed Captain Whiffle and of Whiffle's relationship with Simper, the ship's surgeon: a rumored "correspondence," as the narrator tells us, "not fit to be named."[72] Captain Whiffle, who wears "a curious ring on the little finger of each hand,"[73] is an object of ridicule for his foppishness. He is marked as "effeminate": neither masculine hero, nor feminine hero-ine, that is, but something peskily in between.[74] Captain Whiffle neverthe-less vanishes from the book's plotline without punishment for his erotic preferences. A pirate in Smollet's age, moreover, could often occupy *both* the categories of masculinity *and* sodomite. As a masculine antihero, bearded and bejeweled, the figure of the pirate, in Turley's analysis, "replaced the lib-ertine as a cultural icon."[75] Hence a further generic contrast with the liter-ature of domesticity. According to *A General History of Pyrates*, it was the shore-time custom of Blackbeard (Captain Teach) to emphasize the prior-ity of the male brotherhood to which he belonged by forcibly prostituting his wife to "five or six of his brutal companions . . . one after another, before his Face."[76] The fraternity of shipboard life scrambled, and sometimes merely brutalized, the bourgeois norms of heterosexual domesticity.

In *Middle Passage* Charles Johnson, with accurate emphasis on the power of the ship's captain, revisits this complex of eighteenth-century *topoi*. No romanticized contrast to bourgeois norms results. The reified hypermas-culinity of sailors is described as a "posturing among the crew, a tendency to turn themselves into parodies of the concept of maleness: to strut, keep their chests stuck out, and talk monosyllabically in surly mumbles or grunts because being good at language was womanly."[77] The parallel of ship and jail extends, moreover, to predatory male–male sexuality: the buggering, by Captain Falcon, of the cabin boy (or "bum-boy") Tommy. Nothing utopian can be teased out of this depiction of Falcon's habitual assaults on Tommy. However, Johnson does use the subliminal erotics of the ring ceremony between Falcon and Calhoun to highlight the *complicity* between Captain Falcon's world and the presumably more sheltered life-world of landlubbers.

Domestic life on land is visibly constituted by precisely the sorts of forces that Falcon—in his own eyes a "man's man"—represents. In this sense, even the Allmusseri were linked, as Calhoun muses, by a "cruel connectedness," to Falcon:

> In a sense we all were ringed to the skipper in cruel wedlock. Centuries would pass while the Allmusseri lived through the consequences of what he had set in motion; he would be with them, I suspected, for eons, like an ex-lover, a despised husband, a rapist who, though destroyed by a mob, still comes to you nightly in your dreams: a creature hated yet nevertheless at the heart of all they thought or did.[78]

Middle Passage pointedly declines, moreover, to use an act of heterosexual passion as its tonic chord, its closing figure of reunion. Passion, linked in its etymology to suffering, seems overburdened with undigested memories that need to be shared verbally. The heavy baggage of such memories interferes, in the book's muted "homecoming" scene, with Rutherford Calhoun's erotic reunion with his fianceé, Isadora Bailey. Rutherford Calhoun is not merely a laudably straight male, in contrast to the villainous Falcon, libertine and bisexual pirate. Nor is Johnson advocating a "neo-monastic asceticism."[79] Calhoun is, as the book ends, not yet in the mood to have sex with Isadora Bailey. What Rutherford and Isadora "desire" as the novel concludes is "the incandescence, very chaste, of an embrace that would outlast the Atlantic's bone-chilling cold."[80] The attempt to forge a bearable common history takes precedence over physical desire, and the positive sense in which Rutherford Calhoun "becomes a man"—to cite Douglass again—is quietly delinked from his sexuality. No doubt inflected by Johnson's Buddhist philosophy, this muted conclusion marks one of the ways in which Johnson both recovers and revises the tradition of spiritual autobiography.

Perhaps the truly striking achievement of Johnson's mobilization of eighteenth-century British authors is the surprising new light it casts on the Enlightenment and its challenges to possessive individualism. In *Middle Passage*, a certain self-emptying is brought to bear on Rutherford Calhoun's unresolved anger at his absent father. Rutherford remains angrily haunted throughout most of *Middle Passage* because his father Riley Calhoun, a fugitive slave, had deserted the family and disappeared from his life when he was three years old. In the novel's climax, Rutherford is granted, through his encounter with the Allmusseri's deity, a vision of Riley Calhoun—killed by slave-patrols in Missouri, as it turns out, almost immediately upon his escape. This vision produces a brooding "solution" that is really more of a dissolution: a temporary unraveling of ego boundaries that changes him for the better. Call this fading of the ego the "oceanic feeling" (Romain Rolland) or "syncope" (Catherine Clément).[81] This epiphany—a glimpse around the peripheries of the ego—refuses one sort of standard "recognition" scene for a far more difficult one. The novel refuses to make Rutherford Calhoun whole, that is, by restoring to him his biological father and—no less crucially—the "legitimate" place in the social order of property relations often secured by the father's name. No such resolution is available within slavery-based social relations. Instead, the sublime vision provided by the Allmuseri deity subsumes, "as waves fold back into water," Riley Calhoun's identity into a universal humanity:

> his breathing blurred into a dissolution of sounds and I could only feel that identity was imagined; I had to listen harder to isolate him from the We that swelled each particle and pore of him, as if the (black) self was the greatest of all fictions; and then I could not find him at all. He seemed everywhere, his presence, and that of countless others, in me. . . .[82]

Rutherford Calhoun, in effect, recognizes that he has been "fathered" by all of human history. Rutherford's sense of identity is—and *always has been*—grounded in an illusory father-fixation. In surrendering that illusion, he is granted a redemptive glimpse beyond its limits.

This vision of infinite hybridity provides a solution of sorts, posed earlier in the novel, to the narrator's alienation from a cultural patrimony:

> for was I not, as a Negro in the New World, born to be a thief? Or, put it less harshly, inheritor of two millennia of things I had not myself made?[83]

The oceanic fluidity that revises this earlier "essentialist" view is a product both of spiritual metaphysics and of a certain eighteenth-century history: a useful coincidence that implies, for Johnson, a multilayered significance for the term "Enlightenment." Johnson's daring insistence on the fictionality of the "black self" evokes the medium of water precisely because modern racial formation was so closely tied to the crossing of the Atlantic. The contrast between this uncanny dissolution of self and the garden-variety "finding one's father" plot is highly characteristic of Charles Johnson, who renders similar epiphanies in *Ox-Herding Tale* (1982) and *Dreamer* (1998). The modern "need for recognition" analyzed by Charles Taylor—a need depending, as he observes on "inwardly derived, personal, original identity"[84]—is aligned in Johnson's fiction with susceptibility to illusion, and so contrary to any ethics of authenticity.

Hence an unmistakable edge to *Middle Passage*: if Alex Haley's *Roots* is infinitely preferable, say, to the epic racism of Margaret Mitchell's *Gone with the Wind* (1936), Johnson's skepticism nevertheless works toward a harder truth than Haley's. *Middle Passage* refuses to reduce the quest for identity— a common theme in Johnson's novels—to the sense of affirming membership in an exclusive and singular racial or national community. No contemporary west African griot recites a name supplying the missing genealogical link between Rutherford's American and African family trees. *Middle Passage* does not settle for the compensatory illusions fostered by sagas of racial roots-finding. As Johnson points out in an interview, had Haley tracked his roots on his father's side "he would have ended up probably back in Europe."[85] Indeed, the brief popularity among African Americans of tracing one's genetic homelands through mitochondrial DNA has waned, as Steve Olsen observes, due in part to the significant percentage of male ancestors who proved to have origins in Europe.[86] And though David Hume contributed influentially to an absurd apotheosis of "whiteness"—see page 22–3 above—Humean skepticism, as Johnson shows, tends rather to the dismantling of reified identities. To the extent that such luminaries bring intellectual and aesthetic pressure to bear on the notion of the individual, they prove surprisingly congenial to a novelist searching for literary vehicles to explore Buddhist practice. As in the case of Hegel, the master's tool proves to be handy after all. As Paul Gilroy has recently reminded us, to be "against racism" means, at least in the long run, to be against race as an ideology.[87]

Johnson's remarkable aesthetic coup, in plausibly constructing a dialogue between Buddhism and the British Enlightenment, deserves more attention. While finally affirming that Calhoun belongs to a pointedly mongrelized America, his literary project asserts the prime importance of negotiating creatively with a deliberately cosmopolitan set of literary forebears. In a 1992 interview with Jonathan Little, Johnson describes his preparations for writing *Middle Passage* as follows:

> What I didn't have when I got to *Middle Passage* was knowledge of the sea, so I spent six years reading every book and rereading every book I could on that subject, anything related to sea adventure. I read Homer, Apollonius of Rhodes, the Sinbad stories, Gustavus Vassa. . . .[88]

Middle Passage opens with epigraphs from Thomas Aquinas, Robert Hayden, and the Upanishads. A close reading of *Middle Passage*, moreover, reveals still more layers to his cosmopolitan affiliations: the fact that so many of Johnson's chosen ancestors, with the important exception of Herman Melville, are British authors of the eighteenth century. Johnson mentions, in a speech delivered at Wofford College in 1999, that he wanted a "Swiftian feel" for *Middle Passage*: the sense that the Lilliputians and Brobdingnagians and Houyhynhnms were real.[89] Such eighteenth-century signposting in Johnson serves to reveal as illusory the origination myths that accompanied modern nation-building.

Johnson's refusal to throw out the Enlightenment root and branch is not only a strong achievement, as the basis for a provocative free-standing novel, but a valuable contrarian warning against the reification of identities. His suggestion that one should read masterpieces from all around the globe, moreover—both cosmopolitan and defiantly meritocratic—seems far more interesting than random assaults on the so-called canon. If Johnson rejects an excessive emphasis on orality and the black vernacular, it appears to be because he can appreciate the depth and discipline and perennial challenge represented by literary masterpieces from around the world. Johnson's emphasis on *all* cultures as palimpsestic undermines the epistemological foundation of a commonplace relativism that regards each culture as a discrete universe, hermetically sealed off from all the others:

> What we have are, not different worlds, but instead innumerable different perspectives on *one* world; and we know that when it comes to the crunch, we share, all of us, the same cultural Lifeworld—a world layered with ancestors, predecessors, and contemporaries.[90]

Johnson's views add up to a more useful vision of global literary studies than routinized attacks on canons and on cultural literacy.

PART III

IMMANENT CRITIQUE: THE BRITISH
EIGHTEENTH CENTURY AS RESOURCE

.

CHAPTER 6

SWIFT'S IMMANENT CRITIQUE OF
COLONIAL MODERNITY

> *I assured him, that this whole globe of earth must be at least three times gone round before one of*
> *our better female yahoos could get her breakfast, or a cup to put it in.*
>
> —Jonathan Swift, *Gulliver's Travels*

I have argued at some length that the eighteenth-century moment is marked by a special historical liminality as regards the advent of modernity. The period is known among historians as both the age of nationalism and the age of imperial expansion. I have dwelled in particular on the significance, in these overlapping contexts, of a period especially marked by charged and interesting threshold effects. The eighteenth century is, in this view, a fraught and relativizing moment where the making of "Britishness" and the founding of a global British empire are both peculiarly visible and peculiarly vulnerable to ideological challenge. Precisely this historical character, as I have further argued, begins to explain certain marked acts of literary affiliation by such authors as Salman Rushdie, Wole Soyinka, and Charles Johnson: a conspicuous intertextuality that has more to do with the anti-colonial use of global history than with the freewheeling pastiche often ascribed to "postmodern" authors.

The third phase of my argument—a concluding section focusing on two major authors of the eighteenth century—develops the importance of this moment by way of the notion of *immanent critique*: a dialectical process that transforms "the fixed object," in the words of Theodor Adorno, "into a field of tension of the possible and the real."[1] Immanent critique pries open the retrospective sense of closure—the aura of inevitability—that serves to render the past inert. Each of these authors, Jonathan Swift and Samuel Johnson, realizes the potential of the eighteenth century's immanent critique of British imperial society. Such a claim may seem anomalous both to scholars, who see in the eighteenth century merely the roots of all contemporary ills, and to those for whom the moment represents a stepping stone in a smoothly developmental version of British literary and cultural history. To recognize the full extent to which *Gulliver's Travels* provides an immanent critique of the colonial project disrupts *both* the canonical narratives of literary history *and* their postmodern inversions. Indeed, the expanded context of empire and nation shifts our understanding of the available ideological spectrum and its potential implications. Though Herbert Butterfield suggested as early as 1944 that "the story of British expansion overseas" constituted "the real alternative to whig history in recent times,"[2] few scholars working in the eighteenth-century period have fully grasped the unexpected ways in which a more global unit of analysis might revitalize their field.

The remainder of this chapter demonstrates that two of Swift's most familiar works, *Gulliver's Travels* and "A Modest Proposal," provide a basis for reconsidering some conventional wisdom about literary and cultural history. An expanded context for Swift's texts of the 1720s, restores to them a specific force often lost in merely nation-based contexts. Both "A Modest Proposal" and *Gulliver's Travels* critique the way that "Britishness" and "imperialism" were created within a common economic system whose tentacular reach was, by the 1720s, becoming increasingly vast. Swift's particular mode of dwelling within this history establishes the ground for a striking achievement of his satires: an immanent critique of colonial modernity. Swift inhabits his targets, impersonates them, reduces their inner logic to absurdity. His feat of oppositional inhabitation invites us to understand anew the jarring imbalances of human sociability within the broader horizons of imperial arrogance. In connecting the formal technique of scale-shifting to the issue of colonial domination, Swift finds a universal language for a world operating on a scale beyond nations. And though Swift has often been praised or condemned as a "conservative," the force of his greatest satires is to critique—from within—the violence of a specifically colonial society.

Colonial Modernity: The Space of Critique

To study national and colonial history together overcomes the tendency, common in nation-based histories to reify "modernity" as something developed fully in the metropole and then transplanted wholesale, after a time lag, to the backward colonies. As Tani E. Barlow points out, however, "the modernity of non-European colonies is as indisputable as the colonial core of European modernity."[3] Swift's own historical position, markedly liminal as regards modernity, enables his satirical critique to assert alternative norms that cannot be dismissed as merely premodern or antimodern. During the 1720s, Swift exploited his position on the cusp between English culture and Irish location to confront the arrogance of the splendid and glowering metropole across the Irish channel. His Dublin-based pamphleteering campaign against Wood's Halfpence in the *Drapier's Letters* (1724–1725) mobilized a successful boycott of the British-sponsored coin: a collective action that marks an early chapter in the modernizing of Irish national consciousness. Even Swift's most Irish satire, "A Modest Proposal" (1729), is not about what our easy stereotypes of imperialism might suggest: the imposition of one fully developed national culture onto another. "A Modest Proposal," rather, thematizes precisely the *system* that precipitated the unmistakably combined, if also brutally uneven and discrepant, development of both Britain and Ireland within a connected history. For "A Modest Proposal"—generally read as the despairing shock tactics of a frustrated reformer—demonstrates, along with *Gulliver's Travels*, the significance of eighteenth-century Ireland within the dynamics of an imperial social formation.

If Britain was "the first modern society,"[4] then Ireland was arguably the first territorial unit to be subjected in terms of the "modern" or emergent discourse of political economy. Indeed, the man whom Marx calls the father of political economy, as it happens, invented the science of "political arithmetick" using Ireland as his case study. Sir William Petty is deservedly famed as "a distinguished mathematician, inventor, anatomist, surveyor, cartographer, and pioneer in statistics."[5] Petty, however, also performed the Downe Survey—a massive exercise in mapping seventeenth-century Ireland—that enabled the 1652 Land Settlement to be carried out. In subjecting post-Cromwellian Ireland to his formidable demographic, cartographic, and statistical abilities, moreover, Petty recurs more than once, as Patricia Coughlan points out, to the figure of *anatomy*: a cool, detached comparison of his analytical and quantitative method, that is, with the medical dissection of "cheap and common animals." Petty's "anatomies" of Ireland's population in the later seventeenth century, as Surveyor-General of the Kingdom of Ireland, illustrates the historical link in Ireland between cartography and successive waves of land confiscation. Petty specialized in the numerical representation of populations ("political arithmetic"); he encouraged a centralization of governmental record-keeping; and he began to theorize wealth in terms of domestic production.[6] Simon Schama neatly sums up Petty's role as "the chief scientist of dispossession."[7] After the Cromwellian invasion of 1649, Ireland was thus the first place to bear the full brunt of a specifically colonial modernity: the sophisticated techniques of domination available to a commercially advanced imperial power. And so it "was around the name of Ireland that the moral problems of imperialism first assembled."[8]

Both the colonial roots of British modernity and the inherently modern experience of eighteenth-century Ireland are conspicuous in the emerging science of political economy. The specific discourse that Swift impersonates and parodies in "A Modest Proposal" is precisely that of political economy. The resistance he mounts in "A Modest Proposal," however, lies in bringing to the surface the irrational assumptions and contradictions that permitted the rise of a conspicuously empirical and rationalized "science" of populations alongside conspicuously irrational social relations. This latent violence receives maximum exposure both in "A Modest Proposal" and *Gulliver's Travels*. *Gulliver's Travels* satirizes the vices of arrogance, greed, lying, sycophancy, and cruelty by way of their particular expression in an emerging technical and scientific enterprise that "anatomized" human populations on an entirely new scale. The real bite of *Gulliver's Travels* lies in its satirical engagement with the intensifying sophistication and scale of this colonial project: an escalation manifest in the various forms of technical expertise that enabled, for example, routine circumnavigations of the globe. If "A Modest Proposal" demonstrates the modernity of colonial location in Ireland, then *Gulliver's Travels* demonstrates the colonial roots of metropolitan modernity. Taken together, then, they satirize a specifically colonial modernity from both sides of the colonial conflict.

Dismantling the Colonizer

Gulliver's Travels is a note in a bottle launched in 1726: a time capsule from the eighteenth century. Yet, it is also part of a global lingua franca: words such as *Lilliputian*, *Brobdingnagian*, and *Yahoo* belong to writers and speakers almost everywhere. A book written in English and deliberately published in London—the belly of the colonial whale—has survived because of its diagnosis of that Leviathan. As a satire of the eighteenth-century project of modernity—a project that *Gulliver's Travels* reveals to be colonial at its core—Swift's satire is best understood *both* as rooted in its eighteenth-century moment *and* as universally resonant. This Irish–British conflict, however topical, has a universal resonance precisely because the normative core of the modernity we continue to inhabit is colonial. So the English Gulliver, in the course of his wide-ranging travels, evokes a great many questions of identification and representation. In some of the book's most unforgettable scenes, he discursively "represents" England both to the King of Brobdingnag and to the Master Houyhnhnm, with humiliating results for the judgment on "Englishness" as such. The book's anti-colonial thrust also serves to explain the nature of certain classic cruxes in the critical literature devoted to Swift's masterpiece.

A cluster of related questions has haunted the commentary on *Gulliver's Travels*. There has been frequent debate about whether or not Gulliver is a genuine character, a personality who undergoes conflict and change. Gulliver has many of the trappings of "character"—a proper name, an obtrusively present physique, a family of middling status with its own burying ground, a particularized education, a profession in which he advances (from surgeon to captain), national pride, traits of curiosity and wanderlust, an idiosyncratic and unfailing gift for languages—and yet his outlook is disturbingly unstable. Challengers of Gulliver's personhood thus argue that "Gulliver" is no more than an inconsistently used vehicle for satire, a mere mask to be dropped and reassumed at the whim of the author. A significant domain of interpretation is at stake: for if Gulliver is not seen to some extent as a "character"—and if Gulliver is thus not read both with and against the conventions of the nascent novel—then the entire dimension of the narrative that shows his sequential shifts and changes is rendered meaningless.

Critics likewise debate the extent to which a full reading of *Gulliver* requires recourse to supposed failings, such as misanthropy or neurosis, of Swift. This tradition of reading Swift, residually influential, produces, by way of historical interpretation, only an individual case history. The moral and psychological terms of this debate, precisely to the extent that they condemn or pathologize Swift, tend to depoliticize the interpretation of *Gulliver's Travels*, and, especially, to domesticate its insights into colonial practice and discourse. While gross abuses of psychoanalysis are now mercifully scarce, a less theorized emphasis on Swift's psychology remains common.

A third reiterated critical debate attempts to say just how "historical" *Gulliver* is. It inquires, more specifically, does or does not Swift's mode of satire require us to seek particular historical parallels—in, for instance, the infighting between the Tory cabinet ministers Oxford and Bolingbroke—for every event in *Gulliver*? Is the book a continuous political allegory of long-past events? The parties to such a debate seem to assume history to be little more than the driest of chronicles. Full weight must be given to the colonial resonance of early-eighteenth-century history, especially in Ireland.

Gulliver, responding to an ongoing and supercharged colonial history, is indeed "historical"—but in a less distanced and more urgent sense than is sometimes recognized. As Britain emerged as the leading maritime power in the early eighteenth century, institutionalized languages—a fabric of repeated commonplaces—emerged to legitimate colonial expansion. This colonial discourse reconfigured a matrix of older genres: travel literature, ethnography, cartography, and natural history. The expansionist ethos of these reshaped genres, more than the minutiae of Queen Anne's reign, resonates now with a collectively significant history. Swift's Gulliver goes abroad, as does Daniel Defoe's Robinson Crusoe, because such real-life

British voyagers as Captains William Dampier and Woodes Rogers were creating a vastly popular new genre of quasi-scientific travel writing. Many of the eighteenth-century voyaging narratives were focused on the South Sea because the latter was viewed as the royal road to the most vulnerable flank of the waning Spanish empire. All of these apparently "formal" problems can be reframed by raising a political and ideological issue that links them. My reading, which takes up, as a problematic of form, the cultural representation of "history" in a strong sense—as European colonialism— also offers a possible explanation for certain patterns of misreading *Gulliver's Travels*.

In the long view, the reception of *Gulliver's Travels* has reflected a defensive tendency to foreclose the colonial dialectic on which the full satiric effect of the book depends. The satiric effect of *Gulliver's Travels* depends on Swift's ironizing, literalizing, and, above all, reversing of the commonplaces of seventeenth- and eighteenth-century British colonial discourse. This appropriation of colonial discourse, very typical of Swift's satirical strategies, turns it, through excessive zeal, against the "wrong" object: the Englishman. And though it would be wrong to argue that Swift could have avoided implication in the systems he inhabited,[9] his particular satirical strategies respond to this "inside" position with a withering satire on that system.

From political economy to South-Sea voyage literature, the contemporary modes of colonial discourse constitute Swift's satirical target. To be sure, alternative literary sources for *Gulliver* can be adduced. Ancient travel literature is full of monstrous ethnic "Others," from dog-like men who bark rather than speak to cyclopean beings, from men with eyes in their shoulders to hermaphroditic or pygmy communities. In Swift's time, however, such seemingly timeless discourses were increasingly drawn into orbit of a historically specific project: colonial expansion, based on a combination of commercial and military power, from northwest Europe. *Gulliver* thus responds less to classical or medieval models than to the emerging discourses specific to eighteenth-century colonialism. In order to grasp the dialectic of Swift's satire, then, one must specify the use to which he puts some of the chief *topoi* and narrative strategies of these early colonial discourses. I offer the following *topoi* as a somewhat desultory inventory of the rhetorical resources used to legitimate the colonial project. Alterity is a theme with many variations: cannibalism, abasement, display, exoticism, filthiness, pendulous breasts, and kinship with apes. Absence is likewise a richly elaborated theme: the colonized, it seems *lack* so very many things. Mimicry and the denial of coevalness round out the repertoire.[10] Hence, starting from "inside" a discourse shaped by colonial dynamics, *Gulliver's Travels* works a systematic pattern of reversals. By the time Gulliver has been made the object each of these violent *topoi*, the very identity of the colonizing subject has been dismantled. *Gulliver's* plot, indeed, consists of a narrative in which Gulliver, the English narrator, is himself colonized.

Gulliver Colonized

In *Gulliver's Travels*, Swift hit upon a happy intersection of three related themes: visual scale, empire, and modernity. Shifts in scale permit one to see differently. A broader horizon reframes—and may render strange—objects originally perceived more narrowly. So we enter the anti-colonial theme in *Gulliver's Travels* through Swift's manipulation of scale. Gulliver is huge; the Lilliputians are tiny. Even if they have successfully tied him up, Gulliver's apparent omnipotence promises to enact, all too literally, the dynamics of European encounters with indigenous peoples as Europe has imagined them. Manipulation of scale, then, seems to be a hyperbolic figuration of British colonial power. In this context, we expect to find, and quickly do, evidence of English technological superiority. In a classic colonial *topos*, Gulliver dazzles the Lilliputians with the awesome sound of his pistol:

> The Astonishment here was much greater than at the sight of my Scimitar. Hundreds fell down as if they had been struck dead; and even the Emperor, although he stood his Ground, could not recover himself in some time.[11]

So Robinson Crusoe, having astonished Friday by shooting a parrot, remarks of Friday, "I believe, if I would have let him, he would have worshipp'd me and my Gun."[12] The almost god-like power of one superior European individual over "lesser" non-European beings is perfectly traditional. If Gulliver is a bit vainglorious, the vanity belongs to his position as an omnipotent colonial subject. His omnipotence, however, is short-lived. For we soon encounter, in reversed form, another familiar colonial *topos*. As in *Robinson Crusoe*, this *topos* generally has something to do with kissing, or otherwise groveling near, the feet of the European master. In this case, however, the English-speaking European is the one made abject:

> The Emperor himself in person, did me the honour to be by at the whole ceremony. I made my acknowledgments by prostrating myself at his Majesty's feet.[13]

It does nothing for Gulliver's dignity, of course, that the Emperor is all of six inches tall. And, indeed, no fate could be further from Gulliver's than that of the all-conquering European individual.

Gulliver, mighty as he seems to be, is essentially a hireling used as a one-man mercenary army by the Lilliputians. Moreover, we encounter all too soon the colonial *topos* of exhibition, focusing, as often, on the enlarged private parts of the "native." The Lilliputian Emperor orders Gulliver to stand "like a *Colossus*" with his legs apart. He then orders Lilliputian troops to march between his legs. Unfortunately, as Gulliver confesses, "my breeches were at that time in so ill a condition, that they afforded some opportunities for laughter and admiration."[14] This *topos* recurs throughout *Gulliver's Travels*, as, indeed, it does throughout the colonial discourse; it reappears soon enough in its most objectifying form. After Gulliver has tactlessly extinguished a fire in the Queen's palace by urinating on it, the Lilliputians ponder his punishment. Eventually they decide on the "lenient" course of merely blinding Gulliver. However, the Lilliputians reveal to Gulliver that they had also considered starving him by degrees, cutting his flesh from his bones, and "leaving the skeleton as a monument of admiration to posterity."[15] Gulliver's bones would have figured in some sort of Lilliputian diorama.

What most marks the voyage to Lilliput as an ironic appropriation of colonial discourse, however, is the *topos* of assimilation. Gulliver quickly begins to discard his own culture and to adopt the Lilliputian view of everything. The sharp discontinuities in Gulliver's character thus do not stem merely from the generic sacrifice of character-development in satire. They are, rather, a satiric appropriation, turned against the English, of colonial *topoi* of comic or painless assimilation. Gulliver simply cannot be understood without some minimal concept of an evolving "character." But he exists in a surrealistic historical dimension that cannot be adequately represented within the conventions of formal realism. As he changes societies, the malleability of his character comes to seem so much like soft clay. In this presentation, moreover, Swift's satire does indeed engage with the conventions of the emerging novel. In foregrounding an intimate relation between the novel as a genre and nation-building through print culture,[16] Benedict Anderson hits upon the constellation of identifications that Swift seeks to critique in *Gulliver's Travels*. As a genre, the novel confirms, in Anderson's words, "the solidarity of a single community, embracing characters, authors and readers, moving onward through calendrical time."[17] "Characters" as we know them belong to a world of citizens: they balance a healthy measure of autonomy, once they have come of age, with the solidarity of belonging, usually both to a nuclear family and to a national community (no less effective for being "imagined," often with chauvinistic pride). The plot of Gulliver's "failed assimilation" works with and against this standard narrative, revealing it to be dependent upon the exclusion and oppression of others.

The satisfying trajectory of the realistic novel—the achievement of "ethical autonomy"[18]—has of course been a far-from-universal experience.

Those denied autonomy, as second-class citizens or inhabitants of a territory denied self-determination, lack full access to the ethical. Moreover, the
British eighteenth century as a whole was quite different in this regard from
what came later. "Individuated meaning," as Deidre Lynch writes, "did not
come naturally to British writers and readers in the long eighteenth century."[19] Lemuel Gulliver (1726) is less finely individuated than, say, Henry
James's Maggie Verver in *The Golden Bowl* (1904). A more revealing comparison, however, might juxtapose the inner life of Gulliver, such as it is,
with that of Defoe's *Robinson Crusoe* (1719). Crusoe manifests guilt (for dis-
obeying his father); paranoia (in finding a mysterious footprint on his
island); and ruthlessness (in killing cannibals). He is intermittently religious.
Crusoe is, above all, an exceptionally impervious "individual." Renaming
Friday, Crusoe is both a character and a colonial subject. To hard-edged
Crusoe, Friday must assimilate. Friday's lack of autonomy and the erasure of
his past disrupt any comparable access to ethical subjectivity.

  In *Gulliver's Travels*, however, the protagonist assimilates. Change is abrupt,
mysterious, and far-reaching. So Gulliver suddenly takes pathetic pride in
being—as opposed to Flimnap, his hated rival in Lilliputian court intrigue
and a mere "*Clumglum*"—a lofty "*Nardac*." And indeed, so labile is Gulliver's
identity that he even feels compelled to make an absurdly solemn defense of
the honor of a Lilliputian lady supposedly seen in his chambers. A bawdy
joke, of course: but likewise a sign that Gulliver, entrapped in an increasingly
dehumanizing colonial plot, has lost his own perspective. The assaults on the
coherence of his identity merely intensify as the book goes on. Book II is in
a rather trivial sense the mirror-image reversal of book I. The big man
becomes the little man. More deeply, book II reverses positions between colonizer and colonized. Book I features the aestheticizing and disarming
charms of miniaturization, but book II, by politicizing the prettified "games"
of colonial domination, reveals the perspective of the dominated. The experience of public exhibition, threatened in the Lilliputian plan to display
Gulliver's skeleton, now becomes the "controlling idea of the Voyage":[20]

> My Master, to avoid a Crowd, would suffer only thirty People at a time to see
> me. . . . I turned about several times to the Company, paid my humble
> Respects, said they were welcome; and used some other Speeches I had been
> taught. . . . I drew out my Hanger, and flourished with it after the Manner of
> Fencers in *England*. . . . I was that Day shewn to twelve Sets of Company;
> and as often forced to go over again with the same Fopperies, till I was
> half-dead with Weariness and Vexation.[21]

Despite precautions, moreover, an "unlucky School-Boy"[22] almost
brains Gulliver with a well-aimed Brobdingnagian hazelnut. This traveling

6.1 Drawing of Prince Giolo/Jeoly by J. Sarage, ca. 1700. From *Memoirs of John Evelyn*, 1824. © THE HENRY E. HUNTINGDON LIBRARY AND ART GALLERY.

show—much like what befalls Jeoly, the elaborately tattooed "Painted Prince" (see figure 6.1) brought from the Philippines to England by William Dampier—goes on for some ten weeks. Gulliver performs in 18 large towns, in many villages, for some private families, and, finally, in the Metropolis of *Lorbrulgrud*. His death seems imminent, just as the elaborately tattooed Jeoly died in Oxford of smallpox. And even after Gulliver is rescued by the Queen, who buys him, he graduates only to the status of a pet, a sort of humanoid lapdog or canary. Pets were increasingly anthropomorphized during the Enlightenment, as Keith Thomas points out; and, conversely, certain select favorites among the colonized were elevated to pet-like status: a choice of private playmate over public commodity.[23]

The Brobdingnagians see Gulliver as merely a clever animal, and the Queen's Maids of Honor use him as a sexual toy. But the reversal goes deeper still. What usually passes in the more grotesque descriptions for Swift's neurotic aversion to "the flesh"—note the assumption of universality— is in reality an exemplary demystification of white beauty. The magnified view of the "monstrous Breast" of a Brobdingnagian woman is thus described in terms worthy of the most hyperbolic European voyager:

> It stood prominent six Foot, and could not be less than sixteen in Circumference. The Nipple was about half the Bigness of my Head, and the Hue both of that and the Dug so varified with Spots, Pimples, and Freckles, that nothing could appear more nauseous. . . . This made me reflect upon the fair Skins of our *English* ladies, who appear so beautiful to us, only because they are of our own Size, and their Defects not to be seen but through a magnifying Glass. . . .[24]

We are quickly reminded of the application of this to Gulliver. Reminiscing about his discussion of "Complexions" in Lilliput, Gulliver recalls an intimate friend who said

> he could discover great Holes in my Skin; that the Stumps of my Beard were ten times stronger than the Bristles of a Boar; and my Complexion made up of several Colours altogether disagreeable. . . .[25]

This is not so much an assault on "the flesh" as on a quite specifically color-conscious theme: a *topos* that justifies colonialism by way of the supposed aesthetic superiority of white skin, hair, and breasts. Even Gulliver himself, in this case, draws the tolerant lesson of cultural relativity: a hint of his character-like capacity for reflection.

Among the innumerable "ridiculous and troublesome Accidents" that befall Gulliver in the land of Brobdingnag is an adventure with a "frolicksome" monkey. The adventure is both dangerous and humiliating, insinuating as it does a kinship between Gulliver and a "lower" primate. The monkey holds Gulliver as if to suckle him. "I have good Reason to believe," Gulliver concludes, "that he took me for a young one of his own Species, by his often stroking my Face very gently with his other Paw."[26] Precisely that insinuation is the common currency of colonial voyage literature. As if this were not sufficient humiliation, Gulliver is also revealed to be morally inferior. Gulliver could be said, in some sense, to enjoy a technological superiority to the Brobdingnagians: he knows how to concoct gunpowder. His knowledge, indeed, of gunpowder, cannons, and their military capacities, is expert and detailed, as he informs the King—a secret, as the ingratiating Gulliver sees it, that would make the King "absolute Master of the Lives, the Liberties, and the Fortunes of his People."[27] In this replay of the earlier *topos*, however, the King—far from being dazzled—is merely horrified. Gulliver is shown to be morally lacking, himself a product (as he says of the King) of "*narrow Principles and short Views*."[28] He is himself a parrot-like mouthpiece, uncritically echoing the coarse mentality of his militaristic culture. The sheer passivity of Gulliver's absorption of English culture—the term "brain-washing" comes to mind[29]—disturbs the easy assumption that individual characters can reliably "think for themselves." Because Gulliver has conformed so mechanically to the ethos of his own culture, moreover, he turns out to be defenseless against an external critique of its failings.

In Brobdingnag Gulliver speaks of England in automatic and sanctimonious formulas like the ingenious clockwork toy he appears to be. He spews out the party line. As Clive T. Probyn suggests, Gulliver's "crass complacency" and "smug insularity" are most likely a parody of the scene near the beginning of *Robinson Crusoe* where the elder Crusoe's advice to his son, equally scripted in its tone, becomes a "paean to middle-class values."[30] One of the most famous instances of Swift's supposed misanthropy occurs in this book, during Gulliver's searching conversations with the King of Brobdingnag about the history and social institutions of England. Having interrogated Gulliver's fatuous, cliché-ridden, and yet ultimately damning account of English culture, the King makes the following pronouncement: "But, by what I have gathered from your own Relation, and the Answers I have with much Pains wringed and extorted from you; I cannot but conclude the Bulk of your Natives, to be the most pernicious Race of little odious Vermin that Nature ever suffered to crawl upon the Surface of the Earth."[31] To be sure, the English chauvinist is meant to feel the force of this withering judgment. But the real twist in Swift's satire here comes a few pages later, as Gulliver escapes from Brobdingnag aboard an English ship. Of the English sailors, who first appeared to him as pygmies, Gulliver informs the captain, "I thought they were the most contemptible little Creatures I had ever beheld."[32] The echo of the King's judgment here shows that Gulliver has again adopted the perspective of an alien culture. Self-contempt is the predictable consequence: "For, indeed, while I was in that prince's Country, I could never endure to look in a Glass after mine Eyes had been accustomed to such prodigious Objects; because the Comparison gave me so despicable a Conceit of my self."[33] Unless we assume Gulliver to be at least a rudimentary character, along the lines of Crusoe, the force of this passage is lost. Not painlessly, but in direct conflict with himself and his own kind, Gulliver assimilates. He is indeed a character, but one who redefines himself through the eyes of another.

Although the personal colonizing process of which Gulliver is a victim is largely suspended in book III, the theme of colonial rule is not. What Swift presents instead is a narrative about the collective subjects of colonial antagonisms, nations and peoples. One episode in particular emphasizes the antagonisms that colonial rule inevitably generates. In the Voyage to Laputa, Swift depicts a magnetically powered "flying island" that reigns over, and exacts tribute from, the various dominions on the continent below. When gentler and safer methods of insuring obedience to colonial administration fail, the flying island literally presses down—suppresses—the cities below, making "a universal Destruction both of Houses and Men."[34] As Thomas Metscher observes in an article on the Irish perspective in *Gulliver*, Swift makes clear by implication that in such a situation of colonial suppression, "resistance and insurrections are normal."[35] One episode in particular, censored out in the first and all subsequent editions until the late nineteenth century, deserves more emphasis than it typically receives.[36] It contains "the parable of a successful Irish revolution."[37] Some three years prior to Gulliver's visit, it seems, the King of Laputa declared war on the "proud People" of Lindalino. Gradually escalating his military tactics against their rebellion, the King first caused the island to hover over Lindalino to deprive it of sunshine and rain. When this and harsher tactics were met with defiance, he ordered that preparations be made for his "last Remedy"[38] of "letting the island drop directly on their heads." This tactic, however, which risked cracking the "adamantine bottom"[39] of the island, likewise failed. After an experiment demonstrated that a magnetic force was indeed pulling the island violently toward the towers of Lindalino, the King "was forced to give the town their own conditions."[40] Moreover, as Gulliver was assured by a high official, "if the island had descended so near the town, as not to be able to raise it self, the citizens were determined to fix it forever, to kill the king and all his servants, and entirely change the government."[41] Almost all critics see an allusion here to Ireland's campaign against the debasing currency of Wood's half-pence, led by Swift's *Drapier's Letters* (1724). Metscher correctly insists that the parable of Lindalino's insurrection is also *anticipatory*, a fantasy of "complete national freedom."[42] Both readings, exposing the layers of the real and the possible, make it unmistakably clear that Swift's sympathies "are with the 'proud People' of Lindalino."[43]

The full implications of Gulliver's links with the oppression of Ireland, and with Swift's tracts protesting that oppression, are beginning to be fleshed out. *Gulliver's Travels* must indeed be read as of a piece with Swift's Irish tracts. After the sidelining in 1720 of the Irish Parliament, Ireland was "a colony in all but name," and, thus, "it was a colonial system which the *Drapier's Letters* were written to challenge."[44] The "Irish perspective," however, is not a provincial limitation. As becomes fully clear in book IV, Britain's colonial system extended far beyond the borders of Ireland. This voyage also brings to a gruesome climax the cumulative effects, on Gulliver, of his Friday-like sequence of assimilations and renamings.

If the Voyage to Lilliput is the most popular of the four travels, the most controversial is book IV. The reason lies in its relentless and merciless completion of the colonial dialectic. The depiction of the flat-nosed and droopy-breasted Yahoos is indebted precisely to the colonial voyage literature.[45] But the Yahoos are in fact a hybrid creation, a representation also, as in the description of their violent scramble after *shining Stones*, their drunkenness, and their sycophantic foot- and arse-licking, of European greed, hypocrisy, and brutality. The merging of Gulliver with that image of supposed otherness is inexorable. But the final twist is of course Gulliver's desperate identification with the Houyhnhnms, as an "exceptional" Yahoo, and his violent repudiation of humankind. Gulliver fails to belong at the end, fails to fit in, fails to conform to the norms of character-development that constitute the realistic novel. Not quite a Houyhnhnm, Gulliver comes close to losing his humanity as well.

Gulliver initially takes the intelligent horses, the Houyhnhnms, for magicians. And though he tries to win favor with the Houyhnhnms by presenting them with beads and other such trinkets, he is already in the mystified position of the colonized culture, awestruck by the wonders he sees. That reversal, however, is little compared with his ultimate degradation into a Yahoo "taught to imitate a rational Creature"[46] and endowed with "some small Pittance of Reason."[47] That reversal, of course, is the meaning of the episode in which the lusty blackhaired female Yahoo tries to mate with Gulliver as he is bathing : "For now," says the mortified Gulliver, "I could no longer deny, that I was a real *Yahoo*."[48] A key turning-point of the entire book arrives when Gulliver adopts the self-hating term "Yahoos" to describe his own kind. It occurs as he recounts his own adventures to the "Master" Houyhnhnm:

> I said, my Birth was of honest Parents, in an Island called *England*, which was
> remote from this Country, as many Days Journey as the strongest of his

Honour's Servants could travel in the Annual Course of the Sun. . . . That in my last Voyage, I was Commander of the Ship and had about fifty *Yahoos* under me, many of which died at Sea. . . .[49]

The word *Yahoos* insinuates itself almost unnoticed into Gulliver's language. Yet among the Houyhnhnms, *Yahoo* is the byword for all that is evil or badly made. Its uncritical use represents nothing less than the cultural dispossession of Gulliver, his alienation from his own history and origins. Gulliver becomes more and more the object rather than the subject of his own story and speech.

Hence a crucial point, and far more than a mere "limitation" of the Houyhnhnms: they display "equine chauvinism"[50] in discussion of Gulliver's anatomy. The master Houyhnhnm, in fact, is as complacently ethnocentric as the average smug colonist. He sees only what Gulliver *lacks*, in comparison with a Houyhnhnm:

> He said, I differed indeed from other *Yahoos*, being much more cleanly and not altogether so deformed; but in point of real Advantage, he thought I differed for the worse. That my Nails were of no Use either to my fore or hinder Feet: As to my fore Feet, he could not properly call them by that Name, for he never observed me to walk upon them. . . . He then began to find fault with other Parts of my Body; the Flatness of my Face, the Prominence of my Nose, mine Eyes placed directly in Front, so that I could not look on either Side without turning my Head. . . .[51]

Absurd as this is, even more absurd and more painful is the agreement of "flat-faced" Gulliver under the pressure of such horse-centered scrutiny. As the process of colonization intensifies, Gulliver begins to ape the mannerisms of the Houyhnhnms. Moreover, as in the Voyage to Brobdingnag, his assimilation to the Houyhnhnms is accompanied by extreme self-hatred and self-abasement:

> When I happened to behold the Reflection of my own Form in a Lake or Fountain, I turned away from my Face in Horror and Detestation of my self; and could better endure the Sight of a common *Yahoo*, than of my own person. By conversing with the Houyhnhnms, and looking upon them with Delight, I fell to imitate their Gait and Gesture, which is now grown into a Habit; and my friends often tell me in a blunt Way, *that I trot like a Horse*; which, however, I take for a great Compliment. . . .[52]

Still more violently than before, Gulliver defines himself through the eyes of another. We cannot be surprised, then, that Gulliver is likewise "apt to fall into the Voice and Manner of the *Houyhnhnms*, and hear my self ridiculed on that Account without the least Mortification."[53] Not only has he assimilated, but his assimilation is painfully idiotic and outlandish, confirmation that he is indeed a perfect Yahoo. It makes all the more pathetic his dream that the Houyhnhnms "would condescend to distinguish me from the rest of my Species."[54] No wonder that Linda Colley had suggested that one way of reading *Gulliver's Travels* is as "a narrative of multiple overseas captivities in which the hero finally discards his identity and crosses over to the Houyhnhnms."[55] The cumulative effects of Gulliver's four voyages here produce a conversion—a snapping, an alienation—that completes the colonial dialectic. England makes Gulliver, but the lands across the sea remake him.

Just as Gulliver has achieved the bliss of a conversion that breaks every tie with his past, however, disquiet intrudes into his well-ordered utopia. The Houyhnhnms hold one of their parleys about the sole controversy in their country, the question "Whether the *Yahoos* should be exterminated from the Face of the Earth."[56] The spokesman for genocide, as Gulliver's "Master" recounts the debate, produced a lengthy catalogue of the vices of that "most filthy, noisome, and deformed Animal,"[57] the Yahoo. The spokesman also reproduced a classic colonial *topos*, the denial that the Yahoos have any claim as original inhabitants of the land:

> He took Notice of a general Tradition, that *Yahoos* had not always been in their Country: But, that many Ages ago, two of these Brutes appeared together upon a Mountain. . . . That these *Yahoos* engendered, and their Brood in a short time grew so numerous as to over-run and infest the whole Nation. . . . that those creatures could not be *Ylnhniamshy* (or *Aborigines* of the Land) because of the violent Hatred the Houyhnhnms as well as all other Animals, bore them; which although their evil Disposition sufficiently deserved, could never have arrived at so high a Degree if they had been *Aborigines*, or else they would have long since been rooted out.[58]

This argument is, despite the Houyhnhnms' claim to perfect rationality, a tautology. The Yahoos deserve to be exterminated because they cannot be aborigines; they cannot be aborigines because they deserve to be exterminated. The tautology indeed, is similar to the vicious circle involving the very etymology of the word *Houyhnhnm*, "the *Perfection of Nature*."[59] Such a derivation claims that they are rational, by nature, and so identical with the static perfection they attribute to the natural. The sinister closure of their seeming utopia—their "boring life of certitude"[60]—emerges just at the moment of their discussion of extermination of the group *against* which they define themselves.

We ought not to be surprised that the Houyhnhnms resort to a metaleptic version of history that discredits the claims of the Yahoos to have been there first. The dubious "tradition" they invoke has every feature of colonial mythology. Unmistakably an allusion to the account in Genesis of human creation and "degeneration" prior to the Flood,[61] the citation is a self-serving use, whether the Houyhnhnms know it or not, of that sort of sacred myth. Precisely through the "denial of coevalness,"[62] it seeks to place the degenerate Yahoos in an *other* time: residual but not original. The Houyhnhnms are thus spared the full responsibility for their part in a violent conflict in the same time and place in which the Yahoos exist. Thus, like the "Modest Proposer" of Anglo-Irish cannibalism, the spokesman for the extermination of Yahoos is willing, in the most suave tone imaginable, to appoint himself chief executor of mass death. And though the Houyhnhnm Grand Assembly did not implement this proposal, they did, as Gulliver is informed, adopt the Master's own alternative: an incrementally genocidal program of castration, modeled after the human gelding of horses. Later Gulliver himself goes so far as to use Yahoos' skin and tallow to make the canoe in which he leaves the country.

Citing the Biblical Flood as an authoritative precedent for sanctioned scenarios of mass extermination, Claude Rawson takes the Houyhnhnms straight. He disputes the idea that Swift, in order to discredit the Houyhnhnms, is putting obviously ghastly ideas into their mouths. Rawson has dwelled at some length on the twentieth-century resonance of book IV of *Gulliver's Travels*: flayed skin, the Houyhnhnms' plans to exterminate or at least castrate the Yahoos, the Wannsee Conference, and so on. Rawson asserts that Swift's satire, in the Houyhnhnms' plan to exterminate the Yahoos, is "directed against the victim" and that the satire has "a detailed and unsettling anticipatory resemblance to what the Nazis actually did."[63] Another name for an "anticipatory resemblance" of 214 years is a *gross anachronism*, a term that applies generally to Rawson's sensational emphasis on the Nazis. He seems largely to have abandoned the task of reconstructing the eighteenth-century contexts that would help us to understand what Swift thought he was doing. Consider the following free association about Madagascar: "Much consideration was given by the Nazis to the expulsion of the Jews to an American or African colony, eventually converging on the idea of Madagascar, a land to be made available by the conquered French, and the destination, as it happens, of Gulliver's mutinous crew when they take control of his ship before his arrival in Houyhnhnmland."[64] Madagascar in Swift's time suggested a pirate's nest, just as flaying in his time suggested anatomy theaters.

Rawson describes Swift as "radically hostile to extermination projects and murderous behaviour, but simultaneously capable of strongly charged exterminationist velleities of his own."[65] He suggests that Swift plays riskily along a slippery spectrum of aggressions that reaches from flirtations with the scenario killing all the Yahoos to scriptural "drown-the-world" jokes. The result, in his most nuanced formulation, creates a "volatile combination of 'meaning it', not meaning it, and not *not* meaning it."[66] He prefers to understand such sudden and violent shifts in the text's perspectives as quasi-volcanic "eruptions"—seemingly a psychological notion—that mark Swift's simultaneous contempt and compassion for the oppressed. This reading definitively captures Swift's genius for unsparing self-implication. It deflects attention, however, from the specificity, beyond universal human wickedness, of Swift's particular eighteenth-century targets. To be sure, such a reading produces a momentary *frisson*, a transgressive thrill. It may even seem authentically Swiftian. In fact, however, Rawson's reading *defangs* Swift's satire. For if Swift intends merely a radical inculpation of humanity as a whole,[67] then only those with a special investment in the goodness of human nature need feel the sting and bite of satire.

For the record, scripture brims with atrocities that are divinely caused or commanded: mass infanticide (Exodus 12:29), head-hunting (Numbers 25:4), rape and plunder (Deuteronomy 20:13–14), the ripping open of the bellies of pregnant women (Hosea 13:16), and yes, even cannibalism (Jeremiah 19:9). Certainly Jahweh, whose promised land is already occupied, incites the systematic and merciless destruction of the Canaanites. Jonathan Swift shows few signs of fascination with such scripturally warranted horrors. His jocular drown-the-world reference to Noah's flood (in a letter to Alexander Pope, November 26, 1727), is clearly a bit of posing. It can bear only so much interpretive weight and no more. That Swift does *appropriate* a language of colonial violence in order to satirize it does not make him more complicit than those too willfully innocent to see or hear. To imply that irony is merely another means of sanitizing or legitimating the unthinkable is to imagine that innocence could be a sound foundation for politics. Nothing is more terrible than the flat, unreflective banality of those who preserve their innocence by avoiding the responsibility to think. Swift's satires are in fact aimed precisely at the one-dimensional mentality of those for whom atrocities can be reframed as normal.

When the Houyhnhnms apply the logic of gelding to the "Yahoo Question," their assembly rehearses questions that were actually in the air of early eighteenth-century London and Dublin. An anonymous pamphlet, *Reasons Humbly offer'd to both Houses of Parliament, For a Law to Enact the Castration or, Gelding of Popish Ecclesiastics* (London, 1700; reprinted in Dublin, 1710), illustrates how chilling the Protestant public discourse of the time could be. According to the internal chronology of *Gulliver's Travels*, moreover, *Reasons Humbly offer'd* was reprinted in Dublin just before Gulliver's fourth voyage (1710–1715). Though Swift provides ironic cues, such cues are absent in *Reasons Humbly offer'd*. We too seldom note, for example, that the Master Houyhnhnm, despite his supposed inability to understand lying, *deceives* Gulliver as to the import of the Grand Assembly. He withholds the minor detail, crucial to Gulliver, that he has been banished. Likewise, Gulliver's scandalous speculation (in the first edition; subsequently cut) that the Yahoos are descended from the English gives the lie to Gulliver's claim that he was the first European to set foot in Houyhnhnmland. If neither Gulliver nor the Houyhnhnms are trustworthy, then book IV cannot admit so literal a reading. *Reasons Humbly offer'd*, in a language reminiscent of the theme of official leniency throughout *Gulliver's Travels*, justifies its proposal by means of the following choice between two absurdly cruel alternatives: "[Castration] can no ways be reckoned cruel, since it may be done without hazard of Life, as common experience shews both in Man and Beast, and by consequence less to be complain'd of, than those Laws which condemn them [Catholic priests] to the Gallows."[68] The logic of the assembled Houyhnhnms is no sounder or more attractive than this formulation. Given that critics who emphasize the dark side of the Houyhnhnms have been deemed the "soft" school—an epithet with overtones of squishy pink sentimentality—one must stress that such logic is doubly vicious: both circular, that is, and brutal. The "hard" school might be more appropriately known for its plonkingly literal approach to a story about horses who can talk and thread needles. Whether Swift knew this pamphlet or not, he surely would have known that in 1719 a similar debate, pitting branding (favored both by the Irish Parliament and the English ministry in London) against castration (favored by the Irish Privy Council), preoccupied the elites in Ireland and in England. It would surely not have been lost on him that such proposals were finally defeated due to technical reasons having to do with their impact on lease-law. W. E. H. Lecky refers to this atrocious episode as "a memorable fact in the history of Europe,"[69] and its shadow inescapably falls on the Houyhnhnms.

While it may seem momentarily clever to read Swift literally *à la* Rawson, cancelling out his ironies for the sake of a *frisson*, a longer view will find it more illuminating to see that Swift, as usual, is satirizing all sides of a conflict. The satire against the humanoid Yahoos is sufficiently obvious. The satire against the Houyhnhnms, who define evil only in terms of all things Yahoo, is subtler. Smugly centered around their collective perfection, the Houyhnhnms cannot see nastiness in themselves, but only externally—that is, in the very group on which they depend for slave labor. Houyhnhnms permit no real alternative views: their version of reason does not even admit that such views exist. Hence the inability of the Sorrel Nag, having "no Conception of any Country beside his own," to see a nearby island as anything but a "blue Cloud."[70] So the Houyhnhnms argue over a technical question only: the best means to effect the eradication of the Yahoos. That the

Houyhnhnms may have just a hint of bad conscience can be inferred from their fear that Gulliver may lead a Yahoo revolt. This gives the game away: for all their self-proclaimed perfection, the Houyhnhnms seem to know, after all, that their society is riven by antagonisms for which they are responsible. Is the gelding episode best understood, then, as an eruption of Swift's genocidal feelings? Not at all. Freudian hydraulics aside, Swift was no geyser or volcano, and even his most over-the-top rants, about lawyers, for example, are brilliantly controlled. And though Gulliver identifies with the Houyhnhnms to the point of trotting like a horse, this is exactly where Gulliver and Swift part company.

Along with the evidence presented thus far, the conclusion of *Gulliver* strongly militates against a literal reading of Houyhnhnm perfection. In the closing and most emphatic narrative position comes a passage often attributed to the voice of Swift rather than to the character of Gulliver—a justly famous denunciation of the colonial process:

> A Crew of Pyrates are driven by a Storm they know not whither; at length a Boy discovers Land from the Top-mast; they go on Shore to rob and plunder; they see an harmless People, are entertained with Kindness, they give the Country a new Name, they take formal Possession of it for the King, they set up a rotten Plank or a Stone for a Memorial, they murder two or three Dozen of the Natives, bring away a Couple more by Force for a Sample, return home, and get their Pardon. Here commences a new Dominion acquired with a Title by *Divine Right*. Ships are sent with the first Opportunity; the Natives driven out or destroyed, their Princes tortured to discover their Gold; a free License given to all Acts of Inhumanity and Lust; the Earth reeking with the Blood of its Inhabitants: And this execrable Crew of Butchers employed in so pious an Expedition, is a *modern Colony* sent to convert and civilize an idolatrous and barbarous People.[71]

Preceded by an apologetic account of why Gulliver failed to claim Brobdingnag and the rest for the Crown, this diatribe is followed by one disclaiming, with bitter irony, any possible connection between such "Butchers" and the British nation. Such a disillusioned irony is in fact also consistent with Gulliver's character at this point—or, rather, with Swift's anti-colonial plot against "Gulliver" and against that bourgeois genre, the realistic novel, which often tries to organize reality around a centered and privileged subject or character. Gulliver is himself now the victimized, radically misanthropic—and, indeed, almost insane—product of repeated colonization. The puzzles of Gulliver's disintegrating character and decentered voice thus belong neither to Swift's compartmentalized feelings nor to the genre of Menippean satire, but rather to Gulliver's narrative enactment of that violent colonial process which it so consistently and lucidly condemns. For not only is Gulliver *not* a heroic and conquering European individual, but he so patently lacks true autonomy of voice and thought that he can just barely be said to be an "individual" at all. Gulliver, fragmented among incompatible identities, is the deliberate antithesis of the superbly self-sufficient Robinson Crusoe, a hero whose proud individuality is ruthlessly defined over and against a subordinate "Other."

Near the very end of the book, Gulliver is exiled from the Land of the Houyhnhnms for fear he will lead an uprising of the enslaved Yahoos. Upon departing he again abases himself in a good native fashion (see figure 6.2):

> and then . . . I took a second Leave of my Master: but as I was going to prostrate myself to kiss his Hoof, he did me the Honour to raise it gently to my Mouth. . . .[72]

Moreover, Gulliver's defensiveness about this incident involves his veracity rather than his dignity. "Detractors," he notes, "are pleased to think it improbable, that so illustrious a Person should descend to give so great a Mark of Distinction to a Creature so inferior as I."[73] This sense of inferiority Gulliver carries home to England, where it translates into a hatred of his own kind. Gulliver, for instance, cannot bear the *smell*, another colonial *topos*, of even his own wife and children. Even five years after his return he is so incompletely adjusted to English "Yahoos" that his wife and children, to this hour, "dare not presume to touch my Bread, or drink out of the same Cup."[74] Gulliver is hopelessly alienated. As the prefatory "Letter to his Cousin Sympson" asserts, Gulliver, ensconced in the inhuman and false utopia of his own stable, now claims to prefer the neighing of two "degenerate *Houyhnhnms*" to "the united Praise of the whole Race."[75]

In this powerfully ironic conclusion we register the full force of Swift's critique of the notion of "character" articulated primarily in the intimate life of the private nuclear family. Swift objects to a cozy politics that constitutes "private" individuals, through the political quarantine of domestic life and economic behavior, as truly distinct from the larger public life where public decisions occur. Consumption, to take an example central to Swift's advocacy of boycotts, has public consequences. At the same time, of course, Gulliver seems to be barking mad—the victim of one voyage too many. Gulliver's final misanthropy, as Howard Erskine-Hill argues,[76] is contrasted with the exceptional humanity of Don Pedro de Mendez, the Portuguese captain who rescues Gulliver. Though Rawson asserts that the book's conclusion leaves us with "no alternative perspective to Gulliver,"[77] such a view must perforce discount Don Pedro as an absolute Yahoo.

6.2 Drawing by J.J. Grandville of Gulliver's Kissing the Master Houyhnhnm's Hoof.

Domestication Reframed

Gulliver's loathing of humanity, enforced by his inability to return home, is Swift's last satirical target. Swift laughs at Gulliver's absurd misanthropy. To be sure, Swift also intends to flout the "family values" assiduously promoted by puritan elements in English culture: values that tended to insulate and privatize domestic life. But we are meant to laugh as well at Gulliver, supposedly conversing with ordinary horses. And indeed, jokes about Gulliver's domestic failings began with Swift's immediate circle. Alexander Pope greeted the appearance of the *Travels* with a bawdy verse epistle, "Mary Gulliver to Captain Gulliver," in which Gulliver's neglected wife voices her dissatisfaction with his residence, after returning from his last voyage, in their stable. The influence of the Houyhnhnms has wrecked the ostensibly private space of Gulliver's life at home.

Do we laugh more at Lemuel or Mary Gulliver? Some have felt that Gulliver's repudiation of domesticity confirms his—and perhaps Swift's—loathing of women. Alison Fell's novel, *The Mistress of Lilliput* (1999) continues and revises the story, no doubt intending a certain correction of its perceived "misogyny." *The Mistress of Lilliput* resumes the story of Gulliver subsequent to the scene of his alienated homecoming, after he has again absconded to the South Seas. The novel, however, fleshes out the happily sensual story of Mary Gulliver. In Fell's version Mary dutifully pursues her wandering husband. In the book's wittiest scenes, she experiences a carnal awakening with Lilliputian libertines. Eventually she finds Gulliver deluded in a foreign madhouse; bids him a last farewell; and takes up in France with the far more human Antoine Duchesne, a French naturalist preoccupied with grafting strawberries. The novel swerves away from *Gulliver's Travels* by affirming both domesticity and desire. In this recuperation of domesticity, however, the constellation of norms enabled by an imperial society is reinstated. As felicitous domesticity swims into the foreground, so the issue of imperialism disappears into the inert background. Swift's eighteenth-century satirical fiction, which vexes our grasp of Gulliver's individual character, remains more critical than its late-twentieth-century reinvention as a novel about one English woman's sexual awakening. To laugh at Gulliver's self-righteousness is healthy; to dismiss Swift's critique of the colonial process may be self-serving.

Alison Fell's imaginative retelling nevertheless offers a useful clue to the history of *Gulliver*'s reception more generally. There has been a long-standing urge, in various senses, to "domesticate" *Gulliver*. Swift is too good to be ignored, but he must be housebroken. And so *Gulliver* has often been reduced to a nursery classic, bowdlerized as a Disney animated cartoon, rewritten as a children's book about wee folk peeking out of Gulliver's hair.

Family values serve to eclipse the cosmopolitan perspectives that might make Europe's project of colonial domination seem anything but natural or inevitable. *Gulliver's Travels* was in its own time a riposte to the propagandists for expansion, who have so often ended up speaking for the "winners of history." Coming to terms with this colonial and neocolonial history, for both the British empire and then the American hyperpower, has evidently been considerably more difficult than reconstituting *Gulliver* as a case study in psychopathology, or as a nursery classic, or as an esoteric and remote political allegory, or as a gloomy fable about the human condition. These misreadings are so many awkward attempts to recuperate *Gulliver's Travels* by keeping separate precisely what Swift brings together: the making of empire and the making of the bourgeois individual.

Violent Modernity in Ireland

If *Gulliver's Travels* exposes the colonial roots of modernity in the metropole, then "A Modest Proposal" (1729) addresses the modernity of colonial violence in eighteenth-century Ireland. "A Modest Proposal" satirizes the nature of the social formation constituted by imperial dynamics: a society neither traditional nor organic. The geographical references mentioned in the course of Swift's pamphlet limn the outlines of precisely the trans-Atlantic empire that, by the 1720s, included British colonies in the West Indies and North America. The first paragraph of "A Modest Proposal" claims as a public benefit that its as-yet-unexplained "solution" will save Catholics the trouble of going off to fight for the Pretender in Spain, or of selling themselves into slavery in Barbados. If Irish Catholics go off to fight for the Pretender for reasons that are largely economic; if, indeed, they are situated within a system that inevitably produces forced emigration, their "disloyalty"—their shedding of national ties—has quite a different signifi-cance than would be given it by the usual Protestant paranoia toward a "Jacobite culture." The reference to Barbados, meanwhile, is not merely a further elaboration of bleak options. The additional point is that Ireland is articulated in a vulnerable relationship to a broader system that is busily commodifying large numbers of human beings both as indentured laborers and as slaves.

Consider also the Proposer's later reference to the "very knowing *American* of my Acquaintance in *London*": the source, as it turns out, for the information that "a young healthy Child, well nursed, is, at a Year old, a most delicious, nourishing, and wholesome Food."[78] Jay Macpherson suggests that this reference recalls the visit to London, in 1710, of "Queen Anne's American Kings." The "American kings"—an apt index of the empire's reach—were four Iroquois leaders who were wined, dined, and lodged for a season in Covent Garden as part of a diplomatic effort to shore up a military alliance between the Iroquois and the British against the French and their native American allies. The British forces were preparing for a heightened assault on the French in Canada. The Iroquois kings, then, in their well-publicized audience with Queen Anne, "pressed for the building of new forts," in Macpherson's summary, and "called for the complete destruction of New France."[79] While Swift does not scruple to implicate his native American informant in cannibalism, the logic of "A Modest Proposal" entirely refuses the usual distancing effect of such an implication. For the Modest Proposer's decision to disseminate further this "American" culinary knowledge assumes that the consumption of one human population by another is innate to the system in which he finds himself. The concept of eating children can be seamlessly adapted to the discourse of a jaded gourmet. The Modest Proposer understands cannibalism as entirely appropriate to the decadently cosmopolitan character of London. This "knowing" ethos, then, registers the constitutive impact of empire on an increasingly imperialized metropole.

By focusing on systemic linkages "A Modest Proposal" enacts a direct challenge to the ideological themes of imperial expansion. For the world that Swift's work conjures up is simply not one that can be construed as one in which a benevolent metropolitan power is bringing "civilization" and order to underdeveloped "savages." On the contrary, the Modest Proposer—even as he himself refers to "our savages"—unconsciously reverses the violent logic and direction of such discourse. While explaining that homegrown baby meat will not disoblige England by violating export restrictions, the Proposer explains that "this Kind of Commodity, will not bear Exportation; the Flesh being of too tender a Consistence, to admit a long Continuance in Salt."[80] Swift then throws in a crucial aside: "*although, perhaps, I could name a Country, which would be glad to eat up our whole Nation without it.*"[81] This aside makes it clear that the ultimate and supreme cannibal— the carnivore at the top of the "chain of consumption," as Carol O'Houlihan Flynn puts it[82]—is, precisely, Britain: the metropolitan power directly responsible for the restrictions on the Irish economy. This reversal takes a favorite accusation of colonial discourse—that the natives are benighted cannibals—and firmly redirects that accusation back in the face of its source. To be sure, Rawson terms this "the most uncompromising use of the cannibal slur ever directed at [the native Irish] in modern times."[83] But is Swift's satire really directed against the victim alone? Level by level, "A Modest Proposal" delineates a system, from the imagined product (the native infant) to its producers (the efficiency-minded parents) to the consumer (an Anglo-Irish landlord) to the administrator of the cannibal economy (the British master).

"A Modest Proposal," by defamiliarizing the space of "home," enacts a rhetorical collapse of the distinction between a supposedly external barbarism and a supposedly enclosed and civilized homeland. In "A Modest Proposal," cannibalism is shown to belong *inside*. Couched in a familiar discourse of public-spirited mercantile rhetoric, the proposed cannibalism induces the disorienting discovery, for Swift's reading public in Ireland and Britain, that they are not insulated within the comfortable automatism of their own routines—not securely *inside* their own clothes and dining habits, their own houses and minds and culinary routines. Swift's satire entails the uncanny recognition of a disowned and disavowed brutality. This *unheimlich* quality in Swift's text, this uncanny defamiliarizing of the voice of reason, can properly be understood as a critique of colonial modernity. Swift shows, moreover, that the self-maximizing logic usually associated with economic rationality works within Ireland itself to reinforce intractable social divisions. So profound are class divisions in Ireland, for example, that the Proposer's new concept really concerns only the tables of 1,000 great families: the landlord class. These landlords, the tract notes, having already "devoured most of the Parents, seem to have the best Title to the Children."[84] Costs and benefits, then, are to be evaluated within a framework that takes the logic of such violence as normative.

These class divisions of course correlate strongly with the great religious divide that followed in the wake of the Cromwellian confiscations, the Williamite wars, and the passage of the Penal Laws. A brutally sectarian attitude is thus assumed. One collateral benefit of the proposal, we are casually told, is that it will lead to a "lessening [of] the Number of Papists among us."[85] Rich people, mostly Anglo-Irish Protestants, will do their civic duty by eating poor children, mostly Catholic. Sectarianism can be made to bolster national productivity. Like the English, whom they always seek to emulate, the Anglo-Irish landlords are cannibalistic. One cannot square this representation with an analysis content to rest on the view that Swift is a "colonial" or "settler" nationalist, serving a national interest defined strictly in terms of the Protestant Ascendancy. Cannibalism, it turns out, simultaneously marks and transcends sectarian boundaries. For you are, they say, what you eat: the logic of incorporation thus inherently involves complex dynamics of identification.[86] As a trope, cannibalism is thus a suitable vehicle for paradoxical reversals: above all, for tracing the ironic persistence of a substantial identity between the seemingly incommensurable positions of devourer and devoured, anatomizer and anatomized. In turning cannibalism inside out, so to speak, Swift activates the maximum tension between the real and the possible inherent in the imperial system.

Even within the group targeted for consumption, moreover, there is little solidarity to be expected. The system works instead by a logic of displaced abjection, whereby each member of a hierarchy transmits violence to the one just below. The landless poor are thus envisioned as responding to this policy initiative as petty entrepreneurs whose newfound capital is children. So degraded is their current state that this new view will actually enhance family life. Domestic violence will decline, for formerly abusive husbands—now behaving as conscientious livestock breeders—will place greater value than before on the physical well-being of their wives. The wives themselves, meanwhile—far from attempting any sort of joint sisterly resistance to breeder status—are envisioned instead as competing to see "*which of them* [can] *bring the fattest Child to Market.*"[87] In conditions of scarcity, self-maximization and displaced abjection reduce the horizons of public life to a ferociously privatized dog-eat-dog logic. The Irish are satirized not as a national group, but for their lack of national solidarity.

Even Swift's late pamphlet, "A Proposal for Giving Badges to Beggars in All the Parishes of Dublin" (1737), has an anti-colonial spin. Though sometimes wielded as a trump card by the hard or literalist school, Swift's usual suspects—stingy landlords in the Irish countryside and local authorities in England—remain the villains of this pamphlet. Swift points out that authorities in England are "exporting hither their supernumerary Beggars, in order to advance the *English* Protestant interest among us; and these they are so kind to send over Gratis and Duty-free."[88] Just as Britain eased its task of political integration as a nation by shipping convicts off to the American colonies, so with the dumping ground of Ireland—stuck with the social albatross of Britain's excess poor—within the imperial social formation. Massive poverty is of course a disaster for any social fabric, much less that of a colonial society. Given the already existing poverty in Ireland; and given the simultaneous migration of beggars from rural parishes to an overburdened poor-house in Dublin, children arrived in Dublin only to starve and die. The city, sole support of the poor-house, was faced with a compounding problem. In apparently straightforward language, Swift proposes to revive the enforcement of a law requiring (1) that local parishes be responsible for maintenance of their poor; and (2) that beggars be confined to their own parishes, where they might rely on both on their local parish and on a network of relatives and acquaintances. Hence the cloth "badge" they were already supposed to be wearing on their shoulders. The harsh measures Swift was willing to countenance in order to redistribute this social burden—whipping poor vagabonds out of town, if necessary—suggests how much beyond an ethics of charity he perceived the problem to be. Even so, it is a bridge too far to argue that Swift feels toward the wandering beggars as the Houyhnhnms regard the Yahoos. The beggars, moreover, are *not* entirely from "the tribe of savage Irish," as Rawson says; as he himself notes just few pages later, some are English.[89] Though poverty is usually conceived of as a social problem, something more is involved here. Imperial politics, from restrictions on manufactured woollen goods to the dumping of "surplus" English poor, *constituted* the domain of the social as such in Swift's Ireland.

Swift's *oeuvre* represents a furious engagement with an expanding imperial system and the exploitative social formation it produced. His emphasis on systemic effects may begin to explain, moreover, why certain modes of literary and historical scholarship, retrospectively organized around those supposedly organic, complete, and discrete things called "nations," have been inadequate for understanding his contribution. The anomalies and incongruities in Swift's reception go well beyond the evident ambiguities of Anglo-Irishness as a "hyphenated" culture. One confronts in Swift the complexities of an Anglo-Irish writer who has been variously described as a major Augustan author in the high tradition of English literature; as *the* major Irish author of the eighteenth century; as a sectarian defender of the Ascendancy, and, hence, a colonizer; and as a Hibernian patriot who resisted British arrogance even at the risk of his life. Swift himself, in a famous letter to Pope, remarks that "I have ever hated all nations, professions, and communities, and all my love is toward individuals."[90] This sentiment—which follows a famous line about giving the world "one lash the more at my request"—used to be recruited for discussions of Swift's supposed misanthropy, or Tory gloom. My point about eighteenth-century liminality, in keeping with a structural and systemic approach to the study of empire, is a different one. My own view, while affirming a courageous anti-colonial patriotism on Swift's behalf, emphasizes, above all, the way that his work insistently and eloquently thematizes the workings of a *system* whose dynamics and horizons are not only beyond—but also *prior to*—nation-states and the national cultures they produce. Swift's *oeuvre*, laboring mightily in the negative space between the real and the possible, works against the inside/outside topology that defines nations and nation-based histories.

Roads Not Taken

Swift was a worldly man, all too familiar with the nauseating world of high politics he often satirizes. By refusing to position himself as "outside" the targets of his satire, however, he laughs at the fanaticism to which the self-righteous often become prone. No unwarranted claim to purity grounds his attacks, and Gulliver's expectations that his book will produce sweeping reforms produces another joke on the utopian sensibility. Swift simply refuses to concede that any human place is likely to be free from complicity with pride and cruelty. An agitator in Ireland for clothing boycotts of English woollen goods, he recognizes that systemic harm is as ordinary and banal as the clothes one wears. Swift refuses to offer his readers refuge in any spaces of imaginary innocence—say, domesticity and childhood—because these too reside inside the various systems by which some human beings indirectly consume the lives of others. Swift's satire floats down to us now, on the tides of history and print culture, as an exemplary "inside" critique. Speaking from "within," he stages a battle between really existing British imperial society and ideals that spring also from within its possibilities.

Rawson concludes that Swift attacks dominant groups by equating them with their own despised subgroups: a highly persuasive point, though one not entirely compatible with the emphases that precede it. The breadth of his study, however (from 1492 to 1945), and the disappointing resort, in the end, to comprehensive human depravity and wickedness actually deflects Swift's satire. All modes of constituting "Otherness," from ethnocentrism to white supremacy, are thus steamrolled together in a ceaseless and demoralizing historical pattern. Hope, that sentimental emotion, can find no traction in the face of such an undifferentiated history. Swift's closing attack on pride in *Gulliver's Travels*, however, implicitly appeals to the hopeful virtue of *humility*: the effort, in the words of André Comte-Sponville, "through which the self attempts to free itself of its illusions about itself and—since these illusions are what constitute it—through which it dissolves."[91] The brilliance of *Gulliver's Travels* lies in its simultaneous attack *both* on a specific arrogance of power *and* on the alternative arrogance of the self-righteous reformer.

The discussion of Swift's supposed "misanthropy" has too often conflated, in Eurocentric fashion, his particular targets with the world at large. The satirical targets of the *Travels* in fact comprise concentric circles of increasing intensity and specificity. The colonial project, according to Swift's analysis, *magnifies* the already dismal faults of humankind. For this reason, Europe is named as a special haven for liars. The vanguard of commercial colonizers from northwest Europe—the maritime traders of the Dutch East India Company—are more harshly satirized than other Europeans, especially in book III. At the very center of the target sits a complacently battening Britain, the object of Swift's most lacerating satire. The rush to insist that Swift, that infamous misanthropist, targets the entire human race as a degenerate species is misleading. So he does: but the English remain, after all, at the center of the bull's-eye.

Swift's emphasis on eighteenth-century horrors belies the cliché that assigns an unqualified "dream of mastery" to the Enlightenment. The "modernist" critique of violent modernity, deeply indebted to such earlier thinkers as Sir Thomas More, Michel de Montaigne, and François Rabelais, takes off with full force in the eighteenth century. Swift's grotesque games with scale extend the tradition of Rabelais's *Gargantua and Pantagruel* (1532), which explores the bodily excesses of his enormous character Gargantua. Michel de Montaigne's "On Cannibals" (1580) must have reinforced Swift's recognition that Europe, observed from a sufficient distance, took many cruelties for granted. Looking before and after, *Gulliver's Travels* anticipates a remarkable range of political and aesthetic developments. Swift's satire on colonial modernity belongs to world literature because it remains in dialogue with a premodern international tradition; because it presents human nature as *universally* cussed; because it reserves its most brutal satire for the ascending powers of Swift's own moment; and, above all, because of the violence with which the entire world has subsequently been, unevenly and incompletely, modernized. The grotesque modernity predicted by the harsh adventures of Lemuel Gulliver has, quite simply, come to pass as our norm.

We ought not to be surprised to find Mohandas K. Gandhi—the leader of an anti-colonial struggle that set the stage for decolonization around the world—praising Swift's satire almost two centuries after its publication. Writing from South Africa in 1911, Gandhi, himself an ardent critic of modernity, describes the *Travels* as containing "so effective a condemnation, in an ironic vein, of modern civilization that the book deserves to be read again and again."[92] Swift's achievement compels an acknowledgment of the potential for alternative modernities—roads not taken—that haunts the writings of the eighteenth century more generally. Swift's immanent critique—by compelling the recognition that modern national cultures are themselves constituted by, and within, a larger economic system—can serve as a basis for rethinking familiar accounts of literary and cultural history. *Gulliver's Travels* and "*A Modest Proposal*" have a universal resonance precisely because we continue to inhabit the aftermath of modernity that was colonial. Above all, Swift's satire envisions, through Gulliver's scruples about claiming foreign lands for the British Crown, the possibility of a higher rationality than the world has yet seen: distributive justice *between nations*. In thus repudiating the colonial highjacking of modernity, Jonathan Swift looks forward to a decolonized modernity yet to come.

CHAPTER 7

JOHNSON'S IMMANENT CRITIQUE
OF IMPERIAL NATIONALISM

I do not much wish well to discoveries, for I am always afraid they will end in conquest and robbery.

—Samuel Johnson, letter to William S. Johnson, March 4, 1773

Perhaps no major figure in British literary history has been so perpetually misunderstood as Samuel Johnson. Julian Barnes's amusing depiction in *England, England* (1999) of a Johnson impersonator, carefully packaged for tourists in a historical theme park built on the Isle of Wight, satirizes the distorted terms on which we have too often chosen to remember Johnson. Reduced to a scruffy, floppy-wigged quipster—one more staged experience for Anglophiles, on par with Big Ben, Robin Hood, and the Tower of London—the theme-park "Dr. Johnson" of *England, England* is an actor paid to spout table-talk for tourists. Though "The Island" eventually supplants actual England in Barnes's satirical novel, the Johnson simulacrum overidentifies with his original and remains troublesome: too moody, too abrasively negative about other people's homelands, too unpredictably profound, to blend in with a checklist of Disneyfied icons. Thus "Dr. Johnson," forever blasting Americans, draws "negative feedback" from sightseers to his lair in the Cheshire Cheese. Barnes has hit upon a crux—a tension between the iconoclastic force of Johnson's thought and the accommodating effects of public amnesia—that bedevils the entire history of Johnson's reception.

Johnson's *oeuvre* is indeed a stubborn and recalcitrant index of a road not taken: a body of written work often neglected in favor of the witty and provocative table-talk brilliantly mediated by Johnson's biographer, James Boswell. Backhanded compliments to Johnson legitimate this curious adulteration of public memory: hence Sir Walter Raleigh's verdict that Johnson's greatness is that he is greater than his works. And hence abundant editions of Johnson that amalgamate a few of his writings, some good bits from Boswell's biography, and, say, Thomas Macaulay's *Life*. As Greg Clingham points out, this familiar redaction of Johnson distorts Boswell's emphasis on Johnson as an author and formidable thinker.[1] A sclerotic bottleneck, filtering out aspects of Boswell's biography no less than of Johnson's writings, has worked to convert Johnson into the "titled cliché" of "Dr." Johnson:[2] "Dr Johnson" is a convulsive and overbearing personage best confined, like an eccentric uncle, in some safe corner of public memory.

My attempt in this monograph to recast the overall significance of the British eighteenth century is in part an effort to create the critical context in which the full nature of Johnson's achievement, including his famous intervention in the "Ossian" controversy, can be understood. The challenging crux of Johnson's most misunderstood achievement—his articulation of a cosmopolitan nationalism—awaits a historiography that is prepared to rethink the territorial boundaries, as typically drawn by nation-based historiography, of "inside" and "outside." The purpose of this chapter is precisely to recover in the writings of Johnson the emancipatory energies of his universalist thought: a critique of imperial ideology all the more telling precisely because it arises from within the British Enlightenment.

Cosmopolitan Nationalism

The oxymoron of "cosmopolitan nationalism" is offered as a preemptive recognition that any invocation of belonging to a larger world must nevertheless be locally situated. Hence, as Bruce Robbins notes, the currency of such terms as "rooted" or "vernacular" cosmopolitanism.[3] And hence a new emphasis as well on what Robbins terms "actually existing cosmopolitanisms": solidarities, that is, which—if inevitably less than perfectly universal—do trouble or jump across national boundaries in productively enlarging ways.[4] Given current interest in theorizing the cosmopolitan anew,[5] it should be productive to revisit the Enlightenment through the work of Johnson: the great moment, that is, of both nationalism, on the one hand, and widespread cosmopolitan aspirations, on the other.

The paradox of Johnson's simultaneous investment in nationalism and in cosmopolitanism has given rise to contradictory explanations. Johnson's critical attack on Thomas Gray's "The Bard," for example, has raised questions about the nature of his national loyalties. Howard Weinbrot is alert to this when he writes as follows:

> Johnson's attack on Gray seemed an attack on an energetic and brilliant example of British history and values expressed in the Pindaric mode.

To suggest otherwise was implicitly to obstruct a major path in the lyric's development. . . . In this obstructive sense, the great nationalist Samuel Johnson was a traitor to Britain.[6]

This is perhaps the most sophisticated form of the judgment that Johnson was essentially a "Little Englander": a bulky stumbling-block in the eighteenth-century cultural transition from England to Great Britain. For Katie Trumpener, for whom this same making of Britishness is symptomatic of English hegemony, the target for criticism is Johnson's *Journey to the Western Islands of Scotland* (1773). She sees the *Journey* as an Anglocentric attempt "to establish the primacy of a cosmopolitan and imperial vision of Enlightenment activity over what it sees as Scotland's nationalist Enlightenment. . . ."[7] Here Johnson figures as a quintessential voice of the Enlightenment whose excessively modern cosmopolitanism is merely a disguised form of imperialism. Our perplexities increase further when we turn to J. C. D. Clark. While Clark's claims about Johnson's Jacobitism seem overstated, he does marshal important evidence about a broader range of Johnson's non-Hanoverian affiliations: above all, his residual attachment to a continent-wide and Latin-based Christian humanism.[8] Here Anglo-Latinity—the dynastic high culture inherited from what E. R. Curtius terms "the Latin Middle Ages"—is used to frame Johnson as a poster boy for the wholesale rejection of the modernizing project of building vernacular national cultures. None of these explanations, however, seems adequate to the task of mapping Johnson's sophisticated balancing acts. As regards nationalism, Johnson's interventions are *both* forward-looking (and, hence, internal to the "project of modernity") *and* devastatingly critical of modernity's grossest failings.

The concept of cosmopolitan nationalism offers a productive way of rethinking the paradoxes that surround Johnson's relation to Englishness, to Britishness, and to a cosmopolitan impulse common to many Enlightenment thinkers. This relation can be explained neither as parochial insularity nor as Anglo imperialism. Nor can it be fully understood as the residue of Johnson's investment, in opposition to vernacular culture, in a classical Latinity oriented to a continental elite. One finds instead a hard-earned and sometimes paradoxical effect of Johnson's cosmopolitan engagement with the various nationalisms of his moment. In the wake of the recent emphasis on global perspectives in Anglophone literatures, Johnson's own invocations of a global framework for political analysis deserve to find new contexts and constituencies. By the same token, his negotiations with the progressive potential of a vernacular public sphere demonstrate the possibility of intelligently bridging the gulf between the national and the cosmopolitan.

"Soft" Nationalism: Making Vernacular Englishness

The dual commitment both to a rooted or vernacular culture and to the challenge of going beyond national cultures—the hallmark of a cosmopolitan nationalism—is evident in the way that Johnson conceives of English national culture. When he refers in his biography of Jonathan Swift to England's current status as a "nation of readers,"[9] Johnson locates himself squarely within the eighteenth-century making of a print-based public culture. This was a process of imagining community, as Benedict Anderson has shown, that was intimately connected to the cultivation of new identities on the print-mediated scale of the nation. In his preface to the 1740 volume of the *Gentleman's Magazine*, Johnson writes as follows of the imagined community of readers:

> Every-body must allow that our News-Papers . . . by the Materials they afford for Discourse and Speculation, contribute very much to the Emolument of Society; their Cheapness brings them into universal Use; their Variety adapts them to everyone's Taste: The Scholar instructs himself with Advice from the literary World; the Soldier makes a Campaign in safety, and censures the Conduct of Generals without fear of being punished for Mutiny. . . . and the honest Shopkeeper nods over the Account of a Robbery and the Prices of Goods until his Pipe is out.[10]

Johnson wrote pamphlets on public affairs; he wrote hundreds of periodical essays for a reading public engaged in working through such problems as the tyranny of parents, the social plight of prostitutes, and the ethics of capital punishment. Surveying the Harleian collection of pamphlets generated a century earlier by the English Civil War, Johnson highlights the Habermasian significance of the public sphere that England had developed as inhering in "the form of our government, which gives every man that has leisure, or curiosity, or vanity the right of inquiring into the propriety of public measures, and, by consequence, obliges those who are intrusted with the administration of national affairs to give an account of their conduct. . . ."[11] In "The Duty of a Journalist," Johnson emphasizes the anti-elitist implications of his vocation, asserting that it was the duty of a journalist "to consider himself not as writing to students or statesmen alone, but to women, to shopkeepers, to artisans, who have little time to bestow upon mental attainments, but desire, upon easy terms, to know how the world goes." Precisely to serve the function of public accountability, Johnson reported on parliamentary debates for the *Gentleman's Magazine*, circumventing the laws against such reporting through the tongue-in-cheek fiction that his reports concerned the public affairs of "Magnum Lilliputia." Johnson fully registers the crucial political gain—the increased transparency of political institutions and decision-making at many levels of society—entailed by the building of a vernacular public sphere. In "A Complete Vindication of the Licensers of the Stage" (1739)—a masterpiece of irony—Johnson clinches this theme:

> Unhappy would it be for men in power, were they always obliged to publish the motives of their conduct. What is power but the liberty of acting without being accountable?[12]

Contemporary theorists who attack the Enlightenment ideal of increased social transparency, generally via the thematics of the panoptic "gaze," forget the implications of enabling the politically powerful to operate beyond the vigilance of public watchdogs.

Above all, perhaps, Johnson made such landmark contributions to a vernacular literary culture as his *Dictionary*, his Shakespeare edition, and his *Lives of the English Poets*. Through these achievements, in the words of Nicholas Hudson, "Johnson made a signal contribution to the very concept of 'England' by promoting a general recognition of a common linguistic and literary heritage of English people."[13] Johnson's *Dictionary* was widely seen as single-handedly rivaling the achievement of the entire French Academy; his Shakespeare edition helped to consolidate the reputation of Shakespeare; and his *Lives of the English Poets* gave intellectual substance to his remark in the preface to the *Dictionary* that authors are the "chief glory" of every people. Johnson was a quintessential creature of print culture:[14] a figure effectively engaged in the vernacular production of Englishness.

Yet Johnson's affirmation of Englishness also insistently troubles the ideological closure often represented by national boundaries. In conceding a peculiar bravery to the English common soldier, for example, he refuses to make the occasion of the Seven Years War with France an excuse for glossing over internal social divisions within England. One could easily imagine how the sentimental treatment of "bravery amongst the low" might be used to overstress national unity in the face of an external adversary. That "nationalization" of English society Johnson flatly declines. Thus he demystifies the much-vaunted "liberty" of England in the following terms: "Liberty is, to the lowest rank of every nation, little more than the choice of working or starving; and this choice is, I suppose, equally allowed in every country."[15] He goes on to attribute the bravery of the English common soldier precisely to a contingent social circumstance: his relative insubordination *vis-à-vis* his more feudalized French counterpart, within the social hierarchy. This class-based analysis of uppity plebs then engenders a wry mode of patriotism that allows Johnson to tweak the English elite with the thought that "good and evil will grow up together; and they who complain, in peace, of insolence of the populace, must remember that their insolence in peace is bravery in war."[16] The community constituted by "Englishness," in short, remains a polity imagined as sharing very unevenly in its most cele-brated benefit, and so potentially fissured by its own internal alienation. By targeting easy sentimentality about national fellow-feeling, Johnson opens a seam in the bourgeois public sphere: a glimpse into plebeian perspectives that unsettles rather than reassures. In Johnson, the bourgeois public sphere begins to confront its exclusionary limits.[17]

Johnson represents a distinctly cosmopolitan alternative to the politics of national chauvinism. He is wary of the violent exclusions entailed by an excessive emphasis on the unity or boundedness of national cultures. He warns that "the love of our country, when it rises to enthusiasm, is an ambiguous and uncertain virtue; when a man is enthusiastic he ceases to be reasonable. . . ."[18] This comment comes in the course of a back-and-forth sequence spawned by his review (May 17, 1757), in the *Literary Magazine* of Jonas Hanway's *A Journal of Eight Day's Journey, to which is added An Essay on Tea* (1757). Hanway is best known for his association with the Foundling Hospital, which his book promotes. Hanway was stung by Johnson's droll review (by a self-described "hardened and shameless tea-drinker"), which mentions, as an aside, that the Foundling Hospital had been neglecting the religious instruction of its wards. In the *Daily Gazeteer* (May 26, 1757), the philanthropist replied to Johnson's accusation with some sort of warning to him about the danger of affronting a powerful corporation.[19] Hanway's threatening riposte, now lost, then provoked the further reply by Johnson (June 17, 1757) that includes the sentence cited above. Our inability now to recover Hanway's piece is regrettable. In any case, Johnson's caution against nationalistic excess can be adequately understood as a further response to "An Essay on Tea." Aside from its cranky musings on the risks of drinking tea imported from China, "An Essay on Tea" provokes Johnson precisely because of Hanway's characteristic nationalistic machismo. Here is a sample of "An Essay on Tea":

> Were they the *sons of tea-sippers*, who won the fields of *Cressy and Agincourt*, or dyed the *Danube's* streams with *Gallic blood*? What will be the *end* of such *effeminate* customs extended to those persons, who must get their bread by the *labors* of the *field*![20]

No wonder that Johnson doubted Hanway's "competence" as a social critic.[21] However idiosyncratic, Hanway's fear that tea-sipping is leading to a national decline is consistent with his own habit of channeling humanitarian efforts (saving abandoned infants, for example) to serve a utilitarian national interest (increasing the pool of national labor).[22] Johnson also notes that

Hanway, "amidst his rage against tea . . . made a smooth apology for the East India company (520). . . ." For reasons that may have included the publisher's fear of a libel suit, this little skirmish seems to have ended his association with the *Literary Magazine*.

Johnson's take on English literary history cuts sharply against national mythopoeia. By refusing to invest a specifically sacred awe in any secular national icon, Johnson positions himself outside the mainstream of any cultural nationalism. His cosmopolitanism can likewise be seen in his negative response to the way that cultural nationalism, obsessed with articulating historical time in the mythic terms of national destiny, involves a violent appropriation of religious awe. Nation-based myth-making is the recuperation, in short, of history's randomness. There is no more central icon for the cultural making of later eighteenth-century Britishness, moreover, than that of the bard, supposedly the "indigenous historian of a nation."[23] To quote Trumpener again: "Even while the bard signifies collective and tribal memory, functioning as the repository and transmitter of cultural memory, he becomes the representative of poetic art as a compensatory, secular religion."[24] Johnson resists precisely this: the siren-like lure of a nationalism invested with the aura of sacred narrative. Johnson's biography of Gray illustrates his reservations about sacralizing national icons. What provokes Johnson's ire is, above all, the use of prophecy in "The Bard" to sanctify national icons. Gray's Welsh bard prophesies *ex post facto*, as it were, for one simple reason: nothing could so cheaply convey a sense of destiny as regards "Britannia's issue" as the metaleptic prediction, with the dramatic immediacy of declaimed speech, of events already known.[25] As Gray wrote, wryly, to a friend, "I annex a piece of the Prophecy; which must be true at least, as it was wrote so many hundred years after the events."[26] It is against the stilted hokiness of such rhetoric that Johnson directs his deflationary jabs. Johnson's enunciated standard is "the probable": verisimilitude, rather than truth *per se*, a standard that he insists is historically relative. What he dislikes in Gray's Nostradamus-like prophecy is the author's pretense of naiveté: the sentimentality, in short, of writing like that, now, "at the wrong time." Though visible as an acknowledged fiction in "The Bard," Gray's metaleptic looping of time anticipates Macpherson's more literal writing "at the wrong time."

In the preface to his edition of Shakespeare's plays, Johnson makes a point of withholding "superstitious veneration" for Shakespeare. Enumerating his faults in a sobering disquisition some found shocking, Johnson goes against the grain of a growing Bardolatry that Michael Dobson describes as, in the full anthropological sense, a national religion.[27] By the same token, only a scant handful of Johnson's literary biographies affirm the greatness of the poets described therein. His "soft" or civic nationalism precludes so insular an approach to critical judgments. The two prints reproduced on pp. 177–178 demonstrate the outrage, on these grounds, that greeted his assessment. James Gillray's "Old Wisdom Blinking at the Stars" (figure 7.1) and the anonymous "Apollo and the Muses Inflicting Penance on Dr. Pomposo round Parnassus" (figure 7.2) illustrate the public demand for a more uncritical celebration of literary heroes. Although Johnson regarded authors as the "chief glory" of every nation, it does not follow that his presentation of English authors would be tailored to suit an agenda of English cultural nationalism, much less a British one.

The project of writing English literary history, moreover, does not tempt Johnson to naturalize the national community and its boundaries. Consider the following passage on Samuel Butler's *Hudibras*, which finds and celebrates mixture in its historical analysis:

> We must not, however, suffer the pride, which we assume as the countrymen of Butler, to make any encroachment upon justice, nor appropriate those honours which others have a right to share. The poem of Hudibras is not wholly English; the original is to be found in the history of Don Quixote; a book to which a mind of the greatest powers may be indebted without disgrace.[28]

Merely having English subject-matter, as Johnson knows very well, does not license an overweening claim to cultural autonomy. What may appear to be immanent, or "inside" the national horizon often requires defamiliarization with reference to external history and influences: to a process of construction, that is, that partly works from the outside, and does not serve to illustrate the purity and autonomy of creations from the "inside" of national boundaries.

It is in the same spirit that Johnson is willing to use French critical formulations wherever he finds them useful. He refers, indeed, to almost thirty French authors in the *Lives of the Poets*, including Boileau, Fènelon, Montesquieu, Racine, Rousseau, and Voltaire.[29] At the crucial moment when he requires a framework to approach the epic achievement of *Paradise Lost*, for example, he turns to René Le Bossu's *Traité du poëme épique*.[30] At the same time, Johnson is also an equal-opportunity debunker: he grandly dismisses Voltaire's strictures against Shakespeare, along with those of John Dennis and Thomas Rymer, as "the petty cavils of petty minds."[31] He thus refuses, on the one hand, to bask in the aristocratic aura surrounding all things French in Georgian England: such merely snobbish Francophilia threatened to give cosmopolitanism a bad name. On the other hand, however, Johnson largely declines the populist rhetoric of Gallophobic nativism.[32] During the Seven Years War, indeed, Johnson argued specifically

7.1 Engraving by James Gillray: "Old Wisdom Blinking at the Stars."

7.2 Anonymous engraving: "Apollo and the Muses, inflicting Penance on Dr. Pomposo, round Parnassus."

against an "Englishmen First" rationale for excluding French prisoners of war from charity: a refusal to equate national boundaries with the horizons of moral concern.[33] To be sure, he does briefly entertain the worry that the syntax of the English language is becoming overly Frenchified: "deviating toward a Gallic structure and phraseology," as he puts it in the preface to his *Dictionary*.[34] However, Johnson more often treats the sort of collective identities that can be built through language as inevitably impure, and perhaps as productively porous. The polyglot extravaganza of Sir Thomas Browne's diction, for example—"a tissue of many languages,"[35] as Johnson says—does not tempt him into a policing of linguistic boundaries. He finds both usefulness, and even a certain sublimity, in Browne's daring linguistic importations.[36]

Minimalist Universalism: Resisting Greater Britain

The most remarkable dimension of Johnson's selective negotiations with modernity, however, lies in his consistent critique of the European imperial project in general, and of the British one in particular. His carefully nuanced response to the key ideological theme of "progress" is especially telling in this regard. Johnson is duly skeptical, and often wearily pessimistic, about the likelihood of genuine progress in human affairs. Nevertheless, he tends to embrace "progressive" reforms on the domestic front, without nostalgia, even as he resoundingly rejects the central legitimating theme of imperial ideology: that the invading colonizer confers "the gift of progress" abroad. What makes Johnson's views compelling now, however, is precisely that they cannot be dismissed either as premodern or as a mere stalking-horse for Eurocentrism. Consider how Johnson, in the crucial introduction to his serial coverage of British parliamentary debates for the *Gentleman's Magazine*, understands his ethical and political obligations as a journalist. Though intervening in a highly visible *national* discussion, he insists from the start on extending the boundaries of political concern to humanity as a whole. Thus, in 1738, he frames the affairs of "Magnum Lilliputia," or Great Britain, within the context of a macro-political conflict that he describes as both immoral and as an unlawful violation of sovereignty:

> The people of Degulia, or the Lilliputian Europe . . . are, above those of the other parts of the world, famous for arts, arms, and navigation, and, in consequence of their superiority, have made conquests and settled colonies in very distant regions, the inhabitants of which they look upon as barbarous, though in simplicity of manners, probity, and temperance superior to themselves; and seem to think that they have a right to treat them as passion, interest, or

caprice shall direct, without much regard to the rules of justice or humanity; they have carried this imaginary sovereignty so far that they have sometimes proceeded to rapine, bloodshed, and desolation. If you endeavour to examine the foundation of this authority, they neither produce any grant from a superior jurisdiction, nor plead the consent of the people whom they govern in this tyrannical manner; but either threaten you with punishment for threatening the Emperor's sovereignty, or pity your stupidity, or tell you in positive terms that *Power is right.*[37]

It is precisely through this framing strategy that Johnson maintains a dual allegiance both to a modernizing national project and to a world polity increasingly blighted by the imperial dynamics of European expansion.

A fitting homage to Swift's immanent critique in *Gulliver's Travels*, this passage exposes, as a founding gesture, the broader imperial context within which "British" issues were constituted. Such a globalizing gesture, in the most prominent periodical of the day, belies a common excuse for strictly insular histories of Britain. As David Armitage points out, contemporary historians who wish to minimize the domestic significance of the British empire often invoke as an excuse "the aggressive amnesia of eighteenth- and nineteenth-century Britons"[38] as regards the colonies. That ideologically sanctioned amnesia, however—what Armitage terms "isolationist imperialism"[39]—is far more characteristic of the nineteenth century than the eighteenth, which had not yet consolidated the logical quarantine that would conceive of "British" and "imperial" history as things apart. Indeed, the eighteenth century's much fuller registration of global entanglement was precisely what the nineteenth century had to repress. The visibility of tentacular globalization begat globalizing critiques. Johnson repeats his own globalizing strategy in 1759, when he reframes the contents of *The World Displayed*—a 20-volume collection of European voyage-and-discovery literature—with an introduction instructing readers in the anti-colonial analysis of historical sources. He frames this fraught collection of documents by reading its contents against the grain of its surface content. He foregrounds, and repeatedly comments on, issues of violated sovereignty, pitiless greed, capricious violence, and callow bigotry that permeate this collection.

Johnson never relies on the infamy of Iberian colonial atrocities, moreover—on the "Black Legend" of the uniquely cruel Spanish conquistadors—merely to legitimate by comparison a supposedly more benign British expansionism. In his "Introduction to the Political State of Great Britain" (1756), published just as the Seven Years War with France was heating up, Johnson uses the English phase of early European expansion to unmask the militaristic political ethos of mid-eighteenth-century Britain.

Of the slavery-based colony of Jamaica, Johnson remarks that it continues, even to this day, as "a place of great wealth and dreadful wickedness, a den of tyrants, and a dungeon of slaves."[40] Johnson goes even further in *Idler* 81, an attack on patriotic war-fever that was published some three years later. In this essay, Johnson assumes the perspective of an "Indian" chief dispassionately hoping the competing British and French armies will decimate one another; "Let us look unconcerned upon the slaughter, and remember that the death of every European delivers the country from a tyrant and a robber."[41] This passage concludes as follows: "Let us endeavor, in the mean time, to learn their discipline, and to forge their weapons: and when they shall be weakened with mutual slaughter, let us rush down upon them, force the remains to take shelter in their ships, and reign once more in our native country."

The ripples from this pointed act of ventriloquism continued for some time. In 1765, an anonymous contributor to the *Gentleman's Magazine* versified Johnson's resistance to the imperial forging of Britishness, demonstrating its resonance well after the conclusion of the Seven Years War:

> For See! These sons of rapine have now drawn
> Their swords upon each other, and referr'd
> Their idle and imaginary claims
> To the decision of a war; let us
> Look on with pleasure, still remembering
> That when an *European* falls, there falls
> A tyrant and a robber. . . .[42]

The imaginary occasion for this speech, an explicit amplification of Johnson's native American, was a celebrated national triumph of 1759: the British army's capture of Quebec. Since Major-General James Wolfe died bravely in this battle, the passage implicitly reduces the death of a British hero to the fall of "a tyrant and a robber." Adversarial perspectives likewise kept Johnson's critique in play. In 1783, James Thomson Callender still found it important to defend imperial Britishness against Johnson's attack in the following terms:

> The savages of North America are eloquent and acute. . . . he has given us the oration of an Indian, full of "comprehensive knowledge and delicate elocution." It contains, indeed, many abstract terms of which an Iroquois could have no conception; and this circumstance shews the Doctor's unacquaintance with human manners. . . . And the author has not hinted that this copper-coloured patriot had been taught to read. This absurd opinion . . . arises from Dr. Johnson's narrow views on human nature. He seems to forget for a moment that mankind ever existed under any mode of manners except his own.[43]

Johnson, it seems, is too insensitive to "difference"—to a supposed cultural inferiority that would prevent anything so disturbing as a reasoned critique emerging from the mouth of the colonized.

Callender's attack begins to explain a much broader effort to defang Johnson by relegating him to the land of the quaint. It anticipates the logic of the most infamous evaluation of Johnson's literary *oeuvre*: the broad attack launched by Thomas Babington Macaulay, in his *Encyclopedia Britannica* article of 1856. Macaulay's assessment stands soundly rejected today. Yet what was really at stake in his attack, the discomfort of a Whig historiographer and colonial administrator with the universalist thought of Johnson, is seldom fully understood. Macaulay's views about Johnson's *Rasselas* thus bear quoting at some length:

> Rasselas and Imlac, Nekayah and Pekuah, are evidently meant to be Abyssinians of the eighteenth century; for the Europe which Imlac describes is the Europe of the eighteenth century: and the inmates of the Happy Valley talk familiarly of that law of gravitation which Newton discovered, and which was not fully received even at Cambridge until the eighteenth century. What a real company of Abyssinians would have been may be learned from Bruce's *Travels*. But Johnson, not content with turning filthy savages, ignorant of their letters and gorged with raw steaks cut from living cows, into philosophers as eloquent and enlightened as himself or his friend Burke, and into ladies as highly accomplished as Mrs. Lennox or Mrs. Sheridan, transferred the whole domestic system of England to Egypt.[44]

The object of Macaulay's attack here is quite pointedly Johnson's scandalous association of rationality with non-Europeans. Indeed, what most troubles Macaulay is Johnson's audacious universalism: what an older generation of scholars identified as "Enlightenment Uniformitarianism." Johnson's uniformitarian thought is simultaneously a product of the emancipatory potential of the eighteenth-century Enlightenment and refusal almost in advance, as it were of the Enlightenment's eventual rearticulation from within the exclusive and racial logic of an imperial Eurocentrism. Johnson's principled universalism ultimately fails to harmonize with Macaulay's imperialist worldview.

It is worth noting here that Thomas Macaulay's selective mobilization of Bruce's text also oversimplifies the latter's account of eighteenth-century Ethiopian cultures. Bruce devotes only a page or so of his multi-volume work to the "live steak" incident that so exercises Macaulay.[45] It was nevertheless this sensational incident that had come to characterize the work's public reception, fostering skepticism toward Bruce in many quarters while (as in the case of Macaulay) telling others everything they thought they needed to know about the peoples of Ethiopia.

Though Johnson adhered to the Sons-of-Noah narrative, he manifests no signs of an "ethnic theology" that would justify treating any group of people differently. His resistance to colonial aggression rests on universalist principles that he expresses earlier in 1735 and later in 1777. In his preface to Father Jerome Lobo's *Voyage to Abysinnia* (1735), Johnson argues "that wherever human nature is found, there is a mixture of vice and virtue, a contest of passion and reason; and . . . the Creator doth not appear partial in his distributions. . . ."[46] Some forty years later, these ideas recur in "A Brief to Free a Slave" (1777). In this brief, Johnson made a successful legal intervention on behalf of Joseph Knight, a black slave, suing a court in Scotland for freedom from the Scottish master from whom he had escaped. Johnson bores in on the lack of proof that Joseph Knight has ever—whether as a criminal or as a military captive pleading for life—forfeited his own universal right to liberty:

> He [Joseph Knight] is certainly subject to no law, but that of violence, to his present master, who pretends no claim to his obedience, but that he bought him from a merchant of slaves, whose right to sell him was never examined. It is said that, according to the constitutions of Jamaica, he was legally enslaved; these constitutions are merely positive, and apparently injurious to the rights of mankind, because whoever is exposed to sale is condemned to slavery without appeal; by whatever fraud or violence he might have been originally brought into the merchant's power. . . .[47]

He pauses to register the crude injustice of the race-based legal system that Knight would face if Jamaican law were to be invoked: "The laws of Jamaica afford a Negro no redress. His color is considered as a sufficient testimony against him." He then concludes as follows, with a ringing assertion of universal rights:

> The sum of the argument is this:—No man is by nature the property of another. The defendant is, therefore, by nature free. (368)

Johnson is here explicitly extending human rights beyond any sort of "color line" and beyond the boundaries of nationhood. And though it may seem that Johnson is only now beginning to get his due as an important precursor to the formally organized abolitionist movement,[48] such recognition in fact existed previously, only to be conveniently forgotten. An anonymous abolitionist tract published in Johnson's home town of Lichfield in 1826, addressed to the abolitionist Reverend Thomas Gisborne, Prebendary of Durham, begins as follows:

> The Sugar Colonies of the West present to our sympathy not fewer than 830,000 human beings in a state of slavery.—I think myself happy, Sir, in

being authorized to approach this subject, when virtually addressing the inhabitants of Lichfield, under the protection of the mighty name of SAMUEL JOHNSON. The exertions of this great man, in behalf of the Negroes, preceded by thirteen years, your own efforts, and those of your excellent friend Mr. Wilberforce.[49]

The author praises the universalism that underpins Johnson's reasoning in the case of Joseph Knight as "impossible to refute" and also impossible to confine, in spirit, "to particular parallels of latitude and longitude."[50] Johnson deserves full credit for answering the false universalism of Eurocentrism with a truer one.

Universal Africans

As Macaulay understood, the most telling example of the radical potential of Johnson's uniformitarian thought is indeed *Rasselas* (1759). Although *Rasselas* is ostensibly an "oriental" tale, it is notable above all for the marked absence of a reifying local color. It seems likely, for example, that Johnson picked the setting of Coptic Christianity in the highlands of Ethiopia as a way of reminding his Protestant readers of Christianity's location, during its formative years, in the deserts of West Asia and North Africa. This point requires emphasis. Jack Goody's careless misreading of the characters in *Rasselas* as "heathens" is typical of the way that the nuances of Johnson's achievement get buried by facile debunking gestures.[51] The term "Orientalism," by the same token, does not illuminate *Rasselas*. One finds more emphasis in *Rasselas* on African engineers, philosophers, theologians, astronomers, architects, and poets than on exotic customs and animals. Even the harem in which Pekuah is temporarily confined disappoints all expectations of salacious "Oriental" excess: it is merely a dull prison.

Rasselas, moreover, exemplifies a remarkably sophisticated engagement with those older civilizations whose reputations were becoming increasingly vulnerable to imperial revisionism. Johnson has no difficulty during the book's Egyptian chapters in acknowledging the pyramids as (excepting the Great Wall of China) "the greatest work of man."[52] In Imlac's words to Rasselas: "You are in a country famous among early monarchies for the power and wisdom of its inhabitants; a country where the sciences first dawned that illuminate the world, and beyond which the arts cannot be traced of civil society or domestic life."[53] "The ruins of their architecture," Imlac goes on to say, "are the schools for modern builders."[54] Johnson, furthermore, does not emphasize the pyramids' monumentality merely as a pretext for lamenting the terrible decline of present-day Egyptians from their ancient greatness, a favorite imperial theme. And it is precisely in the spirit of a wholehearted engagement with Egyptian civilization that Johnson's generous admiration does not preclude a criticism of what he considers to be its oppressive features. Thus, he complicates our wonder at the pyramids by introducing a theme of slave-labor, reminding us that the great monuments were built by "thousands laboring without end."[55] This insight, coming as it does at the end of a response to the whole of Egyptian civilization, cannot be taken merely as a gibe at "Oriental despotism." It is, rather, a deflation of the irrational pride and ennui typical of ruling classes everywhere—of a universal "hunger of imagination," as Imlac puts it.[56]

Even when Rasselas seemingly comes closest to incorporating the emergent Eurocentric narrative of the "westering of civilization" and its ubiquitous theme of evolutionary progress, the novella is redeemed by Johnson's scrupulous and overriding commitment to uniformitarian ideals. Thus, in a charged passage, Johnson permits the African characters to confront eighteenth-century imperial conquest directly. Ethiopian Christians, who constantly debate the logic of social and political institutions throughout *Rasselas*, dedicate their acumen to the question of why colonization seems to occur in one direction only. One should not underestimate the salutary shock, moreover, of the simple fact that Johnson's readers are thus placed in the position of registering the violent intersection of their world with that of characters with whom they have been encouraged to identify.

Imlac's musings on the global supremacy of northwest Europe stress naval power and its economic basis: "From Persia . . . I travelled through Syria, and for three years resided in Palestine, where I conversed with great numbers of the northern and western nations of Europe; the nations which are now in the possession of all power and all knowledge; whose armies are irresistible, and whose fleets command the remotest parts of the globe"[57] Imlac's recognition of this current imbalance in power and knowledge led him, as he explains, to an inevitable contemplation of "difference":

> When I compared these men with the natives of our own kingdom, they appeared almost another order of beings. In their countries it is difficult to wish for anything that may not be obtained: a thousand arts of which we have never heard are continually laboring for their convenience and pleasure; and whatever their own climate has denied them is supplied by commerce.[58]

It is worth noting the dispassionate tone with which Imlac registers this difference: he knows, and can calmly assess the value of what he does not know.

To Imlac's description of Europe's apparent monopoly on wealth and power, Rasselas replies with a question about the direction of world history: "By what means . . . Are the Europeans thus powerful? Or why, since they can so easily visit Asia and Africa for trade or conquest, cannot the Asiatics and Africans invade their coasts, plant colonies in their ports, and give laws to their natural princes? The same wind that carries them back would bring us thither."[59] Imlac then replies "They are more powerful, sir, than we . . . because they are wiser. Knowledge will always predominate over ignorance, as man governs the other animals. But why their knowledge is more than ours, I know not what reason can be given but the unsearchable will of the Supreme Being."[60] It might seem in this last exchange that Johnson flirts with the "hemispheric" or "westering" understanding of the "progress" ideal. To be sure, readers familiar with Johnson will sense that the apparently lofty beings are being set up for a fall. But both the animal reference and the phrase "almost another order of beings" may initially suggest the well-known rearticulation of the Great Chain of Being in evolutionary terms.

One must recognize the subtlety with which Rasselas addresses this most powerful of imperial themes. First of all, Imlac does say "*almost* another order of beings"; and the phrase is further deflated in a later passage in which the superficial appearance of happiness in others—"such spriteli-ness of air, and volatility of fancy, as might have suited beings of an higher order"—is revealed to be an illusion. Furthermore, the pointedly nonracial explanation given for the contemporary global imbalance of power—"the unsearchable will of the Supreme Being"—refuses any sort of racial essen-tialism by way of accounting for the imbalance. The supernatural reference introduces contingency rather than inevitability: a point, indeed, that Johnson reinforced some twenty years later to Boswell while pointing to this very passage. "This, Sir," Johnson said, "no man can explain otherwise."[61] Goody has interpreted this very passage as giving European military and economic superiority a "permanent guise":[62] a reading that turns Johnson's attitude—that all empires come and go—upside down.

Finally, one must note the deflating conclusion of this chapter, which fully acknowledges the material benefits of progress without assigning undue significance to their uneven distribution. After Rasselas rhapsodizes about those benefits, Imlac replies as follows: "The Europeans . . . are less unhappy than we, but they are not happy. Human life is everywhere a state in which much is to be endured and little to be enjoyed."[63] This illustrates that the belief in a general human nature provides a crucial check on the ascription of a racial significance to uneven developments in the material infrastructure of cultures. The key point is that Johnson stubbornly refuses to link rationality—in his view, a universal, though also universally fragile and embattled, human characteristic—to any particular geographical site. So in *Rasselas*, and so throughout Johnson's *oeuvre*.

Johnson's scrupulously minimalist universalism, as seen in Rasselas, is to be sharply distinguished from the false universalism inherent in the rhetoric that subtended imperial expansion. A study of Johnson's attitude toward empire shows his systematic and lifelong loathing of imperialism. Moreover, the basis of Johnson's anti-imperialism was precisely his antipathy to the sham universalism by which a racially exclusive notion of "progress" was ideologically deployed to underwrite exploitation abroad. Despite his own patriotism, Johnson had an acute awareness that modern nation-building was profoundly shaped by the brutal oppression of aboriginal populations. He often insisted on the legal, ethical, and political standing of aboriginal rights to annexed land. Johnson's abhorrence of colonialism is so systematic that it leaks into the quotations he selected for his *Dictionary*. Under *native*, for example, he quotes Francis Bacon: "Make no extermination of the natives under pretence of planting religion. God surely will be in no way pleased with such sacrifices."

What is crucial about Johnson's critique of imperial "progress" is that it is not articulated from an antimodern perspective. Johnson, indeed, seems especially agile in negotiating the severest contradictions of the Enlightenment. He engages both with its emancipatory potential at home and its potential abuse as an excuse for imperial domination abroad. Contrary to a widely held critical orthodoxy, Johnson did not propound an anti-Enlightenment position. Johnson, however, utterly rejected the often sentimental resistance to progress found in pastoral and exoticizing genres. Urban to the core, he refused the bad faith of scorning material progress by way of camping out in someone else's condition of rural poverty. What is often caricatured in Johnson as mere Tory politics is thus better seen as a specifically modern resistance to the emerging equation of the Enlightenment with "imperial progress." Johnson's minimalist universalism was heir to the Enlightenment's emancipatory potential. Posterity, however, has too often chosen to deflect the challenge of Johnson's selective and agile negotiations with a critical vocabulary that tends either to push his achievement into a distant past or to neutralize its critical force. It is our loss that Johnson's universalism has yet to be mined and reforged as a tool for contemporary critiques of imperialist and racist ideology.

The potential of Johnson's usefulness for contemporary scholarship has surely been obscured by certain familiar gestures that confine him to the domain of the *passé*. For there is more than a coincidental link between Becky Sharpe's famous "junking Johnson" gesture—her throwing Johnson's *Dictionary* out of the carriage window in the first chapter of Thackeray's *Vanity Fair*—and Macaulay's notorious declaration, as the chief architect of an Anglicizing educational curriculum in India, that "a single shelf of a good European library [is] worth the whole native literature of India and Arabia." In other words, nineteenth-century Anglicizing required not only a rewriting of the colonized, but of the colonizer: a consignment to prehistory of awkward contradictions in Britain's own past. Macaulay thus produced a familiar narrative of literary history in which a caricature of Johnson figures as at best the inevitably doomed foil to later progress. "Like those unfortunate chiefs who were suffocated by their own chain-mail," Macaulay writes of Johnson, "his maxims perish under that load of words which was designed for their defence and ornament."[64] Given that literary history likes to move from Dryden to Ossian (Weinbrot) and from Gaelic to Romantic (Gaskill and Stafford), the "Ossian" controversy has provided an important episode in the making of British literary history. No one should deny Macpherson his place in literary history: his having, as Sir Walter Scott puts it, provided a "new tone" to poetry all across Europe. Yet this development, as Johnson was trying to tell us, was neither inevitable nor necessarily desirable. The pious reading of the "Ossian" controversy has thus provided an especially handy club with which to beat Johnson.

History versus Invented Traditions

As I demonstrated in chapter 2, Macpherson's version of history is inflected to assert the interests of Lowland Scots, by a convenient appropriation of a Highland culture they had often attempted to extirpate, within the unionist and Hanoverian framework of the British empire, at the expense of Catholic Ireland. Johnson's many-faceted response to this famous controversy remains a model for the critical analysis of "invented traditions." His antipathy to roots-finding projects such as "Ossian" was in fact based on a principled suspicion of building any national identity around the mystique of reconstructed origins. Johnson's problem with the fashionable primitivism of his own moment had many levels and dimensions. One such involves the modal distinction between truth and fiction. He saw that the project of cultural nationalism tended toward myth-making gestures that appropriate—or simply invent—a heroic past suitable to the aspirations of the present. To the myth-making aspect of this eighteenth-century project, in Linda Colley's phrase, of "forging" Britishness, Johnson manifests a studied aloofness. Indeed, Johnson himself is the great precursor of such insights into the retrospective inventions of nation-based history. The particular appropriation of Celtic antiquities associated with the making of "Ossian" was to inspire some of Johnson's most trenchant critiques of such claims about natural authenticity and ancient folkish "roots." The vicissitudes of cultural difference, for Johnson, do not trump the integrity of historical scholarship. "If we know little of the ancient Highlands," he urges, "let us not fill the vacuity with *Ossian*."[65]

Another objectionable layer in Macpherson's palimpsest, as Johnson recognized, was its obfuscation of the internal politics of Scotland. Such re-creations of a "unmediated" past often serve to impose a false unity on collectivities otherwise divided in the present, and "Ossian" was no exception. Eighteenth-century Lowland Scots had in fact often actively crusaded to extirpate the Highland's Gaelic culture. Indeed, the Society in Scotland for Propagating Christian Knowledge—founded two years after the 1707 Act of Union—quickly began to displace the Highlands' traditional parish schools; the evangelical society was begun with the express intention of "eliminating the Gaelic language."[66] Johnson registers in his *Journey* the alienating impact of this situation as follows: "Here [in the Hebrides] the children are taught to read; but by the rule of their institution, they teach only *English*, so that the natives read a language which they may never use or understand."[67] And indeed, as in his piece on the English Common Soldier, Johnson refuses in the case of Scotland to paper over internal divisions in the name of a supposedly shared national culture. He observes early on in the *Journey* that Highlanders disdain to learn English from their Lowland neighbors.[68] Near the end of the *Journey* he reflects again on the gulf between the Lowlands and the Highlands, remarking as follows:

> To the southern inhabitants of Scotland, the state of the mountains and the islands is equally unknown with that of Borneo or Sumatra: Of both they have only heard a little, and guess the rest.

"They are strangers to the language and the people," he concludes, "whose life they would model, and whose evils they would remedy."[69]

That Macpherson's bogus translation nevertheless had so many distinguished Lowland illuminati closing ranks behind it provoked from Johnson the following pitiless apothegm: "A Scotchman must be a very sturdy moralist who does not love Scotland better than truth: he will always love it better than inquiry; and if falsehood flatters his vanity, will not be very diligent to detect it."[70] This finely calibrated skepticism is aimed specifically at the Lowland intelligentsia and their opportunistic literary and ethnographic appropriation of Highland culture.[71] The literary myth of the Highlands—based on the suddenly convenient apotheosis of a society otherwise despised as primitive and kept at a great distance—"underpins the Lowland construction of its own identity."[72] With the appearance of *Fingal* in 1761, Lowland Scotland gained what O'Brien describes as "a compensatory myth of origins, an outlet for repressed national narcissism in an age of anglicization."[73] Or, to quote Johnson again: "The Scots have something to plead for their easy reception of an improbable fiction: they are seduced by their fondness for their supposed ancestors."[74] The deadly word *supposed* in this comment glances again at the lack of organic connection in such a genealogy.

Johnson did not, as some have argued, merely drift into the Scottish Enlightenment's developmental paradigm toward the end of his life, when he wrote his famous travel narrative. He is sensitive, in terms of specific policies, to what Michael Hechter described a generation ago as the "internal colonialism" of England toward the "Celtic fringe" (Scotland, Wales, and Ireland).[75] The current celebration of Macpherson is often elaborated along these "anti-colonial" lines, and usually at Johnson's expense. Johnson himself, rather than Macpherson, gives an unflinching contemporary description of the post-Culloden demoralization of Highland culture by English oppression. Of the Highlanders he writes, "Their pride has been crushed by the heavy hand of a vindictive conqueror, whose severities have been followed by laws, which, though they cannot be called cruel, have produced much discontent, because they operate on the surface of life, and make every eye bear witness to subjection."[76] It is again Johnson who directly attacks the Disarming Act of 1746: a law by which, as he writes, "every house was despoiled of its defense."[77] Pointing out that the British sovereign affords the Highlanders no real protection, whether from robbers or armed invaders, he concludes as follows: "Laws that place the subjects in such a state, contravene the first principles of the compact of authority: they exact obedience, and yield no protection."[78] And it is Johnson who recommends, as an antidote to mass emigration out from the Highlands, government concessions both on the arms issue and on the question of traditional plaid, also banned by law in 1746:

> To allure them [Highlanders] into the [British] army, it was thought proper to indulge them in the continuance of their national dress. If this concession could have any effect, it might easily be made. That dissimilitude of appearance, which was supposed to keep them distinct from the rest of the [British] nation, might disincline them from coalescing with the Pensylvanians [*sic*] or people of Connecticut. If the restitution of their arms will reconcile them to their country, let them have again those weapons, which will not be more mischievous at home than in the Colonies. . . . To hinder insurrection, by driving away the people, and to govern peacably, by having no subjects, is an expedient that argues no great profundity of politicks. . . . it affords a legislator little self-applause to consider, that where there was formerly an insurrection, there is now a wilderness.[79]

This last phrase is more resonant still for those who catch the echo of a phrase from Tacitus: *ubi solitudinem faciunt, pacem appellant.* This famous phrase comes from the Scottish campaign, during the time of Boudicca's rebellion, that in AD 84 pitted the Roman general Agricola against the still-unconquered Caledonians. Tacitus quotes a rousing speech by the Caledonian leader Calgacus to his troops that concludes as follows: "To robbery, butchery, and rapine, they [the Romans] give the lying name of 'government'; they create a desolation and call it peace."[80] Here Johnson mobilizes classical learning precisely to indict the "modern Romans" of 1746. Gibes such as these, which seriously annoyed George III, have led some to the dubious conclusion that Johnson was a closet Jacobite. Such labels, in any case, tend to miss the nimbleness of a multi-pronged response that encompasses, among the various mediations of "Ossian," British oppression of the Highlands, Lowland appropriation of the Highlands, and Scottish annexation of Irish antiquities. Such an emphasis on mediations, which gives the lie to a simple developmental paradigm, demonstrates that Johnson did not merely reproduce the themes of social evolution.

As Johnson understood, Macpherson's historiographical project is tainted by agendas that go well beyond the simple issue of forgery. Turning the historical record upside down, Macpherson attempts to reposition the Highlands as the original Celtic motherland. Johnson hints at this problem of highjacked antiquities in the *Journey*, noting that a putatively Earse translation of the Bible proved to be "nothing else than the Irish Bible."[81] He reports in the same vein that he and James Boswell "had heard of manuscripts that were, or had been in the hands of somebody's father, or grandfather; but at last . . . had no reason to believe they were other than Irish."[82] The anti-Irish dimension of Macpherson's "translating" project comes into greater focus, moreover, when juxtaposed with his judgments about that country's history in his subsequent opus, *The History of Great Britain* (1771). As regards William III's "pacification" of Ireland in 1689–1690, for example, Macpherson writes as follows: "The Irish ought to have been considered as enemies, rather than rebels. If, therefore, the pacification was expedient, it was certainly just."[83]

Macpherson's emphasis on pure roots in the Ossianic controversy can indeed be read in part as "a battle of Celtic antiquaries" and "a tribal tug of war between the Scots and the Irish"[84] also involving Charles O'Conor. O'Conor, an Irish Catholic and, in Clare O'Halloran's phrase, "one of the few Gaelic scholars of the time,"[85] had published in 1753 his *Dissertations on the Antient History of Ireland:* a book depicting pre-Christian Gaelic Ireland as "a sophisticated, aristocratic, and, above all, literate society."[86] This anti-primitivist portrayal—a direct challenge to British stereotypes about the "wild Irish"—was especially important at a juncture when Catholics were beginning their campaign to end the odious Penal Laws.[87] Thomas Curley rightly credits O'Conor both with steering Johnson toward an endorsement of Irish Studies and with promoting a blend of Irish patriotism with a conciliatory religious toleration. However, Curley's description of O'Conor's *Dissertations* as "marred by anachronism, credulity, disorganization, and rhetorical imprecision," seems to miss the crucial points of that work.[88] A collection of interlinked essays—on such themes as "faction," for example—O'Conor's work refuses, by discontinuous narration, to harden sectarian identities in the present. O'Conor's scholarly methods are generally cautious and skeptical, and even his weakest argument—the implausible "Milesian" myth that traces ancient Irish civilization back to Egypt via Spanish Galicia—is soberly acknowledged as lacking in evidence.[89] Thomas McLoughlin seems more balanced in describing O'Conor as "the first . . . to ask not for the privileging of Irish national perspectives but for mutual respect and dialogue."[90] O'Conor, neither a charlatan nor a zealot, is a marked alternative to Macpherson in the tiny world of eighteenth-century Gaelic scholarship.

In this dispute, Johnson tilted toward O'Conor. In 1757, having received a copy of O'Conor's book through the offices of the publisher George Faulkner, Johnson wrote to the Irish scholar praising his work and expressing a desire "to be further informed of a people so ancient, and once so illustrious."[91] In the introduction to his subsequent edition of *Dissertations on the Antient History of Ireland* (1766), O'Conor praises Johnson for his receptivity to research in Celtic antiquities: "Far from joining in the current Prejudice versus the present Subject, or oppressing the writer who undertook it with Censure . . . he approved of an Endeavor to revive . . . the antient Language and Literature of a Sister Isle."[92] Johnson wrote again to O'Conor in 1777, expressing a particular desire to know more about the period prior to the English conquest when Ireland was, in his words, "the school of the West, the quiet habitation of Sanctity and literature."[93] He lent support as well to a maverick Scottish researcher in Celtic antiquities, William Shaw, author of a rudimentary Gaelic grammar and dictionary,[94] who refused to rally around Macpherson's attempts to make Scotland, rather than Ireland, the original Celtic motherland. Shaw was a Highland Scot who was sensitive not only to the telling anachronisms in *Fingal* but, perhaps above all, to Macpherson's attempt to aggrandize Scottish "roots" precisely by marginalizing the heavily Irish dimension of extant Celtic antiquities. In Shaw's words, Macpherson, "in order to serve his purpose, wrests facts as they may serve his end, and, apprehensive of a future detection, labours with great zeal to destroy the credit of all Irish history, and with a few bold strokes of his pen, obliterates all the Celtic learning ever known any where, in order to make way for a new system of Celtic emigration and Hebridean and Fingalian history. . . ."[95] The controversy was not bilateral. It was by no means between Macpherson and Johnson only, but between Macpherson and his admirers against a host of skeptics, English, Irish, and Scots. To neglect the Irish dimension, and especially the contribution of Charles O'Conor, distorts and erases history.

Johnson's stance in the "Ossian" affair, entirely consistent with his life-long loathing for the pastoral genre, finally serves to disrupt the touristic pleasure afforded to consumers sighing from Virginia to Weimar over the melancholy fate of weepy warrior-bards. Here is the deflating dish he serves up to a public hungry for underdeveloped forms of life conveniently preserved in the poverty of the Highlands:

> We came thither too late to see what we expected, a people of peculiar appearance, and a system of antiquated life. . . . Of what they had before the late conquest of their country, there remain only their language and their poverty. . . . Such is the effect of the late regulations, that a longer journey than to the Highlands must be taken by him whose curiosity pants for savage virtues and barbarous grandeur.[96]

And though Johnson resolutely refuses to glamorize the Highlands, he does not thereby merely lapse back into an unsympathetic essentialism. He insists instead, with a salutary emphasis on present conditions, that the "primitive manners" of the Highlanders are "produced by their situation rather than derived from their ancestors."[97] Johnson verges here on an insight into the "development of under-development." More broadly, he punctures the tendency of pastoralism to ignore issues of policy and power. The mediation by commerce of "Celtomania," in Weinbrot's felicitous term, illustrates the convenient and unthreatening terms on which the primitivist fad was marketed.

Macpherson wrote precisely to satisfy readers panting "for savage virtues and barbarous grandeur." He appealed to an eighteenth-century sentimental ethos defined by a perceived conflict between the ruggedly "masculine" civic virtue of classical antiquity and the more "effeminate" manners of the refined present.[98] In this sense, it is finally not just a supposedly indigenous Scottish tradition, but also a certain construction of "Britishness," that is ultimately at stake in the controversy over "Ossian." The "voice" of Ossian, published in the wake of the Rising of 1745, conjured up a past that is meant to be Scottish and British simultaneously. The proper name of Ossian "marks the translation of Gaelic culture into England's national myth of Britain."[99] A literary history that unquestioningly celebrates the contribution of "Ossian," then, also risks loving Great Britain "more than truth." "Ossian" represents a case where an obdurate cultural nationalism intersects with a broader imperial agenda, much as Highland regiments were permitted to assert their "traditional dress" while mobilizing at Ticonderoga and elsewhere on behalf of empire. Johnson's interventions, then, were not directed solely at the excesses of Scottish nationalism: they attempted to check an appetite, within and beyond Britain, for commodified access to "British" origins: the selling, in effect, of backwardness. To be sure, the marketability of ancient Celtic romance has proven a mighty force indeed.

"Fingal's Cave" on the tiny Isle of Staffa, remains, along with the Rob Roy Center at Callendar, a significant tourist attraction for touring Scotophiles. But it is not an imperial perspective that determines Johnson's barbed resistance to jumping on the tartan-doll bandwagon. In addition to voicing a generalized suspicion of the staging of national genealogies as such, Johnson recognizes the extent to which the Highlands risk being trapped in someone else's escapist fiction.

Some may still be tempted to argue that Macpherson-the-Trickster was a necessary stimulant to the decolonization of the Celtic peripheries. And there are indeed signs, despite Macpherson's daunting baggage, that Howard Gaskill's campaign to rehabilitate "Ossian" is finding a bit of traction.[100] In a similar vein, Fiona J. Stafford has recently suggested that new critical approaches—"the great interest in colonialism, cultural imperialism, and post-colonial theory"—are likely to consolidate the rehabilitation of Macpherson and deliver *The Poems of Ossian* from the category of "quaint hoax."[101] Over and over again, conventional wisdom in the fields of history and literature isolates Johnson and Macpherson, pits them against one another, and then finds the latter a sympathetic underdog. So the anthropologist and historian Nicholas B. Dirks, for example, describes the benefits of Macpherson's epic poem (which he misnames *Ossian*) without regard either to its truthfulness or to the impact on Ireland of Macpherson's historiographical assaults:

> [The epic] provided Scotland with a heroic and distinctive past, a claim to epic glory, and a legitimate folk tradition. In particular, the epic marked off Scottish history from Ireland's and established the basis for a new cultural nationalism in the wake of England's suppression of the Highland clans after the Jacobite Rebellion of 1745.[102]

Johnson, then, though posing as "a champion of the truth,"[103] merely betrays his bigoted attitude toward Scotland. Dirks follows the position cited above with a caveat about the pernicious effect that historicizing culture or tradition can have because there are "many truths, truths that take many cultural forms."[104] History ought to embrace the sort of relativism once common in anthropology. This pious position is specifically offered in response to, and as an advance over, the influential volume *The Invention of Tradition* (1983), edited by Eric Hobsbawm and Terence Ranger. Satya P. Mohanty, however, articulates an eloquent caveat against such relativist positions: "No matter how different cultural Others are," he writes, "they are never so different that they are—as typical members of their culture— incapable of acting purposefully, of evaluating their actions in light of their ideas and previous experiences, and of being 'rational' in this minimal way."[105] Macpherson, of course, was not merely an outsider who was culturally innocent of empirical epistemological regimes. He was a knowing and stubborn hoaxter who—trapped into defending an untenable lie—made deception and fabrication the center both of his final decade on earth and of his posthumous legacy. Decrying empiricism, in the face of such a story, hardly seems the way forward. And though Dirks emphasizes that David Hume, as a proud Scot, was "deeply offended" by Johnson's attack, Hume was also quite skeptical of Macpherson and justifiably fearful of the embarrassing damage a forged "Ossian"—pregnant with the possibility of its exposure—might do. Hume in fact devised the scrupulously empirical protocol ultimately used by the Committee of the Highland Society of Scotland to investigate the Ossian affair in the early nineteenth century, which concluded in 1805 that "it [was] possessed of no documents, to shew how much of his collection Mr. Macpherson obtained in the form in which he has given it to the world."[106]

Hume's attitude toward public culture was open: he did not rule out the possibility of finding some provisional approximation of the truth, and he did *not*, it seems, love Scotland more than that truth. The "anthropological stop-sign" proposed by Dirks has other problems. How is one to know *which* traditions require special exemption from historical scrutiny? Are some parts of the world better suited to skeptical reflexivity than others? And is it rarer in those tender-minded zones than in England to find that patriotism, as Johnson memorably said, may be "the last refuge of a scoundrel"? One wonders, indeed, if a work such as Wole Soyinka's *Kongi's Harvest*, which satirizes the abusive invention of traditions in post-independence Africa, will have to go onto a new index of prohibited books. To render any group exempt from history would seem to excuse oneself from engaging with that group in the same political space and time. Such evasions, as Edward Said's reiterated emphasis on the political importance of *secular* history makes clear, tend to perpetuate anthropological appropriations whereby societies are culturized "regardless of politics and history."[107]

Perhaps Macpherson is irredeemable, and yet Johnson nonetheless deserves to be tarred as an imperialist? Although the Scottish Highlands come up often in Janet Sorensen's *The Grammar of Empire in Eighteenth-Century British Writing*, she goes beyond the dubious gesture of rallying around Macpherson. Hers is a more sophisticated critique of Johnson's project. Rather than celebrating supposedly discrete local cultures, Sorensen argues for a more multilayered project: the exploration of "the multiple and alternative histories of languages," whether Scots or English.[108] I concur with this; and I likewise concur with her critique of the "anachronistic space" that often marks the commodification of a minority culture such as Gaelic—divorced from economic and political contexts—as it is assimilated by a more powerful one.[109] I disagree with *The Grammar of Empire*, however, in finding far more clues in Johnson's many-layered *oeuvre* than does Sorensen for analytical work in that direction. Her depiction of Johnson's "colonial ambivalence" as a lexicographer—that is, a prescriptive standardizer of the English vernacular who also resigns himself pragmatically to customary usage—seems to dilute the main thrust of his intellectual contribution. I would not concede that Johnson expresses "colonial ambivalence" in the strong sense popularized by Homi Bhabha: that is, a simultaneous desire for, and yet anxiety about, the "mimicry" of the colonized. Because she sees the *Dictionary* as "colonizing" the English no less than anyone else, the word is for Sorensen merely a slippery metaphor for generic domination. To be sure, Sorensen seems to get some mileage out of a simile used in Johnson's plan for the dictionary, in which he compares himself to the soldiers of Caesar looking on Britain.[110] First of all, however, one must note the self-wounding irony in this trope, which recognizes that "it would be madness to invade." More crucially, the trope simply cannot be taken as a telling identification with the colonizer. Here is Johnson's view of the Roman empire: "I know not why any one but a schoolboy in his declamation should whine over the commonwealth of Rome, which grew great only by the misery of the rest of mankind."[111]

The Janus-faced nature of national standardization, whether in England or elsewhere, is an extremely familiar *topos*. I would thus likewise not concede that any attempt to regularize the written language is, by definition, "imperial" merely because (1) linguistic communities are marked by the insider/outsider problematic; or (2) the alphabetic organization of dictionaries enacts a fantasy of rational control. Though focused narrowly on the *Dictionary*, Sorensen's critique casts such a wide net that it immediately implicates virtually every bourgeois nationalism around the globe. The tension between useful leveling and exclusionary homogeneity is inherent to nation-building as such. Any vernacular public culture constitutes itself through linguistic norms, and the horizontal diffusion of such supra-regional norms is not reducible merely to the sidelining of regional difference by the juggernaut of abstract homogeneity. Access to nationally shared norms also potentially enlarges the reach of those otherwise trapped in excessively local and opaque dialects. Moreover, the linguistic currency of written media requires, no less than the currency of monetary exchange, a negotiable set of standardized and shared conventions. While these can be renegotiated, however, like traffic laws, they cannot be dispensed with.

Knees jerk hard and fast against linguistic prescriptivism. Yet an intelligent prescriptivism, as Carey McIntosh argues, can be defended as a means of increasing the clarity of the written language.[112] The gain is practical: to Johnson's *Dictionary*, to take one small example, we owe the refinement of a distinction between "metal" (reserved for chemical elements such as copper) and "mettle"(reserved for spiritual qualities such as courage or spirit).[113] In any case, the frequency with which Johnson yields to the authority of customary spellings and pronunciations makes clear his pragmatic recognition that language—always changing, always teeming with anomalies—can be neither perfectly regularized nor "embalmed." It thus seems reductive to describe the tens of thousands of learned decisions Johnson made in the course of his lexicographical practice—sometimes prescriptive, sometimes descriptive—as constituted by something so vague as "colonial ambivalence." Johnson, as Allen Reddick demonstrates, left unresolved the philosophical crux as to whether etymology or usage determines the meaning of words.[114] As a means of tracking the evolution of usage, moreover, Johnson's practice of including historical illustrations inspired the best feature of the *OED*. Finally, one ought to note that Johnson appeals to *authors* for guidance in usage rather than mere social elitism ("the King's English"). Bourgeois nationalism has its virtues.

Informal, slangy, and vulgar words give the lie to the notion that Johnson was merely seeking to embalm a stuffy and sanitized version of the language. The point is made with a dozen or so of the words that made into the *Dictionary: bamboozle, conycatch, arse, skimbleskamble, puke, snipsnap, asshead, bellygod, fopdoodle, rantipole, turd, balderdash, yellowboy, snot*, and *skipjack*. Johnson's definition of REDSHANK (illustrated from Edmund Spenser's description of the sixteenth-century Ulster plantations) likewise reflects critically on English bigotry, or internal colonialism, toward the Scots:

> This seems to be a contemptuous appellation for some of the people of Scotland. He sent over his brother Edward with a power of Scots and redshanks unto Ireland, where they got footing. (Spenser)

That Johnson marks certain English words as Scots, just as "bohea" and "Calico" are marked as Indian, does not in itself amount to domination. Only the *use* of such words for the specifically colonial function of unequal exchange would implicate such linguistic notations in the dynamics of domination. Entirely in keeping with Johnson's project is his second definition for *national*: "Bigotted to one's country."

Resisting Ethnic Absolutism

It is significant that Johnson maintains a cool distance from any "roots-finding" projects that seek to inflate a supposed national essence by magnifying its glorious origins in antiquity. He thus turns a skeptical gaze as well on Anglocentric antiquarianism, with its parallel program of Saxon revivalism.

Rambler #177 (1751), in portraying the elderly antiquarian Hirsutus, depicts him as introducing his favorite studies "by a severe censure of those who want due regard for their native country."[115] Whereas Hirsutus collects only books printed in Roman or Gothic letters, his ballad-mongering associate Cantilenus "turned all his thoughts upon old ballads, for he considered them as the genuine records of the national taste."[116] Both Hirsutus and Cantilenus seem to prefigure impending developments. By 1764, Thomas Percy's *Reliques of Ancient English Poetry* had generated the figure of the medieval minstrel, of pointedly Saxon ancestry, as an English mirror-image of Macpherson's ancient Caledonian bard. Though Johnson shared membership with Percy in the celebrated literary society of the Club, such fraternization "was not such a fellowship . . . that it resolved differences of taste between Johnson and Percy or prompted Johnson to repress his disagreement with his younger clubmate."[117] Indeed, despite his lengthy acquaintance with Percy, which also led him into ghostwriting the dedication of *Ancient Reliques* to the Countess of Northumberland, Johnson indulged throughout his life in "sportive anathemas" on ballads and their revivalists.[118] His doubts about their literary merits—and especially about the merits of *modern* ballad imitations—were expressed in a number of amusing parodies, the improvisational genius and "merry malice" of which are extensively recorded by Hester Lynch Piozzi.[119]

Johnson was in fact not entirely complacent about the value of supposedly ancient ballads as documents of social history, suspecting, indeed, that Percy's *Reliques* might be placed in the same category as Ossian.[120] Given his attacks on the eager credulity of Scots as regards the antiquity of "Ossian," moreover, it is salutary to register his claim, during his tour of Scotland, that he could produce a ballad-based English equivalent to Macpherson's chorus of true-believers. According to Boswell's *Tour of the Hebrides*, Johnson told Lord Elibank he would undertake "to write an epick poem on the story of Robin Hood, and half England, to whom the names and places he should mention in it are familiar, would believe and declare they had heard it from their earliest years."[121] His particular target, then, is neither old poetry nor popular poetry per se, but rather, as Clark puts it, "the creation of a mythic vernacular literature."[122]

Johnson had little patience with the Gothic revival. Indeed, he rejected the "studied barbarity" of even Edmund Spenser's literary archaisms,[123] never mind the faux medieval diction of a Thomas Warton, or a William Shenstone, or a Thomas Percy. About such contemporary imitators of Spenser, he makes the following comment about stylistic anachronisms: "It would indeed be difficult to exclude from a long poem all modern phrases, though it is easy to sprinkle it with gleanings of antiquity." He closes this disquisition with a Nietzschean disdain for the merely antiquarian: "Perhaps, however, the style of Spenser might by long labour be justly copied; but life is surely given us for higher purposes than to gather what our ancestors have wisely thrown away, and to learn what is of no value but because it has been forgotten."[124] These words, in addition to debunking metaleptic poetics, constitute a salutary warning about reifying the "marginal" as such.

The Modern Critique of Empire

The painfully prolonged triumph of Macaulay's consignment of Johnson to antediluvian irrelevance is perhaps best illustrated by the disingenuous observation in 1924 by a British literary historian devoted to tracing the evolution of imperial literature: "One does not look to the universal wisdom of Dr. Johnson for much of note on matters of empire."[125] Looking with the clearer eyes of a decolonized world, we see that the opposite is true. In deflating the ethos of Percy's *Reliques* Johnson enacts something well beyond the aesthetic or political conservatism that is often ascribed to him. Indeed, precisely this nationalistic recuperation of history into myth arguably marks a fateful ideological appropriation: the redirection of the progressive achievements of the Enlightenment toward empire-building agendas. Johnson's "soft" nationalism remains pointedly civic and antiessentialist precisely because the mystical and folkloric brands of nationalism are so easily highjacked for racial and expansionist myths. While this gesture is of a piece with his general reluctance to mummify national characteristics, it is connected as well to his opposition to imperial expansion. Johnson articulates a universalism that is explicitly opposed to the imperial construction of hierarchies based on "racial difference." Doyle has recently argued that *Reliques of Ancient English Poetry*, a ballad collection framed by the agenda of aggrandizing a people named as *Anglo-Saxons*, constitutes "a new narrative for English culture: a racial narrative."[126] To be sure, Percy could scarcely have foreseen the future deployments of "Anglo-Saxon" identity. Johnson's so-called obstructionism, however, is at least as prescient in its wary forebodings as is Percy's anticipation of the literary achievements of the next age. Knowing in advance how the plots of literary and cultural history "come out," as it were, we have chosen to misunderstand—and, indeed to bury—the striking alternative to nation-based and race-based historiography represented by Johnson.

Johnson's cosmopolitanism disrupts the historical trajectory with which this book begins: the process by which, to quote Howard Weinbrot again, "powerful quasi-European England becomes more powerful and imperial Britain."[127] Johnson's voice, however, belongs neither to a quasi-European *ancien régime* nor to a new imperial Britain. He deflates the emerging myths, to repeat Doyle's apt phrasing, "of an ancient soil-rooted folk fit to become modern, global conquerors. . . ."[128] Perhaps Johnson's most striking achievement, however, is to have demonstrated that "national" and "cosmopolitan" are not necessarily antinomies. His cosmopolitan nationalism challenges us, in a moment that has already made "global" into an annoying buzzword, to write cultural histories that balance attention to global dynamics with the density of analysis available only in local and vernacular frameworks.

Neil Lazarus has recently touched on a renewed interest in universalism by noting, among a wide group of well-known writers and intellectuals—working in the wake of colonial history—a "simultaneous commitment to the 'philosophical discourse of modernity' *and* to its urgent critique."[129] To his list we can add, as a great precursor, Samuel Johnson. Johnson responded to the contradictions of his eighteenth-century moment with a prescient balancing act that evades the usual labels by which we imagine that we have taken the full measure of the past. Johnson attempted to advance the modernizing project domestically while strenuously dismantling its rearticulations as imperial ideology. As a self-conscious public intellectual, he engaged in deliberate and selective negotiations with a nation-making he simultaneously embraces (in the building of a more democratized vernacular culture) and sharply denounces (in its tendency to fabricate mythical national and racial origins). He repeatedly articulates the relations between the national and the global by focusing on Britain's particular implication in a global narrative of colonial exploitation. His writings exemplify an anti-colonial modernity later foreclosed by the Eurocentric and national imperatives of Britain's increasingly imperial trajectory. No wonder it has been more convenient just to misunderstand the nature of his immanent critique.

EPILOGUE: TOWARD A CRITICAL
REAPPROPRIATION OF MODERNITY

there is no more potent tool for rupture than the reconstruction of genesis: by bringing into view the conflicts and confrontations of the early beginnings and therefore all the discarded possibilities, it retrieves the possibility that things could have been (and still could be) otherwise.

—Pierre Bourdieu, "Rethinking the State"[1]

The treatment of the British eighteenth century that I have offered in this book begins with an example of *metalepsis*, as I have explored it through the "Ossian" controversy, and closes with two examples of *immanent critique*. In between James Macpherson's retrospective fabrication of the past and the critiques of imperialism to be digested from Jonathan Swift and Samuel Johnson, *The British Eighteenth Century and Global Critique* explores the political payoff of certain postcolonial affiliations with the British eighteenth century. The aim has been to reveal the British eighteenth century as a valuable resource for constructing an alternative tradition of, and genealogy for, postcolonial critique. This derives from the historical liminality of the period: a unique poise on the cusp of modernity that affords an opportunity for rethinking modernity and its discontents. *The British Eighteenth Century and Global Critique* ultimately attempts to intervene in current controversies about the periodization of modernity. As such, the argument advanced here has implications for our narratives of cultural history. A modification of our standard periodization of modernity, moreover, simultaneously rearranges our understanding of modernity as a political and intellectual project. In that sense, this book argues for a certain sort of break with postmodern critique. I concur with the verdict of Tobin Siebers that the poetics of "skeptical askesis," overly devoted to puritanical suspicion, belongs to the epoch of the cold war.[2] My argument is not—and ought not to be construed as—merely a lapse into a "pre-theoretical" modernism. The angle of vision is prospective.

A few more words, by way of teasing out some further implications of the linked themes of metalepsis and immanent critique, are in order. These implications bear especially on the particular mode of global analysis, and affiliative reading, offered in this book. By opening up the literature of the British eighteenth century to a global reading, *The British Eighteenth Century and Global Critique* repudiates, as partial, the nation-based narrative that construes it as a stepping stone from early to full modernity (the Neoclassical-to-Romantic paradigm). By the same token, the more global reading attempted here exposes the inadequacy of viewing the British Enlightenment, as per postmodern critique, as the harbinger of "Violent Modernity." The reading offered here instead defamiliarizes the material through a unit of analysis constituted by empire as an international system. This reframing opens up eighteenth-century British literature to multiple appropriations that ultimately deconstruct not only nation-based literary canons but also hemispheric divisions between "the West and the Rest." Precisely such a deconstructive gesture follows from the implications of analyzing the affiliations explored here between eighteenth- and twentieth-century texts: affiliations that work *not* merely by "answering back," in some rather formulaic fashion, but, rather, by building and extending a critique already germinating in the older material. Hence the great resources to be found and mined in the British eighteenth century. Especially central to a truly telling critique of the colonial modernity we continue to inhabit are the twin concepts of metalepsis and immanent critique.

Metalepsis and History

Among the metaleptic fabrications discussed above, perhaps none is more worthy of thorough deconstruction than the notion of the "West"—and so of "Western" modernity, "Western" rationality, and so on. The notion of a timeless "West" was precipitated in the process of forging imperial Europe, and by processes analogous to the invention of "Ossian." A considerable massaging of the archives was necessary to convert the Greeks from brilliant conduits of Egyptian wisdom—the standard eighteenth-century view—to miraculous originators. Both the Egyptians and Phoenicians, as Martin Bernal points out, had to be swept off the board of mediterranean antiquity, where the ancient Greeks themselves had acknowledged their influence. Though the ancient Greeks acknowledged, for instance, the Egyptian contribution to mathematics and astronomy, the imperial appropriation of classical Athens, in an age of systematic racism, was far from cosmopolitan. No more egregious racial appropriation could exist than the claim, in a state of miraculous isolation, to have created civilization. The great prominence in this fabricating process of philologists suggests, once again, that linguistic acrobatics—providing supposed access to linguistic genealogies—served to confuse language and "race." To quote Bernal: "Indo-European linguistics, as it developed in the nineteenth century, was influenced by the prevailing racism, anti-Semitism, and Romantic desire for purity, as manifested in the model of a self-generating tree."[3] And once again, the process, by way of "strange loops," was logically circular. Having erased not only the Egyptians and the Phoenicians but also Greek irrationality, the ideologues of nineteenth-century European triumphalism then defined themselves according to a pristine past that they were busily inventing.

Strange loops and Romantic-racialist rewritings: consider the archeologist Heinrich Schliemann, whose professional reputation is now shadowed by evidence of habitual mendacity.[4] Schliemann's dubious archeological claim in 1873 to have excavated Homer's Troy and recovered Priam's treasure (some jewels from which he used to bedeck his wife Sophie), epitomizes the circular logic of a much vaster exercise in European self-legitimation. For it is not the narrative achievement or even the supposedly literal truth of Homer that was energizing Schliemann's fame, but, rather, the *articulation* of ancient Greece as the "childhood"—the privileged origin—of the "Aryan race." Another of Schliemann's finds—the erroneously named "Mask of Agamemnon"—has a markedly thin "Hellenic" nose, arousing suspicion in his biographer William A. Calder III that a modern forgery, based on the physiognomical theories of Winckelmann, was involved.[5] The metaleptic exercise of "excavating Homer" involved both digging and salting the digs and thereby, once again, leading history by the nose.

Once one has recognized that the very concept of "Western history" is itself the relatively recent product of a specifically imperial rewriting of world history, it becomes impossible to sustain belief in some apparently timeless gulf between "East" and "West." For once and for all, then, we need to let go of "Rise-of-the-West" narratives that attribute the phenomenon entirely to some inner dynamics or essence going back to ancient Greece.

Eurocentric historiography depends precisely on crediting "Western culture" with responsibility for the political, economic, and military hegemony of capitalism. Whether the "West" is glorified or bashed, Eurocentric historiography functions to preserve the sense of a natural dichotomy: the idea that the people of one continent had innate characteristics that inevitably led them to dominate others insufficiently blessed with those characteristics. A contingent fact (domination) gets rewritten, through metaleptic reconstruction, as an invariant essence (rationality). The denunciation of rationality, then—blaming "Western culture" for the hegemony of capitalism—does not go far to puncture the unhistorical illusion of an ontological division between the "West and the Rest."

To acknowledge the belatedness of the metaleptic invention of the "West"—its construction during the dynamics of the late eighteenth and early nineteenth centuries—is to reveal the limits of gestures that merely invert the valence, positive or negative, of the East/West divide. Consider one justly famous example, the "dialectic of Enlightenment." The phrase has passed into theoretical parlance as a convenient shorthand for the obscene complicity of a certain rationality with the most lethal and horrific systems of domination. Presented by Theodor Adorno and Max Horkheimer in *Dialectic of Enlightenment* (1944), the phrase responds, in the immediate wake of World War II, to the Nazi appropriation of the term *Aufklärung*. The *Aufklärung* implemented by National Socialists, however, is not immediately deducible from the eighteenth century, much less from the culture of classical Athens in fifth century BC. To be sure, the Odysseus myth serves a variety of rhetorical purposes in *Dialectic of Enlightenment*, including, as Axel Honneth contends, that of defamiliarizing the naturalized horrors of daily life.[6] A thoroughly embarrassing literalism, however, creeps into this more sophisticated use of the myth. Here are Horkheimer and Adorno on the lotus: "The lotus is an eastern food, and even today—finely shredded—plays an important role in Chinese and Indian cooking."[7] For so fine an intellect as Adorno, the collapse of mediations is an appalling lapse, not different in kind from Schliemann's hokey claim, upon examining a mummy, to have "gazed upon the face of Agamemnon." *Dialectic of Enlightenment* thus severely weakens the force of its critique by repeating, through mere inversion, the founding gesture of Romantic-racialist historiography: it demonizes a supposedly "Western" pathology, instrumental reason, by tracing this sinister faculty all the way back to its supposed origins in Greek antiquity. Having failed to acknowledge the rupture produced by the rewriting of history in racialized terms, Horkheimer and Adorno lapse into the anachronism of extending a racially imagined "us" and "them" all the way back to the epoch of ancient civilizations. From Homer to Hitler, as it were, "instrumental reason" has enabled the overly rational "West" to inflict immense harm on a world supposedly operating in its absence. *Dialectic of Enlightenment*, as an early and highly superior example of this flawed genre, can stand for any number of attacks on the Enlightenment that revolve around an unexamined notion of the monolithic "West."

Precisely due to the world-wide impact of imperialism, therefore, a self-described "global" history must foreground what often disappears into the inert background: a great variety of systemic intersections, ranging from alliance to extermination, and ever-shifting patterns of exchange. As such, a truly global history necessarily challenges unmediated claims to cultural achievements in terms of autonomy, authenticity, and purity. The critique offered in this book of metaleptic genealogies is above all an attack on misleading and simplistic narratives. The value of such a critique is that it refuses to surrender "modernity" to the West and thus to limit critiques of

Eurocentrism merely to a disavowal of modernity. Too often the disavowal of modernity leads merely to a dreary religious fundamentalism: a defensive and rigidly mummified reinvention of one "tradition" or another. Moreover, as Thomas de Zengotita points out, the automatic equation of "Western" with the Enlightenment serves to inhibit advocacy for political goals that might be construed as the quasi-imperial imposition of "Western values."[8] The inhibition is paralyzing. What tidy reification of culture gets wheeled in to justify the denial that we are moral agents inhabiting a shared political space, a shared world? I concur with Satya P. Mohanty that "social diversity specifies and extends the critique of false universalism and deepens our understanding of the kind of moral universalism on which so many progressive political movements have been made."[9] Though some will be unable to abide the notion of a universalism that is not false, I await the discovery of a culture that has abolished the law of gravitation.

Immanent Critique and the Past

My argument has proceeded, as Arif Dirlik has argued in a different context, on the assumption that it is now possible to study the past not merely in order to trace the supposedly organic unfolding of the present, but, rather, to see what "alternative historical trajectories" had to be suppressed in order to make the present possible.[10] Such an approach, in this case, highlights the importance of the eighteenth century—a characteristically liminal century on a variety of crucial fronts and registers—as a potential site for providing an alternative narrative, and, indeed, an alternative historical trajectory. As such, the period needs to be seen afresh as the site for an *immanent critique* of the modernity we now inhabit. We find in the British eighteenth century the emergence of a democratizing public sphere that had not been fully coopted by the imperatives of a race-based imperial project. The challenging intellectual positions available at this threshold moment—subsequently closed down and marginalized—continue to resonate with our own dilemmas. Indeed, given a historical contextualization alert to the signature eighteenth-century quality of liminality, many of our current categories for organizing the cultural past stand revealed as so many reifications, abstracted from a field of competing possibilities. Such reifications are both politically inert and intellectually dishonest.

The British Eighteenth Century and Global Critique thus has implications for the so-called canon wars. To attack the metalepsis that constitutes "Western History" does not mean that one is attacking the individual artifacts that have, at one time or another, been said to constitute the so-called Western canon. On the contrary: in denying that any such monolith exists, I urge a more nuanced approach to questions of canonicity, and a criticism that is more historically engaged. We ought to respond to authors and texts in a more case-by-case fashion without assuming that we have already taken the full measure of the past. Homer had nothing to do with Schliemann or the Nazis, though they had all too much to do with him.

This book, though it may seem superficially similar, likewise differs from most exercises in juxtaposing "metropolitan" and "peripheral" texts. Precisely by emphasizing affiliation, the approach offered here eschews an exclusive use of the contrapuntal model proposed by Edward Said. Said has recommended, as a radical technique for rereading the cultural archive, a deliberately non-chronological practice of historical telescoping whereby the "voice of imperialism" in, say, a nineteenth-century British novel is "answered" by a twentieth-century novel bearing the geographically appropriate "voice of decolonization."[11] The historical narrative of decolonization, in such a juxtaposition, is intended to "answer" and thus reframe our interpretative attitude toward the older text. The practice thus produces "alternative narratives,"[12] by which Said evidently means the narratives of anticolonial counter-nationalism. The lesson to be drawn from the cultural archive would seem to be that imperialism is always destined to be "answered" by an always already existing nationalism. However, Said's failure at this point adequately to *periodize* "Orientalism"—or, indeed, the "West"—serves, in the end, to reinforce the very identities that the most powerful dimensions of his work as a whole compel us to question: for the notion of contrapuntal readings invites us, in effect, merely to read a reified version of present identities back into the past. Said's injunction to dispense with historical chronology thus becomes a stumbling-block to the more advanced tendencies of postcolonial critique. "Alternative narratives," nevertheless, do emerge as early as the eighteenth century—and they resonate not only with resistance to empire-building, but to nationalism as well. It is to the crucial project of teasing out those narratives, within a global framework, that I hope to have contributed in *The British Eighteenth Century and Global Critique*. Said himself has more recently described the implications of *Black Athena* as follows: "The principle underlined by Bernal is the extent to which pedigrees, dynasties, lineages, and predecessors are changed to suit the needs of a later time."[13] We therefore ought to cease to reify the "West," even via an elegantly dialectical model such as "contrapuntal reading," as an identity persisting for more than two millennia. To engage with the invention of the so-called West in the very late eighteenth century is to understand its sheer contingency—and hence, its susceptibility to unraveling. The eighteenth century is immensely edifying as regards the contingency of this category of our social imagination.

I contend that the conspicuously elusive nature of the eighteenth century as a distinct period in cultural history derives precisely from its sheer recalcitrance as regards the nature of the critical lenses that have been brought to bear upon it. To the false teleology of Whiggish historiography about "the growth of liberty," the reply must be to invoke the wider context of empire: what Partha Chatterjee has termed the "rule of colonial difference."[14] To the one-sided polemics of contemporary postmodern theorists against the "Enlightenment project," the riposte must be to highlight the crucial *liminality* of the eighteenth-century moment as regards modernity. This liminality frequently exceeds the amnesiac categories of historical periodization transmitted to us by the sedimented layers of imperial and nation-based historiography. And indeed, a surprising reassessment of the British eighteenth century emerges from these amended critical instruments. For a conspicuous element of that historical liminality involves immanent critiques of the global fashioning of imperial Britishness.

In demonstrating that the eighteenth-century British Enlightenment produced an immanent critique of its most oppressive features, I intend as well to expose the now routine reification of the Enlightenment as such in the *mélange* of theoretical discourses self-defined as "postmodern." To return to Dirlik: we have suppressed the alternative modernities that coexisted in the British eighteenth century precisely in order to legitimate the present. I offer this book precisely as an immanent critique of this ubiquitous phenomenon: as an attempt, in effect, to unfreeze the "Enlightenment" that serves as a static foil for so many postmodern claims. What I hope to have performed, then, is a critique of the Eurocentric aspects of modernity that derives not from "outside" the project of modernity but from within a wider understanding of its origins. An immanent critique rooted in the eighteenth century makes visible the way that "modernity" itself was not the exclusive product of the "West," but was indeed of global parentage all along. Alternative modernities were—and still are—possible.

NOTES

Preface: From Crux to Critique

1. Benedict Anderson, *Imagined Communities: Reflections on the Origin and Spread of Nationalism* (London: Verso, 1983), p. 19.
2. See Ernest Gellner, *Nations and Nationalism* (Ithaca: Cornell University Press, 1983).
3. Ibid., p. 125.
4. Benedict Anderson, *The Spectre of Comparisons: Nationalism, Southeast Asia, and the World* (London: Verso, 1998), p. 57.
5. Gellner, *Nations*, p. 48.
6. Anthony Grafton, *Forgers and Critics: Creativity and Duplicity in Western Scholarship* (Princeton: Princeton University Press, 1990), p. 56.
7. See Susan Stewart, *Crimes of Writing: Problems in the Containment of Representation* (New York: Oxford University Press, 1991), p. 23.
8. Paul Baines, *The House of Forgery in Eighteenth-Century Britain* (Aldershot: Ashgate, 1999), p. 2.
9. Slavoj Žižek, *For They Know Not What They Do: Enjoyment as a Political Factor* (London: Verso, 1991), p. 205.
10. Harold Bloom, " 'Before Moses Was, I Am': The Original and the Belated Testaments," in *Poetics of Influence*, ed. John Hollander (New Haven: Henry R. Schwab, 1988), pp. 387–404.
11. See *The Invention of Tradition*, ed. Eric Hobsbawm and Terence Ranger (Cambridge: Cambridge University Press, 1983).
12. See Greg Clingham, ed., *Making History: Textuality and the Forms of Eighteenth-Century Culture* (Lewisburg: Bucknell University Press, 1998) and *Questioning History: The Postmodern Turn to the Eighteenth Century* (Lewisburg: Bucknell University Press, 1998).
13. Noël Carroll, "Interpretation, History, and Narrative," in *History and Theory: Contemporary Readings*, ed. Brian Fay, Philip Pomper, and Richard T. Vann (Oxford: Blackwell, 1998), p. 40 [inclusive, pp. 34–56].
14. Greg Clingham, Introduction, *Making History*, p. 11.

1   The Global Making of the British
Eighteenth Century

1. See Emma Rothschild, "Globalization and the Return to History," *Foreign Policy* 115 (summer, 1999), pp. 106–116.

2. Howard Weinbrot, *Britannia's Issue: The Rise of British Literature from Dryden to Ossian* (Cambridge: Cambridge University Press, 1995), p. 2.

3. Lawrence Lipking, "Inventing the Eighteenth Centuries: A Long View," in *The Profession of Eighteenth-Century Literature: Reflections on an Institution*, ed. Leo Damrosch (Madison: University of Wisconsin Press, 1992), p. 9.

4. See Robert Griffin, *Wordsworth's Pope: A Study in Literary Historiography* (Cambridge: Cambridge University Press, 1995).

5. Douglas Lane Patey, "Ancients and Moderns," in *The Cambridge History of Literary Criticism*, IV: *The Eighteenth Century*, ed. H. B. Nisbet and Claude Rawson (Cambridge: Cambridge University Press, 1997), p. 45.

6. See Robert Markley, "The Rise of Nothing: Revisionist Historiography and the Narrative Structure of Eighteenth-Century Studies," *Genre* XXIII (summer/fall, 1990), p. 79.

7. Greg Clingham, Introduction, *Making History: Textuality and the Forms of Eighteenth-Century Culture*, ed. Greg Clingham (Lewisburg: Bucknell University Press, 1998), p. 11.

8. See R. G. Collingwood, *The Idea of History*, revised edition, ed. Jan van der Dussen (Oxford: Clarendon Press, 1993), for the link between the emergence of "scientific history" and the moment of romantic nationalism.

9. See *The Invention of Tradition*, ed. Eric Hobsbawm and Terence Ranger (Cambridge: Cambridge University Press, 1983); Ernst Gellner, *Nations and Nationalism* (University Press), pp. 53–62; and Immanuel Wallerstein, "The Construction of Peoplehood: Racism, Nationalism, and Ethnicity," in *Race, Nation, Class: Ambiguous Identities*, ed. Etienne Balibar and Immanuel Wallerstein (London: Verso, 1991), pp. 71–85.

10. Alan Richardson, *Literature, Education, and Romanticism: Reading as Social Practice, 1780–1832* (Cambridge: Cambridge University Press, 1994), p. 31.

11. Margit Sicher, "Functionalizing Cultural Memory: Foundational British Literary History and the Construction of National History," *Modern Language Quarterly* 64:2 (2003), p. 217.

12. See Herbert Butterfield, *The Whig Interpretation of History* (1931; New York: Norton, 1965).

13. Norma Landau, "Eighteenth-Century England: Tales Historians Tell," *Eighteenth-Century Studies* 22:2 (winter, 1988–1989), p. 209.

14. Keenan Malik, *The Meaning of Race: Race, History, and Culture in Western Society* (New York: New York University Press, 1996), p. 69.

15. Catherine Hall, "Histories, Empires, and the Post-Colonial Moment," in *The Postcolonial Question: Common Skies, Divided Horizons*, ed. Iain Chambers and Lydia Curtis (London: Routledge, 1996), p. 71.

16. David Theo Goldberg, *The Racial State* (Oxford: Blackwell, 2002).

17. Johann Gottfried Herder, cited in Malik, *The Meaning of Race*, p. 78.

18. Immanuel Wallerstein, "The Construction of Peoplehood," in *Race, Nation, Class: Ambiguous Identities*, ed. Etienne Balibar and Immanuel Wallerstein (New York: Verso, 1991), p. 79.

19. See Paul de Man, *Aesthetic Ideology*, ed. Andrzej Warminski (Minneapolis: University of Minnesota Press, 1996); and Terry Eagleton, *The Ideology of the Aesthetic* (Oxford: Basil Blackwell, 1990).

20. Ivan Hannaford, *Race: The History of an Idea in the West* (Washington, D.C.: Woodrow Wilson Center Press, 1996), p. 9.

21. Brian V. Street, *The Savage in Literature: Representations of Primitive Society in English Fiction 1858–1920* (London: Routledge & Kegan Paul, 1975), p. 94.

22. Hippolyte Taine, *History of English Literature*, revised edition, trans. Henry van Laun, 3 vols. (New York: P.F. Collier & Son, 1900), III, p. 153.

23. John Bender, "A New History of the Enlightenment?" in *The Profession of Eighteenth-Century Literature: Reflections on an Institution*, ed. Leo Damrosch, p. 63.

24. Lester G. Crocker, "The Enlightenment: What and Who?" *Studies in Eighteenth-Century Culture* (1987), p. 336.

25. See Mrinalini Sinha, *Colonial Masculinity: The "Manly Englishman" and the "Effeminate Babu" in the Late Nineteenth Century* (Manchester: Manchester University Press, 1995), pp. 2, 7–11; "Teaching Imperialism as a Social Formation," *Radical History Review* 67 (1997), pp. 175–186; and *Specters of Mother India: The Global Restructuring of an Empire* (Durham: Duke University Press, forthcoming 2006).

26. See "The Enlightenment Project," in *The Routledge Dictionary of Postmodern Thought*, ed. Stuart Sims (New York: Routledge, 1999), pp. 238–239.

27. Michel Foucault, *The Order of Things: An Archaeology of the Human Sciences* (New York: Vintage Books, 1970).

28. See John H. Brooke, "Why Did the English Mix Their Science and Their Religion?" in *Science and Imagination in XVIIIth-Century British Culture*, ed. Sergio Rossi (Milano: Edizione Unicopli, 1987), pp. 57–78.

29. John Gascoigne, *Cambridge in the Age of the Enlightenment: Science, Religion and Politics from the Restoration to the French Revolution* (Cambridge: Cambridge University Press, 1989), p. 3.

30. Robert Markley, *Fallen Languages: Crises of Representation in Newtonian England, 1660–1740* (Ithaca: Cornell University Press, 1993), p. 7.

31. See Charles Webster, *From Paracelsus to Newton: Magic and the Making of Modern Science* (Cambridge: Cambridge University Press, 1982); and Michael White, *Isaac Newton: The Last Sorcerer* (Reading, Mass: Addison-Wellesley, 1997).

32. See Madan Sarup, *An Introductory Guide to Post-Structuralism and Postmodernism*, 2nd ed. (Athens, Georgia: University of Georgia Press, 1993), pp. 143–150; Linda Hutcheon, *The Politics of Postmodernism* (New York: Routledge, 1989), pp. 62–92; Terry Eagleton, The *Illusions of Postmodernism* (Oxford: Basil Blackwell, 1996), pp. 93–130.

33. See Mitchell Dean, *Critical and Effective Histories: Foucault's Methods and Historical Sociology* (New York: Routledge, 1994), p. 57.

34. Satya P. Mohanty, *Literary Theory and the Claims of History: Postmodernism, Objectivity, Multicultural Politics* (Ithaca: Cornell University Press, 1997), p. 11.

35. Mohanty, *Literary Theory and the Claims of History*, p. 131.
36. See Thomas Keenan, *Fables of Responsibility: Aberrations and Predicaments in Ethics and Politics* (Stanford: Stanford University Press, 1997), p. 160ff.
37. Keenan, *Fables of Responsibility*, p. X.
38 P. J. Cain and A. G. Hopkins, *British Imperialism: Innovation and Expansion, 1688–1914* (London: Longman, 1993), p. 24.
39. J. G. A. Pocock, *The Machiavellian Moment: Florentine Political Thought and the Atlantic Republican Tradition* (Princeton: Princeton University Press, 1975), p. 448.
40. Pocock, *The Machiavellian Moment*, p. 447.
41. Cain and Hopkins, *British Imperialism*, p. 64.
42. Colin Nicholson, *Writing and the Rise of Finance: Capital Satires of the Early Eighteenth Century* (Cambridge: Cambridge University Press, 1994).
43. See P. Corrigan and D. Sayer, "Old Corruption," in *The Great Arch: English State Formation as Cultural Revolution* (Oxford: Basil Blackwell, 1985).
44. Pocock, *The Machiavellian Moment*, pp. 460–461.
45. See Michael McKeon, "Cultural Crisis and Dialectical Method," in *The Profession of Eighteenth-Century Literature: Reflections on an Institution*, ed. Leo Damrosch (Madison: University of Wisconsin Press, 1992), pp. 42–61.
46. See Henry R. Rack, *Reasonable Enthusiast: John Wesley and the Rise of Methodism* (Philadelphia: Trinity Press, 1989).
47. See Clement Hawes, *Mania and Literary Style: The Rhetoric of Enthusiasm from the Ranters to Christopher Smart* (Cambridge: Cambridge University Press, 1996); E. P. Thompson, *Witness against the Beast: William Blake and the Moral Law* (Cambridge: Cambridge University Press, 1993); John Mee, *Dangerous Enthusiasm: William Blake and the Culture of Radicalism in the 1790s* (Oxford: Clarendon Press, 1992); Malcolm Chase, *The People's Farm: English Radical Agrarianism, 1775–1840* (Oxford: Clarendon Press, 1988); and Iain McCalman, *Radical Underworlds: Prophets, Revolutionaries and Pornographers in London, 1795–1840* (Cambridge: Cambridge University Press, 1988).
48. Michael Hechter, *Internal Colonialism: The Celtic Fringe in British National Development, 1536–1966*; Murray G. H. Pittock, *Inventing and Resisting Britain: Cultural Identities in Britain and Ireland, 1685–1789* (New York: St. Martin's Press, 1997).
49. See John Guillory, *Cultural Capital: The Problem of Literary Canon Formation* (Chicago: University of Chicago Press, 1993).
50. See Kathleen Wilson, *The Sense of the People: Politics, Culture, and Imperialism in England, 1715–1785* (Cambridge: Cambridge University Press, 1995).
51. Kathleen Wilson, *The Island Race: Englishness, Empire, and Gender in the Eighteenth Century* (London: Routledge, 2003).
52. Street, *The Savage in Literature*, p. 17.
53. Margaret T. Hodgen, *Early Anthropology in the Sixteenth and Seventeenth Centuries* (Philadelphia: University of Pennsylvania, 1964), p. 213.
54. Malik, *The Meaning of Race*, pp. 62–63.
55. Roxann Wheeler, *The Complexion of Race: Categories of Difference in Eighteenth-Century British Culture* (Philadelphia: University of Pennyslvania Press, 2000), p. 5.

56. Malik, *The Meaning of Race*, p. 222.

57. See Michael Omi and Howard Winant, *Racial Formation in the United States from the 1960s to the 1980s* (New York: Routledge, 1986).

58. Henry Louis Gates, Jr., "Editor's Introduction: Writing 'Race' and the Difference It Makes," in *"Race," Writing, and Difference*, ed. Henry Louis Gates, Jr. (Chicago: University of Chicago Press, 1985), p. 5.

59. Gates, "Critical Remarks," in *"Race," Writing, and Difference*, pp. 324–325.

60. See Michael Banton, "Race as Lineage," in *Racial Theories* (Cambridge: Cambridge University Press, 1987), pp. 1–27.

61. Raymond Williams, *Keywords*, revised edition (New York: Oxford University Press, 1983), pp. 248–250.

62. Fiona J. Stafford, *The Last of the Race: The Growth of a Myth from Milton to Darwin* (Oxford: Clarendon Press, 1994), p. 57.

63. Jack Lynch, note, *Samuel Johnson's Dictionary: Selections from the 1755 Work that Defined the English Language*, ed. Jack Lynch (New York: Levenger Press, 2002), p. 593.

64. Stafford, *The Last of the Race*, p. 119.

65. Christopher Hill, "The Norman Yoke," *Intellectual Origins of the English Revolution Revisited* (Oxford: Clarendon Press, 1997), p. 361.

66. Sir Walter Scott, *Ivanhoe: A Romance* (New York: Bantam Books, 1988), p. 2.

67. Kwame Anthony Appiah, "Race," in *Critical Terms for Literary Study*, ed. Frank Lentricchia and Thomas McLaughlin (Chicago: University of Chicago Press), p. 282.

68. Cited in Clare A. Simmons, *Reversing the Conquest: History and Myth in Nineteenth-Century British Literature* (New Brunswick: Rutgers University Press, 1990), p. 90.

69. Appiah, "Race" p. 285.

70. Arendt, *Imperialism*, part II of *Origins of Totalitarianism* (1951; San Diego: Harvest/HBJ, 1990), p. 41.

71. James Shapiro, *Shakespeare and the Jews* (New York: Columbia University Press, 1996), p. 208.

72. Cited in Shapiro, *Shakespeare and the Jews*, p. 208.

73. Paul Stevens, " 'Leviticus Thinking' and the Rhetoric of Early Modern Colonialism," in *Criticism* 35:3 (1993), pp. 441–461.

74. Roxann Wheeler, *The Complexion of Race: Categories of Difference in Eighteenth-Century British Culture* (Philadelphia: University of Pennsylvania Press, 2000), p. 54.

75. See Hodgen, *Early Anthropology*, pp. 424–446; Mary Louise Pratt, *Imperial Eyes: Travel Writing and Transculturation* (New York: Routledge, 1992), pp. 32–33; Michael Banton, *Racial Theories* (Cambridge: Cambridge University Press, 1987), pp. 4–5; and Hudson, "From 'Nation' to 'Race': The Origin of Racial Classification in Eighteenth-Century Thought," *Eighteenth-Century Studies* 29:3 (1996), p. 250.

76. Gates, "Critical Remarks," *Anatomy of Racism*, ed. David Theo Goldberg (Minneapolis: University of Minnesota Press, 1990), p. 320.

77. William Petty, *The Petty Papers: Some Unpublished Papers of Sir William Petty*, ed. Henry W. Landsdowne, 2 vols. (London: Constable, 1927), II, p. 31. See also Gates, "Critical Remarks," p. 320.

78. Carl von Linné, *The System of Nature, in Race and the Enlightenment: A Reader*, ed. Emmanuel Chukwudi Eze (Oxford: Basil Blackwell, 1997), pp. 13–14.

79. See Lisbet Koerner, "Purposes of Linnaean Travel: A Preliminary Research Report," in *Visions of Empire: Voyages, Botany, and Representations of Nature*, ed. David Philip Miller and Peter Hanns Reill (Cambridge: Cambridge University Press, 1996), p. 123.

80. David Theo Goldberg, "The Social Formation of Racist Discourse," in *Anatomy of Racism*, ed. David Theo Goldberg (Minneapolis: University of Minnesota Press, 1990), p. 298.

81. Hans Frei, *The Eclipse of Biblical Narrative: A Study in Eighteenth and Nineteenth-Century Hermeneutics* (New Haven: Yale University Press, 1974).

82. Street, *The Savage in Literature*, p. 94.

83. Edward Long, *The History of Jamaica*, 3 vols. (London, 1774), II, p. 356.

84. Long, *Jamaica*, p. 336.

85. Ibid., p. 364.

86. Edward Long, *Candid Reflections upon the Judgment lately awarded by the Court of King's Bench in West-Minster Hall on What is Commonly Called the Negroe-Cause* (London: T. Lowndes, 1772), p. 48.

87. Long, *Candid Reflections*, p. 49.

88. Alfred David, "An Iconography of Noses: Directions in the History of a Physical Stereotype," *Mapping the Cosmos*, ed. Jane Chance and R. O. Wells, Jr. (Rice University Press, 1985), p. 93.

89. Malik, *The Meaning of Race*, p. 62.

90. See John Block Friedman, "Cultural Conflicts in Medieval World Maps," in *Implicit Understandings: Observing, Reporting, and Reflecting on the Encounters Between Europeans and Other Peoples in the Early Modern Era*, ed. Stuart B. Schwartz (Cambridge: Cambridge University Press, 1994), pp. 64–95.

91. Benjamin Braude, "The Sons of Noah and the Construction of Ethnic and Geographical Identities in the Medieval and Early Modern Periods," in *The William and Mary Quarterly* 54:1 (1997), pp. 103–111.

92. Braude, "The Sons of Noah," p. 131.

93. Ibid., pp. 103–142.

94. Ibid., p. 139.

95. Ibid., p. 142.

96. Wallerstein, "Peoplehood," p. 79.

97. David Hume, "Of National Characters," in *The Enlightenment: A Comprehensive Anthology*, ed. Peter Gay (New York: Simon & Schuster, 1973), p. 532.

98. See Hugh A. MacDougall, *Racial Myth in English History: Trojans, Teutons, and Anglo-Saxons* (Hanover, New Hampshire: University Press of New England, 1982), pp. 81–82.

99. James Beattie, *An Essay on the Nature and Immutability of Truth, in Opposition to Sophistry and Skepticism* (1770), excerpted in *Race and the Enlightenment: A Reader*, ed. Emmanuel Chukwudi Eze (Oxford: Basil Blackwell, 1997), p. 34.

100. Beattie, *An Essay*, p. 35.

101. Ibid., pp. 36–37.

102. Malik, *The Meaning of Race*, pp. 53–54.

103. See John Immerwahr, "Hume's Revised Racism," *Journal of the History of Ideas* 53:3 (1992), pp. 481–486. Immanuel Kant relies heavily on Hume in *On National Characteristics, so far as They Depend upon the Distinct Feeling of the Beautiful and Sublime* (1764). See the excerpt in Beattie, *An Essay*, p. 55.

104. See Norma Myers, *Reconstructing the Black Past: Blacks in Britain, c. 1780–1850* (London: Frank Cass, 1996), p. 27. For a detailed description of the Somerset case, see Gretchen Gerzina, *Black London: Life before Emancipation* (New Brunswick, New Jersey: Rutgers University Press, 1995), pp. 116–132.

105. David Grimsted, "Anglo-American Racism and Phillis Wheatley's 'Sable Veil,' 'Lengthened Chain,' and 'Knitted Heart,' " in *Women in the Age of the American Revolution*, ed. Ronald Hoffman and Peter J. Albert (Charlottesville: University of Virginia Press, 1989), p. 409.

106. Nicholas Hudson, "From 'Nation' to 'Race': The Origin of Racial Classification in Eighteenth-Century Thought," *Eighteenth-Century Studies* 29:3 (1996), p. 250.

107. Long, *History of Jamaica*, pp. 353–354; see also Hudson, "From 'Nation' to 'Race'," pp. 251–252.

108. See Hudson, "From 'Nation' to 'Race'," p. 250.

109. Jennifer Wallace, *Shelley and Greece*: Rethinking Romantic Hellenism (London: MacMillan Press Ltd., 1997), p. 207.

110. For the origins of "Aryan," put into circulation in 1794 by the Sanskrit scholar and colonial judge William Jones, see *Black Athena*, pp. 220, 478 (n.113). For the later history of Jones's tendency to blur linguistic and "racial" categories, see Partha Mitter, "The Aryan Myth and British Writings on Indian Art and Culture," in *Literature and Imperialism*, ed. Bart Moore-Gilbert (Surrey: Roehampton Institute, 1983), pp. 69–92. For the origins of "Caucasian," first put into print in 1795 by Johann Friedrich Blumenbach, see Stephen Jay Gould, "The Geometer of Race," in *Discover* (November 1994), pp. 65–69.

111. Romila Thapar, *Interpreting Early India* (Oxford: Oxford University Press, 1993), pp. 27–33. See also Thomas R. Trautmann, *Aryans and British India* (Berkeley: University of California Press, 1997).

112. Martin Bernal, *Black Athena: The Afroasiatic Roots of Classical Civilization*, 2 vols. (New Brunswick, NJ: Rutgers, 1987), I: *The Fabrication of Ancient Greece 1785–1985*, p. 28.

113. Vasant Kaiwar, "The Aryan Model of History and the Oriental Renaissance: The Politics of Identity in an Age of Revolutions, Colonialism, and Nationalism," in *Antinomies of Modernity: Essays on Race, Orient, Nation* ed. Vasant Kaiwar and Sucheta Mazumdar (Durham: Duke University Press, 2003), pp. 13–61.

114. Mark Edmundson, *Literature Against Philosophy, Plato to Derrida: A Defense of Poetry* (Cambridge University Press, 1995), p. 128.

115. Peter Osborne, *The Politics of Time* (London, 1995), p. 157.

116. Kwame Anthony Appiah, *In My Father's House: Africa in the Philosophy of Culture* (New York: Oxford University Press, 1992), p. 58.

2   When Fingal Fought and Ossian Sang: Eighteenth-Century Metalepsis

1. *The Norton Anthology of English Literature*, Vol. I, ed. M. H. Abrams and Stephen Greenblatt (New York: W.W. Norton and Company, 2000), p. 2882.
2. Linda Colley, *Britons: Forging the Nation 1707–1837* (New Haven: Yale University Press, 1992).
3. Ian Haywood, *The Making of History: A Study of the Literary Forgeries of James Macpherson and Thomas Chatterton in Relation to Eighteenth-Century Ideas of History and Fiction* (London: Associated University Presses, 1986), p. 21.
4. Ibid., p. 35.
5. W. A. Speck, *Literature and Society in Eighteenth-Century England 1680–1820: Ideology, Politics and Culture* (London: Longman, 1998), p. 98.
6. See J. G. A. Pocock, *Barbarism and Religion*, 2 vols. (Cambridge: Cambridge University Press, 1999), II: *Narratives of Civil Government*, pp. 268–270.
7. Richard B. Sher, " 'Those Scotch Imposters and Their Cabal': Ossian and the Scottish Enlightenment," in *Man and Nature: Proceedings of the Canadian Society for Eighteenth-Century Studies*, ed. Roger L. Emerson (London, Ontario, 1982), p. 55.
8. Richard B. Sher, *Church and University in the Scottish Enlightenment: The Moderate Literati of Edinburgh* (Princeton: Princeton University Press, 1985), p. 254.
9. Ibid., p. 257.
10. Kathleen Wilson, *The Sense of the People: Politics, Culture, and Imperialism in England, 1715–1785* (Cambridge: Cambridge University Press, 1998), p. 211.
11. Pat Rogers, "Coffee Houses," in *The Blackwell Companion to the Enlightenment*, ed. John W. Yolton, Roy Porter, Pat Rogers, Barbara Maria Stafford (Oxford: Blackwell, 1991), p. 95.
12. Charles Churchill, *The Prophecy of Famine: A Scots Pastoral* (Dublin, 1763), p. 13.
13. Pat Rogers, *Johnson and Boswell: The Transit of Caledonia* (Oxford: Clarendon Press, 1995), p. 198.
14. Ibid., pp. 20–21.
15. Fiona J. Stafford, *The Sublime Savage: A Study of James Macpherson and the Poems of Ossian* (Edinburgh: Edinburgh University Press, 1988), p. 134.
16. Colley, *Britons*, p. 121.
17. David Armitage, *The Ideological Origins of the British Empire* (Cambridge: Cambridge University Press, 2000), p. 196.
18. Ibid., p. 23.
19. Janet Sorensen, *The Grammar of Empire in Eighteenth-Century British Writing* (Cambridge: Cambridge University Press, 2000), p. 186.
20. Rogers, *Johnson*, p. 195.
21. Colley, *Britons*, p. 130.
22. Ibid.

23. Tom Nairn, *The Break-Up of Britain: Crisis and Neo-Nationalism*, 2nd ed. (London:Verso, 1981), p. 129.

24. Henry Home, Lord Kaimes, *Sketches of the History of Man*, 2 vols. (Edinburgh, 1774), I, p. 102.

25. Robert Crawford, "Scottish Literature and English Studies," in *The Scottish Invention of English Literature*, ed. Robert Crawford (Cambridge: Cambridge University Press, 1998), p. 231.

26. James Macpherson, *The Highlander:A Poem in Six Cantos* (Edinburgh, 1758), p. 64.

27. Colley, *Britons*, p. 130.

28. See Susan Stewart, *Crimes of Writing: Problems in the Containment of Representation* (New York: Oxford University Press, 1991), pp. 66–74.

29. Joan H. Pittock, "The Scottish Enlightenment," in *Cambridge History of Literary Criticism*, vol. IV, ed. H. B. Nisbet and Claude Rawson (Cambridge: Cambridge University Press, 1997), p. 555.

30. See George Kubler, *The Shape of Time: Remarks on the History of Things* (New Haven: Yale University Press, 1962), p. 6.

31. James Macpherson, "A Dissertation Concerning the Antiquity . . .," in *The Poems of Ossian and Related Works*, ed. Howard Gaskill (Edinburgh: Edinburgh Press, 1996) p. 477, n.38.

32. Haywood, *Making*, p. 83.

33. Hugh Blair, Preface to James Macpherson, *Fragments of Ancient Poetry* (London, 1760), pp. v–vi.

34. Ibid.

35. John J. Dunn, Introduction to James Macpherson, *Fragments of Ancient Poetry* (Los Angeles: William Andrews Clark Memorial Library, 1966), p. iii.

36. Murray G. H. Pittock, *Inventing and Resisting Britain: Cultural Identities in Britain and Ireland, 1685–1789* (New York: St. Martin's Press, 1997), p. 155.

37. Blair, Preface to James Macpherson, p. vii.

38. Sher, *Church*, p. 257.

39. Fiona J. Stafford, *The Sublime Savage: A Study of James Macpherson and The Poems of Ossian* (Edinburgh: Edinburgh University Press, 1988), p. 128.

40. See Howard Gaskill, Introduction, *Ossian Revisited*, ed. Howard Gaskill (Edinburgh: Edinburgh Press, 1991), pp. 1–18; and Donald E. Meek, "The Gaelic Ballads of Scotland: Creativity and Adaptation," in the same volume, pp. 19–48. The phrase "mainly oral" is intended to cover whatever use Macpherson made of "The Book of the Dean of Lismore," an early sixteenth-century compilation, in Roman characters, of Highland ballads.

41. See Derick Thomson, " 'Ossian' Macpherson and the Gaelic World of the Eighteenth Century," *Aberdeen University Review* 40 (1963), pp. 7–20.

42. Stafford, *Sublime*, p. 141.

43. Malcolm Laing, *The Poems of Ossian*, (Edinburgh, 1805), p. 328.

44. Hugh Blair, *A Critical Dissertation on the Poems of Ossian, the Son of Fingal*, 2nd ed. (London: T. Becket and P.A. De Hondt, 1765), p. 112.

45. Malcolm Laing, *The History of Scotland* (London and Edinburgh, 1800), II, p. 399.

46. Leith Davis, "Origins of the Specious: James Macpherson's Ossian and the Forging of the British Empire," *The Eighteenth Century* 34:2 (1993), p. 132.

47. James Macpherson, "Dissertation Concerning the Poems of Ossian," in *The Poems of Ossian* (1773). Rpt. in *The Poems of Ossian and Related Works*, ed. Howard Gaskill (Edinburgh, 1996), p. 477, n.45.

48. Ibid., p. 412.

49. Adam Ferguson, in *Report of the Committee of the Highland Society of Scotland Appointed to Enquire into the Nature and Authenticity of the Poems of Ossian*, ed. Henry Mackenzie (Edinburgh: Archibald Constable & Co., 1805), p. 65.

50. See John M. Mackenzie, "Essay and Reflection: On Scotland and the Empire," *International History Review* 15:4 (November 1993), pp. 714–739; and Michael Fry, *The Scottish Empire* (Edinburgh: Tuckwell Press, 2001).

51. P. J. Marshall, *Problems of Empire: Britain and India 1757–1813* (London: George Allen and Unwin, 1968), p. 30.

52. Dafydd Moore, "Heroic Incoherence in James Macpherson's *The Poems of Ossian*," in *Eighteenth-Century Studies* 34:1 (2000), p. 47.

53. James Macpherson, *The History and Management of the East-India Company, from Its Origin in 1600 to the Present Times* (London, 1779), note, p. 267.

54. I am indebted for most of the information in this paragraph, including the quotation from Burke, to George McElroy, "Ossianic Imagination and the History of India: James and John Macpherson as Propagandists and Intriguers," in *Aberdeen and the Enlightenment*, ed. Jennifer J. Carter and Joan H. Pittock (Aberdeen University Press, 1989), pp. 363–374.

55. Macpherson, Preface to *The History and Management*, p. 3.

56. Grafton, *Forgers*, p. 59.

57. Ibid.

58. Kames, *Sketches*, p. 43.

59. Haywood, *Making*, p. 87.

60. Mary Poovey, *A History of the Modern Fact: Problems of Knowledge in the Sciences of Wealth and Society* (Chicago: University of Chicago Press, 1998), p. 221.

61. Stephen Jay Gould, *Questioning the Millennium: A Rationalist's Guide to a Precisely Arbitrary Countdown* (New York: Harmony Books, 1997), p. 121. His topic is Bishop Ussher's sacred historiography of 1650.

62. See Haywood, *Making*, p. 88.

63. John Macpherson, *Critical Dissertations on the Origin, Antiquities, Language, Government, Manners, and Religion, of the Antient Caledonians. . . .* (Dublin, 1768), p. 208.

64. Anonymous, *Fingal King of Morven, a Knight-Errant* (London, 1764), p. 47.

65. Weinbrot, *Britannia's Issue*, p. 548.

66. See John Dwyer, "The Melancholy Savage: Text and Context in the *Poems of Ossian*," in *Ossian Revisited*, pp. 164–206.

67. Grafton, *Forgers*, p. 67.

68. James Macpherson, Preface to *Fragments of Ancient Poetry in The Poems of Ossian and Related Works*, ed. Howard Gaskill (Edinburgh University Press, 1996), p. 6.

69. Kames, *Sketches*, p. 308.

70. Ferdinando Warner, *Remarks on the History of Fingal, and Other Poems of Ossian* (London, 1762), p. 10.

71. Charles O'Conor, *Dissertations on the Ancient History of Ireland* (Dublin, 1766), p. 38.

72. Ibid., p. 22.

73. Ibid., p. 59.

74. See Gauti Kristmannsson, "Ossian: A Case of Celtic Tribalism or a Translation without an Original?" in *Transfer: Übersetzen—Dolmetschen—Interkulturalität* (Sonderdruck: Peter Lang, 1997), pp. 449–462.

75. Clare O'Halloran, "Irish Re-Creation of the Gaelic Past: The Challenge of Macpherson's Ossian," *Past and Present* 124 (1989), p. 74.

76. James Macpherson, "Preface" (to 1st ed. of *Fingal*, 1761–1762), in *The Poems of Ossian and Related Works*, ed. Howard Gaskill (Edinburgh: Edinburgh University Press, 1996), p. 37.

77. Derick S. Thomson, *The Gaelic Sources of Macpherson's "Ossian"* (Edinburgh: Oliver & Boyd, 1952), p. 72.

78. Warner, *Remarks on the History*, p. 31.

79. Robert and Catherine Coogan Ward, "The Catholic Pamphlets of Charles O'Conor (1710–1791)," *Studies* 68 (winter, 1979), pp. 259–264.

80. S. J. Connelly, "Introduction: Varieties of Irish Political Thought," in *Political Ideas in Eighteenth-Century Ireland*, ed. S. J. Connelly (Dublin: Four Courts Press, 2000), p. 24.

81. Thomas McLoughlin, *Contesting Ireland: Irish Voices against England in the Eighteenth Century* (Dublin: Four Courts Press, 1999), p. 143.

82. Charles O'Conor, *Dissertations,* p. 50.

83. Ibid.

84. Maurice Colgan, "Ossian: Success or Failure for the Scottish Enlightenment?" in *Aberdeen and the Enlightenment*, ed. Jennifer J. Carter and Joan H. Pittock (Aberdeen University Press, 1989), p. 348.

85. John Macpherson, *Critical Dissertations on the Origin, Antiquities, Language, Government, Manners, and Religion of the Ancient Caledonians* (London: 1768), p. 83.

86. Anonymous editor, Introduction, John Macpherson, *Critical Dissertations*, p. 72.

87. The Reverend Mr. Whitaker, *The Genuine History of the Britons Asserted in a Full and Candid Refutation of Mr. Macpherson's Introduction to the History of Great Britain and Ireland* (Dublin, 1773), pp. 3–4.

88. William Shaw, *An Inquiry into the Authenticity of the Poems Ascribed to Ossian* (London, 1781), pp. 34–35.

89. Dauvit Brown, *The Irish Identity of the Kingdom of the Scots* (Suffolk: Boydell Press, 1999).

90. Hugh Kearney, *The British Isles: A History of Four Nations* (Cambridge: Cambridge University Press, 1989), p. 224.

91. Richard Brodhead, "Regionalism and the Upper Class," in *Rethinking Class: Literary Studies and Social Formations*, ed. Wai Chee Dimock and Michael T. Gimore (New York: Columbia University Press, 1994), p. 150.

92. Trever-Roper, "Highland Tradition," pp. 28–31.

93. Shaw, *Inquiry*, p. 33.

94. Andrew Gallie, Letter of March 4, 1801, in Henry Mackenzie, *Report of the Committee of the Highland Society of Scotland* (Edinburgh: Archibald Constable, 1805), p. 44.

95. Malcolm Laing, editorial note, in James Macpherson, *The Poems of Ossian*, 2 vols., ed. Malcolm Laing (Edinburgh: James Ballantyne, 1805), p. 328.

96. Stafford, *Sublime Savage*, p. 169.

97. Maurice Colgan, "Ossian: Success or Failure for the Scottish Enlightenment," in *Aberdeen and the Enlightenment*, ed. Jennifer J. Carter and Joan H. Pittock (Aberdeen University Press, 1989), p. 346.

98. Nick Groom, *The Forger's Shadow: How Forgery Changed the Course of Literature* (London: Picador, 2002), p. 129.

99. See Pocock, *Barbarism*, II, pp. 269–270.

100. *Report of the Committee of the Highland Society of Scotland*, ed. Henry Mackenzie (Edinburgh, 1805), pp. 151–152.

101. Weinbrot, *Britannia's Issue*, pp. 541–553.

102. Colin Kidd, *British Identities before Nationalism: Ethnicities and Nationhood in the Atlantic World, 1600–1800* (Cambridge: Cambridge University Press, 1999), p. 200.

103. Martin Bernal, *Black Athena: The Afroasiatic Roots of Classical Civilization*, 2 vols. (New Brunswick: Rutgers University Press, 1987), I, pp. 206–223.

104. William Julius Mickle, *The Prophecy of Queen Emma . . . To which is added, by the editor, An Account of His Discovery and Hints towards a Vindication of the Poems of Ossian and Rowley* (London, 1782), pp. 17–18.

105. Kames, *Sketches*, p. 10.

106. Charles Mackinnon, "On the Authenticity of Ossian," in *Essays on the Following Subjects*, 2nd ed. (Edinburgh, 1785), p. 73.

107. Kidd, *British Identities*, p. 201.

108. John Locke, *An Essay Concerning Human Understanding*, ed. Peter Nidditch (Oxford: Oxford University Press, 1975), p. 405.

109. Nicholas Hudson, *Writing and European Thought 1600–1830* (Cambridge: Cambridge University Press, 1994), pp. 76–91.

110. Stuart Piggott, *Ancient Britons and the Antiquarian Imagination: Ideas from the Renaissance to the Regency* (New York: Thames and Hudson, 1989), p. 235.

111. See Rosemary Sweet, "Antiquaries and Antiquities in *Eighteenth-Century England*," in *Eighteenth-Century Studies* 34:2 (2001), p. 182, pp. 196–198.

112. William Stukeley, *Abury, A Temple of the British Druids* (London, 1743), p. 78.

113. Stukeley, *Abury*, p. 98.

114. Ibid., p. 16, p. 67.

115. Locke, *Essay*, p. 405.

116. Sorensen, *Grammar*, p. 193.

117. Prys Morgan, "From a Death to a View: The Hunt for the Welsh Past in the Romantic Period," in *The Invention of Tradition*, ed. Eric Hobsbawm and Terence Ranger (Cambridge: Cambridge University Press, 1983), pp. 68–74.

118. See Kidd, *Subverting Scotland's Past* (Cambridge: Cambridge University Press, 1993), p. 224.

119. William Maitland, Preface, *The Histories and Antiquities of Scotland* (London, 1758), p. i.

120. See Kristmannsson, "Ossian: A Case of Celtic Tribalism," pp. 452–453.

121. John Clark, *An Answer to Mr. Shaw's Inquiry into the Authenticity of the Poems Ascribed to Ossian* (Edinburgh, 1781), p. 13.

122. See Nicholas Hudson, "Theories of Language," in *The Cambridge History of Literary Criticism*, 4 vols. (Cambridge: Cambridge University Press, 1997), IV, p. 247.

123. I borrow this term and its analysis from Douglas R. Hofstadter, *Gödel, Escher, Bach: An Eternal Golden Braid* (New York: Vintage Books, 1979).

124. James Macpherson, *The Poems of Ossian and Related Works*, p. 520, n.40.

125. O'Conor, *Dissertations*, p. 48.

126. James Macpherson, *An Introduction to the History of Great Britain and Ireland* (London, 1771), p. 150. See Baines, *House*, p. 114.

127. Hugh Blair, *Critical Dissertation*, pp. 7–8.

128. See David Couzens Hoy, *The Critical Circle: Literature, History, and Philosophical Hermeneutics* (Berkeley: University of California Press, 1978), p. vii.

129. See Katie Trumpener, *Bardic Nationalism: The Romantic Novel and the British Empire* (Princeton: Princeton University Press, 1997), pp. 70–71.

130. Derrick S. Thomson, "James Macpherson: The Gaelic Dimension," in *From Gaelic to Romantic: Ossianic Translations*, ed. Fionna Stafford and Howard Gaskill (Amsterdam: Rodopi, 1998), p. 26.

131. Ibid.

132. See Stewart, *Crimes*, p. 68.

133. Baines, *House*, p. 106.

134. Pat Rogers, *Johnson and Boswell: The Transit of Caledonia* (Oxford: Clarendon Press, 1995), p. 207.

135. Samuel Johnson, *A Journey to the Western Islands of Scotland*, ed. Mary Lascelles (New Haven: Yale University Press, 1971), p. 118.

136. Nick Groom, *The Making of Percy's Reliques* (Oxford: Clarendon Press, 1999), p. 92.

137. See Paul J. deGategno, *James Macpherson* (Boston: Twayne Publishers), p. 107.

138. Derrick S. Thomson, " 'Ossian' Macpherson and the Gaelic World of the Eighteenth Century," in *Aberdeen University Review* 40 (1963), p. 14.

139. *Report of the Committee of the Highland Society of Scotland*, ed. Henry Mackenzie (Edinburgh, 1805), p. 79.

140. K. K. Ruthven, *Faking Literature* (Cambridge: Cambridge University Press, 2001), p. 13.

141. Sir John Sinclair, Baronet, *A Dissertation on the Authenticity of the Poems of Ossian* (London, 1806), pp. xiii–xiv.

142. Derick S. Thomson, *Gaelic Sources* (Edinburgh: Oliver & Boyd, 1952), p. 89.

143. Thomson, " 'Ossian' Macpherson," p. 14.

144. Hugh Trever-Roper, "The Invention of Tradition: The Highland Tradition of Scotland" in *The Invention of Tradition*, p. 26.

145. Gaskill, The *Poems of Ossian*, pp. 541–542, n.1.

146. See Geoffrey Treasure, *Who's Who in Early Hanoverian Britain (1714–1789)* (London: Shepheard-Walwyn Ltd., 1992), p. 425; Stafford, *Sublime Savage*, p. 4; Colin Kidd, *Subverting*, p. 221; Speck, *Literature*, p. 98. The most incautious effort to exploit the "mixed verdict" on Macpherson in this vein can be found in Howard Gaskill, "Ossian: Toward a Rehabilitation," in *Comparative Criticism: An Annual Journal* 8 (1986), pp. 113–146.

147. DeGategno, *James Macpherson*, p. 143.

148. Bernard Bailyn and Philip D. Morgan, Introduction to *Strangers within the Realm: Cultural Margins of the First Empire* (Chapel Hill: University of North Carolina Press), p. 27.

149. Oscar Wilde, "The Decay of Lying," *The Artist as Critic: Critical Writings of Oscar Wilde*, ed. Richard Ellmann (New York: Vintage Books, 1968), p. 292.

150. Stewart, *Crimes*, p. 92.

151. *Norton Anthology*, p. 2882.

152. Groom, *Making*, p. 9.

153. William Shenstone to Thomas Percy, February 3, 1762. In *The Percy Letters: Correspondence of Percy and Shenstone*, ed. Cleanth Brooks (New Haven: Yale Press, 1977), p. 137.

154. See Arthur Johnston, *Enchanted Ground: The Study of Medieval Romance in the Eighteenth Century* (London: Athlone Press, 1964), p. 79.

155. Gwendolyn A. Morgan, "Percy, the Antiquarians, the Ballad, and the Middle Ages," in *Studies in Medievalism* VII (1995), p. 26.

156. G. Malcolm Laws, Jr., *The British Literary Ballad: A Study in Poetic Imitation* (Carbondale: Southern Illinois University Press, 1972), p. 5.

157. Joseph Ritson, Introduction to *Ancient Songs from the Time of King Henry the Third to the Revolution* (London: J. Johnson, 1792), p. xxi.

158. Groom, *Making*, 242.

159. Haywood, *Making*, p. 105.

160. John W. Hales and Frederick J. Furnivall, "The Revival of Ballad Poetry in the Eighteenth Century," *Bishop Percy's Folio Manuscript*, ed. John W. Hales and Frederick J. Furnivall (London: N. Truber & Co., 1868), p. xxix.

161. Ibid.

162. Thomas Percy, *Reliques of Ancient English Poetry* (1765), p. 356.

163. Laura Doyle, "The Racial Sublime," in *Romanticism, Race, and Imperial Culture, 1780–1834*, ed. Alan Richardson and Sonia Hofkosh (Bloomington: Indiana University Press, 1966), p. 15. It can scarcely be a coincidence, moreover, that Percy's American contemporary, Thomas Jefferson—a staunch white supremacist—was likewise the insitgator of Anglo-Saxon Studies as an academic subject both at William and Mary and the University of Virginia. I am grateful to Jim Basker for pointing out this connection to me.

164. Ibid., p. 101.

165. Thomas Percy, "An Essay on the Ancient Minstrels in England," in *Reliques of Ancient English Poetry*, ed. Henry Wheatley, 3 vols. (New York: Dover, 1966), p. 347.

166. Kwame Anthony Appiah, *In My Father's House: Africa in the Philosophy of Culture* (New York: Oxford University Press, 1992), p. 51.

167. Doyle, "The Racial Sublime," p. 15.

168. Horace Walpole to William Mason, May 25, 1772, *Horace Walpole's Correspondence with William Mason, 1756–1779*, ed. W. S. Lewis, Grover Conin, and Charles Bennett (New Haven: Yale University Press, 1955), p. 36.

3   Leading History by the Nose: Reading Origins in *Midnight's Children* and *Tristram Shandy*

1. Linda Hutcheon, *The Politics of Postmodernism* (New York: Routledge, 1989), p. 63.

2. Ibid., p. 65.

3. Salman Rushdie, *Midnight's Children* (London: Penguin, 1980), p. 177.

4. See Rushdie's essay " 'Errata': Or, Unreliable Narration in *Midnight's Children*," in *Imaginary Homelands: Essays and Criticism 1981–1991* (London: Granta Books, 1991), pp. 22–25.

5. Aijaz Ahmad, "*Orientalism* and After: Ambivalence and Metropolitan Location in Edward Said," in *In Theory: Classes, Nations, Literatures* (London: Verso, 1992), p. 184.

6. For instances of this ubiquitous list, see Linda Hutcheon, *The Politics*, p. 65; Rudolf Bader's "Indian *Tin Drum*," *International Fiction Review* 11:2 (1984), 75–82; and Tariq Rahman's, "Politics in the Novels of Salman Rushdie," *Commonwealth Novel in English* 4:1 (1991), p. 25.

7. See Kumkum Sangari's critique of this emphasis in "The Politics of the Possible," *Cultural Critique* 7 (1987), pp. 157–186.

8. Hutcheon, *The Politics*, p. 104.

9. See Una Chaudhuri, "Imaginative Maps: Excerpts from a Conversation with Salman Rushdie," *Turnstile* 2:1 (1990), p. 37.

10. Keith Wilson, "*Midnight's Children* and Reader Responsibility," *Critical Quarterly* 26:3 (1984), p. 34.

11. Robert Alter, "The Novel and the Sense of the Past," *Salmagundi* 68–69 (1985–1986), pp. 104–105.

12. Damian Grant, *Salman Rushdie* (Plymouth: Northcote House, 1999), p. 51.

13. George Kubler uses this image more generally for all efforts at reconstituting the past. See his *The Shape of Time: Remarks on the History of Things* (New Haven: Yale University Press, 1962), p. 19.

14. David Blewett, "Introduction," *Reconsidering the Rise of the Novel*, ed. David Blewett. Special Issue, *Eighteenth Century Fiction* 12:2–3 (2000), p. 141.

15. William B. Warner, *Licensing Entertainment: The Elevation of Novel Reading in Britain, 1684–1750* (Berkeley: University of California Press, 1998), p. 1.

16. I have in mind, in addition to books otherwise cited in this chapter, such accounts as Michael McKeon, *The Origins of the English Novel 1600–1740* (Baltimore: Johns Hopkins, 1987); J. Paul Hunter, *Before Novels: The Cultural Contexts of Eighteenth-Century Fiction* (New York: Norton, 1990); Patricia Meter Spacks, *Desire and Truth* (Chicago: University of Chicago Press, 199); Simon Varey, *Space and the Eighteenth-Century Novel* (Cambridge: Cambridge

University Press, 1990); John Zomchick, *Family and the Law in Eighteenth-Century Fiction* (Cambridge: Cambridge University Press, 1993); Christopher Flint, *Family Fictions* (Stanford: Stanford University Press, 1998); Ros Ballaster *Seductive Forms: Women's Amatory Fiction from 1684 to 1740* (Oxford: Clarendon Press, 1992), Robert Mayer, *History and the Early English Novel* (Cambridge: Cambridge University Press, 1997); James Thompson, *Models of Value: Political Economy and the Novel* (Durham, NC: Duke University Press, 1996); and Deidre Lynch, *The Economy of Character: Novels, Market Culture, and the Business of Inner Meaning* (Chicago: University of Chicago Press, 1998).

17. Charles Johnstone, *Chrysal: or, The Adventures of a Guinea*, Introduction by Malcolm Bosse, 4 vols. (New York: Garland Publishing Company, 1979), I, pp. 12–13.

18. John Richetti, *The Novel in English History 1700–1780* (London: Routledge, 1999), p. 3.

19. Anderson, *Imagined Communities* (London: Verso, 1983), pp. 30–31.

20. Warner, *Licensing Entertainment,* p. 20.

21. Ibid.

22. Homer Obed Brown, *Institutions of the English Novel: From Defoe to Scott* (Philadelphia: University of Pennsylvania Press, 1997), p. 183.

23. Lennard Davis, *Resisting Novels: Ideology and Fiction* (New York: Methuen, 1987), p. 63.

24. Tobias Smollett, *The Expedition of Humphrey Clinker*, ed. James L. Thorson (New York: Norton, 1983), p. 34.

25. David Armitage, "Greater Britain: A Useful Category of Historical Analysis?" in *American Historical Review* (April 1999), p. 439.

26. Ibid.

27. Tom Keymer, *Sterne, the Moderns, and the Novel* (Oxford: Oxford University Press, 2002), pp. 212–213.

28. Lennard J. Davis, *Resisting Novels: Ideology and Fiction* (New York: Methuen, 1987), p. 151.

29. Ibid.

30. Ibid., p. 150.

31. Ibid., p. 151.

32. Tom Keymer, *Sterne*, p. 25.

33. James Boswell, *Boswell's Life of Johnson*, ed. George B. Hill and L. F. Powell (Oxford: The Clarendon Press, 1934–1950), Vol. II, p. 449.

34. Viktor Shklovsky, "A Parodying Novel: Sterne's *Tristram Shandy*," *Laurence Sterne: A Collection of Critical Essays*, ed. J. Traugott (New Jersey: Englewood Cliffs, 1968), p. 89.

35. Richard Lanham, *Tristram Shandy: The Games of Pleasure* (Los Angeles: Berkeley Press, 1973), p. 27.

36. Patricia Waugh, *Metafiction: The Theory and Practice of Self-Conscious Fiction* (London: Methuen, 1984), p. 70.

37. Milan Kundera, "The Depreciated Legacy of Cervantes," *The Art of the Novel*, trans. Linda Asher (New York: Harper & Rowe, 1986), p. 6.

38. Keymer, *Sterne*, pp. 6–7.
39. Edward Young, *Conjectures on Original Composition*, ed. Edith J. Morley (Manchester, England: The University of Manchester Press, 1918), p. 34.
40. See Gauri Viswanathan, *Masks of Conquest: Literary Study and British Rule in India* (New York: Columbia University Press, 1989).
41. Una Chaudhuri, "Writing the Raj Away," *Turnstile Press* 2:1 (1988), p. 29.
42. Rushdie, *Midnight's Children*, pp. 129–130.
43. Grant, *Salman Rushdie*, p. 11.
44. Timothy Brennan, *Salman Rushdie and the Third World* (London: Macmillan, 1989), p. 166.
45. See Salman Rushdie, "Outside the Whale," in *Imaginary Homelands: Essays and Criticism 1981–1991* (London: Granta Books, 1991), pp. 87–101.
46. Chaudhuri, "Writing the Raj Away," p. 29.
47. Indira Karamcheti, "Salman Rushdie's *Midnight's Children* and an Alternate Genesis," *Pacific Coast Philology* 21:1–2 (1986), p. 83.
48. Ibid.
49. Richard Dyer, *White* (London: Routledge, 1997), p. 68.
50. Vasant Kaiwar, "Racism and the Writing of History," Part I, *South Asia Bulletin* 9:2 (1989), p. 33.
51. Kaiwar, "Racism," p. 35.
52. Aijaz Ahmad, *In Theory: Classes, Nations, Literatures* (London: Verso, 1992), p. 181.
53. Ibid., p. 163.
54. Ibid., p. 181.
55. Ibid., p. 335.
56. Meera Nanda, "Is Modern Science a Western, Patriarchal Myth? A Critique of the Populist Orthodoxy," *South Asia Bulletin* 11:2 (1991), pp. 32–61.
57. Meera Nanda, "The Science Question in Post-Colonial Feminism," *Economic and Political Weekly* (April 20–27, 1996), p. 6.
58. Kaiwar, "Racism," p. 32.
59. Ibid., p. 34.
60. See *Averroës and the Enlightenment*, ed. Mourad Wahba and Mona Abousenna (Amherst, New York: Prometheus Books, 1996).
61. Kaiwar, "Racism," p. 32.
62. Nicholas B. Dirks, *Castes of Mind: Colonialism and the Making of Modern India* (Princeton: Princeton University Press, 2001), p. 49.
63. Herbert H. Risley, *The People of India* (London: W. Thacker & Co., 1915), p. 17.
64. Nanda, "Is Modern Science a Western, Patriarchal Myth?" p. 37.
65. Ibid.
66. Ibid.
67. Lawrence Lipking, "Inventing the Eighteenth Centuries," p. 18.
68. Kaiwar, "Racism," p. 40.
69. Laurence Sterne, *Tristram Shandy*, ed. Howard Anderson (New York: Norton, 1980), p. 160.

70. Alfred David, "An Iconography of Noses: Directions in the History of a Physical Stereotype," in *Mapping the Cosmos*, ed. Jane Chance and R. O. Wells, Jr. (Rice University Press, 1985), p. 79.

71. David, "An Iconography of Noses," p. 80.

72. Ibid., pp. 81–82.

73. Sterne, *Tristram Shandy*, p. 159.

74. Ibid., p. 160.

75. Here I am loosely adapting and paraphrasing a more general point about the historiographic confusion of consequences and causes from Vasant Kaiwar's "On Provincialism and 'Popular Nationalism': Reflections on Samir Amin's *Eurocentrism*," *South Asia Bulletin* 11:1–2 (1991), p. 71.

76. Sterne is forever being constructed as "our contemporary": a practitioner of Chaos Theory, according to one recent claim. See Stuart Sim, " 'All That Exist Are *Islands of Determinism*': Shandean Sentiment and the Dilemma of Postmodern Physics," in *Laurence Sterne in Modernism and Postmodernism*, ed. David Pierce and Peter de Voogd (Amsterdam: Rodopi Press, 1996), pp. 109–122.

77. David, "An Iconography of Noses," p. 89.

78. Ibid.

79. Ibid.

80. Ibid., p. 93.

81. Risley, *The People of India*, p. 29.

82. Sander Gilman, " 'I'm Down on Whores': Race and Gender in Victorian London," in *Anatomy of Racism*, ed. David Theo Goldberg (Minneapolis: University of Minnesota Press, 1990), p. 166.

83. See George Eliot, *Daniel Deronda*, ed. Barbara Hardy (New York: Penguin, 1969), p. 415.

84. Sterne, *Tristram Shandy*, p. 174.

85. Laurence Sterne, letter to Stephen Croft of December 25, 1760. In Sterne, *Tristram Shandy*, p. 466.

86. Howard Anderson, note, in Sterne, *Tristram Shandy*, p. 163.

87. See *Gentleman's Magazine* (October 1790), p. 894. The illustrations are on p. 884.

88. David Lloyd, *Nationalism and Minor Literature: James Clarence Mangan and the Emergence of Irish Cultural Nationalism* (Berkeley: University of California Press, 1987), p. 21.

89. Sterne, *Tristram Shandy*, pp. 258–259.

90. Rushdie, *Midnight's Children*, p. 548.

91. Ibid., p. 136.

92. Ibid., p. 291.

93. George Eliot, *Daniel Deronda*, ed. Barbara Hardy (New York: Penguin, 1969), p. 689.

94. Rushdie, *Midnight's Children*, p. 109.

95. Appiah, "Race," p. 282.

96. Ibid., p. 136.

97. Ibid., p. 221.

98. Tejaswini Niranjana, *Siting Translation: History, Post-Structuralism, and the Colonial Context* (Berkeley: University of California Press, 1992), p. 21.

99. Rosane Rocher, "British Orientalism in the Eighteenth Century: The Dialectics of Knowledge and Government," in *Orientalism and the Postcolonial Predicament*, ed. Carol A. Breckenridge and Peter van der Veer (Philadelphia: University of Pennsylvania Press, 1993), p. 242.

100. Michael Gorra, *After Empire: Scott, Naipaul, Rushdie* (Chicago: The University of Chicago Press, 1997), p. 147.

4 Singing the Imperial Blues: Reading Nation and Empire in John Gay and Wole Soyinka

1. Peter Sabor, "Wole Soyinka and the Scriblerians," in *World Literature Written in English* 29:1 (1989), pp. 43–52.

2. Ibid., p. 44.

3. Aparna Dharwadker, "John Gay, Bertolt Brecht, and Postcolonial Antinationalisms," *Modern Drama* 38 (1995), pp. 4–21.

4. Ibid., p. 7.

5. Diane Dugaw, *"Deep Play"—John Gay and the Invention of Modernity* (Newark: University of Delaware Press, 2001), p. 51.

6. John Bender, "A New History of the Enlightenment?" in *The Profession of Eighteenth-Century Literature: Reflections on an Institution*, ed. Leo Damrosch (Madison: University of Wisconsin Press, 1992), p. 63.

7. Dhardwadker, "John Gay," p. 7.

8. Wole Soyinka, *The Burden of Memory, the Muse of Forgiveness* (Oxford: Oxford University Press, 1999), p. 140.

9. Wole Soyinka, "Neo-Tarzanism: *The Poetics of Pseudo-Tradition*," *Art, Dialogue, and Outrage*, 2nd ed. (New York: Pantheon Books, 1993), p. 305.

10. See Mrinalini Sinha, *Colonial Masculinity: The "Manly Englishman" and the "Effeminate Babu" in the Late Nineteenth Century* (Manchester: Manchester University Press, 1995), pp. 2, 7–11; "Teaching Imperialism as a Social Formation," *Radical History Review* 67 (1997), pp. 175–186; and *Specters of Mother India: The Global Restructuring of an Empire* (forthcoming, Duke University Press, 2006).

11. One such was Philip Quaque (1741–1816), from whose correspondence selections can be found in *Black Writers in Britain 1760–1860*, ed. Paul Edwards and David Dabydeen (Edinburgh: Edinburgh University Press, 1991), pp. 101–116.

12. See, among others, David Dabydeen, *The Black Presence in English Literature* (Manchester: Manchester University Press, 1985) and *Hogarth's Blacks* (Manchester: Manchester University Press, 1987); Peter Fryer, *Staying Power: The History of Black People in Britain* (London: Pluto Press, 1984) and *Black People in the British Empire: an Introduction* (London: Pluto Press, 1988); Keith Sandiford, *Measuring the Moment: Strategies of Protest in*

Eighteenth-Century Afro-English Writing (Selinsgrove: Susquehanna University Press, 1988); Folarin Shyllon, *Black People in Britain, 1555–1833* (Oxford: Oxford University Press, 1977); Edward Scobie, *Black Brittania: A History of Blacks in Britain* (London: Pall Mall Press, 1972); James Walvin, *The Black Presence: A Documentary History of the Negro in England, 1555–1860* (London: Orbach and Chambers Ltd., 1971); Paul Edwards and James Walvin, *Black Personalities in the Era of the Slave Trade* (Baton Rouge: Louisiana State University Press, 1983); Gretchen Gerzina, *Black London: Life before Emancipation* (New Brunswick: Rutgers University Press, 1995); and Moira Ferguson, *Subject to Others: British Women and Colonial Slavery, 1670–1834* (New York: Routledge, 1992).

13. Paul Gilroy, *The Black Atlantic: Modernity and Double Consciousness* (Cambridge: Harvard University Press, 1993), p. 88.

14. Soyinka, *The Burden of Memory*, p. 38.

15. Equiano is mentioned by Soyinka in his essay "The External Encounter," in *Art*, p. 231. The 1770s and 80s, indeed, saw the appearance not only of Equiano's pathbreaking autobiography but of works by several other Black Britons as well: most notably, the letters of Ignatius Sancho (published posthumously in 1782) and the powerful antislavery treatise of Ottabah Cuguano (1787). This is not to mention the appearance in 1773 of Phillis Wheatley's *Poems on Various Subjects*, which was first published in London, where it was effectively exploited for abolitionist purposes.

16. David Nokes, *John Gay: A Profession of Friendship* (Oxford: Oxford University Press, 1995), p. 436.

17. John Gay, *The Beggar's Opera, John Gay: Dramatic Works*, ed. John Fuller, 2 vols. (Oxford: Clarendon Press, 1983), II, p. 62.

18. Dugaw, "*Deep Play*," p. 21.

19. Wonyosi was a type of imported lace banned in Nigeria during the 1970s: a symbol, hence, of conspicuous decadence. The play's title, in addition to playing on the first syllable of *Wole*, puns on the Yoruba phrase *ópèrà*, meaning in Yoruba "A fool buys. . . ." I am very grateful to Robert Elliot Fox for this information, and for sharing with me his private collection of program notes and other materials relating to the original production of *Opera Wonyosi*.

20. See Douglas Hay, "Property, Authority, and the Criminal Law," and Peter Linebaugh, "The Tyburn Riot against the Surgeons," in *Albion's Fatal Tree: Crime and Society in Eighteenth-Century England*, ed. Douglas Hay et al. (New York: Pantheon Books, 1975), pp. 17–117. See also Peter Linebaugh, *The London Hanged: Crime and Civil Society in the Eighteenth Century* (Cambridge: Cambridge University Press, 1992).

21. Mpalavi-Hangson Msiska, *Wole Soyinka* (Plymouth: Northcote House, 1998), pp. 25–26.

22. Wole Soyinka, *The Man Died* (London: Rex Collings, 1972), p. 182. Some more recent musings by Soyinka on the fate of the Nigerian nation deal with the period leading up to the hanging, by the military government of Sani Abacha, of writer Ken Saro-Wiwa and eight fellow activists in the Movement for the Salvation of the Ogoni People. See Wole Soyinka,

The Open Sore of a Continent: A Personal Narrative of the Nigerian Crisis (New York: Oxford University Press, 1996).

23. Msiska, *Wole Soyinka*, p. 26.

24. Wole Soyinka, "The Writer in a Modern African State," *Art*, p. 17.

25. See Johannes Fabian, *Time and the Other: How Anthropology Makes Its Object* (New York: Columbia University Press, 1983).

26. Soyinka, *The Burden of Memory*, p. 9.

27. Wole Soyinka, *Opera Wonyosi* (London: Rex Collings, 1981), p. 24.

28. Ibid., p. 82.

29. Martyn Lyons, *Napoleon Bonaparte and the Legacy of the French Revolution* (New York: St. Martin's Press, 1994), p. 138.

30. See Edward Said, *Orientalism* (New York: Vintage Books, 1978), pp. 79–89.

31. See J. A. Downie, "Gay's Politics," in *John Gay and the Scriblerians*, ed. Peter Lewis and Nigel Wood (New York: St. Martin's Press, 1988), pp. 43–44.

32. Both Paul Gilroy and Gauri Viswanathan warn against the theoretical conflation of empire and nation. See Paul Gilroy, *"There Ain't No Black in the Union Jack": The Cultural Politics of Race and Nation* (Chicago: The University of Chicago Press, 1991); and Gauri Viswanathan, "Raymond Williams and British Colonialism," *The Yale Journal of Criticism* 4:2 (1991), pp. 47–65.

33. See Arnold Rampersad, *The Life of Langston Hughes*, 2 vols. (New York: Oxford University Press, 1988), II, p. 325.

34. See Soyinka's discussion of the electrifying impact on him of first hearing Leadbelly's (Huddie Ledbetter's) version of "Irene, Goodnight" in "Climates of Art," *Art*, p. 191.

35. For historical work toward such a global narrative, see L. S. Stavrianos, *Global Rift: The Third World Comes of Age* (New York: Morrow Press, 1981); and Samin Amir, *Eurocentrism*, trans. Russell Moore (New York: Monthly Review Press, 1989). See also Dugaw, "Deep Play," pp. 31–51.

36. See Colin Nicholson, *Writing and the Rise of Finance: Capital Satires of the Early Eighteenth Century* (Cambridge: Cambridge University Press, 1994), pp. 123–138; and P. G. M. Dickson, *The Financial Revolution in England: A Study in the Development of Public Credit 1688–1756* (London: Macmillan, 1967).

37. Nicholson, *Writing and the Rise of Finance*, p. 120.

38. See Terence Bowers, "Great Britain Imagined: Nation, Citizen, and Class in Defoe's *Tour through the Whole Island of Great Britain*," *Prose Studies* 16:3 (1993), pp. 148–178.

39. John Gay, *Polly*, in *John Gay: Dramatic Works*, ed. John Fuller, 2 vols. (Oxford: Clarendon Press, 1983), II, p. 137.

40. Diane Dugaw, *Warrior Women and Popular Balladry, 1650–1850* (Cambridge: Cambridge University Press, 1989), p. 201.

41. John Richardson, "John Gay, *The Beggar's Opera*, and Forms of Resistance," in *Eighteenth-Century Life* 24:3 (2000), pp. 19–30.

42. Ibid., p. 206.

43. See Peter Lamborn Wilson, *Pirate Utopias: Moorish Corsairs and European Renegadoes* (Brooklyn: Autonomedia, 1995).

44. Edward Long, *The History of Jamaica*, 3 vols. (London, 1774), I, p. 300.

45. See Peter Hulme, *Colonial Encounters: Europe and the Native Caribbean 1492–1797* (London: Methuen, 1986), pp. 181–188.

46. See P. Corrigan and D. Sayer, "Old Corruption," in *The Great Arch: English State Formation as Cultural Revolution* (Oxford: Basil Blackwell, 1985).

47. Nokes, *John Gay*, pp. 439–440.

48. See Joshua Hammer, "Nigeria Crude: A Hanged Man and an Oil-Fouled Landscape," *Harper's Magazine* 292:1753 (June 1996), pp. 58–68.

49. Gilroy, *Black Atlantic*, p. 49.

50. Soyinka, "*The External Encounter*," *Art*, p. 182.

51. For an appreciation of Soyinka's political engagements, see Adewale Majd-Pearce, *Who's Afraid of Wole Soyinka?* (London: Heinemann, 1991).

52. See Gabriel Gbadamosi, "Wole Soyinka and the Federal Road Safety Commission," in Essays on African Writing: A Re-evaluation, ed. Abdulrazak Gurnah (Oxford: Heinemann, 1993), pp. 159–172. For a discussion of Soyinka's journalism in Nigeria, which has included several articles about bad road conditions there, see James Gibbs, "Tear the Painted Masks. Join the Poison Stains: A Preliminary Study of Wole Soyinka's Writings for the Nigerian Press," in *Research in African Literatures* 14:1 (1983), pp. 3–44.

53. See Brian Crow and Chris Banfield, "Wole Soyinka and the Theatre of Ritual Vision," in *An Introduction to Post-Colonial Theatre* (Cambridge: Cambridge University Press, 1996), pp. 78–95.

54. Soyinka, *Opera Wonyosi*, p. 80.

55. The best treatment of this dimension of Soyinka's work is found in Derek Wright's *Wole Soyinka Revisited* (New York: Twayne Publishers, 1993).

56. See *The Invention of Tradition*, ed. Terence O. Ranger and Eric Hobsbawm (New York: Cambridge University Press, 1983); and Albert Memmi, *The Colonizer and the Colonized* (New York: The Orion Press, 1965), p. 98.

57. Wole Soyinka, *Kongi's Harvest*, in *Wole Soyinka: Collected Plays*, 2 vols. (Oxford: Oxford University Press), II, p. 81.

58. See Gayatri Chakravorty Spivak, "Can the Subaltern Speak?," in *Marxism and the Interpretation of Culture*, ed. Cary Nelson and Larry Grossberg (Urbana: University of Illinois Press, 1988), pp. 290–291; Jonathan Arac and Harriet Ritvo, Introduction, *Macropolitics of Nineteenth-Century Literature: Nationalism, Exoticism, Imperialism* (Philadelphia: University of Pennsylvania Press, 1992), p. 1; and Rosemary Hennessy, *Materialist Feminism and the Politics of Discourse* (New York: Routledge, 1993), pp. 16–22, 64–66.

5 Rutherford's Travels: The Palimpsest of Culture in Charles Johnson's *Middle Passage*

1. Charles Johnson, Interview with Diane Olsen, in *The Book That Changed My Life: Interviews with National Book Award Winners and Finalists*, ed. Diane Olsen (New York: The Modern Library, 2002), p. 38.

2. Charles Johnson, *Oxherding Tale* (New York: Plume, 1995), p. 152.

3. Charles Johnson, Introduction to *Oxherding Tale* (New York: Plume, 1995), p. xvii.

4. See Paul Gilroy, *The Black Atlantic: Modernity and Double Consciousness* (Cambridge, MA: Harvard University Press, 1993).

5. W. Jeffrey Bolster, *Black Jacks: African American Seamen in the Age of Sail* (Cambridge, MA: Harvard University Press, 1997), p. 37.

6. Olaudah Equiano, *The Interesting Narrative and Other Writings*, ed. Vincent Carretta (New York: Penguin, 1995), pp. 55–56.

7. George Berkeley, "On the Prospect of Planting Arts and Learning in America," in *Eighteenth-Century English Literature*, ed. Geoffrey Tillotson, Paul Fussell, Jr., and Marshall Waingrow (New York: Harcourt Brace Jovanovich, Inc., 1969), p. 1521.

8. Henry Steele Commager, *The Empire of Reason: How Europe Imagined and America Realized the Enlightenment* (Garden City, NY: Anchor Press, 1977), p. 87.

9. Eric Foner, *Who Owns History? Rethinking the Past in a Changing World* (New York: Hill and Wang, 2002), p. 144.

10. Francis Jennings, *The Creation of America: Through Revolution to Empire* (Cambridge: Cambridge University Press, 2000), pp. 294–295.

11. Ibid., p. 337.

12. Charles Johnson, *Middle Passage* (1990; New York: Plume, 1991), p. 50.

13. Ibid., p. 49.

14. Johnson, *Middle Passage* (New York: Penguin, 1991), p. 29.

15. Ibid., p. 143.

16. Ibid., p. 30.

17. Marc Steinberg, Charles Johnson's *Middle Passage*: "Fictionalizing History and Historicizing Fiction," *Texas Studies in Language and Literature* 45:4 (2003), p. 375.

18. Ibid., p. 146.

19. Ibid.

20. Ibid., pp. 144, 145.

21. Georg Wilhelm Friedrich Hegel, "The Geographical Basis of World History," in *Race and the Enlightenment: A Reader*, ed. Emmanuel Chukwudi Eze (Cambridge: Blackwell, 1997), p. 142.

22. Martin W. Lewis and Kären E. Wigen, *The Myth of Continents: A Critique of Metageography* (Berkeley: University of California Press, 1997), p. 107.

23. Johnson, *Middle Passage*, p. 51.

24. Ibid., pp. 52, 95.

25. Ibid., p. 66.

26. Ibid., p. 124.

27. Ibid., p. 125.

28. Ibid., p. 153.

29. Ibid., p. 154.

30. Ibid., p. 67.

31. Ibid., pp. 56–57.

32. Ibid., p. 33.

33. Johnson, *Middle Passage*, p. 75.

34. Ashraf Rushdy, *Neo-Slave Narratives: Studies in the Social Logic of a Literary Form* (Oxford: Oxford University Press, 1999), p. 22.

35. Peter Hallward, *Absolutely Postcolonial: Writing between the Singular and the Specific* (Manchester: Manchester University Press, 2001), p. 142.

36. Marion Rust, "The Subaltern as Imperialist: Speaking of Olaudah Equiano," in *Passing and the Fictions of Identity* (Durham: Duke University Press, 1996), pp. 21–36.

37. Seyla Benhabib, *The Claims of Culture: Equality and Diversity in the Global Era* (Princeton: Princeton University Press, 2002), p. viii.

38. Ibid., p. 177.

39. Angelo Costanzo, *Surprizing Narrative: Olaudah Equiano and the Beginnings of Black Autobiography* (Wesport, CT: Greenwood Press, 1987), p. 70.

40. Equiano, *The Interesting Narrative*, p. 3.

41. Ibid., p. 176.

42. Joseph Fichtelberg, "Word between Worlds: The Economy of Equiano's Narrative," *American Literary History* 5:3 (1993), p. 466.

43. Srinivas Aravamudan, *Tropicopolitans: Colonialism and Agency, 1688–1804* (Durham: Duke University Press, 1999), p. 38. Aravamudan, p. 237.

44. Walvin, *Black Personalities*, p. 193.

45. See Paul Edwards, "The Invisible Chi in Equiano's Interesting Narrative," *Journal of Religion in Africa* XIX, 2 (1989), pp. 146–156.

46. Equiano, *The Interesting Narrative*, p. 72.

47. See S. E. Ogude, "Facts into Fiction: Equiano's Childhood Reconsidered," *Research in African Literature* 13:1 (1982), pp. 31–43.

48. See Olaudah Equiano, *Equiano's Travels*, ed. Paul Edwards (Oxford: Heinemann, 1967).

49. Vincent Carretta, "Olaudah Equiano or Gustavus Vassa? New Light on an Eighteenth-Century Question of Identity?" in *Slavery and Abolition* 20:3 (1999), pp. 96–105. See also the introduction to Olaudah Equiano, *The Interesting Narrative and Other Writings*, ed. Vincent Carretta, revised edition (New York: Penguin Books, 2003), pp. ix–xxxii.

50. Ibid., p. 96.

51. Johnson, *Oxherding Tale*, p. 152.

52. Ibid., p. 97.

53. Equiano, *The Interesting Narrative*, p. 188.

54. Fritz Gysin, "The Enigma of the Return," in *Black Imagination and the Middle Passage*, ed. Maria Diedrich, Henry Louis Gates, Jr., and Carl Pedersen (New York: Oxford University Press, 1999), p. 187.

55. Equiano, *The Interesting Narrative*, p. 208.

56. Johnson, *Middle Passage*, p. 102.

57. V. S. Naipaul, *The Overcrowded Barracoon* (New York: Vintage, 1984), p. 206.

58. Robert Wess, *Kenneth Burke: Rhetoric/Subjectivity/Postmodernism* (Cambridge: Cambridge University Press, 1996), p. 28.

59. Alasdair McIntyre, *A Short History of Ethics: A History of Moral Philosophy from the Homeric Age to the Twentieth Century* (New York: MacMillan, 1966), p. 151.

60. "An Interview with Charles Johnson Conducted by Jonathan Little," *I Call Myself an Artist,* p. 227.

61. Johnson, *Middle Passage,* p. 38.

62. Ibid., p. 7.

63. Ibid., p. 88.

64. Ibid., p. 111.

65. Ibid., p. 190.

66. Ibid., pp. 149–150.

67. Ibid., p. 187.

68. Ibid., p. 208.

69. Ibid., p. 90.

70. Ibid., p. 92.

71. Ibid., p. 25.

72. Tobias Smollett, *Roderick Random* (London: J.M. Dent, 1927), p. 200.

73. Ibid., p. 196.

74. See Han Turley, *Rum, Sodomy, and the Lash: Piracy, Sexuality, and Masculine Identity* (New York: New York University Press, 1999), pp. 41–42.

75. Ibid., p. 39.

76. Charles Johnson [possibly a pseudonym for Daniel Defoe], *A General History of the Pyrates,* ed. Manuel Schonhorn (Mineola, NY: Dover Press, 1999), p. 95. At this writing, the attribution to Defoe remains contested, p. 76.

77. Johnson, *Middle Passage,* p. 41.

78. Ibid., p. 144.

79. Hallward, p. 666.

80. Ibid., p. 209.

81. See Sigmund Freud, in *The Letters of Sigmund Freud,* trans. Tania and James Stern, ed. Ernst L. Freud, 2 vols. (1960; New York: Basic Books, 1975), I, Letters 214–242 to Romain Rolland in 1929, pp. 388–389; Catherine Clément, *Syncope: The Philosophy of Rapture,* trans. Sally O'Driscoll and Deirdre M. Mahoney (Minneapolis: University of Minnesota Press, 1994).

82. Johnson, *Middle Passage,* p. 171.

83. Ibid., p. 47.

84. Charles Taylor, *The Ethics of Authenticity* (Cambridge: Harvard University Press, 1991), p. 48.

85. "An Interview with Charles Johnson Conducted by Jonathan Little," *I call Myself an Artist,* p. 241.

86. Steve Olsen, *Mapping Human History: Genes, Race, and Our Common Origins* (Boston: Houghton Mifflin, 2002), p. 235.

87. See Paul Gilroy, *Against Race: Imagining the Political Culture beyond the Color Line* (Cambridge, MA: Harvard University Press, 2000).

88. Charles Johnson, "An Interview with Charles Johnson Conducted by Jonathan Little," in *I Call Myself an Artist: Writings by and about Charles Johnson* (Bloomington: Indiana University Press, 1999), p. 230.

89. Charles Johnson, personal communication to Linda Selzer (to whom I am grateful). From Johnson's talk delivered on September 17, 2002, at Wofford College, Spartanburg, South Carolina.

90. Charles Johnson, *Turning the Wheel: Essays on Buddhism and Writing* (New York: Scribner, 2003), p. 154.

6 Swift's Immanent Critique of Colonial Modernity

1. Theodor W. Adorno, "Sociology and Empirical Research," in *The Positivist Dispute in* German Sociology, trans. Glyn Adey and David Frisby (London: Heinemann, 1976), p. 69.

2. Herbert Butterfield, *The Englishman and his History* (Cambridge: Cambridge University Press, 1944), p. 81.

3. Tani E. Barlow, "Introduction: On 'Colonial Modernity,'" in *Formations of Colonial Modernity in East Asia*, ed. Tani E. Barlow (Durham: Duke University Press, 1997), p. 1.

4. See *The First Modern Society: Essays in English History in Honour of Lawrence Stone*, ed. A. L. Beier, David Cannadine, and James M. Rosenheim (Cambridge: Cambridge University Press, 1989).

5. Patricia Coughlan, " 'Cheap and Common Animals': The English Anatomy of Ireland in the Seventeenth Century," in Literature and the English Civil War, ed. Thomas Healy and Jonathan Sawday (Cambridge: Cambridge University Press, 1990), p. 213.

6. Mary Poovey, *A History of the Modern Fact: Problems of Knowledge in the Sciences of Wealth and Society* (Chicago: The University of Chicago Press, 1998), pp. 120–138.

7. Simon Schama, *A History of Britain*, 2 vols. (New York: Hyperion, 2001), II: *The Wars of the British*, 1603–1776, p. 236.

8. James Morris, *Pax Britannica: The Climax of an Empire* (San Diego: Harcourt Brace Jovanovich, 1968), p. 478.

9. Swift had invested in the South Sea Company, brainchild of his Patron Sir Robert Harley; moreover, the Treaty of Utrecht (1713) "for which the Tory ministry pushed" included the *Asiento* clause, giving Britain the right (exclusive, but undermined by smugglers) to supply an annual quota of slaves to the Spanish colonial possessions.

10. I have elaborated in detail on these *topoi* in "Three Times Round the Globe: Gulliver and Colonial Discourse," *Cultural Critique* 18 (1991), pp. 187–214.

11. Swift, *Gulliver's Travels*, ed. Herbert Davis (Oxford: Basil Blackwell, 1965), p. 37.

12. Daniel Defoe, *Robinson Crusoe*, ed. Michael Shinagel, 2nd ed. (New York: W. W. Norton, 1994), p. 153.

13. Swift, *Gulliver's Travels*, p. 44.

14. Ibid., p. 34.

15. Ibid., p. 57.

16. Benedict Anderson, *Imagined Communities: Reflections on the Origins and Spread of Nationalism* (London: Verso, 1983), Ch. 3, pp. 41–49.

17. Ibid., p. 33.

18. David Lloyd, *Nationalism and Minor Literature: James Clarence Mangan and the Emergence of Irish Cultural Nationalism* (Berkeley: University of California Press, 1987), p. 21.

19. Deidre Shauna Lynch, *The Economy of Character: Novels, Market Culture, and the Business of Inner Meaning* (Chicago: University of Chicago Press, 1998), p. 9.

20. Aline Mackenzie Taylor, "Sights and Monsters and Gulliver's Voyage to Brobdingnag," *Tulane Studies in English* VII (1957), p. 56.

21. Swift, *Gulliver's Travels*, pp. 97–98.

22. Ibid., p. 79.

23. See Keith Thomas, *Man and the Natural World: Changing Attitudes in England 1500–1800* (New York: Oxford University Press, 1983), p. 117; and Srinivas Aravamudan, *Tropicopolitans: Colonialism and Agency, 1688–1804* (Durham: Duke University Press, 1999), p. 38.

24. Swift, *Gulliver's Travels*, pp. 91–92.

25. Ibid., p. 91.

26. Ibid., p. 122.

27. Ibid., p. 135.

28. Ibid.

29. Denis Donoghue, *The Practice of Reading* (New Haven: Yale University Press, 1998), p. 171.

30. Clive T. Probyn, *Jonathan Swift: The Contemporary Background* (Manchester: Manchester University Press, 1978), p. 184.

31. Swift, *Gulliver's Travels*, p. 132.

32. Ibid., p. 147.

33. Ibid.

34. Ibid., p. 171.

35. Thomas Metscher, "The Radicalism of Swift: *Gulliver's Travels* and the Irish Point of View," *Studies in Anglo-Irish Literature*, ed. Heinz Kosok (Bonn: Bouvier Verlag Herbert Grundmann, 1982), p. 14.

36. This five-paragraph passage was transcribed by Swift's friend Charles Ford in an interleaved copy of *Gulliver's Travels* (Ford's Book) in which he made corrections for subsequent editions. Scholars cannot determine if it is a correction or if Swift added something new after the first edition. Ford's Book, now in the Forster Collection at the Victoria and Albert Museum, is the sole surviving source for the passage.

37. Metscher, "The Radicalism of Swift," p. 14.

38. Jonathan Swift, *Gulliver's Travels*, in *Gulliver's Travels and Other Writings*, ed. Louis Landa (Boston: Houghton Mifflin, 1960), p. 138. Because the "resistance-of-Lindalino" episode is omitted from the Davis edition, I cite Landa's edition.

39. Landa, ed., in *Gulliver's Travels and Other Writings*, p. 138.

40. Ibid., p. 140.

41. Ibid.

42. Metscher, "The Radicalism of Swift," p. 14.

43. Ibid.

44. David Nokes, *Jonathan Swift: A Hypocrite Reversed: A Critical Biography* (Oxford: Oxford University Press, 1985), p. 286.

45. R.W. Frantz, "Swift's Yahoos and the Voyagers," *Modern Philology* 29 (1931), pp. 49–57.

46. Swift, *Gulliver's Travels*, p. 235.

47. Ibid., p. 259.

48. Ibid., p. 267.

49. Swift, *Gulliver's Travels*, p. 243.

50. Robert C. Elliot, "The Satirist Satirized," in *Twentieth Century Interpretations of Gulliver's Travels: A Collection of Critical Essays*, ed. Frank Brady (Englewood Cliffs: Prentice, 1968), p. 52.

51. Swift, *Gulliver's Travels*, p. 242.

52. Ibid., pp. 278–279.

53. Ibid., p. 279.

54. Ibid., p. 278.

55. Linda Colley, "Going Native, Telling Tales: Collaboration, Captivity, and Empire," *Past and Present* 168 (2000), p. 174.

56. Swift, *Gulliver's Travels*, p. 271.

57. Ibid.

58. Ibid., pp. 271–272.

59. Ibid., p. 235.

60. Donaghue, *The Practice of Reading*, p. 184.

61. William S. Anderson, "Paradise Gained by Horace, Lost by Gulliver," in *English Satire and the Satiric Tradition*, ed. Claude Rawson (Oxford: Basil Blackwell, 1984), pp. 160–163.

62. See Johannes Fabian, *Time and the Other: How Anthropology Makes Its Object* (New York: Columbia University Press, 1983).

63. Claude Rawson, *God, Gulliver, and Genocide: Barbarism and the European Imagination, 1492–1945* (Oxford: Oxford University Press, 2001), p. ix.

64. Ibid., p. 275.

65. Ibid., p. 35.

66. Ibid., p. 12.

67. Ibid., p. 9.

68. Swift, *Gulliver's Travels*, p. 294.

69. W. E. H. Lecky, *A History of Ireland in the Eighteenth Century*, 5 vols. (1892; London: Longmans, Green and Co., 1913), I, p. 163.

70. *Gulliver's Travels*, p. 282.

71. Ibid.

72. Ibid., pp. 289–290.

73. Ibid., p. 8.

74. Ibid., pp. 289–290.

75. Ibid., p. 8.

76. Howard Erskine-Hill, *Swift: Gulliver's Travels* (Cambridge: Cambridge University Press, 1993), p. 81.

77. *Rawson, God, Gulliver, and Genocide*, p. 271.

78. Ibid., p. 11.

79. Jay Macpherson, "Swift's Very Knowing American," in *Lumen*, XIII, ed. Donald W. Nichol and Margarete Smith (Edmonton: Academic Printing and Publishing, 1994), p. 110.

80. Ibid., p. 117.

81. Ibid.

82. Carol Houlihan Flynn, *The Body in Swift and Defoe* (Cambridge: Cambridge University Press, 1990), pp. 150–151.

83. Rawson, *God, Gulliver, and Genocide*, p. 91.

84. Swift, "A Modest Proposal," *Prose Writings*, XII, p. 112.

85. Ibid., p. 114.

86. See Maggie Kilgour, *From Communion to Cannibalism: An Anatomy of Metaphors of Incorporation* (Princeton: Princeton University Press, 1990).

87. Swift, "A Modest Proposal," p. 115.

88. Swift, "A Proposal for Giving Badges to Beggars in All the Parishes of Dublin," *Prose Works* 13 (1959), p. 136.

89. Rawson, *God, Gulliver, and Genocide*, p. 229, p. 243.

90. Swift to Pope, September 29, 1725.

91. André Comte-Sponville, *A Small Treatise on the Great Virtues*, trans. Catherine Temerson (New York: Henry Holt, 1996), p. 147.

92. Mohandas K. Gandhi, Letter to Maganlal Gandhi, May 18, 1911, in *The Collected Works of Mahatma Gandhi*, 90 vols. (Delhi: Publications Division, Ministry of Information and Broadcasting, Govt. of India, 1958), vol. 11, letter #63, p. 77.

7 Johnson's Immanent Critique of Imperial Nationalism

1. Greg Clingham, *Johnson, Writing, and Memory* (Cambridge: Cambridge University Press, 2002), pp. 2–3.

2. Thomas Curley, "Johnson and the Irish: A Postcolonial Survey of the Irish Literary Renaissance in Imperial Great Britian," *The Age of Johnson: A Scholarly Annual*, vol. 12, ed. Paul Korshin and Jack Lynch (NY: AMS Press, 2001), p. 106.

3. See *Cosmopolitics: Thinking and Feeling beyond the Nation*, ed., Pheng Cheah and Bruce Robbins (Minneapolis: University of Minnesota Press, 1998), pp. 2–3.

4. Ibid., p. 3.

5. See also Martha Nussbaum, *For Love of Country: Debating the Limits of Patriotism*, ed. Joshua Cohen (Boston: Beacon Press, 1996); Timothy Brennan, *At Home in the World: Cosmopolitanism Now* (Cambridge: Harvard University Press, 1997); and Karen O'Brien, *Narratives of Enlightenment: Cosmopolitan History from Voltaire to Gibbon* (Cambridge: Cambridge University Press, 1997).

6. Howard Weinbrot, *Britannia's Issue: The Rise of British Literature from Dryden to Ossian* (Cambridge: Cambridge University Press, 1993), p. 389.

7. Katie Trumpener, *Bardic Nationalism: The Romantic Novel and the British Empire* (Princeton: Princeton University Press, 1997), p. 70.

8. See J. C. D. Clark, *Samuel Johnson: Literature, Religion and English Cultural Politics from the Restoration to Romanticism* (Cambridge: Cambridge University Press, 1994); and "The Cultural Identity of Samuel Johnson," in *The Age of Johnson* 8 (1997), pp. 15–70.

9. Samuel Johnson, "Swift," *Lives of the English Poets*, ed. George Birkbeck Hill, 3 vols. (New York: Octagon Books, 1967), III, p. 19.

10. Samuel Johnson, "Preface," *Gentleman's Magazine* 10 (1740), pp. iii–iv.

11. Samuel Johnson, "Introduction to the Harleian Miscellany: An Essay on the Importance of Small Tracts and Fugitive Pieces," in *The Oxford Authors: Samuel Johnson*, ed. Donald Greene (Oxford: Oxford University Press, 1984), p. 123.

12. Samuel Johnson, "A Complete Vindication of the Licensers of the Stage," in *Samuel Johnson: The Oxford Authors*, ed. Donald Greene (New York: Oxford University Press, 1984), p. 75.

13. Nicholas Hudson, Review of John Cannon's *Samuel Johnson and the Politics of Hanoverian England* (Oxford: Clarendon Press, 1994), in *The Age of Johnson* 9, ed. Paul Korshin (New York: AMS Press, 1998), p. 342.

14. Alvin Kernan, *Printing Technology, Letters, and Samuel Johnson* (Princeton: Princeton University Press, 1987); Robert DeMaria, Jr., *Samuel Johnson and the Life of Reading* (Baltimore: Johns Hopkins University Press, 1997); and Lawrence Lipking, *Samuel Johnson: The Life of an Author* (Cambridge: Harvard University Press, 1998).

15. Samuel Johnson, "The Bravery of the English Common Soldiers," in *The Yale Edition of the Works of Samuel Johnson, X: Political Writings*, ed. Donald J. Greene (New Haven: Yale University Press, 1977), p. 283.

16. Ibid., p. 284.

17. See Jürgen Habermas, "Further Reflections on the Public Sphere," trans. Thomas Burger, in *Habermas and the Public Sphere*, ed. Craig Calhoun (Cambridge, MA: MIT Press, 1992), pp. 421–461.

18. Samuel Johnson, "Reply to a Paper in the Gazetteer of May 26, 1757," in *The Oxford Authors: Samuel Johnson*, p. 520.

19. See Ruth K. McClure, "Johnson's Criticism of the Foundling Hospital and Its Consequences," *Review of English Studies*, n.s., 27: 105 (1976), pp. 2–26.

20. Jonas Hanway, "An Essay on Tea," in *A Journal of Eight Days Journey from Portsmouth to Kingston upon Thmas through Southampton, Wilstshire, & c. With Miscellaneous Thought, Moral and Religious; in Sixty-Four Lettres: Addressed to Two Ladies of the Partie. To which is added An Essay on Tea*, 2nd ed., 2 vols.) (London: 1757), II, p. 273.

21. *Samuel Johnson as Book Reviewer: A Duty to Examine the Labors of the Learned* (Newark: University of Delaware Press, 2002), p. 145.

22. James Stephen Taylor, "Philanthropy and Empire: Jonas Hanway and the Infant Poor of London, *Eighteenth-Century Studies* 12:3 (1979), p. 288.

23. Haywood, *Making*, p. 36.

24. Trumpener, *Bardic Nationalism*, pp. 294–295, n.14.

25. For views of "The Bard" that highlight Gray's self-reflexivity, see Suvir Kaul's *Thomas Gray and Literary Authority: A Study in Ideology and Poetics* (Stanford University Press, 1992); and Paul Odney's "Thomas Gray's 'Daring Spirit': Forging the Poetics of an Alternative Nationalism," in *Clio* 28:3 (1999), pp. 245–260.

26. Thomas Gray to Stonhewer, August 21, 1755. *Correspondence of Thomas Gray*, ed. Paget Toynbee and Leonard Toynbee, 3 vols. (Oxford: Clarendon Press, 1935), I, pp. 432–433.

27. Michael Dobson, *The Making of a National Poet: Shakespeare, Adaptation, and Authorship, 1660–1769* (Oxford: Clarendon Press, 1992), p. 6.

28. *Yale Edition of the Works*, VII, p. 149.

29. See James Gray, "Arras/Hélas! A Fresh Look at Samuel Johnson's French," in *Johnson after Two Hundred Years*, ed. Paul J. Korshin (Philadelphia: University of Pennsylvania Press, 1986), p. 88.

30. Samuel Johnson, "Milton," in *Lives of the English Poets*, ed. George Birkbeck Hill, 3 vols. (New York: Octagon Books, 1967), I, p. 171.

31. *Yale Edition of the Works*, VII, p. 66.

32. For a study of social class in the shaping of English attitudes toward French culture, see Gerald Newman, *The Rise of English Nationalism: A Cultural History 1740–1830* (New York: St. Martin's Press, 1997).

33. Samuel Johnson, "Introduction to the Proceedings of the Committee on French Prisoners," in *Works*, X, pp. 287–289.

34. Samuel Johnson, Preface to *A Dictionary of the English Language, in The Oxford Authors: Samuel Johnson*, ed. Donald Greene (Oxford: Oxford University Press, 1984), p. 319.

35. Samuel Johnson, "Browne," in *The Works of Samuel Johnson, LL.D.* (1825; New York: AMS Press, 1970), vol. X, p. 500.

36. Ibid.

37. Samuel Johnson, "The State of Affairs in Lilliput," in *The Gentleman's Magazine* VIII (June 1738), p. 285.

38. David Armitage, "Greater Britain: A Useful Category of Historical Analysis? in *American Historical Review* (April 1999), p. 439.

39. Armitage, "Greater Britain," p. 439.

40. Samuel Johnson, "An Introduction to the Political State of Great Britain," in *Political Writings*, p. 137.

41. Samuel Johnson, *Idler* #81, in *The Idler and The Adventurer*, ed. W. J. Bate, John M. Bullitt, and L. F. Powell (1963), p. 254.

42. Anonymous, *An Indian's Speech to His Countrymen. Imitated from the second vol. Of the* IDLER. *Gentleman's Magazine* (November 1765), p. 526, ll. 80–86.

43. James Thomson Callender, *A Critical Review of the Works of Dr. Samuel Johnson* (Edinburgh: Dickson and Creech, 1783), p. 59.

44. Thomas Babington Macaulay, "Samuel Johnson," in *Selected Writings*, ed. John Clive and Thomas Pinney (University of Chicago Press, 1972), p. 145.

45. See James Bruce, *Travels to Discover the Source of the Nile in the Years 1768, 1769, 1770, 1771, 1772, & 1773*, 2nd ed., 8 vols. (Edinburgh: James Ballantyne, 1804). I am grateful to the John J. Burns Library, Boston College (Williams Collection), for access to *Bruce's Travels*.

46. Samuel Johnson, "Preface to Lobo's *A Voyage to Abyssinia*," in *The Oxford Author*.

47. Samuel Johnson, "A Brief to Free a Slave," in Boswell's *Life*, II, p. 368.

48. James G. Basker, "Intimations of Abolitionism in 1759: Johnson, Hawkesworth, and Oroonoko," in *The Age of Johnson: A Scholarly Annual* 12 (New York: AMS Press, 2001), pp. 47–56.

49. Anonymous, *Reflections on Recent Occurrences at Lichfield; including an Illustration of the Opinions of Samuel Johnson, L.L.D. on Slavery, and the General Distribution of the Scriptures* (London: J. Hatchard & Son, 1826), p. 22.

50. Ibid., p. 23.

51. Jack Goody, *The East in the West* (Cambridge: Cambridge University Presss, 1996), p. 2.

52. Samuel Johnson, *Rasselas and Other Tales*, ed. Gwin Kolb, *The Yale Edition of the Works of Samuel Johnson* (New Haven: Yale University Press, 1990), Vol. XVI, p. 117.

53. Ibid., p. 111.

54. Ibid.

55. Ibid., p. 119.

56. Ibid., p. 118.

57. Ibid., p. 46.

58. Ibid.

59. Ibid., pp. 46–47.

60. Ibid., p. 47.

61. Boswell, *Life*, IV, p. 199.

62. Goody, *The East in the West*, p. 2.

63. Johnson, *Rasselas*, p. 50.

64. Macaulay, *Life*; and *Clive and Penney*, p. 532.

65. Samuel Johnson, *A Journey to the Western Islands of Scotland*, ed. R. W. Chapman (1924; London: Oxford University Press, 1978), p. 108.

66. Paul J. Degategno, " 'The Source of Daily and Exalted Pleasure': Jefferson Reads the Poems of Ossian," in *Ossian Revisited*, ed. Howard Gaskill (Edinburgh University Press, 1991), p. 103.

67. Johnson, *Journey*, p. 103.

68. Ibid., p. 36.

69. Ibid, p. 88.

70. Ibid., p. 108.

71. Karen O'Brien, "Johnson's View of the Scottish Enlightenment in *A Journey to the Western Islands of Scotland*," in *The Age of Johnson* 4 (1991), p. 64.

72. O'Brien, "Johnson's View," p. 64.

73. Ibid., p. 63.

74. Johnson, *Journey*, p. 108.

75. See Michael Hechter, *Internal Colonialism: the Celtic Fringe in British National Development, 1536–1966* (Berkeley: University of California Press, 1975).

76. Johnson, *Journey*, p. 89.

77. Ibid., p. 90.

78. Ibid., p. 91.

79. Ibid., p. 97.

80. See Tacitus, *The Agricola and the Germanica*, trans. H. Mattingly, revised by S. A. Handford (London: Penguin, 1970), p. 81.

81. Johnson, *Journey*, p. 117.

82. Ibid., p. 118.

83. James Macpherson, *The History of Great Britain from the Restoration to the Accession of the House of Hanover*, 2 vols. (London: W. Strahan and T. Cadell, 1775), I, p. 697.

84. Kritmannson, "Ossian," p. 449, p. 452.

85. O'Halloran, "Irish Re-Creation of the Gaelic Past," p. 75. See also her *Golden Ages and Barbarous Nations: Antiquarian Debate and Cultural Politics in Ireland, c. 1750–1800* (Notre Dame: University of Notre Dame Press, 2005).

86. Ibid., p. 77.

87. Ibid., p. 75.

88. Curley, "Johnson and the Irish," p. 91.

89. See Thomas McLoughlin, *Contesting Ireland: Irish Voices against England in the Eighteenth Century* (Dublin: Four Courts Press, 1999), p. 142.

90. Ibid., p. 138.

91. Samuel Johnson, *The Letters of Samuel Johnson*, ed. Bruce Redford, 5 vols. (Princeton, N.J.: Princeton University Press, 1992–1994), I, p. 152.

92. See note to *Letters*, I, p. 151.

93. *Letters*, III, p. 24.

94. See Richard Sher, "Percy, Shaw, and the Ferguson 'Cheat': National Prejudice in the Ossian Wars," in *Ossian Revisited*, p. 240, n.33.

95. William Shaw, *An Enquiry into the Authenticity of the Poems Ascribed to Ossian* (London: J. Murray, 1781), pp. 35–36.

96. Johnson, *Journey*, pp. 57–58.

97. Ibid., p. 44.

98. See Adam Potkay, "Virtue and Manners in Macpherson's Poems of Ossian," *Publications of the Modern Language Association* 107:1 (1992), pp. 120–130.

99. Martin Wechselblatt, "The Canonical Ossian," in *Making History: Textuality and the Forms of Eighteenth-Century Culture*, ed. Greg Clingham (London: Associated University Presses, 1998), p. 31.

100. Howard Gaskill, " 'Ossian' Macpherson: Towards a Rehabilitation," in *Comparative Criticism* 8 (1986), pp. 113–146.

101. Fiona J. Stafford, "Introduction: The Ossianic Poems of James Macpherson," in *The Poems of Ossian and Related Works*, ed. Howard Gaskill (Edinburgh University Press, 1996), p. xvii.

102. Nicholas B. Dirks, "Is Vice Versa? Historical Anthropology and Anthropological Histories," in *The Historic Turn in the Human Sciences*, ed. Terence J. McDonald (Ann Arbor: University of Michigan, 1996), p. 41.

103. Ibid., p. 41.

104. Ibid., p. 45.

105. Satya Mohanty, *Literary Theory and the Claims of History: Postmodernism, Objectivity, Multicultural Politics* (Ithaca: Cornell University Press, 1997), p. 198.

106. *Report of the Committee of the Highland Society of Scotland*, ed. Henry Mackenzie (Edinburgh, 1805), pp. 151–152.

107. See Edward Said, "Representing the Colonized: Anthropology's Interlocutors," in *Reflections on Exile and Other Essays* (Cambridge, Mass.: Harvard University Press, 2000), p. 302.

108. Janet Sorensen, *The Grammar of Empire in Eighteenth Century British Writing* (Cambridge: Cambridge University Press, 2000), p. 26.

109. Sorensen, *The Grammar of Empire*, pp. 174–175.

110. Ibid., p. 89.

111. Samuel Johnson, "Review of Thomas Blackwell," *Memoirs of the Court of Augustus*, in *The Oxford Authors*, ed. Greene, p. 496.

112. Carey MacIntosh, *The Evolution of English Prose, 1700–1800: Style, Politeness, and Print Culture* (Cambridge: Cambridge University Press, 1998), pp. 171–181.

113. Bill Bryson, *Bryson's Dictionary of Troublesome Words* (New York: Broadway Books, 2002), pp. 131–132.

114. Allen Reddick, *The Making of Johnson's Dictionary 1746–1773*, rev. ed. (Cambridge: Cambridge University Press, 1996), p. 45.

115. *Works*, V, p. 170.

116. Ibid., p. 171.

117. Bertram H. Davis, *Thomas Percy* (Boston: Twayne Publishers, 1981), p. 117

118. Sigurd Bernhard Hustvedt, *Ballad Criticism in Scandanavia and Great Britain during the Eighteenth Century* (London: Humphrey Milford, 1916), p. 218.

119. See Hesther Lynch Piozzi, *Anecdotes of the Late Samuel Johnson, LL.D.*, ed. S. C. Roberts (Westport, CT: Greenwood Press, 1975), pp. 44–48.

120. Alice C. C. Gaussen, *Percy: Prelate and Poet* (London: Smith, Elder, & Co., 1908), pp. 46–47.

121. See Boswell, *Tour*, p. 423; and Hustvedt, *Ballad Criticism*, p. 216.

122. Clark, *Samuel Johnson*, p. 82.

123. See Jack Lynch, "Studied Barbarity: Johnson, Spenser, and the Idea of Progress," in *The Age of Johnson*, 9, ed. Paul J. Korshin (New York: AMS Press, 1998), pp. 81–108.

124. Samuel Johnson, *Rambler* 121, in *Works*, IV, p. 286.

125. Edward Salmon, *The British Empire*, ed. Hugh Gunn, 12 vols. (London: W. Collins, 1924), II: *The Literature of the Empire*, p. 83.

126. Doyle, "The Racial Sublime," p. 15. It can scarcely be a coincidence, moreover, that Percy's American contemporary, Thomas Jefferson—a staunch white supremacist—was likewise the instigator of Anglo-Saxon Studies as an academic subject both at William and Mary and the University of Virginia. I am grateful to Jim Basker for pointing out this connection to me.

127. Weinbrot, *Britannia's Issue*, p. 2.

128. Laura Doyle, "The Racial Sublime," p. 22.

129. Neil Lazarus, *Nationalism and Cultural Practice in the Postcolonial World* (Cambridge: Cambridge University Press, 1999), p. 8.

Epilogue: Toward a Critical Reappropriation of Modernity

1. Pierre Bourdieu, "Rethinking the State: Genesis and Structure of the Bureaucratic Field," in *State/Culture: State-Formation after the Cultural Turn*, ed. George Steinmetz (Ithaca: Cornell University Press, 1999), p. 57.
2. Tobin Siebers, *Cold War Politics and the Politics of Skepticism* (New York: Oxford University Press, 1993), pp. 27, 29–70.
3. Martin Bernal, *Black Athena Writes Back* (Durham: Duke University Press, 2001), p. 125.
4. See *Excavating Schliemann*, ed. David A. Traill (Atlanta: Scholars Press, 1993); *Myth, Scandal, and History: The Heinrich Schliemann Controversy and a First Edition of the Mycenaean Diary*, ed. William A. Calder III and David A. Traill (Detroit: Wayne State University Press, 1986); and David A. Traill, *Schliemann of Troy: Treasure and Deceit* (New York: St. Martin's Press, 1995).
5. William A. Calder III, "Is the Mask a Hoax?" in *Archaeology* 52:4 (1999), pp. 53–55.
6. Axel Honneth, "The Possibility of a Disclosing Critique of Society: The *Dialectic of Enlightenment* in Light of Current Debates in Social Criticism," *Constellations* 7:1 (2000), p. 124.
7. Max Horkheimer and Theodor W. Adorno, *Dialectic of Enlightenment*, trans. by John Cumming (New York: Continuum, 1989), p. 63.
8. Thomas de Zengotita, "Common Ground: Finding Our Way Back to the Enlightenment," *Harper's Magazine* (January 2003), pp. 35–44.
9. Satya P. Mohanty, *Literary Theory and the Claims of History: Postmodernism, Objectivity, Multicultural Politics* (Ithaca: Cornell University Press, 1997), p. 242.
10. Arif Dirlik, *The Post-colonial Aura* (Boulder, CO: Westview Press, 1997), p. 3.
11. Edward Said, *Culture and Imperialism* (New York: Alfred A. Knopf, 1993), p. 51.
12. Ibid.
13. Edward Said, *Reflections on Exile and Other Essays* (Cambridge: Harvard University Press, 2000), p. 586.
14. Partha Chatterjee, *The Nation and Its Fragments: Colonial and Post-colonial Histories* (Princeton: Princeton University Press, 1993), p. 10.

INDEX